D1270512

Praise for *Gerta*

Winner of the Magnesia Litera Readers' Award; short-listed for the Jiří Orten Award, the Josef Škvorecký Award, and the Magnesia Litera in the prose category.

"I think [*Gerta*] is beautiful and relevant. One of its basic themes is the expulsion of the German population from Czechoslovakia after the Second World War, but as a whole the novel carries a much broader theme that seems crucial to me today—that the mutual problems between people and nations will not be solved simply by an acknowledgment, and not even by an apology. An apology is just the beginning. We can admit our own guilt, take it on ourselves, but an even more difficult and important step, which is not spoken of so much and for which there are no laws or entitlements, is forgiveness—whether toward others or toward ourselves. For me, *Gerta* is a book about forgiveness."

—Alice Nellis, director of the Czech TV adaptation of *Gerta* (English translation by Véronique Firkusny)

"A great book . . . Immediately after reading, [*Gerta*] is unforgettable . . . Kateřina Tučková wrote a novel that should be required reading."

—Jan Hübsch, *Lidovky*

"The central story of Gerta Schnirch can be captured in one word, the clichéd adjective *powerful*. Its power lies particularly in its vivid depiction of frightful experiences immediately after World War II, experiences resembling terrible nightmares. To achieve this, the author did not need to make use of cheap effects or explicit, detailed, or shocking descriptions."

—Petr Hrtánek, iLiteratura

"The author describes, with a great writing talent and empathy for human suffering, Gerta's life from the moment she stood at her mother's grave in 1942 . . . We have read of various marches, but few are as dreadful as the one depicted with deep compassion by Kateřina Tučková. The story is as forcefully described as if [Tučková] were Gerta, experiencing it all firsthand."

—Milena Nyklová, *Knižní novinky*

"[*Gerta*] masterfully fulfills one of the potential and important functions of literature. It is a means of self-reflection for a particular community, in this case the Czech nation."

—Pavel Janoušek, *Host*

GERTA

GERTA

A NOVEL

KATEŘINA TUČKOVÁ

TRANSLATED BY VÉRONIQUE FIRKUSNY

AMAZON **CROSSING**

Text copyright © 2009 by Kateřina Tučková
Translation copyright © 2021 by Véronique Firkusny
All rights reserved.

Previously published as *Vyhnání Gerty Schnirch* by Host in the Czech Republic in 2009. Translated from Czech by Véronique Firkusny. First published in English by Amazon Crossing in 2021.

Published by Amazon Crossing, Seattle

www.apub.com

Amazon, the Amazon logo, and Amazon Crossing are trademarks of Amazon.com, Inc., or its affiliates.

ISBN-13: 9781542043151 (hardcover)
ISBN-10: 1542043158 (hardcover)

ISBN-13: 9781542043144 (paperback)
ISBN-10: 154204314X (paperback)

Cover design by Kimberly Glyder

Printed in the United States of America

First edition

AUTHOR'S NOTE

My thanks to the survivors of the death march who spoke to me with such openness. My thanks also to those authors whose expert texts and research helped me to flesh out the story, especially historians Jan Perníček and David Kovařík. Thanks to the latter for inspiring me to write this book and for the thirty kilometers we walked together at night in memory of the victims of the transport.

PROLOGUE

The edges of the rough road crumble into the ditch. Grass grows through the gravel, and the wheels of the baby carriage bump over the stones. Her left foot has just slipped on the loose pebbles; there's a dull throbbing in her ankle; perhaps she's pulled a tendon. She tries to avoid putting her full weight on the foot. For several hours now, they've been walking slowly, shuffling along, their baby carriages side by side. From time to time, they steady each other, take turns pushing. For a long while, it's been impossible to make out the road clearly. Only every so often do the beams of a flashlight or the headlights of a truck sweep over them, but then they huddle even tighter, hasten their steps, and throw their coats over the carriages to cover the children.

She can't tell for certain how long they've been walking. It seems as though their journey has taken ages. And yet dawn hasn't even broken, so it can't have been more than a few hours. She's tired, and so is her companion. Should she try to stop and rest?

A few times they have passed people sitting either on the ground or on the suitcases they have been dragging along. Several times they have also seen one of the armed youths rush over and bash in these people's heads with the butt of a rifle. She was scared to stop. In spite of the stitch in her side and the pain in her left foot, she forced herself to keep taking steps.

The young mother walking beside her was whispering about being thirsty.

Gerta said nothing. She had hidden away some water for herself and her child, but she couldn't offer any, not knowing what still lay ahead. Although she, too, was thirsty, she remained silent and shuffled along, step by step, only God knew to where.

God? She had lost faith in him long ago. Once upon a time, she had prayed to him, begged him to help her, to do something—anything—that would have changed her life. Then, little by little, she realized that God wasn't about to do a thing for her. But by then, it was too late.

From that moment on, she had stopped praying and didn't think about God anymore. She wanted to be self-sufficient, even at times like this. Because God had no idea where they were driving her; only those crazed schoolboys knew, and maybe in the end, not even they. Those harebrained brats—she choked with rage; their voices would reach her and then disappear again, becoming lost in the cries of the people ahead of her. A few times, she caught a glimpse of them riding in the backs of passing trucks. With their upraised, tangled weapons, they reminded her of Medusa and her twisted hair of snakes. A seething, raging Medusa, a murderess with the sinister, drunken maw of vulgar riffraff. Look upon them and you would die. You would turn to stone, or they would shoot you. She hated them, but that was all she could do. Only hate. And above all, not let it show if she wanted to survive. She walked meekly beside her companion and kept her mouth shut. The night was inching toward a gray morning, and ahead of her stretched a column of quiet, exhausted people. The sounds of their steps, the swish of winter coats, and words uttered in low voices were interrupted only by the shouts of the guards, the moans of the wounded, and occasional gunshots. How many? Gerta could no longer keep count.

Where exactly had this nightmare started?

By the time the flowers had fallen to the bottom of her mother's open grave, everyone was already sensing it, as if they already knew. Even her father was getting anxious, although he still blindly believed.

When Gerta shot him a sidelong glance, she saw how he was holding himself together, how he was clenching all the muscles in his face, keeping his eyes fixed and then hiding them behind a profusion of blinking, how hard he was trying not to cry. But he should cry, thought Gerta, he should. He should smear the top of his bald head, from which the last wisps of fair hair were receding, with the earth from her mother's grave; he should rub the earth onto his face, let it mix with his tears, and, above all, cry for forgiveness. That he should do. Not stand there preening in his uniform like a pigeon on a perch with his chest puffed out, watching her mother's coffin disappear under clods of dirt. *Stop!* Gerta wanted to cry out, but Friedrich held her back. He grabbed her arm so abruptly, it startled her. Was Friedrich not crying either? But of course, how could he, faithful image of his father that he was? Gerta looked again into the deep hole, where by now the dark gray of the coffin was showing through only in spots. It had been a modest funeral. But this, after all, was not where it had started. This funeral was just one link in a chain of calamities that had come month by month, year after year. All through the war.

And yet the life ahead of her had once seemed so full of promise. And not just her life—Friedrich's, too, and her father's and her mother's, and Janinka's and Karel's; all of their lives had been meaningful and had made sense. They had all been moving as a unified whole toward a future, the contours of which Gerta could make out perfectly. Yet by the winter of 1942, when Mother disappeared beneath the Schnirch headstone, that vision of the future was already disintegrating. The last semblance of security would be trampled by the mob on the Feast of Corpus Christi in 1945. But first, a whole series of other events was still to come.

PART I

Living Through the War

Branded a Schnirch

I

Janinka was delicate, almost translucent. She was like the green lacewing with its pellucid wings woven with golden threads, its tiny pistachio-colored body, and its exceptionally long antennae with which it was fencing against the glass of the windowpane, trapped in a corner by the windowsill until Gerta released it into the warm July night. Janinka, delicate as eiderdown, was a tall, lanky girl with slightly rounded breasts, skinny legs, and flaxen, shoulder-length, carelessly cropped hair that fell across her face like a veil. The first time Gerta met her, she was quiet, and it wasn't because she was shy. She was, for the most part, always quiet, lost in her inner world full of tropical flowers, brilliant butterflies, exotic fauna and flora whose tendrils entwined to form ornamental canopies of fantastic designs. She would allow Gerta and the other children to approach the outskirts of her inner landscape, but it was Mr. Kmenta whom she liked best, and he was always the first one she invited to enter. He would creep in among the foliage of the primeval growth, densely populated by flowers with jagged and smooth, elongated petals. Mr. Kmenta always seemed deeply affected by the aroma wafting from the thickly painted sheet of paper. He would stand over it for a long time and with a slight smile would wander along the pathways of her inner topographies that exuded tranquility. Then he would stroke

Janinka's blonde hair and convey an unspoken compliment to her questioning blue eyes, at which she would lower her stubby, pale eyelashes and smile at her creation. After that, the others could come and have a look as well, to see what Janinka had conjured up this time. Gerta stood beaming proudly behind her, as if it were the work of her own hands, as if her work and Janinka's were one and the same.

"Very good," she'd say.

And of all the children, Gerta was always the last one to return to her table to complete her own drawing of the pitcher with flowers, or the palm of a hand, or whatever the lesson's assignment had been. Janinka's illustration would then sparkle among the plain pictures like a precious gem held by two clothespins on a long line stretched along the wall. It would dangle in their midst like the eye of an eagle among the blind, a jungle of flowers amid the crudely drawn stumps of human arms and the misshapen forms of angular pitchers.

Afterward, she and Janinka would head home, making their way along the wall of St. Jacob's Church, past the Jesuit church, through the park stretching from the Künstlerhaus to the intersection of Pressburger Straße, then on past the first few houses until they reached Blatná Street. Gerta would be talking and swinging her canvas bag carrying all her watercolors and her set of brushes in rhythm with her steps; Janinka would be following along, always a few steps behind. Throughout the prewar years, they had returned home together the same way, and then suddenly everything came to an end. Mr. Kmenta vanished from their lives, and back then, her mother had said that it was bound to end anyway, because Gerta was starting secondary school, and that made her too old to be listening to schoolmaster Kmenta's stories about famous artists, like Michelangelo and Rembrandt, and to be bringing home drawing assignments.

Janinka could have gone on taking Mr. Kmenta's class for another year, but the school secretary had abruptly declared over the telephone that this year Mr. Kmenta's courses weren't open, that they weren't even going to be taking place, and that as for where else Mr. Kmenta might be teaching his art class, she had no idea. Gerta sadly hung up the receiver in the public telephone booth at the post office. Janinka's eyes welled up with tears, and her gaunt little hand trembled. Afterward they sat together on a bench in the park, hand in hand, Janinka silent with her head hanging, looking down at the dark blue shoes that encased her narrow feet, Gerta staring out at the bushes that were slowly turning into golden cascades. It was 1939, Indian summer, and the disappearance of Mr. Kmenta and their art class, for which they had been signed up since the end of the previous school year, had perhaps been foreshadowed by her mother's enigmatic words, now so often heard in their home.

"Everything's going to be different now, and no one will be as happy as they were before," said Gerta, turning to Janinka. Janinka kept the heels of her shoes tapping against the footrest of the bench in a steady rhythm. She nodded her lowered head as if she understood, and remained silent.

II

The war was long. It began inconspicuously, with Gerta barely noticing, and then spread until by the end, it had infiltrated every corner of their lives. It had begun with the cancellation of Mr. Kmenta's art class and then crept along until it reached into their home, right inside their kitchen, where Father chortled as he read aloud from the paper about a Jew who had been stripped and chased out of the Esplanade Café, running so fast that he fell and broke his neck on the steps. That time, her mother burst into tears over such an undignified ending to a human life. This didn't go by without a quarrel, just as when she had given half a liter of milk to Mrs. Goldstein next door, who hadn't managed to go shopping during the hours designated for Jews. Back then, Gerta thought that these were only domestic disasters, earthquakes happening within the walls of their apartment, threatening the peace between her parents. In her room, she would then pray that Mrs. Goldstein wouldn't come to them next time she needed milk, prayed that her mother wouldn't soften at the sight of little Hannah in Mrs. Goldstein's arms, her big dark eyes like freshly peeled chestnuts. Or she prayed that the people sitting on the sidewalks alongside carts heaped with furniture would disappear from the city soon. They always brought such sadness to her mother's face, as did every encounter with Mrs. Kocur from next door, whose son, Jirka, had shot himself because of the "betrayal in Munich." That time, Gerta couldn't understand why her father sent her mother away to their bedroom while he explained the situation to a dismayed Friedrich, who in Jirka had lost a classmate. He dispelled his misgivings with a single word: *sissies.* And Friedrich, that Aryan apple of his father's eye, their little Friedrich, understood, as he always did. Nothing could come between him and his father.

So the war advanced, step by step, while Gerta stubbornly strove not to allow any of the changes that were happening into her life. Except with Janinka, whom she had invited to share her bedroom when Janinka's own was taken over by relatives who had been expelled from Frývaldov.

"They had to make room for people like you," Janinka explained quietly with downcast eyes before refusing Gerta's offer, not even wanting to tell her what was now being said in her house about the Schnirchs. Gerta shook her head, not understanding. What did she mean, *people like you*? After all, hadn't she always been just like Janinka? She had attended drawing class, was about to start secondary school, and rather than being interested in the pictures of Hitler lit by flickering candles in apartment windows, she was much more curious, in the darkness of her bedroom, about the delicate nipples budding from the areolas of her naked breasts. In short, she was absorbed in her own life, which now, as she was about to start attending a new school, had become so engrossing.

Every October morning during that first wartime year, Gerta woke to an inky-blue darkness, unpierced by the slightest glimmer of light, full of curiosity and eagerly anticipating the new day. The window through which she looked out onto Pressburger Straße while she was getting dressed offered her only a view of deep shadows, darker where silhouettes of massive plane trees blocked the approaching light. Gerta never stayed at the window longer than it took her to dress. She was motivated to hurry by the thought of her mother's kind smile at breakfast, heralded by the muffled clinking of cups and spoons that floated to her from the kitchen.

Quietly shutting the door of her room behind her, she slipped down the hallway and stepped into the dining room, where her mother was just setting down a loaf of bread covered by a blue-checkered dish towel. Her father was sitting at the table, leafing through yesterday's paper, as he did each morning. It was only on his way to work that he bought the new one at Mr. Folla's newsstand, which had changed ownership that year, as they discovered from the shop sign that now read "Konrad Kinkel–Trafik."

"Good morning," said Gerta in Czech, at which her mother shot her father a nervous glance before smiling at her and nodding, whereas her father replied in German, glanced up at her mother from behind his paper, gave it a meaningful shake, and dropped his eyes back to the page. Gerta scrunched her lips into a tight pucker, blew her mother a kiss, and relaxed them back into a broad smile. She loved her mother for who she was: simple, kind, with an ample, soft embrace and strong, rounded arms. She was on her side regardless of the circumstances, even these new ones that Gerta didn't really understand, unlike Friedrich Jr., who seemed to have been born already knowing everything. With his polished *Weltanschauung,* or worldview, and even in his appearance, he was the spitting image of his father. He had the same lock of hair on his forehead, narrowed his eyes the same way when he smiled, and did the right thing even before his father articulated it. Friedrich was a true Schnirch, and that was why their father looked upon him differently from the way he looked upon Gerta. Because with Gerta, things had been different since childhood.

Like Friedrich, she spoke both German and Czech, and could sing *"Deutschland, Deutschland über alles"* at her father's request in a way that set his foot tapping in rhythm in its heavy shoe, from which a tall white knee sock protruded. She even wore a boar's bristle on her hat with her dirndl to please him, yet she never held the same worth in his eyes as Friedrich, and she didn't know why. For a long time, she had tried to win over her father, to charm him, before something inside her finally broke. She realized that no matter how hard she tried, she would never be as perfect as Friedrich. In the revolt that took hold of her in the wake of this realization, she tried to refute everything her father had introduced them to and became even more attached to her mother. Around then, their household split into opposing factions, Czech and German, and only she and her mother were on the Czech side. A rift emerged between Gerta and her father. She put away the green dirndl bordered with red flowers and along with it all of her father's rules. Among them was her father's ban on speaking Czech.

It was sometime in the spring of 1939 that he had a long talk with them at home and ordered them to speak only in German. He no longer wished to hear the Czech language. Friedrich complied right away and from that moment on, didn't utter a word in Czech, not even when he and Gerta were alone together. She, however, found this absurd.

"Why don't you speak normally?" she asked, perplexed, when one Sunday at lunch even her mother served in German. She couldn't believe it—her mother had always spoken exclusively in Czech. "It's never been like this," Gerta protested. Not that she objected to the German language; on the contrary, she liked it. Besides, it was as natural a language for her as Czech. She spoke it outside playing games, when they went visiting, at school or even in class, depending on whom she was addressing. She didn't even think about whether to speak Czech when saying something to her friends or to speak German when she saw her father. Several times her father got angry with her, overhearing her speaking in Czech outside and going so far as to lock her in her room for an entire Sunday afternoon. And several times it also happened that he went into his bedroom and came back with a switch and gave her a thrashing, without even batting an eye. Mother tried to catch hold of his hand, pleaded with him in tears to ground her instead, Mother who then would bring Gerta a warm dinner. A warm dinner served in German.

Friedrich stepped into the dining room with a groggy *Grüß Gott*—"Good day." Beyond the window that looked out onto the unkempt garden of the inner courtyard, there was still the same darkness, although Gerta had already eaten half of her slice of bread, and her father had set down the paper and was finishing his cup of tea. Mother pushed a thick slab of buttered bread sprinkled with chives and a cup of tea toward Friedrich and pointed out, as she did every morning, that he had gotten up late.

"I hope you make it on time, children."

The three of them would then step out into the raw morning together.

Father would hurry them down the stairwell, but by the time they set foot outside, they were in step, their collars turned up and their hands clasped at their throats against the cold and relentlessly blowing wind. At the corner of Pressburger Straße and Ponawkagasse, they split up. Father turned to go through the park toward Adolf-Hitler-Platz, and Gerta and Friedrich went on to Horst-Wessel-Straße, where their school was situated.

Gerta's enrollment in the German commercial academy had been her father's choice. She would have preferred to attend the small school that had opened just a few years ago and offered an expanded curriculum in fine arts. How she longed to be in one of those studios, sketching designs for the ceramic bowls and pitchers that she had seen lined up along the windows when she and her mother had gone to the open house. Or she wanted to be creating marionettes of fairies and water sprites and sewing clothes for them out of fabrics with patterns that looked as though they had come out of Janinka's paintings. She saw studios like that there as well. And then others, where there were pedestals on which stood giant human figures made out of white and brown material, fashioned after models as naked as the day God had made them; and then still others, where easels held canvases covered with landscapes, fields, and forests, and paintings of people who looked nothing like people, not even when Gerta examined them for a second and third time, laughing at their angular shapes and faces with two noses. And finally, there were paintings that Gerta couldn't figure out at all, and not even her mother knew what they were supposed to represent. It was a visit Gerta never forgot, so enthralled had she been by the quantity and variety of art that she encountered there. Nor would she ever forget the aroma permeating that school, which remained in her memory for years to come, with the greatest adventures she could imagine wrapped up in it.

That had been her wish, but her father enrolled her in the German commercial academy as he had done with Friedrich. It was a complicated time, and the nation needed competent clerical workers, whom her father could then employ in the *Oberlandrat* office, the newly established supreme regional council, a lower-level branch of the German administration, where he himself worked.

Gerta didn't resist. To be an artist, after all, was just a dream, possible to live out only if you were one of the elect, those who knew they never could or would do anything other than serve a higher calling. And Gerta was not among them; she was merely the daughter of Barbora Ručková and Friedrich Schnirch of Sterngasse, who could draw a little bit with charcoal and pastels, do some handiwork that her mother had taught her, and excelled in computation at school. *Someone like me doesn't become a famous artist,* she told herself, and in September 1939, she entered the German *Handelsakademie*, and it was a good thing she did, since they closed the fine arts school shortly thereafter.

III

At the very beginning of that first year of secondary school, her father signed Gerta up for the League of German Girls. There was nothing she could do about it. She went, same as the other girls from her class, same as Anne-Marie Judex, the daughter of the city's *Regierungskommissar*, the government commissioner, about whom there had been so much talk that year. Gerta avoided her and the others and hid out every day in the applied arts studio until four o'clock, when at the corner of Kotgasse she could meet up with Janinka, whose parents had stopped keeping an eye on her, as they had both been deployed full-time to a bullet factory in Líšeň.

"It looks good on you," said Janinka once, when Gerta came running over late, still in her uniform. "But if my parents saw you like this, I probably wouldn't be allowed to spend time with you anymore."

They turned in the direction Gerta had just come running from and set out for the closest bench in the nearby park off Koliště Street.

"We had practice," said Gerta, running her hand from her black necktie all the way down the front of the long dark skirt, embarrassed. "If I didn't have to, I wouldn't wear it."

"But you still go there anyway."

Gerta walked on in silence.

"I've started taking art class again," she then said. "They have their own studio there. They believe that everyone should develop their natural talents. Mr. Kmenta used to say the same thing. I could ask Frau Wirkt if you could come too."

Janinka shook her head.

"They won't let me if I'm not in the League. And I can't be in the League. My parents won't allow me. And I don't really want to be. I don't even know what you do there."

"Well, you do what you want. I do Art Studio, Chorus, and Sports. I never imagined it would be this much fun. Had my father not signed me up, well, you know." Gerta shrugged. "At the beginning, I was nervous, too, and my mom didn't want me to go either. But now I just go to those classes."

"I'm not sure," murmured Janinka softly.

Eventually they reached the park, ran across the empty street, and made a beeline for the bench. Gerta thought about the concerns her mother expressed early on. While feebly trying to protest to her father, she had said, and Gerta had heard her, "They're going to brainwash her there." That was what she had said. Brainwash, which Gerta had thought was strange. Had Friedrich said it, with his closetful of horror pulp fiction, she wouldn't have been surprised. But her mother saying it to her father? Her father became furious and sent her mother to their bedroom, after which there was silence. In the end, all Gerta knew was that she was supposed to show up at the League the second week of school, so she did. And she did so at her mother's behest, even though she understood how much it went against her mother's way of thinking.

In the end, though, all the girls ended up going there after school. It seemed perfectly normal, and what could be wrong—one went to art class and occasionally rehearsed some German songs and practiced marching in uniform for revues in various parades. Or was there something wrong?

Gerta wasn't sure, and this made her uneasy. Sometimes she felt she didn't belong among them. If only she could just be normal! A normal German girl who was thrilled to stay in the sightlines of their *Führerin* lady leader and show off what a worthy representative of the League she was. Her schoolmates, for example, had tittered with excitement during those trials held early on, designed to reveal what hidden talents lay within each one of them. Gerta was embarrassed because she couldn't toss a ball or throw a javelin, wasn't good at long jump, and was a slow runner. Naturally, she wasn't the only one to be jeered at by the more competitive girls. But might she have done better had the image of her mother's troubled face not been before her at all times?

But then she noticed she wasn't alone. Over time, it struck her that she wasn't the only one doodling on blank scraps of paper during breaks, reading a book under her desk, or even staring out of the window into the street for minutes on end. That was how she first ended up in conversation with Karel. This made them the first two to breach what up to then had been an awkward barrier between the handsome young men strutting around in their uniforms, who were actually painfully shy, and the attractive girls in their League uniforms, who, however, had eyes only for Anne-Marie Judex, and ears only for the high-society gossip she brought back to them.

A slight little girl who had been playing in the sandbox approached the bench on which she and Janinka were sitting. She ran over from the grass to the sidewalk, which offered a better surface for drawing with chalk, a short, fat stub of which she held in her small fist. She squatted on the sidewalk and started drawing numerical figures that she looked barely old enough to know, and sang, "Five, six, seven, eight, Hitler's little head of hate! Prague, Brno, Paris wail, let the villain rot in jail!"

Gerta froze. One wasn't allowed to say such things, for God's sake. What if someone overheard?

"Don't say that!" Gerta shouted at her, panicked.

The girl looked up with her round blue eyes and asked in surprise, "Why?"

Gerta turned to Janinka, whose gaze was darting back and forth from one to the other in consternation.

"It's not allowed. You could go to jail for that."

The child looked at her.

"And so could your mother, if you keep on saying it."

The little girl stood up, brushed the sidewalk grit off her knees, and ran back to the sandbox and the women chatting on a bench beneath a shrub.

Gerta and Janinka looked at each other, decided they'd better get up, and set out across the intersection back toward Pressburger Straße.

"And what about your new classmates, what're they like?" asked Janinka a little later.

"I'm not sure. I haven't really gotten to know anyone yet," answered Gerta indifferently.

"Maybe in time," said Janinka.

Maybe, thought Gerta, but it wasn't something she felt like discussing with Janinka. No one could compete with Janinka's place in Gerta's life anyway, so why should Gerta add to Janinka's worries, when as of last summer she'd been assigned to a cleaning job at an insurance company, because she wasn't allowed to go on to secondary school? She was lucky. Because of her weak heart, they hadn't sent her directly to the Reich as they had many others. This way they could go on meeting secretly for their afternoon walks in the park or along the Zábrdovický embankment by the Svitava River, tucked away behind the rear facades of sumptuous villas. They would sit by the dam, in the shadows cast by the Petersdom and Špilberk Castle, where the sound of rushing water drowned out even the sound of the nearby streetcar, wondering how it was possible that the people of Brno had forgotten about this river, which had been edged out of the sightlines of the promenades.

Back then, Gerta lived for such moments, and later on also for the short breaks by the window, when Karel would politely come over to keep her company. Who would have suspected that before long, his image would accompany her even on her afternoon walks with Janinka, and would linger in her bedroom in the evenings, so that she could barely wait for the morning? She herself was surprised when she couldn't keep him out of her mind. It was as if the sense of harmony and inner balance that he exuded kept drawing her thoughts back to him. Who back then would have suspected that he would be the one to hold her so close during dance lessons that the fabric of her skirt, pulled tight across her thighs, would crease? That he would be the one to walk her home and hold her hand under the plane trees, long after the light in her parents' bedroom had gone out. Nor back then had she ever imagined that he would be the one, some years later, to say he would marry her when the war was over and the Germans had lost, even though her last name was Schnirch. At that she had burst out laughing and protested that he knew perfectly well just how German she was. And finally, she had never imagined that for years this would be the last joyful laughter to come bubbling so freely and easily from her lips. As the memory of a final moment of happiness, it would arc over many long years to come.

IV

She had no problem with it, and why should she have; it could only work to her advantage. The fact that she was acting as a cover for

Anne-Marie and Friedrich didn't bother her in the least. She did her own thing, and whether Friedrich chose to spend his time in the Hitler Youth, or elsewhere, she didn't really care. Besides, she had risen in his esteem and for the first time felt that Friedrich wasn't looking down on her with contempt. In fact, he seemed to be downright grateful. And the effect on Gerta's classmates seemed to be the same.

It hadn't taken long for Anne-Marie to discover that the youth leader of the Turner gymnasts, who had cut such a dashing figure waving his flag at the head of his division in the parade honoring Reich Protector von Neurath's official visit, was Gerta's brother. It was sometime toward the end of November that she sidled up to Gerta in the girls' bathroom and asked her about him. Gerta burst out laughing at her covetous look, lamely disguised under the pretext of a conspiratorial friendliness, as if she were being sincere. Nonetheless, Gerta proceeded to lay her brother at Anne-Marie's feet. She introduced them one Friday afternoon at the stadium where Friedrich was training with his division.

He thus became Gerta's admission ticket to a clique of girls who up until that moment had excluded her. Not that it helped her to finally feel normal, nor did it manage to dispel the misgivings that she brought to school with her from home, and then carried back home again, but at least she could feel that she was almost one of them. Anne-Marie started sitting next to her on the school bench and, wonder of wonders, resolved to become her best friend. Gerta was tickled, yet at the same time it made her nervous, and she felt uncomfortable. Next to Anne-Marie, she felt like a turnip beside a hyacinth. Every night she smelled her intoxicatingly fragrant bench mate on her clothes and envisioned the delicate wrists, from which dangled golden bracelets, and the carefully manicured bright red fingernails. She understood why Friedrich was so smitten with her, elegant Anne-Marie, always tastefully swathed in dark dresses made of fabrics that hadn't appeared on the shelves of ordinary shops in a very long time. The girl with blonde tresses falling in loose waves to her shoulders, with pencil-thin black eyebrows arching over her pale blue eyes, and her full lips always meticulously coated with a layer of bloodred lipstick. Anne-Marie easily could have given competition to the beautiful movie star Adina Mandlová had they been in the same room, and she might even have had the advantage, not only in looks, but also in eloquence. She spoke with astonishing ease about her papa's connections; in his capacity as *Regierungskommissar*, he sent a chauffeur to pick her up from school every day. She also spoke of dinners with the Reich Protector or the police commissioner, and about the gowns she and her mother wore for each occasion. She was exquisite, living proof of the superhuman realm. Her effect on the other girls in the class was magnetic as she instantly became their arbiter, and each one wanted to spend at least a moment bathed in the glow of her attention. And Friedrich was no different. He had succumbed to her at once.

It was hard to say what he imagined might come of it, being the son of a mere clerk in the *Oberlandrat* office, but that was no longer Gerta's concern. Maybe he thought of himself as a Teutonic demigod— after all, he had looked like one in that procession of Turners, a chosen one not obliged to deny himself anything. Maybe he sensed a way to advance himself toward more-important responsibilities and a position beyond a career in administration or the *Wehrmacht*, although he had been genuinely looking forward to that. To Gerta, it was all the same.

She existed in her own insulated world. Had the arguments at home not started and had she not met Anne-Marie—such irrefutable proof that the Reich was real—she might have remained deaf and blind to it all, hiding out on the secluded banks of the Svitava River with Janinka until the very last day of liberation. By then, she would have welcomed her looting neighbors escorted by the Red Army, oblivious to the fact that she was now one of the guilty. And the defeated. But she had met Anne-Marie Judex, and from there, it was just one more step to Oskar Judex and the red banners with swastikas on a white background, streaming down from both sides of the New Town Hall balcony.

V

Oskar Judex knew it in advance. Throughout the eve of the declaration of the Protectorate, he had been waiting, so that at three o'clock the next morning, immediately upon receiving the order by telephone, he and a squad of *Ordners* took over the municipal administrative office in the New Town Hall, where he promptly pronounced himself chief commissioner of the city. Meanwhile, Karl Schwabe, his colleague from the NSDAP—that is, Nazi Party—leadership, occupied the police headquarters on Palacký Street and, under the protection of the Fifth Army and General List, took over the office of the commissioner of police. On the morning of March 15, 1939, the residents of Brno, without even realizing it, woke up to a different city. As did the hapless Dr. Rudolf Spazier, the First Republic mayor of Brno, who that morning, arriving at work as usual, discovered upon reaching the door to his office that he was to be escorted inside by two armed *Ordners*. Seated in the upholstered visitor's chair opposite his usual place, in which Judex, seven years his junior, arrogantly sprawled, sporting a fashionable toothbrush mustache on his round, fleshy face, the mayor was informed that on this day the city council as well as the municipal government had been dissolved and were henceforth forbidden to congregate, that all offices had been taken over by trustworthy employees who were NSDAP members, and that it would behoove him, Spazier, to go on furlough, before it was officially announced that the newly appointed chief administrator of the city was Oskar Judex.

"And if you haven't listened to the radio yet today, allow me to inform you that Czechoslovakia is now history and, as the Protectorate of Bohemia and Moravia, has been incorporated into the Third Reich. I accept your congratulations. *Heil Hitler!*"

The two *Ordners* tapped Spazier on the shoulder and escorted him out of the building. Spazier made his way to the Czech Besední dům, where over the course of the day, other city officials who had been dismissed from their posts were gathering. Once he finally pulled himself together, he decided that he would refuse to acknowledge Judex as mayor and returned to the town hall, to which he continued to go regularly for another week. After that week, however, as a warning to others, Judex had him removed to Palacký Street just as the headquarters of that building were swarming with hundreds of Gestapo officials in black SS uniforms, who had been transferred over from Vienna and Stuttgart. These days, no one had time to worry about the fate of the former mayor. Brno was changing its colors. Buildings were being taken over, and signs were going up on street corners, calling for calm and order, and warning against any attempts to resist the course of events. Streets were redirected, and amid the confusion, cars drove the wrong way, on the right side. Over the next few weeks, this cost many pedestrians their lives, and that was just in Brno.

But order was order. As an old patriot with an understanding of order, Spazier refused to accept the revocation of his post without confirmation by the city council and the municipal government, let alone when it came from someone who had appointed himself to the position. In the end, though, on September 1, 1939, during the first wave of arrests, he was dragged out of bed before dawn, taken to the casemate prison at Špilberk Castle, sent from there to the concentration camp in Dachau, and from there directly to Buchenwald. And Judex had peace.

During the first days of the occupation, Judex officially accepted the position of *Regierungskommissar*, government commissioner, as well as personal congratulations from Hitler, who was passing through the city and chose to show himself to his people on the balcony of the New Town Hall, the *Neues Rathaus*, from where he blared his unforgettable speech to a cheering crowd of Brno Germans, ecstatic to be *Heim ins Reich*, "home" again.

On that occasion, Anne-Marie with her mother and siblings had stood in the room behind the balcony, looking out at the backs of the great Führer and her father, who stood proudly at his side, newly in charge of the city, which now belonged to them. Hitler then paid a gallant compliment to her beauty and to her mother's beauty, congratulated Papa Judex, this time not on his superbly executed takeover of the city of Brno but on his lovely family, sure to become a pillar of the Reich, and took off for Vienna.

Judex, bolstered by the confidence of the Great One, went to work with gusto. He wanted to leave a mark on the history of his hometown. An indelible one. He broke ground to complete what was left unfinished of the Ringstraße, the section from Horst-Wessel-Straße, Husová Street, and the Stadthofplatz down to the train station, thus creating a complete circular boulevard, a project the Czech municipal government had been planning for years but never managed to realize. For Judex and the new city council, it was a convenient development, mostly because it allowed for their National Socialist parades to be carried out in an even more grandiose manner, circling the entire city. He put in a tram line on Französische Straße, connecting the center of the city to the fashionable Černá Pole residential district, and had a second line put in that went all the way to the suburb of Líšeň. All the roads under Petrov Hill were paved, new buildings were designed, and old ones renovated, until finally, in June 1941, a law banning all construction of nonmilitary buildings went into effect. He determined that this thwarted his plans and was detrimental to the city, so he carried on undeterred. Brno was to become the cultural center of the Protectorate, destined one day to surpass even the nearby metropolis of Vienna. Soon people would be talking about visiting Brno and only afterward Vienna. The glorious Brno *Deutsches Haus*, the Petersdom cathedral, Spielberg castle, a lecture at the university, and a performance in the concert hall of the German Theater on Richard-Wagner-Platz would belong on every itinerary. Such were Judex's goals, and to ensure he could go on to achieve them undisturbed, he ordered some three hundred cultural and political public officials imprisoned, thereby giving the Brno Gestapo its first major assignment. Once the Czech universities were shut down, the Gestapo took over two university buildings, Kounic College and Sušil Dormitory, from which emerged confused students with half-packed personal belongings, those who hadn't yet been arrested on the spot, interned, and sent directly to Dachau. The German Technical University was expanding, and the troublesome Czechs were being eliminated just in time. And as if that weren't enough, the Gestapo had seized even the new law school building at the end of Eichhorner Straße, or Veveří Street, where they were now holding their assemblies in the hall facing the wall where, before the war, there had hung a monumental painting by Antonín Procházka depicting Prometheus bringing fire to mankind, now rolled up and hidden in some basement by Czech patriots. And it was toward this wall that they now pointed the fingertips of their rigidly extended arms, raised in a thunderous *Heil Hitler!* delivered with such conviction, it seemed as if they were saluting Hitler himself, Hitler-Prometheus, Hitler the hero, who had brought them fire.

Yet how could Gerta, when she announced at home that her new classmate was Anne-Marie Judex, have known all that? Her mother had blinked in alarm but continued her work at the kitchen table, where Gerta was helping her glaze with honey the delicate angel-wing pastries they were making for Friedrich's birthday. Friedrich had just shrugged his shoulders, and her father had murmured, "*Sehr gut,*" immediately adding a satisfied, "He's doing a good job, the *Regierungskommissar.*" Then he meaningfully raised his eyebrows, continued what he was doing, and with that, the subject was closed. The only thing that had changed since then was that the air in their household was now tinged with the fragrance of Anne-Marie's French perfume, which came off not only Gerta's clothes but also Friedrich's.

It was only several years later that Judex turned Brno into a city of war, marching in precise step under a baton of terror, where one could detect the odor of resistance fighters and saboteurs, cooking up their kitchen-table plots and sweating in fear, alongside the smell of money being raked in by the munitions industry and by the factories supplying the *Wehrmacht*. And that was just one of the reasons why some people hated Judex while others praised him, although this didn't strike Gerta as in any way unusual. After all, it had always been like that; what pleased some people displeased others. And in the end, people said it was thanks to Judex that during the war, the city had fared so well. That it didn't end up like Frankfurt or Dresden.

As the industrial center of the Protectorate, it could have fared much worse. The munitions industries, rubber plants, engine factories, and textile mills that were spread out all over the city easily could have invited destruction, which not even the historical center could have withstood, had Judex, at the very last minute, with the front lines just a few kilometers south of Brno, not ordered the dissolution of the statutory law for the city's defense. Fortification efforts were aborted. The city was declared open, and the Red Army poured in through the broad access roads that were now being defended only by the local People's Militia.

Both the *Regierungskommissar*, Oskar Judex, and the vice president of the Provincial Council, Karl Schwabe, were by then already bringing up the rear of the first wave of fugitives fleeing west. Their cars were piled high with Brno's insignias and treasures, including Rubens's painting *The Head of Medusa*, which Judex had ordered to be removed from the exhibition hall of the Moravian Gallery and had personally confiscated, so that for the duration of the war, it hung in his town hall office. They were fleeing toward Jihlava. Judex drove off in his car, closely behind an automobile laden with his personal effects, where on the seat beside the driver, wearing a silver fox fur coat, huddled the corpulent, racially pure birth mother, the fair Gabrielle Judex, and behind her Anne-Marie, her sister, Eugenie, and little Otto-Adolf, the youngest. Judex could have decided to allow the city to be torn up by the Russian swine, as he liked to say in certain settings, such as among the men in the SS units up at Špilberk Castle. Between the *Wehrmacht* soldiers and the armed militia, there were still enough German defenses in the streets of Brno that a clash with the Red Army could have left the city in ruins. He also could have allowed it to be flooded by the Moravian Sea, the waters of the Brno Dam Lake, but unlike SS Hauptmannführer Römer, under whose authority it also could have fallen, the order to blow up the dam above the city was one he didn't give. In spite of his ruined career, he took off without any feelings of animosity and left the city to its fate, which at that moment didn't seem to be particularly tragic. Perhaps he thought that developments at the front would take a different turn and that Hitler's secret weapon would flush the allied armies out of the southern tips of the Protectorate, where they were trying to break through at any cost, and that someday he might still return. Regarding his return, he wasn't entirely mistaken. He had about five days before he was recognized in Jihlava, apprehended, and handed over to the Brno people's court, which on December 2, 1946, sentenced him for life. He was lucky. Schwabe had already been hanged in September 1946, mere hours after a heated trial. With his tongue lolling and his eyes bulging from their sockets, he had soiled his pants just like all those whom he had ordered strung up on the three gallows standing side by side like sisters in the Kounic College courtyard. But luckiest of them all would be their third colleague, with whom they had spent many gaming nights in the Špilberk casemate barracks. On the very last day before the city was taken by the Red Army, the head of the Brno Gestapo, Hugo Römer, still managed to order fourteen Czech civilians to be executed on the shooting range in Medlánky for having willfully damaged the city's fortifications along the rear lines. At the same time, like Judex and Schwabe, he had packed his suitcases and hightailed it unobserved out of the city and remained unpunished, as he was never found. Judex learned all this only long after receiving his sentence, which granted him eight years to ponder how things had turned out for all his *Kameraden*, for himself, and for his family, who had been left with nothing but a health certificate issued for the American occupied zone, the few layers of clothing they were wearing, and a tiny Russian fang stuck in Anne-Marie's womb, because a muzhik from the Caucasus, who had made it as far as the Bohemian-Moravian Highlands, didn't bother to ask first. And after those eight years in the Cejl Street prison, just a few meters away from the new home of Gerta and Barbora Schnirch, on September 11, 1953, he died, feeling like a forgotten hero, accustomed to being smiled upon by the gods who had stood by him throughout his life, on the Russian front during World War I and later during those five years in Siberia, which he had barely survived. And then even back home in Brno, until at the very end, literally the last few minutes, when it would have taken so little for him to drive out of nighttime Jihlava into the American zone, where he could have disappeared into the crowd, those gods had forsaken him.

VI

She hadn't quite figured it out yet; there was still something childlike about her. The concerns she would bring home, the worries on her mind—a few times Gerta's mother had genuinely had to laugh. She tried to put off Gerta's clash with reality for as long as she could. She would gather up Friedrich's newspapers as soon as he set them down on the table and asked that he and Freddy listen to the radio in his room, and not in front of Gerta. For Friedrich, it was a given that he would initiate their son into politics, but not Gerta, because as far as he was concerned, girls and women had no business mixing with politics. So it had been possible to spare Gerta from having to witness the calamity that was spreading through their country. And for this, Barbora was very grateful to him, although his motivation wasn't love for their daughter, but rather disdain. A woman's place was elsewhere, as she very well knew.

He hadn't always been that way. When she married him, he had been gentle, caring, and extremely chivalrous. She, Barbora Ručková, a farmer's daughter, never would have questioned the roles of a man and a woman, as she understood perfectly well who had which responsibilities. It was therefore surprising to her when Friedrich tried to help her with everything, accompanying her to go shopping, and even discussing masculine topics with her. He would ask for her opinion on the political situation, and when he returned home from work, he seldom went out again. That was in the early twenties. By the time she gave birth to little Freddy and later Gerta, it was 1925; Friedrich seemed to worship the ground she walked on. Only much later did it dawn on her that the extraordinary level of care that her husband lavished on her had in fact been a ploy to control her completely. Little by little at first, and then after she'd had the children, with increasing rapidity (although they always kept her so busy, there was barely time to notice), she realized more and more that she had slipped into an isolation in which her only contact was with him and with a few of their neighbors in the building. She had never given it much thought, because after all, she'd had such a loving and attentive husband. So when had things begun to shift? Bit by bit, after they started listening to Hitler's barking speeches on the radio. She disliked them from the start, couldn't stand that modulation of his, those outbursts of hysterical shouting, at first euphoric and then moments later dark and menacing. It made her ears ring and her head hurt. But Friedrich, after listening to those speeches, seemed practically transformed. That must have been when it started. Up until then, he had busied himself cultivating the garden of his family, never moving even a step away, and then all at once he fenced it in, put a roof over it, stuck everyone inside as if into a jail, and turned his attention to the garden of mankind, which that histrionic charlatan on the radio promised would be his. Back then, the more Friedrich got involved, the more vertically he rose. Not only professionally, but even physically. Seeing him walk around ramrod straight and with a stuck-up air, she struggled to remember how laid-back he had looked when he used to play volleyball at the public outdoor swimming pool. Could this even be the same person? The one who now, twenty years later, spoke to her only in terse commands, even behind the closed door of their bedroom? But no, she would never dream of challenging him. She was grateful to him for her two beautiful children, her respectable home, her comfortable life. She was grateful to him for her social status, one that, when she had first arrived in Brno, before he took her under his wing, she never could have imagined. She wouldn't dare to rebel against him, not even for the way he reproached her daily for her Czechness. She wouldn't dare, but Gerta did. It was, after all, completely natural. Why wouldn't Gerta want to know why he forbade her to speak in Czech? They had raised both children to be bilingual. The two of them would slip from one language into the other as if it were nothing, in the same way as at least half of all the other children they knew. Wasn't everyone in Brno also a little bit Viennese? Who in Brno couldn't at the very least understand both languages? No one. Friedrich spoke to them in German, she in Czech. Until this cursed war changed him so completely. And it changed her too. Now she felt like a maidservant beside him, like some domestic burden that was tolerated but brought shame down on the house of Schnirch. He had succeeded, without much effort, in pulling Freddy away from her. Exactly when had it happened? When had she lost him? Her little boy, who would wrap himself in her skirts and beg for a kiss? When did her son first give her that cold look, as if she were some lowly Czech servant? Maybe even before he started trade school, when he first started attending those Hitler Youth meetings in the evenings. What a handsome Turner he then became. He even made that young Judex girl's head spin. Several times her car with its uniformed chauffeur had pulled up in front of their house, and all three of them had jumped out—first Gerta, to whom no one paid any attention and who immediately dashed into the building, then the Judex girl, and finally Freddy, who would gallantly kiss her hand. She watched it from the window but said nothing as she set lunch on the table. *They're still just children,* she had thought. *This soon will pass.* But it didn't. She mentioned it to Friedrich. She might as well have doused him with ice-cold water. He wasn't about to risk ruining his career because of a little romance his son was having with the daughter of the *Regierungskommissar*, who had suitors of a different rank in mind for her.

"It has to stop," he declared sternly one evening after dinner, having folded his napkin and placed it on the table.

All the blood seemed to have drained from Freddy's veins. He shot a glance at Gerta, who sat rigid and stunned, and then at her, his own mother, as if she were a spy and a traitor. That was the moment she lost him for good.

But Gerta stuck by her. It had been her own decision not to renounce the Czech language; she, Barbora, never would have dreamed of forcing her. Gerta made her decision because she loved the language; it was what they spoke at school, and it was what her friend Janinka spoke, she who barely spoke at all. She made her decision with the recklessness of a child and let all of Friedrich's commands go out of her head. How often had he brought her home in tears, having caught her on the corner whooping happily in Czech with some of her girlfriends? Barbora tried to convince him not to be so hard on Gerta, but he didn't let up. In their household, ridicule and contempt for all things Czech became the norm. If a Czech, then a flunky; the Czechs were a nation of sissies, easily bought off. They had no honor. He said this, looking straight into her eyes, the eyes of his wife, and she didn't say a word. Not even on those nights when he ordered her out of their bedroom. She said nothing, just took her quilt to the couch in the kitchen. Stared at the ceiling for a long time, unable to sleep, wondering where the gentleness with which they used to hold each other through the night had gone. Those loving, tender caresses with which he used to take her body, where had they disappeared? What remained were sullen, gruff gestures with which he would grab her for a moment, and then, as if ashamed of his weakness, would move away to the farthest edge of the bed and turn his back on her in silence. Barbora didn't understand. All she understood was that she mustn't cry, because even silent sobbing would infuriate him so much that he would order her into the kitchen again.

About the pain in her chest, which appeared out of the blue toward the end of November, she said nothing to anyone. As it was, she had heard enough about how weak, lazy, and good at lying the Czechs were, and besides, she didn't want to worry Gerta. Coming home from school these days, she seemed different, somehow more grown up. *It's the age,* Barbora thought, contemplating her daughter who had suddenly transformed from a child into a young woman. Could she be in love?

Who would have anticipated how quickly she would grow so weak? She, the youngest child born to a farmer from Moutnice married to the daughter of an old Austrian tenant-farming family, whose dowry had been stamina and strength. But it overpowered her, nonetheless.

Yet maybe it wasn't just the pain that had settled in her chest. Maybe it was also that her love of life was evaporating like air seeping out of a carnival balloon. She knew she should make an effort, that she should rally and find the will to live again. But for whom, other than for Gerta, who stayed beside her, devoted, vigilant, hugging her burning, sweat-soaked body? Like this she had only one other desire—to sleep untroubled by thoughts of the present or future.

Never would she be able to apologize enough to her daughter for abandoning her, for cutting short her adolescence, for hurling her into real life. No amount of regret would ever suffice. But going on had become simply impossible.

VII

It happened a few months after her mother's funeral. As if her death had brought devastation down on the whole family. The embrace that had held everyone in their household together had fallen away. They scattered, and silence settled into the apartment. What remained of their family life was a deliberate passing of each other through the vacant rooms and scraps of paper with orders that her father started leaving for her. And one day, a draft notice appeared beside them.

First her mother, she thought, and now Friedrich. Freddy, the family's prize stallion, apple of his father's eye, the boast of his German blood. Hitler Youth squad leader, standard bearer, the most dashing Turner in the city of Brno.

For her father, it was a terrible blow. His own Friedrich, whose career path he had been paving, toiling to secure a better place for his own blood at the banquet feast, all for nothing, as now even his Friedrich was being sent to the front. Hell, he should be there already, Gerta thought to herself after she got home from school that afternoon and was tucking Friedrich's draft notice behind the cupboard glass.

A few days later, she watched her father firmly set his jaw and jut his chin forward, determined to take this civic obligation like a man and to be proud of this calamity. It was, after all, an honor.

"It's your duty, boy," he said through clenched teeth on March 23, 1943, the day Freddy reported for duty at the German House on Adolf-Hitler-Platz, the day they had to say goodbye to him.

How had her father so far managed to grease all the right palms without ever missing the mark? Gerta wondered. What had happened? Why was twenty-year-old Friedrich, up to now a seemingly indispensable minor clerical worker, suddenly being called to the front? Could it be that all those SS men from Stuttgart and Vienna, for whom her father, at Schwabe's orders, had obligingly danced, were by now too comfortably settled in their posh villas in the Černá Pole neighborhood?

Were there no more wishes left to fulfill? Was no one lacking for anything? Or had someone wanted to take revenge, someone from under whose nose he might have snatched a coveted apartment vacated by persons who had been displaced, or had he perhaps displaced the wrong families? Gerta was aware of how her father and brother took advantage of their official posts. By the fourth year of the war, it was obvious to Gerta why they were never lacking for meal tickets, sugar, or meat. During those evenings in the kitchen when they tried to keep her out of their discussions, they were wrong in thinking that Gerta was either hard of hearing or couldn't understand anything. She knew as much as they did about those nets of theirs, which they would cast randomly over whomever they pleased, reallocating apartments belonging to families that had not yet been displaced and trafficking in their belongings. *Human traffickers, scavengers,* she thought to herself as she listened to the insatiable urgency with which they bartered people who were still passing them in the street, shopping at the same grocery store, going to the same movie theater. But from the moment Friedrich was drafted, her father was left alone to his double-dealing. Gerta felt not even a shred of pity. On the contrary, she found herself feeling a wicked glee. *As he did unto Mother, so may God do unto him,* she said to herself.

From the window, she watched them—her father and his son, her father and her brother—as they left the building on March 23, and never shed a tear. She felt nothing. Had it been Karel's back she was watching instead of theirs, she would have felt something. Or Janinka's, had she been sent away to one of the labor camps in the Reich. But everything else left her feeling empty. Even the question as to when the war would end, which was on everybody's lips. And who would be the victor, now that Hitler had set out for Russia? For Gerta, it all went in one ear and out the other. She had been indifferent before and was indifferent even now, since her mother had died. And she was indifferent when it came to the future, even though her brother was now in the war. She felt no fear for him. She feared only the loneliness that was about to close in on her and keep her inside the apartment alone with her father and his pedantic ways, harsh commands, and uncompromising rules.

She stood by the window that March morning in the middle of a war with no end in sight, four months after she had buried her mother and mere minutes since her brother had gone. In that moment, she still had no idea how radically her life was about to change. Had anyone told her that her father would make her join the German Winter Relief Program, most likely she would have laughed out loud. But back then, there were still an untold number of things that she, Gerta Schnirch, faithful to the Czech legacy of Barbora Ručková, never could have imagined, not even in a nightmare.

VIII

A few weeks after Friedrich's departure, Gerta stopped showing up at the League of German Girls. She couldn't stand that stifling heroic feeling to which she couldn't relate. And Anne-Marie was insufferable.

Papa Oskar Judex, at his daughter's request, had ordered a giant map of Europe to be put up on the clubhouse wall, with movable push-pin flags to indicate the front lines and tiny German flags to mark the major cities that had already come under the Reich's control. Each week, these would be adjusted by an *Ordner* who would accompany Anne-Marie and her driver to the *Handelsakademie* and make sure that they were kept up to date. All the girls would reverentially listen to Anne-Marie, tears in her eyes, as she used a pointer, its tip hovering over the region of Volhynia, from where Friedrich's first letters had begun to arrive.

Very soon it became practically fashionable to have someone at the front. Anne-Marie basked in the aura of Gerta's brother, a crusader for their future, and with a suffering expression would drape her arm around

Gerta's shoulders and lay her head against Gerta's in a display of com-
miseration of grief that not even Adina Mandlová could have portrayed
more convincingly. At the same time, in the *Brünner Tagblatt* daily
newspaper, there were always photographs of the *Regierungskommissar*
surrounded by his family at festive gatherings in which there was invari-
ably a tall and handsome SS officer standing at Anne-Marie's side.

Gerta could do without having to listen as letters from her brother
or from some of the other girls' relatives were read aloud. She wasn't
interested in being part of the Nordic Heroes fan club or in cheering
every time a little red flag on the map moved. Instead of attending
the League's assemblies, she took refuge in the art studio. She didn't
even need to make up excuses. The zeal with which her father had
initially overseen her pro-German activities had long since dissipated.
Occasionally he would ask her where she'd been, and Gerta would say
that she and some of the other girls had been in the studio, which
sometimes, when the League assemblies would take place during art
period, was even true. Then she would quickly turn the conversation
to the map in the clubhouse on which they were trying to keep track
of Friedrich's footsteps, and that was all she needed to do. Her father
would immediately be overcome by a surge of pride and concern that
would occupy him for the remainder of the brief moment of interaction
with his daughter.

During this period, Gerta was happiest when she was working with
clay. She delighted in its consistency, pliable as plasticine, its slickness
in her wet hands, the way it would slip between her fingers, gradually
growing warm under the intensity of her touch. It would become more
and more malleable, until it allowed itself to be shaped into forms. At
first simple ones, based on prototypes Frau Wirkt would give them to
copy, then eventually more complex ones, and finally a bust, in which
she struggled to capture her mother's likeness. Was it possible that she
had already forgotten the details of her features?

When everyone was gathered in the studio with the *Führerin*, Gerta found that she couldn't concentrate. She would toss the clay from one hand to the other, pull on it and squeeze it into a ball while listening to fantastic visions about the future of the Reich. Back then, the girls were still trying to outdo one another in their praise for the nation, cheering upon hearing the names of new cities through which the front line had passed on its way to Russia and expressing concern when the colorful flags on the map moved backward toward the west. Forward and backward, it was like a game that was running them ragged. Indoctrinated at home with blind faith in the Führer's genius and in his mysterious secret weapon, they speculated about Hitler's strategies and dreamed up various scenarios.

"Girls, listen up . . . Hush, listen, here's what I know."

"The entire German race has joined forces . . . There's only one way it can end—within a month, Moscow will belong to us!"

Or:

"*Endsieg*, final victory, we're almost there! Moscow is practically ours, and the Führer is sending them on to Stalingrad!"

Or:

"I heard the business in Kharkov was a ruse, that at first they retreated, then doubled back and attacked with renewed force, and in the end, those Stalinists lost a million men! A million! Now, that's a massive blow!"

And then also:

"Have you heard, Goebbels wants to divorce Magda? For Lída Baarová . . . Yes, seriously!"

Or:

"Did you know that in the Caucasus Mountains, there are Jewish tribes that kill every firstborn child and drink its blood?"

There were more and more such stories going around, implausible, surreal, and always ending with the girls exclaiming the same surefire victory: "Whatever happens, in the end, victory will be ours!"

Apparently, Gerta was the only one looking on with any consternation as the little red flags inched back westward. The other girls would all cluster around a different point on the map and would whisper conspiratorially about confusing the enemy, about the *Wehrmacht* finally proving itself, that this was no retreat, but just a shift from offense to defense, just like Goebbels said, and they would go on to discuss next steps, tactics 100 percent guaranteed to succeed. They grew increasingly frenzied, and their language escalated. What had started out as a quest to liberate the racially pure German people and provide them with *Lebensraum*, living space, had turned into a battle against Jewish Bolshevism and forced de-Germanization. The *Wunderwaffen*—miracle weapons—that were supposed to rescue besieged German folk living outside the Reich's borders turned into *Vergeltungswaffen*—weapons of retribution; targeted *Blitzkrieg* warfare turned into *totalen Krieg*, all-out war. The level of agitation was steadily rising.

Meanwhile, Gerta's father was coming home more and more seldom, and often he was drunk, perhaps because Friedrich had virtually stopped writing. When he did write, his letters were terse and spoke only of retreats or the fight for a particular city somewhere in Volhynia.

Everything was in a terrible state of turmoil. The wheels of war had been set in motion; they were gaining speed and spinning at full tilt. For Gerta, it was unfathomable, as if they were moving simultaneously in every direction, yet hurtling inexorably from one major event to the next: Moscow; Kharkov; forward and backward, then forward again; Stalingrad; the offensive in the Ardennes; Normandy; backward and then again forward. The wheels were turning somewhere far away, in other countries, on foreign soil, but the groaning axles and popping bolts, their threads worn out, could be heard all the way back to her street in Brno.

What was even more puzzling to her was that Karel seemed to be living in the same state of heightened excitement and zeal as the League girls from the *Handelsakademie*. A state of excitement in which he talked to her long into afternoons that spilled into days, during which her excitement kept pace with his, even though they stood on opposite sides of the barricades.

"To stal'n'selth," he wished her in the entrance door to their building on New Year's Day.

When she asked him what sort of gibberish that was, he gave an impish smile.

"To Stalin's health, huh?" he repeated, shaking his head at her slowness.

She hated that. At such moments, he reminded her of her father when he had tried to indoctrinate her with the proper worldview. Suddenly, he was shouting out similar slogans, and then, during the final days of January 1944, he changed completely. He became exuberantly optimistic, spent much less time with her, was up to his eyeballs in work but couldn't talk to Gerta about any part of it, and finally it was she who found that she could no longer talk to him. Everything snowballed, grew bigger, swelled, and finally burst, and Karel disappeared, perhaps to avoid being deployed, but most likely because of her. The wheels were in motion, spinning, spewing gravel and grit, and then one day, before too much longer, they came to a grinding halt.

IX

Catastrophe hung in the air. The lack of success was visible not only on her increasingly stooped father, but even on the faces of the people in the streets. Gerta walked alongside them like an automaton, unable to break out of the orderly ranks that carried her along, until she found herself standing in the collection center at the German House, where they hung a money box around her neck and sent her and Ulrika Köhnerová into the streets. Ulrika was a true Aryan. Blonde and well built, and above all she radiated enthusiasm. What did they call it? Being active and engaged. She was typically the one to collect the lion's share of what went into the *Winterhilfswerk* kitty for the German Winter Relief fund. Her father sat on the executive board of the arms factory, and her mother was the chair of the Brno branch of the *Nationalsozialistiche Frauenschaft*, the National Socialist Women's League.

They walked side by side, Gerta looking down at the late-afternoon February shadows that spilled out of dark corners and crept across the streets, when suddenly the sky seemed to grow so dark that, with her eyes still fixed on the shoelaces of her winter boots, she stopped short. She looked up only as Ulrika shrieked, grabbed her sleeve, and yanked her sharply off the edge of the curb. A hand slipped off her shoulder. The cuff adorned with a decorative button came off, the shiny button clinking against the sanded sidewalk tiles, but by then Ulrika was already dragging her away, running as fast as she could in the direction of the Reduta Theater and toward the busier Cejl Street. The stiff soles of her boots clattered and creaked as they skidded in the splattering slush. Ulrika, one hand holding on to Gerta, the other clutching her rattling money box, kept on running, farther and farther, until Gerta had to stop her, saying she couldn't go on.

"That had to be a Jew . . . for sure . . . *Mutti* told me . . . be careful . . . They could be anywhere, like stray dogs. For a crust of bread, they're even ready to go after a girl. Are you all right?" Ulrika uttered between gasps.

"I'm fine."

Ulrika glanced down at the money box hanging around Gerta's neck. "How could you have been so oblivious? What were you looking at?"

"When?"

"Just now, by that passageway."

"I don't know. I was probably just thinking. I didn't notice."

"And I'd just been thinking that somebody could be lurking in there . . . I just had a feeling. At least I've got it, you know, a sixth sense.

Just as we were nearing that gate, I was thinking to myself, *That's the courtyard with the scrap heap. Someone could easily be hiding in there.* And you see, there was. We've got to report it right away. There's sure to be a patrol on Cejl Street, come on."

Gerta reluctantly moved forward. Her heart was still pounding, and she had barely caught her breath. Step by step, she followed Ulrika, her eyes cast down again, watching her shoes moving side by side. From the beginning, she had thought it was a stupid idea to head out into those narrow alleyways, where people didn't even open their doors, let alone hand out money. They had been ringing doorbells all afternoon, knocking, trying to get into people's homes. And they could consider themselves lucky if even a caretaker opened up. How much could they have collected? Seven marks? Eight?

That would certainly land Ulrika in trouble when she got home. Or, God forbid, she'd decide not to call it a day and would resolve to try to bring the amount up to what she'd collected on the previous days. Gerta's fingers and toes were frozen, and she felt as if her knees, in spite of being wrapped in thick stockings, were creaking with the cold. She would have liked to go back to the German House, turn in what they had collected, and go home. Since that morning, the only thing she had really wanted was to go back home. But what could she do? Her father, along with the others, was waiting back at the German House, ready to start tallying and noting down the names of who had contributed and who had been surly, and where the latter people lived. Gerta would keep quiet, but Ulrika, her cheeks reddened either by the frost or by the attention of the change collectors, would blush and carry on, ready to embellish her story with exaggerated details. Today Gerta would certainly end up having to hear her describe the vicious attack and their hairbreadth escape. Gerta would have preferred to give Ulrika a kick. With her heavy boot with its stiff sole and crude shoelaces that could withstand a thing or two. Her mother bought her those shoes, saying that whatever happened, she wanted them to last Gerta through the end of the war.

But Gerta was far too tired to give anyone a kick. She was sleepy, and felt numb and empty. Like a sheep, she went along with everything, did what she was told, and wanted in exchange only to be left alone. Which was why it hadn't taken her father much of an effort to make her join the *Winterhilfswerk*, but God, how ashamed she was of the begging! Still, her father's cursing made her go, and at times even his tears, on those evenings when he'd been hitting the bottle too hard. He would then pursue her from room to room, one minute full of humility and remorse, prostrate before her, making her feel almost sorry for him, and the next, exploding in uncontrollable rage to the point where she feared he might hurt her.

"Come on, Gerta, there's a guard!"

No doubt her father would approve of Ulrika. Ulrika, who never talked about how, no sooner had the war started than her family had moved into the Černá Pole villa that had been confiscated from Mr. Rosenkraus, as Gerta found out from Karel. With her shameless smile, she had no qualms about blocking someone's way and didn't think twice about threatening, "You'd better make a donation, or my father . . ." Or, "Make a donation, why surely you must want victory for our soldiers! You mean you don't? And your name is?"

Gerta would just stand there, staring down at the tips of her shoes. She was afraid of meeting someone's gaze and worried that, even without looking up, she might recognize a familiar voice somewhere up over her bangs asking in Czech, *Gerta dear, and how are you doing? Aren't you cold?* Or, *Gerta dear, how is it that even you are willing to gouge us this way?*

Gerta didn't know what she would do were she to run into Mr. Kmenta, for example. Or Janinka's mother. Ulrika would certainly march right up to them with her money box held out, and if they didn't make a donation, she would pull out her little notebook and jot down either their car or bicycle license number, or maybe a physical description that wouldn't necessarily help to identify them, but just might. Wasn't Gerta being an accomplice? She was. She was collecting winter relief for German soldiers to help Germany win the war, when in fact she really didn't care one way or the other. All she wanted was for the war to be over. She wished no ill to Friedrich, but at the same time wanted everyone like him and like her father to be silenced. Then she could go back to taking Mr. Kmenta's art class with Janinka, continue seeing Karel, and begin her studies at the university, whether in Czech or in German; to her it didn't matter. She wanted peace, for herself and for everyone else, but especially for Janinka, who was no longer allowed to have anything to do with Gerta, the daughter of Germans like those in the Reich who had imprisoned and then murdered her uncle from Frývaldov, and for whom Janinka's aunt then had to pay off debts. The debt for detention was one and a half marks per day, twenty marks for court expenses, three hundred marks for execution by decapitation, five marks for cleaning the blood off the blade, one hundred marks for funeral and cremation; supposedly, it was all itemized on the receipt and broken down on the payment schedule they drew up for Auntie, whose weekly pay was seven marks, which on the black market wasn't enough to buy her even a cup of lard. When Janinka told Gerta this, she was sobbing, for her uncle, whom she said they had killed just because he was a Communist, for her exhausted parents, and for herself, worn out after long days of menial work at the insurance company. Gerta hugged her and wished for it all to be over, and for the Germans, who had been the cause of so much misery, to lose, and to lose as quickly as possible.

X

That morning, Gerta was catching up on the sleep she'd missed out on during the night when her father had been drunkenly raging again.

The apartment was steeped in darkness; not even a glimmer of light came through the blacked-out windows. She was awakened by a dull, drawn-out sound. She opened her eyes wide and listened closely to the unfamiliar noise. It didn't subside. It sounded like the rumbling of thunder before a storm but was coming at regular intervals. Ominous and booming and growing louder. This was then interrupted by another sound, which flared and faded in a single flash, during which it swelled and subsided in intensity, and then came again. It was booming outside the windows, and everything had to be very close. Gerta flew out of bed, reached toward her bedside table, and knocked the flashlight she kept there to the floor. She dropped on all fours and fumbled around the cold floor under the bed until she finally felt the flashlight. She aimed it straight ahead of her and in its cone of light made out the handle on the door to the kitchen. She ran toward it, threw it open, and shone the light inside. The kitchen materialized out of the darkness, but the noise of planes flying overhead didn't stop; it continued and was growing louder. The door to her father's bedroom was closed. *He may as well die in there,* she thought, and instead of going over to see if he was even inside, she spun around and raced through the vestibule and out the main door into the hallway. Wearing only her nightgown and with bare feet, she made for the cold, damp stairwell and was swept up in the chaos of terrified people who were rushing down from the upper floors. Some clutched objects in their hands, others bags they had prepared, and the sound of screaming and children's crying reverberated through the building. From up above, she recognized the frantic whimpering of Granny Novotná. She had to drag herself along as she couldn't stand on her feet and had long ago stopped leaving her apartment. Gerta hoped someone would help her. She herself simply had to get downstairs, away from here, at any cost.

"*Schnell, schnell,* air raids," someone from down below shouted; perhaps it was the caretaker.

Terrified, she inched forward toward the stairs, the stone floor cold against the soles of her feet. Suddenly, a surge of booming sound engulfed her, and the wall against which she was leaning with her palm shuddered beneath her fingers. Gerta pressed herself back hard against it and felt the vibrations, along with the unceasing roar of aircraft engines, go through her entire body. There was a loud explosion. Her foot slipped as she raced down the stairs. She tripped and remained lying on the ground, her mouth and eyes full of plaster that had rained down on her. Before she had a chance to stand up, the entire building shuddered again; this time it had to be somewhere extremely close by. Gerta got up, shielding her stomach with her hand, and made her way down the stairwell filled with dust, bits of bricks, and fallen chunks of stucco, ready to run for the front door. She wanted to dash outside, but her foot caught on a body huddling by the bottom step, just ahead of the bend in the staircase that led into the basement. Someone grabbed her foot, and she cried out, kicking in all directions as the next blast hit. She cowered against the male figure and buried her face into his warm woolen sweater. The roar lasted interminable seconds during which someone was shouting at her, the voice coming from the chest against which she was leaning, but she didn't understand a word; she couldn't because she had covered her ears with her hands, but even if she hadn't, the noise of the airplanes, explosions, shattering glass, and falling bricks was so deafening, she couldn't have understood a word anyway.

The caretaker grabbed her and pulled her up to her feet before she had a chance to move a finger. He put his arm around her waist and, panting, started to drag her down to the basement. Gerta kicked at him; after all, she was trying to get outside, away from this building, which at any moment was going to bury her alive, was going to come crashing down around her, couldn't possibly hold out.

"Into the shelter," she heard right by her ear.

She stopped struggling. As he opened the door, the next roar was already approaching. She felt a chill against her feet, her loins, and even her stomach, her nightgown having ridden up under her armpits as she had tried to squirm out of the caretaker's hold. The intensity of the roar was increasing, growing louder, coming closer, and Gerta knew that she wouldn't be able to fend it off. The roar would come, and her heart would again stop; every hair on her body would stand on end, and she would feel sick, because this had to be the sound of death. She wrenched herself free of the woolen grasp. Her nightgown fell back down along her sides, and she raced down the few-remaining steps and into the shelter, where people were huddled together on wooden benches along the concrete walls in the flickering light of a pale light-bulb, which, seconds later, went out for good.

No one kept track of how much time elapsed. Leaning against the feet of the residents who had still found room to sit on the benches, Gerta sat on the floor, her head tucked between her thighs. It was possible that a long period of silence had passed. No one dared to say a word; not even the children made a peep. A stifling, oppressive still-ness prevailed, and then, in a single, abrupt instant, she became aware of being able to hear the silence. It was as if she had woken up, as if with the wave of a magic wand, like the one her mother used to tell her about in fairy tales, she had been brought back to life. One wave, and you would get everything you wished for. Gerta's wish would have always been to have an infinite number of additional wishes, and she was proud to have come up with a way to outwit the magic wand. Now, someone had waved such a wand, and Gerta's senses had returned. Silence. Darkness.

With her face still pressed to her knees, she could smell her own urine, which had trickled down her inner thighs and had by now grown chilled. She inhaled that pungent smell and the odor of her bare sex, and in that blend of primal scents, she also breathed in the knowledge that she was alive. She inhaled over and over and with exhilaration, and then finally dared to lift her head and look around.

She saw nothing. She was surrounded by darkness, but no longer that sepulchral, terrible one. This was a darkness in which one could discern, like luminous splashes of color, the shuffle of feet, the sniffling of noses, shallow breathing, and even an occasional sigh. Finally, a child began to cry, its inconsolable, shrill wail filling the cramped space of the stone chamber. Gerta wasn't a whole body; she was just a torso, a heavy, leaden rib cage from which arose, ever so slowly, a first sob that almost ripped her throat apart as it forced its way past her shriveled tonsils, her slackened tongue, and her clenched teeth. It forced its way out through the dark cave of her mouth like the head of a serpent, followed by a long, thick, round body that then slid out easily, and suddenly her sobs were flowing freely in a steady rhythm between tears and fitful gasps for breath. The entire basement was astir with sounds of relief, first words, exclamations, embraces, and then some more hissing—*hush, hush, what if it's not over yet!*

Gerta had a feeling that it was over. If it wasn't, she would lose her mind on the spot. It had to be over!

Someone tripped over her; then another person did. People were getting up and stepping on her. Bracing her hands against the knees of a woman beside her who by now was also stirring, she prepared to straighten up, tried to stand. Her knees had stiffened from being in that cramped position for so long that she was like a mummy; her joints and muscles wouldn't move. Someone grabbed her by the armpits and helped pull her up. And then somebody opened the door.

A faint gleam of light filtered into the basement. Not even the corridor into which the door was opening had much light. Suspended in the air were smoke and dust motes from the masonry that had come crashing down in the stairwell. The door was wedged against the rubble and wouldn't open farther. Through the demolished front door, at which those below gazed up as if beholding a miracle, the August afternoon light came pouring in.

XI

Slowly they ascended the steps behind the caretaker, who went ahead as far as the front door to have a look in the street. He quickly turned back and motioned impatiently with his hand for everyone to keep coming.

"All right, folks, come on, *schnell*, it's all over," he said, and then he ran out into the street where a few disoriented, disheveled people were aimlessly wandering about. He stopped after a few steps, spun around, and ran back inside the building, as if he had dashed out only to make sure the air outside was also possible to breathe.

"It's over," Gerta heard from all sides, in Czech and in German, as she made her way up the basement steps in the cluster of people.

"It's over; we survived."

"We're alive, thank God."

Even Gerta was grateful. She cautiously stepped out in front of the building where almost everyone had come to a standstill. They were all paralyzed by the overwhelming emotion of what they had just lived through. Then behind them, from inside the building, they heard a scream. No one had helped Granny Novotná down into the shelter. Gerta didn't turn around and didn't run inside to look as did some of the other women. She didn't even go upstairs to see if there was a hole in the wall of their apartment or if any of their furniture was left. Something else had crossed her mind: *Janinka*.

She quickly set out walking along the row of buildings, the sidewalk littered with fallen plaster and shattered glass, until she came across someone who hadn't managed to get inside fast enough, had been struck by the falling bricks, and now lay on the ground, a pool of blood spreading out under his head. She stared at the scene, transfixed, unable to turn her eyes away. Then a man carrying a shovel bumped into her, hurrying in the opposite direction, toward the head of the square. She turned to look after him. The building in which Anička Horáková lived and where Gerta's mother had regularly brought her food-ration coupons, stamped with the large *D* for *Deutsch*, was no longer standing. The collapsed upper stories, of which only some jagged walls jutting aimlessly up at the sky remained, were now nothing but a mountain of rubble, bricks, and sections of staircases, which had completely inundated Pressburger Straße. The prolapsed bowels of the apartment building spilled out onto the asphalt of the street and trailed off in long veinlike lines as far as the plane trees in the middle of the square. Everyone standing there beheld the unfamiliar panorama of the rooftops of the buildings of the parallel-running Cejl Street before them. Gerta couldn't stop staring at the new look of this familiar place. She peered through the haze of dust rising over the ruins and tried to imagine their original height. There was suddenly much more light. More space. The square seemed to have appropriated the new space, as had the plane trees, whose crowns, as Gerta saw when she looked up, were now spread out against a clear blue sky.

"Jesus Christ, give me a hand!" a man shouted toward her shoulder. He was approaching her with his hands behind him, each one gripping a handcart. He rushed past her in the direction of the rubble. She followed him all the way to where a crowd of people were either standing about or scurrying over the debris, shouting and pointing, coming together and then dispersing, hoping the mountain would open up and surrender its innermost treasures. Alive or dead. Or some remaining survivors, still trapped down below, waiting for someone up above to notice that their home had disappeared beneath a mound of rubble. Gerta's chest grew tight at the thought of those below not even knowing whether it was over or if the horror was still raging. Not knowing if they would stay buried under the rubble, or if someone would find them before they used up all their oxygen.

Gerta took off, running in the direction of Pressburger Straße, and then kept going straight ahead to where Janinka lived. What if Janinka was buried underground, wondering if anyone would come looking for her?

Gerta ran and tried to see down the full length of the street. Janinka's building wasn't far. But she couldn't see anything. Soot kept falling, making it impossible to see; the entire street was full of it. Not to mention the smoke from the building she had just passed, whose weight had collapsed into the courtyard behind it. The residents were bringing out one body after another; none of them had even been covered yet.

Gerta was out of breath by the time she reached the corner of Schöllergasse. The silhouette she was able to make out through a wall of dust and smoke gradually took on contours. The house on the corner with Konrad Kinkel's newsstand was gone, swallowed by a wave that had swept away the front part of the house clear across the intersection, all the way to the mouth of Pressburger Straße and practically to Gerta's feet. The next two houses weren't standing either. Schöllergasse had become a funnel, its cone overflowing with debris. From the other side of the street, she heard the helpless wail of a fire-truck siren.

Gerta fixed her gaze on Janinka's house. It was standing next to a corner building that had caved in and was missing an exterior wall, making it look naked. But it was still standing. Except that it didn't have a bomb shelter in which the Horn family could have hidden. The bomb shelter was in the building next door. Gerta aimed straight for the rubble and cautiously began to clamber up the mound. She scrambled over fragments of wreckage, bricks, beams, and broken roof tiles, splintered bits of furniture, and household items, everything piled up to the height of the second floor, where the building stopped. All that remained were shaky remnants of collapsed walls that jutted upward. Every time her foot slipped on the loose debris, she felt the sharp edges of the stones scrape the soft, untoughened flesh on the soles of her feet. She used her hands, pulling herself up on protuberances. Then suddenly a pair of knees appeared right in front of her face and blocked her way. She tried to stand up but faltered, and had this person not grabbed her arm, she surely would have fallen backward.

"Don't go any farther; it's still crumbling," he said, and gruffly gestured for her to go back down.

"Let me go!"

"You can't go there right now; it hasn't been stabilized. I'm telling you, it's still coming down."

"Janinka could be somewhere in there."

"If she's in there, we'll find her. Wait down there."

"I'll help."

"You'd better go find some clothes. Wait down there," he repeated unyieldingly, giving her a nudge while steadying her at the same time so that she wouldn't fall.

Gerta turned her head in the direction that her body was now facing, and, unstable as she was, fell onto her rear end and slid down for a stretch on the loose dirt. The soiled nightgown had again ridden up to her waist. She quickly pulled it back down over her bare stomach to hide her swollen belly. She looked around in dismay, to make sure no one had seen her, then shakily stood up and gingerly continued making her way down. Others cut across her path, shouting instructions at each other: forward or backward, push or toss, hold on or let go. The din of voices, the constant wail of the siren, the occasional screams— it was earsplitting. Then something exploded. At the deafening blast, Gerta instantly dropped into a squat on the rubble. Something struck her shoulder, and her head was showered with debris. Then there was silence. She looked up. All around her, people were as covered in soot and dirt as she was. They were shaking their heads, trying to remove the dirt. Some were already rising to their knees; others had turned onto their backs and were sliding down.

A man's voice from up above shouted, "The gas blew!"

Gerta was struggling to get down as everyone returned to action. She felt a dull twinge in her shoulder, but she could move it without pain; she must have been struck by a rock or a piece of wood. The lacerated soles of her feet were more painful. Then, just as she reached for a beam to steady herself, she saw the tip of a foot underneath. It was sticking out, covered with dirt, filthy, with a disjointed big toe. A foot that made it look as if someone below were doing a handstand.

Gerta froze. Janinka's foot wasn't that big, but a foot that size could have belonged to her father. She reached out and touched it. It was soft and warm. A real human foot. She screamed. She turned to the left and to the right and kept on screaming, looking around for someone in charge, who, unlike her, would know what to do. From over to the right and from down below, people were advancing toward her. Within moments, some men had formed a close circle and had pushed her to the outside, telling her to get out of the way.

Gerta forced her way back into the midst of the huddle around the foot, reached between the bricks under the beam, pulled out a handful of rubble, tossed it behind her, and, working around the men's legs, tried to help clear away the dirt from the discovery.

"This one's beyond help," someone else shouted. "Go back down!"

Gerta didn't move; she stared at the toiling bodies, mesmerized. One slipped and tumbled, coming to a stop only when his black boot was practically on top of her.

"Jesus. Get out of here; didn't you hear? You're in the way; you can't help here!"

"Who is it? I have to know who it is," said Gerta, close to tears and not budging.

Just then from beneath the beam, where the foot and part of the shin were now exposed, a small avalanche of pebbles came loose, so that a part of the other foot was also uncovered. One of the men grabbed hold of it and gave it a yank. Out from the debris came a stump no longer attached to a knee. Gerta felt sick. She turned her face away and clambered back down as fast as she could, holding on to her stomach with both hands while tumbling and sliding the rest of the way down, until she landed on the hard pavement of Pressburger Straße and finally came to a stop.

On the sidewalk in front of the nearest buildings sat people, lean-ing back against the facades. Some sat with their heads hanging down; others reached out with imploring gestures to anyone who was hurrying by. From Koliště Street came people with stretchers to take away the wounded. They left the dead bodies. Around those, people were gath-ering. Gerta knew many of them by sight and also recognized some of the bodies over which they were bending. All around, one could hear wailing and the calling out of names, some of which Gerta recognized as well.

"Janinka Hornová!" she shouted at the top of her lungs.

No one answered. The only responses were other names.

"Janinka Hornová!"

The woman beside her shook her head. Gerta crossed over to the other side of the street where more wounded people were sitting against a building. She walked past them quickly, peering into their faces.

"Janinka Hornová!" Her voice broke. She was terribly afraid that she might be calling out in vain. She kept going until she got as far as the Ponawkagasse intersection, where the noise level suddenly subsided. The farther away she went from the epicenter of the calamity, the more slowly people were moving. They were no longer cutting in front of each other in their frenzied scurrying. Instead of the shouting and tur-moil near the wreckage, here, apart from the moans of the wounded and the concentrated work of the stretcher-bearers and medics, a sense of calm prevailed. If Janinka was here, there was no way Gerta could have missed her. She turned around and headed back down Pressburger Straße, toward the Horn family's building. She walked slowly, her arms crossed, her hands resting on her shoulders. She stepped carefully, pro-tective of the painful, scraped-up soles of her feet, her legs weak at the knees.

Then she saw something very strange. On the mountain of rubble, bobbing up every so often above the other heads, was a small head with flaxen hair. Gerta hastened her step, threading her way through the crowd that now, closer to the wreckage, had become dense again, and jumped up onto the sidewalk, stepping over the legs of the wounded. Then she saw her. A slight figure hopping from one foot to the other on top of the rubble heap, moving up and down, a few steps up, step-slide-step-left, step-slide-step-right, then several jumps down. She was moving in a peculiar dance, clearly to the rhythm of some inner music, holding the hem of her long, soiled skirt between her fingertips and wagging her head from shoulder to shoulder. Gerta stood still in astonishment.

Janinka had just completed a rotation and with her gaze lowered and a slight smile playing on her face, made several even jumps. Then she squatted down, stood back up, and remained standing there for a while, her head hanging down. Gerta kept her eyes fixed on her until she climbed all the way up to where she was and grabbed her by the hand. Janinka turned toward her, and the slight smile vanished. She scowled and shrank back, angrily snatching away her hand, freeing herself from Gerta's grasp. Out of her mouth came a guttural sound as her lips twitched. She frowned and stared right through Gerta with a look of bitterness, but also emptiness, an emptiness Gerta had never seen before.

XII

Mugwort. On shadowy waste heaps, by roadsides, in the underbrush, along banks and embankments, in the sultry heat of summer. Clusters on rigid, angular, branched stems on purplish hollow stalks. Lobed lower leaves, four to four-and-a-half inches long, smaller, sessile upper leaves. The undersides white with fine, downy hairs, feltlike. Flowers—small, yellow or yellowish-brown. The base of each bloom nestles inside a greenish funnel, and when the blossom drops off, what's left is a small green bun riddled with pinprick dimples. One heaping teaspoon of the delicate blossoms tipped into a porcelain cup—the water on the stove is already bubbling.

European yew. How much is fifty grams of needles? A handful, not more. It's poisonous and can be lethal. Fifty grams, no more, preferably less. The fine needles cover the yellowish-brown mugwort blossoms in the bottom of the cup. The steam from the kettle on the stove is rising. The water comes spurting out in a cascading swirl and fills the porcelain cup. The water level rises, and the needles and blossoms twirl in a wild, death-bearing dance. One cup four times a day. For one whole week. And every evening, a mallow root drizzled with twenty drops of lemon juice inserted into one's body and left inside overnight, until the bleeding begins, until the womb is cleansed. Don't fear the cramps; don't fear the nausea.

What could have gone wrong? Why hadn't she succeeded in evicting this goblin? Was it the missing lemon? But where now, five years into the war, could she find a lemon? She had managed to acquire the European yew and mugwort; she had managed to procure a mallow root through a woman who dealt on the black market, but a lemon, there simply was none to be had. Lemons were beyond the reach of even the black-market profiteer.

Gerta was desperate. She was terrified. She was at her wits' end, dying of fear. Never, not even during the air raids of the previous few nights, had she been as terrified as she was these days. These weeks. Weeks upon weeks, while her womb remained occupied, as new life already pulsed through the openings of her pores, shifting, turning over, swimming, making sure she knew it was there.

Later on, she regretted the blows. The blows to her stomach that had only made her feel sicker and seemed to have had no effect whatsoever on the life by now deeply rooted inside her. They only hurt. She gave in. The goblin growing inside her had won.

XIII

Gerta made her way up the street where the sanded road inclined. She walked, looking down at the ground; she had no desire to look around. Instead, she turned her gaze inward and was rummaging among memories. In front of her eyes, her feet in black shoes with separating soles were moving in alternating steps, but all she saw was her father's face, contorted in one of his nighttime spasms, and his sweat-drenched body, rocking back and forth through her half-closed eyelids. Since the time a giant drop of sweat had rolled off his round, bald head right into her eye, she had preferred to look aside. That time the salt had spilled into the white of her eye, and it had stung like hell. In between her father's heavy panting and his *Look at me! Look at me!* commands, she had tried to rub her eye, but as his thrusts became harder, the pressure of her fist just caused a deeper, duller pain. By the next morning, his expression had shriveled into a mournful grimace that hardened into an ugly scowl whenever she inadvertently glanced his way.

Gerta walked along the street, turned the corner, and followed the wide curve of the cemetery wall toward the entrance that faced a snow-covered field. She was alone, and the city lay far behind her. She found it hard to walk. By now, her stomach was heavy, her back sore, and her feet swollen and stiff. It was easier to shuffle than to pick them up and take proper steps, so she shambled along, wobbly, breathing heavily. She couldn't wait to be free of it, for the moment when she could expel it from herself.

Today she wanted to honor the memory of her mother. At the end of November, it had been exactly two years since her mother had left her. She would never forget those final hours. She had kept her warm with her own body, had held her burning hand when she was delirious with fever, had hugged her whenever she called out her name. Gerta hadn't left her side for even a moment. Her father and Friedrich, on the other hand, had sat nervously at the kitchen table, waiting for it finally to be over. During those last few days of her mother's life, they ran off at every opportunity, to go to work or to meetings, to fetch the paper or to listen to the radio; anything took priority over the process of her dying. But for Gerta, it had been the most important time of her life. Otherwise, she never would have discovered how brutal her father had been to her mother. It took a while before she connected the red welts across her mother's back with the frenzied cries that would invade her dreams. How was it possible that she hadn't noticed it sooner? Gerta's eyes filled with tears.

In the gatehouse beyond the cemetery's wide entryway sat an old porter. He was resting his head in his hands and looked as if he had nodded off. Gerta turned left, leaving footprints on the snow-covered path between the graves. No one had yet walked there that day. All around her rose tall cypresses. She found herself in a place where there were no signs of any war happening. Far from the bombs that had been dropping on Brno since the summer, far from the fear brought on by each darkening night, far from the shortages, the poverty, and the empty shops. Far from the uncertainty and the anxiety, and also far from the absurd, maniacal euphoria of Hitler's speeches that her father was still tuning in to on the radio. *We will obliterate their cities!* would come booming from her father's bedroom. But the louder Hitler's proclamations, the more one could hear the panic in his voice. How long did her father's optimism last after such a broadcast? One hour? It was ridiculous, and by the time the hour passed, he himself felt ridiculous. His shoulders would slump; he would hang his head and flee his home, where his daughter, her belly as big as a drum, had locked herself inside her room.

But here there reigned a graveyard silence, disturbed only by the soft swish of the branches of the aspens and poplars along the cemetery wall, the majestic swaying of the cypresses, and the flickering of two or three votive candles that some of the wealthier families had left for their dead. One couldn't even find candles in regular shops anymore. Gerta came to a stop in the lee of a thicket of several bare hazelnut bushes in front of the Schnirch tomb. What a joke, burying Mother here of all places, in the Schnirch family plot.

Here I am, she greeted her mother in her mind. She stepped right up to the tombstone on which there were three names engraved alongside three photographs.

"Gertrude Schnirch, b. Leitzmann, died 1931. Leopold Schnirch, died 1922. Barbora Schnirch, b. Ručková, died 1942." Her mother smiled at her from an oval frame, looking just as she remembered her from the years before the war. As if nothing in between had really happened. Gerta sat down on a low stone pillar and tenderly ran her hand in its knitted mitten over the glass. She wiped away a few ice crystals.

"I can't love this child," she said softly.

In the silence of this place, her voice sounded strange. She drew her shawl more closely across her forehead and tucked in the ends on either side of her neck. Her mother in the photograph kept on smiling. Gerta knew what she would tell her. That God had his reasons for sending her this child. That she should stop worrying and put herself into his hands. And that every life was deserving of love. And that a mother's love for her child was a sacred duty. *And a natural one, Gerta, don't you forget. The first time you hold that bundle in your arms, helpless and entirely dependent on you alone, you'll feel something you've never felt before. It will rise up inside you and overflow, sweeping away all your misgivings.*

Gerta didn't believe that God had his reasons for sending her this child. Maybe God had wanted to punish her, not just with the child, but with everything that had happened this past year. God had permitted her to suffer. First her mother, then Janinka, and finally even Karel had disappeared from her life, Friedrich, too, although she didn't care as much about that, but now only her father remained. What sort of ghoulish plan of God's was it to have left Gerta all alone with her father?

"Why did this have to happen to me?" Gerta asked, shaking her head. "He ruined my life, God."

The wind lifted the hem of her skirt as it draped down over her parted knees. Gerta braced her hands against the freezing pillar and with great effort, moving sideways to get around her swollen belly, stood up.

"I can't love this child," she repeated once she was standing and had turned back to the gravestone.

"But what I can do is try to imagine not that God sent it to me, but that you sent it to me. As a sign, on the anniversary of your death. So that I wouldn't be all alone. If I can manage to think about it that way, it'll be easier."

The wind overhead was chasing through the needles of the cypress trees and the branches of the hazelnut bushes. They seemed to be nodding. Large snowflakes slowly began to fall and settle on the tombstone as she pulled her coat closer around her and watched their silent, swirling, stately dance.

XIV

Winter at the turn of that year was bitterly cold. As if man-made catastrophe weren't enough, nature added its own. January and February passed, and Gerta barely noticed; she was permanently bent over swaddling clothes and was aware only of the shrinking allotments on the meal tickets that her father, his ration book for race-certified families in hand, would go each week to collect and bring home to her. She had delivered Barbora into a time of poverty. And into a time of fear.

At night she couldn't sleep. Behind her closed eyelids, she would see bits and pieces of stage scenery sailing through the air as she had witnessed that time in November, when a siren had caught her by surprise in the city center. She had ducked into a shelter, and once the shocks subsided, she climbed back up the stairs, emerging into a blinding, sunlit afternoon, in which, in addition to ash from the fresh demolition, thousands of multicolored scraps of paper were raining down. Carried by the wind, they danced along Ratwitplatz and fluttered through the bowels of the Czech National Theater, which had been cleft in two, along with shreds of tattered fabrics, sets from never-performed Czech plays, and the fine residue of what had been the house curtain during the time of the First Czechoslovak Republic. The collapsed facade mockingly revealed the red velvet of the balcony box seats, the wide floorboards of the stage that for Brno had once represented the world, and the stucco of the rear wall, the only one left standing, like a silent witness, on the square. For the rest of that day, Brno shuddered with time-bomb explosions, to the left, to the right, far off in the distance, and terrifyingly, unimaginably close by.

Then in April, day after day passed during which everyone waited anxiously for the American planes to appear and finally liberate the city. The sirens signaled air raids two or even three times a week. Then for a time they would fall silent again, and people sank back into their dejected thoughts about the Reich and the world's indifference to the plight of a small nation. This was the mood Gerta picked up on in the empty stores when she occasionally had to run out for something. It was a troubled time. Emotions were running high; neighbors were whispering secretively among themselves, women trying to find out what each one knew, Czechs and Germans alike. Their muffled cries resembled the lines of a seismograph recording the rising and falling frequencies of their emotional fluctuations, whether in hope or in tearful resignation, that served as a barometer for that entire tense, nerve-racking period. Gerta navigated it in a strange frame of mind. As if the world's afflictions had ceased to affect her. The so-often invoked freedom seemed trivial compared to the cup of milk that the Hamšíková woman could get her on the black market. Not even the ubiquitous dispute, would it be the Soviets or the Americans, meant anything to her if Barbora wouldn't nurse. Only bombs snapped her out of her lethargy.

By now, she and Barbora had been through air raids too many times to count. In the basement bomb shelter on Sterngasse; in the *Luftschutzraum* shelter in Akátky forest park that she'd found by following arrows drawn on the walls of the buildings in the Židenice quarter, where she'd gone searching for a black marketeer; in the cellar under the New Town Hall when she was on her way to take Barbora to see Dr. Heinz. Barbora hated it, cried after each blast, and Gerta couldn't get her to stop. Only at moments such as these did Gerta feel somehow in touch with reality again. She would never forget the panicked, excruciating fear that gripped her when she realized that she could die, and that Barbora would be left on the basement floor at the mercy of the feet of a terror-stricken crowd. Or that Barbora could die too. She held her close and tried to stifle her own tears along with Barbora's, but to no avail. After the shelter in butcher Šíma's huge ice cellar was hit, however, and the armor-plated, concrete-slab ceiling collapsed, crushing sixty people, while the apartments in surrounding buildings remained intact, she no longer bothered to leave her home. At the end of the day, not even the safest bomb shelter in Brno had been able to protect them; everyone had died. From then on, she never slept for more than two hours at a time, not at night and not in the day, half-crazed with dread of the next long, double wail of the siren. Usually she just lay awake while the limerick that had seared itself into the mind of every Brno resident went around and around in her head: *Get your rest by moonlight, we'll get you in the sunlight.* That was what they used to say back then about the Allied air strikes. And it was true. How many nights had she spent awake with her eyes wide open, staring at the stained, damp wall of her room? And then suddenly, one day it was over.

XV

It was April 26, 1945, at around eight o'clock in the evening, when the Red Army officially flooded into Brno. Its arrival was preceded by heated debates on every Brno street corner. Had they reached Hodonín yet, or might they be in Veselí, where one couldn't get through to anyone by phone anymore, or could they already have come as far as Židlochovice, or maybe even Heršpice? The army's arrival had also been preceded by air-raid warnings, at first twice a week, then once every three days, then every other day, and finally on April 17, the sirens went off no less than twenty-one times. There had been frantic rushes into the nearest shelters, where several times a building's German residents had doors slammed in their faces. In the faces of those who still believed in "the final victory" and refused to be evacuated, but also in the faces of those who had tried throughout the war to steer clear of the political apparatus. Although each day families passed through the city with fully loaded carts heading in the direction of Tišnov, toward Jihlava, and then on to the Bayreuth district where evacuees from the Protectorate were being taken in, there were still plenty who stayed behind, fervidly believing in the V-3, Hitler's secret weapon that he was to deploy on the occasion of his fast-approaching birthday. It was from among their ranks that the Brno *Volkssturm* recruits were assembled, a pathetic national militia made up of old men who were the only ones not to have been called up to the front line, and to whom the people of Brno promptly assigned the infamous nickname "V-3."

Squadrons of feeble or crippled old men fanned out through the city streets, piled up wooden boards and scraps of junk into anti-tank barriers, and dug ditches. Life in Brno began to choke under all the barricades and excavated trenches. Getting around the city became more difficult every day. But it wasn't long before the already sparse street traffic came to a complete stop.

On April 12, the municipal authorities decided not to sound the sirens so as not to disrupt the work in the factories; every minute of production for the Reich was precious. The German air-traffic watch on Petrov Hill didn't announce the air strike, which then decimated several factories full of workers. In the hat factory on Cejl Street, not far from the house in which the Schnirchs lived, a bomb landed in the middle of the main hall, leaving thirty women dead. And on Joštova Street, another one fatally struck a streetcar full of passengers, sweeping it off the rails upon which it exploded with such force that the limbs of its wretched occupants had to be scraped off the facades lining the broad avenue for hundreds of feet. The next day, people didn't go to work. They stayed at home, and offices and certain factories remained closed. Life in Brno came to a halt, and people took leave of each other, saying, "See you after the war." Then, in the privacy of their homes, night after night, they would unfold a map of Europe and follow the advance of the Allies, switching it out in early April for a map of Moravia, which some days later they switched out in turn for a map of Brno and its immediate surroundings. Suddenly, Brno was on the front lines.

Her father's moods fluctuated between states of manic hysteria and total lethargy. He stayed inside his room, glued to the radio. Occasionally, in a fit of spasmodic laughter, he shot out to inform Gerta with glee of one of the short-lived successes of Field Marshal Schörner's Army Group Center. That they'd blown the Vranov Dam sky high, and the water had poured through the Dyje River into the Morava, which even with all its tributaries hadn't been able to absorb such volume, so it flooded a stretch one and a half kilometers wide, stopping Malinovsky's army between Lanžhot and Hodonín. And because the Russians had been intercepted near the Moravian villages of Ořechov and Šitbořice, there was already talk of calling it a Moravian Stalingrad, but this time the outcome would be different. And almost ten thousand Red Army soldiers had already been captured. But then the transmission broke off. The radio jammed; there was static and the sound of clicking; and then it went silent altogether, and with it her father. As Gerta moved around inside the apartment, his door remained shut. On some nights, she could hear him behind it, shouting in his sleep, and on some days, softly sobbing. The last time he appeared in his doorway was after a quiet weekend, when loudspeaker-equipped cars drove blaring through the streets, urging people to return to work and announcing that the shops had reopened, all the while trying to drown out the noise of gunfire and commotion from the nearby battlefront. Her father was confused. Just the previous day, they had heard from the caretaker that four Soviet scout tanks had been sighted near the cemetery and that the Red Army was assembled six kilometers south of Brno. Incredulous, he paced back and forth across the narrow expanse of the kitchen while Gerta and Barbora stayed barricaded behind their bedroom door. And then the city of Brno began to shudder with new detonations. The German army's destruction units blew up the munitions warehouse in the barracks of the former Pod Kaštany concentration camp. Tonguelike flames leaped at the sky. Gerta could see them even from Sterngasse, and above them rose a column of thick, black smoke. Soon rumors were flying: the German army base and Slatina airport had also been blown sky high, as had the depot by the train station, where they had still managed to deploy explosives, blasting all the locomotives to bits and knocking out the railroad switches. Brno was cowering under clouds of smoke; all was gray, like before a thunderstorm. A film of fine ash settled on the sidewalks and on the leaves of the trees.

Gerta's father looked just like the streets. Ashen gray, with parched lips and circles under his staring eyes. He was bone thin, because even the little that Gerta managed to scrape together from the meal tickets he wouldn't touch. Just as well; at least there was more for her and Barbora, who sucked on her ravenously, eating away at her by day as well as through the sleepless nights, which she spent listening for *Little Ivan*, the nickname people in Brno had given to the Russian biplane. Every night, during those last days of April, it crisscrossed the sky over the darkened, sleeping city. At first, one would just hear a steady clatter, and then two tiny Christmas trees would come into view, flares that floated slowly down to the ground on little parachutes, illuminating the city that spread out beneath them practically as if in broad daylight. And right behind them, dropping onto the brightly lit targets, fell demolition bombs, two at a time. As soon as the home guard or remaining Gestapo on the Špilberk started scanning for the biplane with floodlights and firing at it, its motor would fall silent, and *Little Ivan* would quietly disappear into the darkness beyond the city limits. The Red Army was laying its groundwork for the decisive attack, and Gerta wished for it to happen.

And then it happened, early one morning, after a night interrupted by Barbora's crying, *Little Ivan*'s clattering, and the racket made by *Volkssturm* militia deserters who were ransacking houses, grabbing whatever they could so that by morning they could be as far away from the front lines as possible. Day was just breaking when swarms of rockets began to appear over the city, leaving behind blazing trails, columns of smoke, and booming thunder mixed with the droning of oncoming planes overhead.

It's happening, flashed through Gerta's mind, her stomach in knots and her rib cage shuddering with fear. She flew out of bed as the first bombs fell, grabbed Barbora, who was just waking up, and her emergency bag, and fled from her bedroom.

"It's happening!" she shouted toward the door of her father's room, but didn't wait, hurrying on, out into the corridor and down to the basement, into the shelter, as she must have done some hundred times already since last summer. But this time would be different. "The Russians are here!" shouted someone from up above.

Gerta ran straight into the shelter, sat down against the back wall, and with Barbora in her arms and her bag under her feet, waited for the basement to fill up. And to see if her father would appear. He didn't. Twice more the caretaker opened the door to the shelter, which shook from the falling rockets and bombs, to let in some last stragglers, but her father wasn't among them. Whenever a silence spread through the basement, the caretaker would go out to look around, only quickly to return, shaking his head, *No, not yet.* The hours passed. A few times Gerta even nodded off into a light, fitful sleep. Then someone began to bang on the basement door, repeatedly, forcefully, over and over again, until the caretaker opened it and an old man practically fell inside shouting, "The Russians are here; it's finally over!"

After almost two days, the inhabitants of the house on Sterngasse staggered out into the daylight. The square around them was destroyed, the streets rutted by the treads of army tanks, and under the windows lay bodies of *Volkssturm* defenders who had fallen out of their barricaded machine-gun lairs.

"There's still fighting up at the Špilberk. They're driving them north toward Královo Pole and Řečkovice!"

"The German House was hit; they've surrendered!"

"František Šikula and his loyal boys saved the Brno Lake Dam!"

Such were the snippets of conversation Gerta overheard along with the Russian songs blaring from the radio-equipped vehicles slowly moving through the streets. On the curbs of the torn-up sidewalks sat weary soldiers, smoking and heating up over makeshift fires whatever was left of their meager supplies. The few Brno residents who had joined them, so that at the eleventh hour they could at least feel they'd contributed to the effort of liberating their city, were making the rounds of nearby buildings, going into shelters and basements and bringing up others from their hiding places, just as that old man had brought them out.

And then the deep, familiar voice of Levitan, the radio announcer from Moscow, echoed through the streets:

> *Moskva govorit, govorit Moskva! The army of the second Ukrainian front under Army General Malinovský, continuing its attack today, on April 26, employing a masterful pincer movement and a frontal assault, has gained control of the large industrial center of Czechoslovakia, the city of Brno, a major transportation hub and a bastion of support for the German defense . . .*

XVI

During those first days of liberation, Gerta would hear that voice coming from the loudspeaker on the military truck every few minutes. It carried over from Cejl, where Red Army soldiers had moved into the corner building on Bratislavská Street, formerly known as Pressburger Straße, drifted through courtyards and across open courtyard balconies, and floated all the way to her windows, from which she had finally been able to remove the blackout material. The rowdy Russian voices echoed through the empty streets late into the night, disrupting her and Barbora's fitful bouts of sleep. The last few weeks had left Gerta completely exhausted, from lack of sleep, lack of food, the nightly carousing of the Red Army soldiers, and from work, for which she was collected daily. Early in the morning, the Brno Germans were picked up from their front doors and brought wherever they were needed, to collapsed buildings, first to dig out shelters that had caved in, and then to clear away rubble. More than once, she witnessed mutilated corpses being pulled out. They were buried immediately in the closest parks, because the Brno cemeteries were already overflowing.

The city had changed. One could see it on every other house, even the one in which Gerta lived with her father and Barbora. The walls facing the spacious garden were pockmarked with round craters left by embedded bullets. The worst to be hit in their quarter were Französische Straße, Köffillergasse, and even Sterngasse, which had lost most of its odd-numbered buildings. A whole row of houses opposite theirs had collapsed. Zeile, or Cejl, and Pressburger Straße looked as if they had been the victims of some demonic counting rhyme. *Eeny meeny miny moe, and you are it*—every second or third house was missing. Of the corner buildings at the intersection of Schöllergasse and Ponawkagasse, only rubble-strewn lots remained. Entire streets had disappeared from the map of Brno. Gerta was sent to work on Koliště Street and on Údolní Street, of which one entire side, including the Convent of the Sisters of Mercy of St. Borromeo, had collapsed. Also destroyed were the Palace of Noble Ladies on Kozí Street, the JEPA department store and Hotel Astoria on Svoboda Square, and one whole side of Fröhlichergasse, in Czech Veselá Street, where three blocks of buildings had been reduced to ruins. Half of Mendel Square, the public spa on Hlínky Street, and most of the houses on Dornych Street were gone. Meanwhile, the large synagogue in the Trnitá district had been burned out, and only a few brick stumps pointing up to the sky were left. And that was just the damage in her immediate neighborhood.

The city was huddling in the deep craters of its mutilated streets, but within its bowels, a spine-chilling drama was being played out by the most sundry ensembles. The local Czech players included prisoners who had streamed out of the gates of Kounic College, having survived interrogations by the Gestapo, and mothers with their children who, as Gerta witnessed, in an onslaught of euphoria threw themselves at the legions of haggard and exhausted foreign soldiers, who with hungry eyes kept on demanding more slivovitz. Also participating were the self-important men who were busy organizing the Revolutionary Guard and the National Committees, and finally the youths running wild through the streets, wearing helmets far too big for their small heads and with hands full of found shells and unexploded grenades. Then there were the local German players, the ranks of enfeebled women and their children bending over the rubble for whom the bell had begun to toll, as it had for their husbands and fathers. The few German men who still remained were taken outside of the city and interned in camps, where it was said they were worked to the bone in retaliation. And then there were the Red Army soldiers and the Romanians, those who hadn't followed Schörner's army on to Prague. They, too, had a part to play. Meanwhile, solo parts were divvied up among those who had returned from forced labor or concentration camps, as well as among opportunists and fortune seekers who picked through any leftover German property, people with no history who were just passing through the city on their quest for new horizons.

The city was regrouping, reorganizing itself. Occupied apartments were being vacated; vacant apartments were being occupied; new jails were cropping up on its outskirts. Brno floundered in the postwar chaos, transforming day by day. The city no longer belonged to its inhabitants, accustomed to straddling its Czech-German feuds and rivalries; every day it was becoming more foreign.

XVII

May 12 found Gerta standing at the edge of a crowd. She had positioned herself at the corner, right under the Church of St. Michael's baroque statues that looked down on her from the edge of its terrace platform—St. Paul seemingly with compassion, his head bowed, a book tightly clasped to his breast. She leaned sideways against the flaking masonry. In the midst of this large gathering, she felt lightheaded; perhaps she shouldn't even have come.

But she couldn't allow herself to miss the opportunity to find out what lay in store and what was to happen next. She hadn't been able to resist, so she'd set out on her own, not wanting to rely on reports skewed ten different ways from neighbors, at least those who for now were still talking to her. She wanted to hear it for herself.

She stood, periodically switching Barbora over from her right arm to her left, shifting the weight of her body away from the wall and in toward the street. She studied the sidewalk beneath her feet up to where it disappeared under the heels of the densely packed, restless crowd. It was mostly broken up into bits, and any paving cubes that remained had been loosened. Full of gaps, like drum notes, her mother would have said.

Gerta was frightened. Extremely frightened. The fear sat deep inside her chest, resembling a spider with eight legs spread into every part of her body. The heavy, massive, broad body of this creature swelled inside her chest, against which from the outside she pressed Barbora, whose little head bobbed back and forth, again and again, in time to her rocking.

She knew she was violating the decree issued the day before and that failure to comply had been declared punishable by death. The only Germans now allowed to stay in their apartments were infirm old women, and even they were forbidden on pain of death to look out of their windows. Forbidden to look out of their windows! Outrageous. What would they do with her for violating the decree and attending the rally on the Rathausplatz?

If someone recognized her, if they swarmed around her and dragged her off to the Revolutionary Guard, those burly men sporting the big, red letters *RG* on their shirtsleeves, it would all be over. She would disappear, as had so many others from her neighborhood over the past month. The situation had affected everyone; not a single person remained who hadn't lost an acquaintance or a family member. In the best-case scenario, they found out where the abducted person had been dragged off to. Worst case, one day the person simply didn't return from their rubble-clearing work and disappeared without a trace. Among the Germans Gerta knew, fear ruled, and each new regulation was treated with reverence.

The previous day, for the personal safety of President Edvard Beneš, the authorities had decided that all Brno Germans would be removed and placed outside the city limits. No one dared to protest this new decree. Nor did they protest when their apartments were cleared out, nor when they were assigned to labor for which they weren't paid a crown or given an extra crumb of food. No one dared to complain; everyone just waited. What would this retribution, about which Beneš had spoken from his London exile, look like, a retribution to be sealed in blood and imposed in the near future? For this reason, no one resisted, and word came uneasily through the grapevine to comply with the orders of the decree. Word had reached Gerta as well, but she decided not to remove herself to any camp.

If old women were allowed to stay at home, then why couldn't Gerta also manage to go undetected and stay in the city so that she could hear what was being planned? After all, she, too, was Czech, through her own free will but above all through her mother, and she carried her birth certificate with her at all times as proof. Besides, during the war, she hadn't begged anyone to stamp her food ration coupons with the letter *D*.

She only feared those who might recognize her, identify her as Gerta Schnirch. Those who would take satisfaction in seeing the daughter of Friedrich Schnirch—who had managed to make plenty of enemies in the northern part of Brno—being led away by the Revolutionary Guard, or getting beaten up and having her child taken away. That thought gave Gerta pause. What if they took Barbora away from her? What if they beat her up and dragged her off and left Barbora lying someplace on the street, someplace where no one would notice her? What if no one fed her because she was the child of a half-German mother? What then? She would go out of her mind, that much she knew.

Still, she took the risk. She had to know what was coming, what the future held for her and for Barbora, as both Czechs and Germans. Nothing would happen, she reassured herself, and on the afternoon of May 12, she put on the best dress she could find, picked up Barbora, and walked slowly toward the Rathausplatz. In her pocket, she carried her father's old glasses and the scarf her mother used to wear to church on Sundays, hoping this way no one would recognize her, even if they were walking right beside her. Besides, she had Barbora, about whose existence barely anyone knew. She would be Gerta's protective shield.

So at five o'clock, Gerta was standing beneath the edge of the terrace surrounding St. Michael's Church in a crowd buzzing with excitement, waiting for President Beneš to step out onto the balcony of the *Neues Rathaus*, now known once again by its Czech name, the *Nová Radnice*, or New Town Hall. Then the doors opened, and the crowd's murmur swelled into an aroused clamor with the occasional victory whoop or shout of good luck thrown in.

XVIII

On that next-to-last evening of May, Gerta came home after a grueling day of work and sensed that something was brewing. All this time she had been waiting, and suddenly now, on this day, the city abuzz with whispers, guards loitering on every street corner, policemen patrolling up and down Bratislavská Street in pairs, everything seemed to indicate that something was imminent. Now the predictions of the frightened neighbors would come to fruition; now the worst fears harbored by all those who wore a white armband with a large black *N* for *Němec*, the

Czech word for *German*, would burst through the floodgates. They had been suspended in the air, taking on contours with each new account of yet another neighbor, or friend of a friend, gone missing, each newly reported suicide, each successive execution.

Gerta had been expecting it any day, ever since that late afternoon on May 12, when she had returned home terrified by the rally at which Beneš delivered his rousing speech. What a fool. He had turned that mass of ordinary people into servile dogs, those petty officials, workers, shopkeepers, those frightened little people, who all through the war had striven to maintain civil relations with the Germans. She had observed it hundreds of times, and hundreds of times had felt ashamed for those neighbors, and even the strangers, who had come around subserviently in the evenings to seek out her father. And who among them was now being viewed as a collaborator? Not a single one. They were all just Czechs, pure and simple Czechs, who had suffered under the yoke of occupation. And that some of them had grown fat as maggots under that yoke, that they had gotten their hands on handsome properties, acquired what otherwise they would never have been able to acquire, that was of no interest to anyone.

It would have been of no interest to Gerta either, as she was all for live and let live, except now the riled-up mob had it in for her and for Barbora. Her father? Fine, let him reap his just deserts for what he had helped to cook up, wherever he might be, even if that was Kounic College, as the caretaker had relayed to her when her father hadn't come home after that first night following liberation. Let her brother pay his dues as well; both of them deserved it. But this? Such fervid zeal? Germans out? All Germans? With this Gerta did not agree.

At home, she locked herself in the kitchen and was just getting ready to warm up Barbora's bottle of milk, when she heard the thud of heavy boots all over the building, followed by pounding and shouting. Right away she knew it was upon them, the rage that had surged in the breasts of those Czech nationalists on the Rathausplatz, drummed into them by that new revivalist, who, when things had become dicey, had run off to London. Now, someone was knocking on her door, and Gerta knew that Beneš's threats and promises had caught up with her.

She opened the door, and there stood the caretaker. He waved a piece of paper right in front of her face. It took Gerta a moment to bring it into focus.

> *Decree . . . Germans living in the district of Brno, meaning women and children, further men under fourteen years of age and over sixty, as well as those who are invalids or infirm, are to be expelled from the city. The aforenamed persons are permitted to take with them only what they can carry, with the exception of jewelry or savings books . . . effective on this day, May 30, 1945, at 9:00 p.m.*

She read no farther. The caretaker's hand holding the paper went limp, and for a moment he stood there, awkwardly staring into Gerta's wide-open eyes. His jaw slackened as if he were about to utter a long *ahhhh*, but then he just said in a hoarse voice, "There's no other way." He turned on his heel and sped down the stairs without looking back.

Gerta slowly shut the door, leaned back against it, and slumped to the floor. Before a single sob could escape her throat, she heard Barbora's loud cries echoing through the apartment. She ignored them. Through her mind there again flashed the words that two weeks earlier had flown down from the balcony of the New Town Hall to a tumultuous crowd, the same ones that one day later, in the silence of her kitchen, Beneš shouted at her from the newspaper she had bought. Printed there was his entire speech, which on that stifling afternoon, as she was leaning against the wall of St. Michael's Church, she hadn't been able to hear in full, as it was partially delivered behind the closed doors of the assembly room in the New Town Hall, packed with attentive city officials. Now, at this very moment, two weeks after that May 12 rally, his rhetoric had become reality.

Do you remember how, already in the spring of 1938, Hitler was getting ready for us? Do you remember, starting already in 1934, the actions of Henlein and Frank and their entire party, whose ranks included at least 80 percent of the German people in Czechoslovakia? Do you remember the Nazi hate speeches against us at the Nuremberg Rally in 1938? Do you remember, how on September 26, 1938, Hitler rudely insulted me, calling out to his followers like a town crier and telling them that they had to make a resolute choice between him and me? Do you remember all his wartime speeches, from the fall of Poland to the occupation of Belgium and Holland and France, and the attempted occupation of England, to the attack on Russia, to his declaration that Russia had been decimated, that the Red Army no longer existed, that the Balkans had been surrounded, and that the Caucasus and Africa would be next?

The crowd had rumbled; here and there, exclamations had rung out; and the buzz had turned into a roar from which curses against Hitler and the Germans rang out on all sides. Beneš had waved his hand dramatically in the air and, full of anger and indignation, had gone on with his speech, knowing full well its ramifications. He had kneaded the crowd below him as if it were made of dough, soft and pliable, ready to be molded.

And do you remember his wartime speeches, when suppos-edly he had defeated practically everyone and had crushed all his adversaries, and his raving about how the Third Reich would last through the next millennium? Do you remember the crude threats made against our nation over seven long years, the gruesome marauding, the infamous Petschek Palace headquarters, the Gestapo jails and torture chambers, the concentration camps, the annihilation of Lidice and Ležáky, and all the massacres and executions?

Gerta remembered leaning back against the wall of St. Michael's Church as if suddenly she needed a sturdier support to help her bear what was to come. The harsh words kept coming, landing with precision in the fertile soil of memories that were still fresh. And real. Somehow everyone had known; even Gerta had heard rumors, but they were always said to be grossly exaggerated. People, after all, had seen with their own eyes the Jews making their way to the assembly points and waiting to be taken away, whole families. And everyone had also seen those who couldn't wait for them to be gone, circling them and calling them Jewish swine. And Gerta had even seen small boys chasing after people wearing a yellow star, pulling on their suitcases, trying to trip them, pummeling them. That was before the Jews had disappeared completely, from the streets, from the shops, and from the cafés. Had it just been a matter of moving them east and their needing to wait in camps playing soccer all day, as she'd once seen in a newsreel at the cinema, they probably wouldn't have worn such expressions on their faces. And Anička Goldová wouldn't have felt the need to jump out of the window, unless someone truly had helped her. At least, that was what was rumored later, but who knew what really happened. Yet having listened to Beneš, she thought that it most likely had been suicide after all, even though she was reluctant to believe everything that emigrant with his mopey wife, Hana, at his side was saying.

And the daily dismantling of our culture, our schools, our national pride, the daily insults against our people, the way they kicked us and spat at us with their talk of the enlightened Herrenvolk, the master race!

The crowd had roared.

Those were words no one ever wanted to hear again. *Enlightened Herrenvolk, Superman, Aryan.* Gerta felt a peculiar tingling in the very pit of her stomach at the sound of them. She remembered her father repeating them like a mantra.

Gerta recalled the people around her seething with genuine rage. She could relate to them, to their raised fists and incensed voices. She, too, was one of them, one of the outraged, one of the vengeful, one of those who wanted retribution for all those long-suffered humiliations, countless concessions, and irreparable losses. The loss of her mother. Even Gerta wanted to condemn the past that she had in common with the crowd around her, and in so doing indict both her father and Friedrich, see them both put in a pillory, and with them all the *Herrenvolk* and the racial purity they stood for.

The arms raised over the heads of the people in front of her looked like porcupine quills, swaying menacingly in all directions and threatening to stab. She, too, would have raised her arm over her head if she hadn't needed to keep on rocking Barbora who had started to cry, frightened by the commotion. She pulled the corner of the blanket into which she had swaddled her over her little head and placed her hand protectively on top of it. She tried to quiet her by jiggling her on her hip, but not even she believed it would help to soothe her. Not when Gerta's own heart was pounding like mad. It was racing, spurred on by the hatred that was pouring from the balcony where President Beneš stood with his wife. *For Mother, for Mother,* throbbed inside Gerta's breast as the shouting around her grew louder.

But now the Nazi war is over! Up to the very last minute, it drove the German people into a fanatical battle, and these people willingly went along. What seems unthinkable truly happened: The German people threw themselves into bloody murder as if they were deaf and blind. They didn't resist; they didn't think; they didn't stop—they went on, either fanatically or unthinkingly, butchering and allowing themselves to be butchered. Over the course of this war, that nation ceased to be human, and ceased to be tolerable to humanity. Today it appears to us as a human monster. And for that, the nation must be forcefully and harshly punished!

The crowd went wild.

"Now we'll get right to work," shouted Beneš from the balcony, "and we'll restore order among ourselves, especially here in the city of Brno, among the Germans and among everyone else. My plan is—and I make no secret of it—regarding the German question in our Republic, it must be liquidated."

Shouting erupted in the square, and the crowd began to chant.

"Death to the Germans, death to the Germans!" rang out on all sides.

"Liquidate!"

"Punish the Germans!"

"Death to the Germans!"

"Germans out! *Raus!*"

The louder the commotion around her grew, the wilder the gesticulations, the more menacing the fists, the higher the leaping of the boys, barely out of school, eager to prove their readiness to start liquidating Germans, the smaller did Gerta's own desire for revenge become. It shrank and shriveled up, until all that was left of it was a small, hard, dense ball in the pit of her stomach. Fear.

Punish the Germans? All the Germans? Or punish the Germans who were guilty, who had helped build the Reich, who had tried to snatch more for themselves of what rightfully belonged to the Czechs or the Jews? Which Germans?

"Punish the Germans!"

"Germans out!"

"Germans out!"

The square thundered with the clamor of thousands of people. Gerta buried her face in Barbora's hair and pulled her in toward her chest, into her belly, into herself. In sheer terror. Because at that moment, amid all the shouting and whistling around her, she realized that she could never be part of that crowd, that mass of individuals who would relieve their pangs of conscience and the pain of losing family members, friends, and acquaintances, by taking revenge. Revenge was something that she would never be able to take. Against whom would she take it? Who were the Germans? She, Gerta Schnirch, thought of herself as Czech, but at the same time, she was the daughter of Friedrich Schnirch, a clerk in the *Oberlandrat* office, fully half-German, a former member of the League of German Girls, one who had volunteered for the *Winterhilfswerk*.

XIX

Naturally it had occurred to her even beforehand: the Germans would have to be paid back in their own currency. What other way? There had been plenty of talk about it, after all. This was also why, when it became clear that the Germans weren't going to win the war, some of them had fled like rats abandoning a sinking ship. How many shops and apartments were now empty? For instance, the formerly Jewish grocery store on the corner of their street that had been confiscated, or the villa of their erstwhile Sterngasse neighbor Mr. Hovězák, who when the war started had suddenly become Herr Hortek. The likes of him had all taken to their heels. But this was also why Gerta had stayed. What reason did she have to flee, she whose mother was Czech, and who, up until the beginning of the war, had attended a Czech school as well as Mr. Kmenta's art classes, for as long as she possibly could? Why should she leave Janinka, Pressburger Straße, where she had grown up, their apartment, where Barbora had been born? Why should she go away from here, when after all, she was one of those whose conscience was clean?

But she hadn't taken into account that there would be no opportunity to explain to anyone how she had lived and what she had thought. That there would be no time to assess people based on their actions, that there would only be time to flip through the certificates of race and separate out the people whose papers were stamped with a capital *D*. And judging by that, she was German. And like all other Germans, she was an object of the loathing with which all the Czechs in Brno were seething, even boys barely old enough to be out of school. Gerta's hair stood on end as she thought of the fanatical zeal with which these boys, their teeth clenched in anger and their fists balled, had been leaping up in the crowd below the balcony. Just to show Beneš how bold and ready they were to carry out his plan. She had often witnessed the same zeal during the war. But this time, it was inciting people in the streets to chant, "Death to the Germans! Germans out!"

How naive of her to have thought that instead, they would be chanting, *Out with those who took action against our Republic! Out with those who are guilty!* How stupid to assume that by now, passions had cooled. She had spotted Mr. Kmenta in the crowd in front of the New Town Hall, but in that setting, she couldn't approach him for help. With half of the city running amok, how could she explain to him that she thought of herself as Czech, just like her mother? Whom could she turn to? Who could vouch for her credibility? Who could get her the piece of paper that these days everyone was after?

She thought of the caretaker. He, after all, had known her family and had lived through everything with them.

If offering herself to him and allowing him to do whatever he pleased to her meant that in the end she would have that paper, then she would think of those two weeks as a survival strategy. Afterward she would try to expunge them from her memory. By then she would have secured her apartment, which she would eventually exchange for a smaller one where she would raise Barbora, and she would find some kind of work. She wouldn't waste any time worrying about what had become of her father. She wouldn't worry about Friedrich either; it had been, after all, what he wanted, and as for Karel and his broken heart, it no longer mattered either. Janinka was the only one she would try to find again. Nothing else from the past, from the war years, would be welcome in her new life. Everything else she would bury somewhere deep down inside herself, for good.

For two weeks, she went down to see him regularly. She would leave Barbora upstairs alone on the bed, swaddled in a blanket and sur-rounded by pillows so that she couldn't roll around and fall off. It never took more than a few minutes; she wasn't gone long.

He promised to get her a certificate that would allow her to stay in Brno. He promised to testify that she had always spoken Czech, that she was Czech like her mother, that she was dependable and an anti-fascist. He promised to vouch for her and not let her and Barbora go down with those who had *Sieg Heiled*, informed, seized Czech or Jewish property, or been avid supporters of the Reich. He said she could rely on him, because, after all, he knew how things had been at home. All she had to do was to show him a little affection now and then, and wait for the certificate of credibility to arrive from the town hall, where the new National Committee had established its seat. She needed to be patient and wait.

While she was waiting and going to work clearing away rubble, spending fourteen to fifteen hours a day moving around the city with Barbora strapped to her back or to her chest, barely managing to find enough food to feed herself, she was witness to a perverse drama. Those who had once greeted her father by raising their arm in a salute were now standing behind the ranks of toiling Germans, kicking them to make them work faster, or beating them for no reason at all, just on a whim. Even Gerta caught a few kicks, and from people she knew well; she did all she could do to keep Barbora out of their way. It was as if they had never set eyes on her before. And who was among them? Petr Pitín, Friedrich's Hitler Youth buddy, who with the butt of his rifle smashed in Frau Mayer's head because she looked at him in surprise. Mr. Vlk, who during the war had always signed himself Herr Wolf, and the one-armed Mr. Bednařík, whose sleaziness had made even her father spit on the floor once he'd walked out the door. But Mr. Kmenta and Janinka's father were also among the supervisors, making sure to mete out fair punishment on the bony, hunched-over backs of those who were feverishly working away. These and others like them stood by the heaps of rubble on Bratislavská Street or along the tram tracks on Cejl, where Gerta worked. These days, the law was in their hands. They were the ones to decide who would be paired with a ten-year-old child to haul away heavy, collapsed beams or slabs of a stone staircase, who would collect and clean off bricks, or who would pull a fully loaded cart. Occasionally, they would beat up someone just for having a coughing fit in the dusty surroundings, or for having eyes bloodshot with conjunctivitis, or they would fire a random shot into the midst of their stooped bodies. Sometimes they would stand a woman up with her face to the wall and hit her across the back of the neck with a cudgel so hard that her nose would become a shapeless blob in the middle of her face, spurting blood down her chest all the way to the ground. That spring, Gerta saw for the first time the sheer horror in the eyes of mothers forced to strike the faces of their own children when their supervisors felt they were working too slowly. The more tentatively they hit, the harder the club would end up coming down on both of them. And she witnessed the despair of women whose daughters were led away from the rubble heaps to go peel potatoes for the Russians or wash their laundry on the platforms of the Židenice train station. Even Gerta was chosen for such tasks. And always she would return home, her back raw, and welts and bruises on her thighs, depending on how hard she had tried to resist. A woman who, in the eyes of the Ukrainians and Kazakhs, had ceased to be a person. But at least she had Barbora, and she was still alive. Unlike others, who every day would be taken away, never to be seen again by any of those who regularly showed up for work on the corner of Cejl and Koliště Streets.

It went on like this for the rest of May. Each day she would receive from the caretaker's hands ever-dwindling ration books, stamped with a large letter *D*. At night, she would barricade her front door with a wardrobe, just as she had done in the days before liberation, when she had gone from being a resident of Brno to being a second-class citizen. And so it continued up until May 30, the eve of the Feast of Corpus Christi in 1945, when the caretaker appeared waving the decree in front of her face.

PART II

When Felling a Forest,

Splinters Will Fly

I

Justice does not exist. Until recently, she had believed that it did and had thought it was somehow related to a person's degree of guilt. Until recently, she had thought that in the end, truth would prevail. How wrong she had been!

Gerta looked around for familiar faces among the people who, along with her, were taking such ignominious leave of Brno, driven toward an uncertain future. The informer Frau Braun was plodding along a few steps ahead of her with her daughter who was barely fifteen. Between them, they were dragging a suitcase wrapped around with a cord that was tied together on top in loops just the right size for their hands to slip through. Every so often, they would exchange a nod, set the suitcase down at the edge of the road, and switch sides. Every so often, Frau Braun would nod and grab both handles herself, hauling all that was left of her possessions on her own. Gerta lost sight of them when she and the young woman, who had been pushing her child in the baby carriage alongside Gerta's since they had set out from Brno, dared to stop for a moment by the side of the road, just before daybreak.

Herr Liebscher and his frail, stooped wife shuffled past them. In less than an hour, Gerta would in turn pass them, but wouldn't dare look back as a youth with maniacally blazing eyes stood over the old couple, curled up together in the grass by the side of the road, firing one shot after another, one to the right of the old lady, one to the left, between the sprawled legs of Herr Liebscher, until a blasted clod of earth buried his trouser leg. Gerta didn't think that those two, cradling each other's heads and huddled together as once upon a time in a lovers' embrace, would get up again. She didn't want to see it. She would keep walking, walk faster, quicken her step like the young woman beside her. Better not to look; after all, she had Barbora with her—better to get away fast, and above all, inconspicuously.

Just then, Frau Freiberg passed her. Frau Freiberg had a little fabric shop on the corner of Schöllergasse and Pressburger Straße. Or once had. She was the one who had pointed out that Annie Goldová, who up until then had managed to avoid the transport, was in hiding with Mr. Šrámek, the button maker. It was because of her that Annie Goldová had jumped out of the window, that was unless she'd been helped along, although supposedly Mr. Šrámek had tried to protect her with his own body. Still, nobody knew what had really happened. Then even Šrámek disappeared. A German white-collar family moved into his empty apartment and very soon blended into the neighborhood. So now it was the turn of the Germans to be on the move, thought Gerta. Her own suitcase was loaded onto the netting underneath Barbora's baby carriage, and they were being moved somewhere to the south, vaguely characterized as being outside of the city, because within the city, Germans, even those like her, were no longer welcome.

Holding her breath, she wondered what might be lying in store for her and Barbora.

Would they be trampled underfoot? Would the two of them become casualties on a victim list, names in the column between two black lines where one always found the names of the executed? Victim? That was not what this list was going to be called, she thought wryly as she looked around at the armed youths.

Neither she, nor Barbora, nor the young woman beside her—none of them was marching in a procession of victims, she thought to herself. No one would bother to count them. For that matter, all through May, no one had counted them, and no one had bothered to inform them, the Germans who remained and were clearing the streets, about what had happened to the ones who disappeared.

Gerta stopped. She felt sick to her stomach. Her unsteady legs gave way beneath her, and suddenly it seemed as if the world around her had been switched off. It stopped making sound; it stopped being audible; it stopped being visible, and as her limbs grew heavy, it seemed to vanish somewhere above her, flying up as fast as she was falling down.

She was aware of a blow to her head. Then there were just a dull ringing and darkening circles spiraling in toward the center of her vision, narrowing as new ones formed around the outer edges.

She felt a smack, first one and then a second. The flat palm of someone's hand was slapping her face. Slowly the world started to come back into focus. The dull ringing separated into distinct voices; the black circles slowly took on contours, and out of their dark, symmetrical curves emerged a round face framed with blonde hair. She was staring into the eyes of the young woman whose face was right up against hers. She could smell her hungry breath as the muffled waves of her voice wafted past her nostrils. Slowly she began to discern the words as well.

"Get up, you hear me! Get up. Pick yourself up. You can't stay lying here."

She was frightened.

Little by little, Gerta recalled what had happened. She began to feel sick again, felt the rising pressure in her stomach and the acidic saliva rushing into her mouth.

"They're going to do something to us. To get back at us for everything that happened . . . they're going to do something to us. They're not just sending us out of the city; they're sending us to our deaths, I'm sure of it," she rasped.

"Hush! What're you saying?"

"We're marching to our deaths; they're going to shoot us—what else do you think they're planning to do with us? They want us to die like dogs, do you understand? We can't go on."

"You're crazy! My God, what's wrong with you? You have to, you hear me? You have to go on. I don't have the strength to help you, so come on. You have to keep going. They're not going to kill us; why would they? They're just taking us to the border; it's not that far."

"Then why are they taking the old people who'll never make it that far? Don't you get it? There are too many of us here. Once we get past the city limits, they're going to shoot us!"

"Don't shout, you hear me?" said the girl, looking around in alarm at the people who were passing close by.

Gerta couldn't hold herself any longer. She rolled over on her side and began to retch, spewing pungent gobs of sour phlegm and half-digested bits of food from her mouth.

The young woman stood up, grabbed the handlebars of both baby carriages, jiggled them as if she were quieting the children, and looked around. Then she quickly dropped back down to kneel beside Gerta.

"Come on, get up, quickly, before they see us. Right now, you have to keep on walking; we're leaving the city, you understand? We're only leaving the city, and then they're going to leave us alone. Or they'll take us across the border. I have an aunt in Vienna. We can stay with her until my husband comes. They're not going to kill us. Get up!"

But Gerta saw it. Saw how even this young woman, who now was standing up again and rocking the carriages, all at once had grown afraid. Afraid that what she still believed for now might in one hour no longer be true. As had been the case all through the war.

Gerta slowly sat up, wiped her mouth, and got to her feet. Her head was ringing, and the cramps racking her stomach compressed it into a hard, shriveled-up ball. It was as if a walnut were now lodged in her bowels, chafing the walls of her other organs with its tough, gnarly shell. She brushed off her dress and grabbed hold of the carriage in which Barbora was sleeping. Her knee joints seemed to have turned into gelatin. Unsteady, as if lacking the support of bones or a spine, she leaned, feeble and limp, on her companion's shoulder.

"What good are we to them in the city? They just want to get us out. We're in the way, understand? Lots of people have come back since the war ended, and there's no place for them to live. We just have to make room for them, just until it all gets sorted out; they just need to get us out of the way, that's all," whispered the young woman, shaking her head as if trying to get rid of a pesky fly buzzing by her ear. She grabbed Gerta around her waist, put her other hand on the handlebar of her own baby carriage, and slowly set off again.

Gerta followed her. She felt empty. Figuratively and also literally, her stomach was in knots.

"We have to come up with a plan. We have to think," she said. "What's your name?"

"Helga Bartl."

"Gerta. Schnirch. We have to figure out a way to get out of here. To get away, as quickly as possible."

II

But it wasn't just Frau Freiberg and the Brauns; there were others as well, those who had steered clear of the political situation all through the war, and who, now that the war was over, still held no political interests. Even so, on that May night in 1945, before being driven out of the city, they all stood in the same long line of people that wound from the Augustinian cloister across Mendelplatz, all the way past the brewery where it disappeared into the dusk, and stretched in the other direction past St. Anne's University Hospital and continued beyond the bend of Annagrund Street.

The Liebschers, Granny Pawelka from Köffillergasse with bleeding earlobes, from which moments ago her earrings had been ripped, the shopkeeper Frau Mayer with little Ingrid and Irma, who spent school holidays sitting around on stools in front of the grocery store—they all stood in the same crowd. The girls huddled together, cowering at the loud yelling of the armed Revolutionary Guards, and right near them stood Herr Tomaschek, Herr Gollo, and a few others whom she recognized from the *Winterhilfswerk*. What had Frau Mayer ever done to anyone, or Granny Pawelka, or Gerta, or Barbora, to deserve being lumped together along with the likes of those others and driven out of the city? What had Gretl Schumann ever done, slumped against the cloister wall on top of her small suitcase next to her husband on crutches and their twin boys, who at the checkpoint soon would be taken away from her anyway, once it was discovered that she hadn't given their real age. What more would they still put her through? And how much more could Gretl still bear? Mere hours had passed since old Frau Herrscher decided not to come along. Supposedly they had all been there, even the twins, standing around the bathtub as Gretl cradled her mother's head and her husband cut. Into the clear water spurted two red threads, swirling in meshlike eddies around the outstretched forearms, and they said the old lady just kept on smiling. She wouldn't have made it very far; she wasn't well, and who knew what would have happened had she stayed behind in the empty apartment. It would have depended on who walked in first.

They had all been standing there since nine o'clock that night, the residents of Sterngasse, crowded into a corner of Mendelplatz. All the people who wore a white armband marked with a big, black *N*. They stood there in the order in which they had arrived, driven through the darkening streets across Cejl, through the park at Koliště, down Dornych and Silniční Streets, all the way to the square. A small group of men not yet taken away to the camps had stayed behind. The caretaker from their building, Sterngasse 142, had turned over three families to the Revolutionary Guard. As he handed in Gerta's papers, he looked directly over her head, as if she weren't standing right there. *He hasn't done a thing for me,* she thought bitterly.

As if to feel any more bitterness or shame was even possible after what she had been through this past month, during which she had completely lost her sense of being a person. Her sense of being a woman. What was left of her was a stooped and disfigured body, toilworn and loathsome, her face furrowed by indignity and fear. Fear above all, which forced her inwardly screaming lips to remain outwardly mute. So as not to draw attention to herself. She felt as hollow as an empty nutshell. Hollow and withered, worthless. It was only for Barbora that she was doing all this, for her alone. Her mother would have been right about that business of one's love for one's child. But not even the baby had softened the caretaker. That evening, under the flowering plane trees on Sterngasse, he hadn't had the decency to look her even once in the eye.

III

From the edge of the wooden barn's roof, which was directly above her face, a large drop fell right onto her cheek. It had rained. Out of the solid mass of dense noise, individual sounds were beginning to emerge. She was able to discern an erratic banging, commotion, shouting, and long-drawn-out weeping women's voices. Gunshots. Male voices.

She was regaining her senses.

The soldier who had just gotten off her looked down as she rolled over onto her side, relieved finally to be able to bring her knees together, and gave her exposed buttocks a hard kick.

"Stinking sow!" He spat on her, then turned away and quickly strode off. As of the past few weeks, this was nothing new for her. For that matter, it seemed as if for her whole life it had been written across her forehead that anyone was welcome to help themselves to her body with impunity. But in this case, in contrast to when her father had done things to her, she knew exactly why she had it coming. It was because of him. Because of that German half, which came from him and was part of her.

She sat up, wiped off her face, and smoothed her disheveled hair, then finally stood to see why Barbora wasn't crying. She really had slept through the whole thing. Gerta left her lying as she was, on her back with her arms stretched over her head. She started to fumble around the netting under the carriage for one of Barbora's diapers, wanting to dry her soiled thighs. But then she let the diaper be and pulled out one of her blouses instead. Who knew when she would next have a chance to launder Barbora's diapers; she didn't have enough with her to afford to waste a single one, having no idea when and how this journey would end.

Slowly she wiped off her inner thighs and smelled the musk seeping out between her legs, her sweaty armpits, her own familiar odor mingled with an alien one, the distasteful smell of male semen. Her heart was still pounding in her throat but was slowly being drowned out by the more painful pressure of stifled sobs, which had germinated deep below her diaphragm and now fought their way up past her larynx, which had started to bob as she tried to force the first sobs back down.

She couldn't hold them back for long. She broke into a violent weeping that came out sounding more like a desperate wailing than sobbing. The dry sobs made her feel as though she were choking, the fitful exhalations and wheezing gasps for breath threatening to suffocate her, but she couldn't stop them. They came on uncontrollably. Powerless, she gave in to them. They were impossible to stop despite her fear that they might attract another soldier, might again betray a hiding place that had already once been discovered.

Gerta's shoulders shook as she huddled by the wheels of the baby carriage, and this was how Helga found her. She shuffled over quietly, her child in her arms. She sat down beside Gerta, very close, practically on top of her protruding hip. Gerta spun around, doubled over, buried her head in Helga's lap, and let her grief pour into her skirt. Helga sat motionless, made no attempt to comfort Gerta. She stayed sitting, gently rocking her little boy, while Gerta tried to master her own rage and sense of shame, self-pity, and disgust, her feeling of revulsion directed as much against herself as at the Russian soldier who had discovered their hiding place. She shook and sobbed, and then abruptly sat up and fixed her wet eyes on Helga's profile, inscrutable in the night's gloom. She reached out and with her hand brought Helga's left cheek toward her. Helga stared through her and began to rock the child more intensely.

"What did they do to you?" asked Gerta.

Helga was nodding in rhythm to the rocking.

"What did they do to you? Can you hear me? Say something! Helga!"

Gerta nudged her with her shoulder.

"Can you hear me? Can you talk?"

Helga kept on nodding, making no other motion. With her hand resting on the back of the boy's head, she went on rocking the child in silence.

Gerta freed the hand on which she was leaning, grabbed the young woman by the shoulders with both hands, and gently shook her. No reaction. She shook harder.

"Helga, can you hear me?"

Nothing.

From the other side of the barn behind which they were hiding, there still came sounds of banging, crashing furniture, and a jumble of men's voices and women's screams.

Gerta looked around. The hiding place behind the barn had saved them from what was going on in the farmstead courtyard, which earlier that evening the drunken guards had so generously offered to them as a place to spend the night, but it was only a matter of time before the next soldier would stumble across them, again looking for a place to relieve himself. Like the one who had wandered over a little while ago, before intending to jump on one of the women inside the farmyard. The soldiers had arrived in the night about an hour or so after the women, who, exhausted from the march to the point of collapsing, had barely managed to drag themselves inside. Also leaping out of the back of the truck were some of the same guards who had directed them here, who then just howled with laughter as they watched the soldiers light into the women. This gruesome activity was still going on in the farmstead courtyard. Gerta needed to find a better place to hide. Over where the long shadow cast by the barn ended, alongside a fence overgrown with tall grass, she spied a low pile of heaped logs.

"Do you see that pile? Helga?" No reaction.

"Grab your things. We'll hide behind it."

Helga didn't move an inch, just went on rocking the child.

Gerta braced herself against the ground, threw her skirt down over her knees, and stood up. She tucked the blouse and other scattered objects in beside Barbora who was still sleeping and backed the carriage up a bit, past her seated companion.

"We're going. I'm wheeling Barbora over there," said Gerta, turning the carriage toward the woodpile. Staying in the barn's shadow, she slowly moved off.

Between the fence and the log pile was a narrow gap, just enough room for two bodies but not for a sturdy carriage as well. Gerta lifted Barbora out of the bassinet and bundled her up in the bedding and the coat that she had tucked underneath her the night before. She pushed through the undergrowth and squeezed behind the logs, the slightest crackle paralyzing her with fear.

She laid Barbora down in the grass behind the logs, making a little nest for her out of the bedding and the coat. Barbora gurgled and smacked her lips but went on sleeping. The baby carriage sat looming ominously in the grass. It stood by the pile of logs so naturally, as if someone had just left it there for a moment. Gerta toppled the carriage onto its side and left it lying on the ground. The wheels jutted into the air and slowly revolved; out of the netting and bassinet tumbled bed-clothes and what was left of their provisions. Gerta angled the underside of the carriage in the direction from where the soldiers had come and placed a few branches across the wheels. This way, under the cover of darkness, it wouldn't occur to anyone that it was anything but a discarded old baby carriage, let alone a screen shielding two huddled women.

Gerta turned back to look at Helga. She was still sitting there, rocking with her child. Gerta ran back to her.

"Come on, I'll help you."

Helga didn't budge. Gerta positioned herself with her legs spread apart and reached down, scooping her hands under the young woman's armpits to try to pick her up. As soon as Helga sensed the pressure, however, she leaped up on her own and, with her left arm clutching the boy to her chest and a frightened, semi-audible gasp, lashed out at Gerta with her right arm.

"Shh." Gerta grabbed hold of her arm and managed to keep them both in balance. Then she noticed how the small boy's head had fallen backward at an impossible angle, like the head of a rag doll held on only by a few remaining threads that still attached the neck to the colorful little shirt.

IV

By the time the commotion in the farmstead courtyard behind them had died down, it was almost daybreak. The deep, dark blue of night, in which one couldn't see beyond at most a few feet, had turned into a grayish haze, and the stars had grown pale. Helga was lying behind the bulwark of branches and the two carriages, curled up into a tight ball, her forehead pressed against her knees and her heels hard against her buttocks. She was convulsively wrapped around the infant's body, clutching him tightly in her arms, as if trying to force him back into her stomach. She had fallen into a stuporlike sleep and looked so rigid and stiff that it seemed she wasn't even breathing. Gerta peered out from behind the barricade.

The barn that had sheltered them during the night allowed her to observe only a sliver of what was going on in the courtyard. In the pale light of the breaking day, she could see a military truck surrounded by several soldiers who were nervously snapping at each other. The words weren't Czech; it was a foreign language, although she could have easily been mistaken since the wind carried over only snippets of words that were further fragmented by the obstruction of the barn. The nervousness and agitation, however, Gerta could make out clearly. Some of the men were standing around the truck; others were running off; still others were slowly approaching, bearing bundles that they either carried slung over their shoulders or dragged behind them on the ground. As one of the bystanders bent down to give a soldier a hand with a bundle he had just dragged over, Gerta saw that it was a human body with strangely contorted limbs. They swung it up into the back of the truck, where another soldier grabbed the lifeless female body by the armpits and dragged it deep inside the truck's interior. He soon reemerged, ready for the next load, which the newly arriving soldiers were already heaving up.

Gerta watched the tedious process in dismay. Men kept on coming to the truck, carrying or dragging bodies. Some were so slight that all it took for the men to lift them into the back of the truck was to grab and toss them. One of the soldiers keeping watch by the open back of the truck broke into a run toward Gerta, but doubled over after just a few steps, his hunched back shuddering convulsively, and vomited. This got him a few surly catcalls, but none of the other men interrupted the frantic pace of their grim cleanup work.

From the section of the courtyard that was hidden behind the barn and that Gerta couldn't see came the sound of a heavy motorcar starting up. The men paused. Some raised their arms and waved; others just lifted their heads and went back to work. The hum of the motor grew louder, and then the sound seemed to indicate that the vehicle was moving. In one of the outbuildings, a child began to cry. As the truck pulled out of the gate of the courtyard, which was surrounded by wooden sheds, Gerta caught a glimpse of bodies through the slats of the sides of the truck bed, bodies piled on top of each other with limply dangling arms and legs. Then the vehicle went around a bend and disappeared from her sight.

The soldiers she had been observing were now piling into another similar vehicle, also loaded up with bodies.

Gerta drew herself back behind the barricade of wooden boards, baby carriage, and branches. The gray of the dwindling night gradually gave way to dawn, and Gerta quietly wondered what to do next. She could still hear a child crying and soldiers shouting off in the distance. Her gaze darted back and forth between Helga's sleeping body and Barbora, wrapped in her coat. Soon Barbora would wake up; Gerta knew her rhythm. What would happen if she woke up cranky and started to cry? She would alert the soldiers to their hiding place. Having massacred all the women in the camp, they wouldn't be about to spare them. Gerta kept her eyes riveted on Barbora, waiting for her to start stirring and opening her delicate little mouth, making smacking noises. Ready for the moment when her daughter would open her eyes and make the first gurgle, Gerta slowly unbuttoned her blouse, prepared to slip a nipple into the baby's mouth in case she woke up hungry. In the morning chill, goose bumps ran up along Gerta's rib cage.

Several minutes passed, and then she heard the truck's motor. She dropped down onto her knees, braced her hands on the ground, and cautiously peered out. The back of the truck was again piled with bodies, lifeless limbs protruding through the slats, just as they had from the vehicle that had driven off some moments ago. The soldiers moved to the far side of the courtyard, where Gerta couldn't see them. She heard the sound of another motor, and then yet another. All the vehicles, the one carrying the women's bodies and the two in which the soldiers rode, were driving off in the same direction from where they had originally come, toward Pohořelice. The sound of the motors grew fainter and then finally faded away completely. The farm was steeped in an eerie silence. To Gerta, the complex of buildings that she continued to observe seemed alive, as if the oppressive silence were merely the calm before the storm, at which point the roofs of the buildings would fly off and one structure after another would erupt in massive explosions. She waited for that suspended, practically palpable horror to descend, for the moment when it would come crashing down and when she, too, would finally be able to burst into tears. But instead, the only sounds she could hear were the chirp of awakening birds, the rustle of the breeze, and the occasional creak of something inside the wooden buildings.

Gerta crawled back to Barbora and Helga. Barbora was still not waking up.

"Helga!"

Gerta reached out her hand and touched her shoulder.

"Helga, wake up."

As Gerta shook her shoulder, she heard a low guttural sound emerge. She didn't let up, and Helga finally opened her eyes, and, taking deep, gasping breaths, slowly came back to life. She was breathing as if she had just finished running a marathon. Little by little she extended her legs, her face reflecting the pain of moving her stiffened limbs, and then moments later, the eerie silence of the farm was rent by a primal scream—Helga's.

V

The way back from the farmstead to the main road leading to the town of Pohořelice took the small group of women, those who had survived the night's rampage, just under a half hour. In the darkness, when they had been going in the opposite direction, the stretch of road had seemed endless. Exhaustion from the past night and the march of the previous day was showing on all of them.

Now they were standing on a field road amid still-green corn, where the wheels of heavy vehicles had left tracks of broken stalks, flattened into ruts. One such vehicle was steadily approaching along the main road with a convoy of slowly moving people. In the back sat several youths, and from the short distance between the intersection of the two roads, most visible were their rifles, jutting up between their seated, upright bodies.

"What're you up to here?"

"Trying to disappear, are you?"

The vehicle pulled up, and the men jumped out of the back. An anxious murmur rippled through the group of women. One look made it obvious that they were part of the Brno convoy. They looked just like the people trudging along in the marching column. Dirty, wrapped in as many layers of clothing as possible, with baby carriages, carts, or suitcases.

"They took us to a farm for the night," said one of the women in Czech. "They pulled us off the march at night and . . ." Her voice broke before she was able to finish her sentence, and she burst into tears.

"You women German?"

Some nodded anxiously; the woman who was crying tried to choke back her sobs. Gerta held on to Helga and, staying in the middle of the group, observed the men. They were all still boys. They looked as though they could be sixteen or seventeen years old; they were wearing work clothes, and their rifles looked completely out of place. She could imagine them still just a few days ago, finishing their shift, removing their coveralls and hanging them up in their lockers, rinsing off their faces, and heading home to their mothers for dinner in one of the streets in the Brno-Židenice or Brno-Líšeň neighborhoods. Now, here they were with weapons in their hands, aiming them at unfamiliar women, some of whom were older, some considerably so. They appeared to be tired. Perhaps they had been marching with the convoy throughout the night, and throughout the previous day and night, and now this morning, they lacked the energy to be aggressive. *Whatever happens, don't provoke them,* Gerta reminded herself, remembering from the day before what these boys, masters of the moment, were capable of. She could still see the rock in one of their hands as he used it to knock gold teeth out of an old man's mouth. She recalled the ruthlessness with which they ripped earrings from women's ears, some of the women fighting back tears as they placed their hands over their ears, and how the blood spurted through their fingers. How a few steps later, they sank to the ground, unconscious, and how their companions, if they had any, tried quickly to revive them, or hastily rolled them into the roadside ditch, before they themselves got kicked or slammed by the butt of a rifle. She saw them chop off a corpulent woman's finger when she couldn't pull off her ring. And when the woman wouldn't stop shrieking, saw them slit her throat as if she were a hog. Gerta wasn't about to say a word or do anything to attract their attention.

"I'm Czech," said one of the women, beside whom stood her small daughter, barely ten years old.

Gerta looked over at her in alarm. The other women stood frozen, trembling with fear, what was left of their belongings set down by their feet, waiting to see what would happen next. *We're acting like sheep,* thought Gerta, as worn out and exhausted after the night of horror as the others.

The young men looked to be annoyed by this information.

"Which one of you is Czech?"

The woman held up her hand. After her, a few others also timidly raised their hands.

"So what're you doing here?"

"They took us to a farm just off the road for the night. Some soldiers. Probably Russians. We're just coming back. We'd like to go back to Brno; we're here by mistake."

The one who had asked the question was a short, pudgy youth. His dark eyes scanned from one to the next. It was obviously not easy to get a handle on the situation. Fifty filthy and frightened women with children, flocked together where the main road to Pohořelice intersected a field road, standing like pillars of salt, not trying to run away but not joining the marching column either. A furrow creased his forehead, distorting his eyebrows. By now he was fed up with everything. He hadn't slept in two nights and a day, just trying to get these damn fascists out of town. And all without taking even one sip of booze, unlike the others, who got drunk on the very first night. What they then did to the women along the way was something he would never be able to forget. Jožka Rejsek tore a screaming kid away from one of them and tossed it into a field like a football. Then he riddled the woman's back with bullets when she went running after it. They had all been blindingly drunk, and he alone had tried to maintain some control. After all, he was in charge. Better not to dwell on it and let it be a thing of the past. These women looked like they were German. Someone had put them on the march. Why was not his concern. Maybe they were collaborators.

"Collaborators," declared the dark-haired spokesman for the group, and pointed to the convoy.

One of the women standing behind Gerta got shoved with the butt of a rifle. She yelled out in fright, and the flock of women huddled closer together.

"I don't give a damn why you're here. Whether you're Czech or German. You're joining the transport, now."

He gestured to the young men with weapons and then waved at the driver. The vehicle set into motion and veered off the main road to cut across the flattened section of the field, heading straight toward the flock of women. With a frightened yammering, the women grabbed their bags and suitcases. The back row set off, after which the whole group began to move, the young men on either side and the vehicle bringing up the rear. They quickened their step as the vehicle bore down on them. The small children began to cry. As soon as Barbora heard their sobs, she made a face, opened her drooly mouth, and began to cry as well. Red-faced with anger, she wouldn't settle down, not even when Gerta started to rock her or tried to calm her with hushed words, although her own quivering voice betrayed her. Helga walked like a ghost by her side.

"Move!"

After several hundred yards, they reached the tail end of the straggling column of people, mostly elderly, limping along, supporting one another. A convoy of the most wretched of the wretched, thought Gerta. Privately, she reproached herself for having let herself be talked into going back with the other women to the main road toward Pohořelice. As if every one of them had lost her mind. And actually, Gerta as well, since she had been afraid to remain alone in the fields in the middle of nowhere. Setting off in the opposite direction, all alone, seemed just as dangerous as risking the aim of some Czech kid who was a bad shot. And so she found herself in the middle of this flock of women, among whom were some Czechs and even some Germans who wanted to return to Brno at any cost. It hadn't occurred to a single one of them that they might still run into the convoy of exiles that continued to stretch on for miles. Altogether how many could there be, if all through the horrific night Gerta and the other women had spent at the farmstead they had continued to flow in an uninterrupted stream along the Pohořelice road?

Gerta trudged on, pushing her carriage in front of her, with Helga convulsively latched on to the handle. They were both silent; even Barbora had quieted down. Gerta jiggled her on her left arm while Helga walked on her right, clutching the dead little boy to her chest. It was the only thing she still carried; she had left her carriage at the farm and with it all her things. It hadn't helped when Gerta had tried to pick out and hand her some essentials; Helga took nothing with her, and Gerta couldn't add any more to her own load. From that moment when she had come running over in the night with her dead child, Helga hadn't said another word. In the morning, she had stayed near Gerta, as if they were somehow connected, but never altered her expression, not even when Gerta was helping to carry out the last of the dead bodies that the soldiers had left behind in the barns. She squatted down on her haunches a short distance away, watching as the remaining others brought out several young girls and grown women who had escaped the night's horrors by taking their own lives.

Not one of the women they found lying in various places around the farmstead was still alive. They laid out six bodies side by side under the overhang of the roof and covered them with burlap, of which there was plenty to be found in the sheds. It was a grim sight.

The group of women from the farmstead slowly dispersed among the convoy of exiles. The vehicle with the guards who had forced them back into the marching column had long since passed them. Along the road stood young men from the Zbrojovka Arms Factory, keeping watch over the steady stream of exiles. They were no longer bullying. Gerta even saw them lift an old couple into the back of a truck when they couldn't walk any farther, so that they could be driven ahead to Pohořelice. Even these war heroes had grown weary, and from time to time, the compassion within them overcame their callousness. Or perhaps they had sobered up and became aware that there would be consequences to what they had wrought in their state of victorious ecstasy. Gerta had already seen a couple of groups head back to Brno.

And along with the armed guards sitting in the backs of the trucks, their heads jammed between their knees, there were some women and a few children. So not everyone was being forced to leave—there was still hope that she, too, might be able to stay, thought Gerta.

They passed a sign at the edge of the road that said "Pohořelice," and then the first houses came into sight. This was the first time since Gerta had left Brno that she was seeing people other than exiles and their armed escorts. Since the small town of Modřice, where some other expelled families had joined them, they had walked only through fields, skirting the town of Rajhrad and the village of Ledce in the night. It wasn't until Thursday late morning that they encountered some residents of the villages along the way. Gerta had no expectations. It never even occurred to her that something might happen. In her mind's eye, all she saw were houses with darkened windows and deserted streets. This was why she was so surprised when they finally reached Pohořelice.

The town seemed to have come to a complete standstill; no one had gone to work. It was as if everyone wanted to be present when the procession came through. In front of the houses along the road stood women with their children, dipping cups into buckets of water at their feet, and reaching out to offer them to the exhausted and dehydrated Germans. But only rarely did anyone accept. From within the group voices warned, "They want to poison us!" And, "Don't take it. Why do you think they are offering it to us?" Mothers slapped their children's outstretched hands and gripped them tightly by the shoulders, making sure they didn't stray from the middle of the road, keeping them away from the villagers. Only a few dared to drink. One of them was Gerta, who along the way hadn't drunk from either the Modřice stream or from the well in Ledce, where those who hadn't brought any water with them were all bending over. Later on, she even saw people bending down to lap water from puddles and ditches like dogs. One time she saw a drunken guard go over and kick two kneeling old men, sending them tumbling headfirst into the bottom of the ditch. Gerta hadn't dared to look back to see what happened next.

Along the way, she didn't drink from puddles or streams. She took only the tiniest swallows of water from the bottle she had brought with her from home. And she did so only at night, when Helga couldn't see. She couldn't afford to share the little bit that might save Barbora's life and her own. She drank from the bottle when Helga bent down over a stream, and drank when she stepped away to squat down and relieve herself. Always making sure nobody was looking. Into the empty bottle she would then express from her breast whatever Barbora hadn't drunk. It wasn't much; her milk was drying up. She was exhausted, depleted. Observing this, she grew panicked at the thought of her milk drying up altogether. What would then happen to Barbora?

But this time she did reach out her hand, as did Helga, for a cup filled with water from an aluminum pail being offered by a woman wearing a scarf, with two small children peeking out of the window behind her.

"Go ahead; have some; don't be afraid. Take some; have a drink," the woman wearing the scarf repeated in clumsy German, reaching out over and over again toward the marching column with a cup in each hand. Gerta laid Barbora down in the carriage, took the cup in both hands, and drank greedily.

"Please, one more," said Gerta in Czech.

"You speak Czech?"

"One more, please, quickly," Gerta begged, and hastily grabbed a second cup of water, while behind her back she could hear words full of indignation and reproach.

"Hell, you can't trust the Czechs anymore; that girl's going to be dead soon."

"It's poisoned; don't drink any, you two," a woman shouted at Gerta and Helga as she went by, "and watch out, there are guards right behind us."

Gerta pulled Helga back to the carriage. They both still had cups in their hands. She managed a fleeting glance backward and out of the corner of her eye caught a glimpse of one of the young guards approaching. She braced her back, dropped her head down between her shoulders, and grabbed Helga around the waist. She was expecting a blow from his rifle butt. Instead, she overheard him ordering the village woman back into her house. And then up ahead, she saw something that the guard hadn't yet seen—more villagers lined up in a row, extending their arms toward the convoy. She felt her empty stomach contract with hope. Was it possible that farther ahead the guards had already relented?

VI

Even though up ahead she didn't see a single guard, no youth brandishing a weapon, even though all she saw was a crowd of curious or concerned people, the convoy kept going. No one stopped. They continued in a slow-moving and weary column right through the town, across the main square, until finally the number of houses around them began to dwindle. The more sparse and remote cottages tapered off, and in their place appeared several large buildings enclosed by a fence. When Gerta next looked up from her carriage, she discovered that the convoy of travelers had apparently arrived at its destination. Just up ahead, the course of their procession was veering off the main road onto a dirt lane leading toward a large fenced-off area full of wooden structures. Everyone was moving in the same direction, the old men, all the women and children. No one was staying on the main road. Only in the bend where the dirt road branched off and the column of people had to go around the curve was there a group of young men standing with weapons. Others stood by the entrance to the compound, and Gerta glimpsed a few more positioned along the fence line. They were no longer by themselves. Standing alongside them were small groups of Russian soldiers smoking cigarettes that they were offering around to the Czech guards. Moving in the opposite direction of the incoming column came a Zbrojovka Arms Factory truck, heading in the direction of Brno, the back full of guards.

Gerta, plodding along in the column, took a good look at them as they passed by her. They were all young, some even younger than she was, and they all looked tired and indifferent. Then she and Helga entered the fenced-off area.

There were people everywhere, either sitting or lying down. The carpet of human bodies extended to the right and to the left. It spread among the tall wooden buildings and seemed to be pulsating with voices, moans, and the calling out of names of missing family members. Gerta had never seen so many people in one place. She would have stood a bit longer to take in the dismal scene, but the ranks of new arrivals were already pushing her from behind. They pressed past her, jostling her, and Helga was swept away in the crowd. Gerta suddenly spotted the back of her forlorn figure, picking her way among the bodies lying all over the ground and moving to the left, toward the entrance of one of the barracks.

"Helga! Wait! Helga! Helga!" she shouted after her.

Her voice blended with the desperate voices of those who had arrived before her. Gerta leaned into her carriage and set off after Helga. She wasn't sure why, as she barely knew her, and given Helga's current condition, there wasn't much they could really share. But she went after her nonetheless; anything was better than being completely alone.

She bumped into the feet of people who were lying down, tried to get around them, asked them to let her pass. Again and again came voices from down below.

"Have you seen my Jorkl? I lost sight of him along the way."

"Have you seen my wife? They put her in the back of a truck and drove ahead with her."

Gerta shook her head and pushed her carriage, trying to catch up to Helga, who had just come to a standstill by the entrance to a large wooden building. She stood there until Gerta pulled up beside her. Then together they went inside. They were met with the sound of groaning, as if they had stepped inside an infirmary.

They made their way along one of the walls until they reached the far corner, where Helga slumped down, settled her little boy on her lap, and sat motionless, staring out across the expanse of the hall.

Gerta parked her carriage up against the wall, picked up Barbora, spread out the now-soiled and foul-smelling coat with her other hand, and sat down on it beside Helga. All around sat other people talking over each other, although several were just lying there. They looked as if they had a fever. Beads of perspiration stood out on their foreheads, and their bodies trembled uncontrollably. The stench of excrement permeated the space.

"Excuse me, I'm Gertrude Schnirch from Brno, from Sterngasse," said Gerta to one of the women seated beside her.

"You two just got here, didn't you?" replied the woman, nodding toward her and Helga. "I'm Hilde, Hilde Wessely. We lived in Komárov, if you know where that is."

She nodded toward an older woman lying in front of her, and two girls, sitting quietly alongside, about nine and eleven years old.

"Mother's sick. We carried her almost the whole way. At first, she could still walk a little, but by last night, not another step. Trudi Lang helped us," she said, pointing a short distance away to a small, stout woman who sat with her legs crossed, and smiled back at her.

"We've been here since last night. They brought us in around eleven, soaked by that rain. Did you get caught in it too? Since then, Mother's been lying here, but she doesn't look well. They say there's dysentery going around because so many people drank from puddles along the way."

Hilde's daughter, sitting across from her, began to cry.

"She's terribly thirsty; they both are. But I won't let them drink anything. I won't let them die of typhoid fever. This morning, the Russians gave them soup; that'll have to do for now."

"You got some food?"

"Those who moved fast enough. Runny slop, basically water with a bit of potato, but thank God for that. As they handed it out, they said they'd be giving out rations every morning."

"And how long do they plan to keep us here, any idea? What's going to happen next?"

"Nobody knows a thing. Everyone's looking out for themselves. Except nobody has much of anything left, no food, no water. People have been picking dandelions, but as you probably saw outside, whatever hasn't been trampled yet has already been eaten."

"We can't last long here without any water. They have to move us someplace else."

"No idea. Nobody knows. Supposedly at the Austrian border they turned the first group away. They don't want us over there either, and besides, where are they supposed to put us, when they don't even have enough food for themselves? So I wouldn't be surprised if one night they just set this whole place on fire. It would solve the German problem."

Another woman leaned toward them.

"They'd better solve it quick. Just look around for yourselves. Have you seen the latrines? No? There aren't any. And the dysentery is bad, maybe because of the water or something. They've dug a ditch outside, but it's always mobbed. So people are just going, wherever they can. There's no way we can stay here for long; the locals won't have it."

"There's something going around here, fever and diarrhea." Hilde nodded in agreement.

"I already told you, it's dysentery. My brother was a doctor. Don't eat or drink a thing around here."

"But for how long?" asked Gerta in desperation.

"Nobody knows. But take a look around. It's all women and old men. And loads of kids. They can't just go and kill us. It would be an international scandal."

"These days? If they did, they'd most likely think it was just as well, a few less Germans. You're not thinking straight."

Hilde's daughter was still crying.

"Have you seen Erna? Erna Bayer? A petite lady in her forties, might she have been walking with you?" Bending down to them was a young woman, barely twenty years old. Her face was filthy. One of her teeth had been knocked out, and her lip was split open.

Gerta shook her head no, she could no longer remember anyone who had been walking with her.

"I hope you find her," said Hilde, sadly shaking her head.

"So many people missing, families torn apart. I've seen so many mothers crying here. I've seen some dead ones too. Exhaustion. They got here last night, lay down, and never woke up in the morning. They've been carrying them out to that fence next to the army barracks. Maybe that way, those soldier boys will take notice and do something about it, when they start to smell right under their noses."

Hilde grew silent. She looked over at her mother, and her eyes filled with tears.

"We had a little house, and my husband had his tailor shop in it. We sewed custom men's shirts for the well-to-do families. No mass production. We did everything by hand, with white stitching along the collar. We were hoping to send the girls to school. And now we have nothing. We haven't been back since Beneš returned and made his speech. For twenty days, we stayed with friends. Each of us had just the one small suitcase we were allowed to bring. That was before they drove us out. But my husband was in the party, so who knows where he is now. I've heard people talking about labor camps somewhere right near Brno."

She was shaking her head, dabbing the corners of her eyes with a handkerchief, as if trying to avoid smudging eye makeup. Barbora began to stir.

Trudi Lang smiled and said to Gerta, "I saw what they did to some babies along the way. And how they treated their mothers. One woman with her baby in her arms, they knocked her into a ditch. They wouldn't stop kicking her until she stopped screaming. I didn't see what happened next. Poor thing."

Gerta leaned back against the wooden wall. She cradled Barbora in her arms, rocking her gently, resting her little head against her chest. She tilted her own head back, closed her eyes, and hoped for at least a few moments of sleep.

VII

The road was unmaintained and full of potholes. At any given moment, the wheels of the horse-drawn cart would hit one, and its occupants would be catapulted up and dropped back down onto the hard bench. Each of the women did all she could to keep one hand either on her baby carriage, the child on her lap, or the suitcase at her feet, and the other gripping the side planks of the wagon. They were proceeding slowly behind an equally laden horse-drawn wagon, and behind them, in turn, came a line of women with older children, as well as a few men on foot. They were walking more quickly than they had walked on the march. They were spurred on by hope, opportunity, and, above all, the desire to get away from that rank field with its ramshackle wooden buildings where they had spent the previous two horrendous nights. The flow of those forced to leave Brno had let up by early evening of the day on which Gerta arrived. Most of the Czech guards had gone back to Brno. Those who remained were mainly older supervisors, a few volunteers from Pohořelice, and some Russian and Romanian soldiers, who night after night would pull women out from among them, just as they had previously done at the farm. But this time, Gerta was spared. The camp was teeming with several thousand exhausted deportees, lying or standing around on the grounds of the former brickyard, and it was rumored that there were two more similar compounds just past Pohořelice. The first two mornings, dead bodies were carried out of the buildings by the dozens. Gerta, when she finally dared to move away from the corner of the wooden hall where she and Helga had taken refuge, saw them with her own eyes. She had waited until the morning, when word went around that the Romanian soldiers were doling out soup rations, before daring to venture outside the wooden hall. She had then dashed out twice, forcing her way through the crowd, both times with Barbora clasped tightly to her chest and the cup from the woman in Pohořelice clutched in her hand. Since the previous day, when she had drunk the water from the aluminum pail, she hadn't put anything in her mouth. Although it took an almost superhuman effort to quell her thirst, the murky water that some of the others were pulling up from the well by bucketfuls terrified her. For Barbora, she kept repeating to herself, for Barbora's sake, she must resist.

Not everyone, however, was able to suppress their thirst, in spite of two old German doctors among them who were giving strict orders not to drink the water because it was contaminated. People drank the water anyway and brought it back to their relatives who were lying all over the brickyard, burning up with fever. The plaintive sound of the word *water* echoed from every corner of the camp; there wasn't a single person who didn't utter the word like an incantation. Gerta could hear that word and the names of missing family members all the way in the corner of the building where she sat, not moving, trying to sleep. The most essential thing was to avoid any unnecessary exertion. Beside her sat Helga, completely immobile. She neither got up to get soup, nor did she get up to go outside to empty her bladder; the small amount that seeped out of her was soaked up by her skirt. Gerta left her a bit of soup in the bottom of her cup, which Helga gulped down ravenously, but then turned her face once more to the wall. The only change Gerta noticed was that after the first night, she no longer could see the dead baby's body. Helga had swaddled him in her own tattered blouse. Now the small bundle was again resting in Helga's lap, the sleeves of her blouse knotted tightly under the infant's chin. Helga had on just her buttoned jacket. She must have rearranged her clothes during the night, while Gerta slept. That she had dozed off at all was a miracle, given the screams of the women whom the drunken soldiers were dragging out yet again from the wooden buildings. How many could there have been? And how many had come back? Trudi Lang wasn't there the next morning, and up until the moment of Gerta's departure when she was loaded onto the wagon, Trudi had not yet returned. Hilde Wessely had spent the whole first night lying on top of her older daughter, having hidden her younger one in the long skirts of her mother, who died later that same night. Gerta then held Hilde in her arms all morning until someone carried her mother's body out to the fence. All three of them looked terrible. Hilde was overwhelmed by grief; her daughters, their features haggard and unchildlike, were begging for water. Their mother, however, refused to give in. The one cup of soup from that morning had to suffice.

The wagon lurched again as a wheel hit another pothole. "Whoa," the farmer up on the box seat yelled to the horses, and the wagon swung back up. The fields around them rippled in the gentle breeze. Gerta stared into the fresh green until her eyes stung. It all looked so idyllic and peaceful, as if the war and all the horrific events that followed never happened.

She tried not to think about what lay ahead. She tried not to allow herself to hold out any hope, tried at the same time not to imagine what might happen if they had been lied to. Maybe they just needed to break them up into smaller groups to make it easier to exterminate them. But then why would they be transporting them in wagons? And why would they have so carefully picked out the more able-bodied ones? If they had just been planning to kill them, would it have mattered? Once more she forced away her dark thoughts. She had made a conscious decision to believe as soon as she heard the voice of one of the Pohořelice volunteers calling out the names of the local villages: Perná, Dolní Dunajovice, Horní Věstonice, Bavory. All of them needed laborers to do agricultural work. Women were preferable to men. The important thing was that they still had their strength. Gerta had leaped to her feet at once, had put Barbora back in her carriage, had left behind the coat, and finally also Helga, who had refused even to look at her. Gerta had shaken her by the shoulders, but when she reacted by striking out, without even opening her eyes, she hadn't tried to persuade her. The guard had already left the building, trailed by several women with their children as well as by a few men. Anyone with their wits still about them who understood Czech must have realized that here was a chance to get away from this contaminated wooden box, where sooner or later they would all die like dogs. More and more people were scrambling to their feet. Women were gathering up the scattered contents of their suitcases, calling for their children, and the first group of contenders was already heading out. Gerta pushed her carriage along the edge of the wall. She never said goodbye to Hilde. Neither Hilde nor her two daughters were anywhere to be seen.

Gerta was among the first to reach the camp entrance. Standing around on the dirt road were several men dressed in country clothes, talking among themselves, with riding whips tucked in the belts of their trousers. Some were smoking and intently examining the crowd assembling before them. Behind them stood teams of horses, and milling about were children, probably from Pohořelice. Although the makeshift Pohořelice camp was situated a good stretch beyond the last of the houses, several women wearing headscarves were also standing by the side of the dirt lane, looking as if they had just dropped by for a friendly chat. They stood there, folded arms tucked under their bosoms, gossiping, laughing, occasionally giving a shout to the children who were playing around the horses. Gerta raised her hand and, like all the others who were swarming around the entrance being blocked by the Russian soldiers, tried to call attention to herself.

"I know how to work!" called out one of the women beside Gerta.

A slew of subsequent offers followed. The main thing was to get out of here.

"I speak Czech!" shouted Gerta.

"I know shorthand; I studied at the commercial academy!"

"I'm Czech; I shouldn't even be here; pick me!"

"I used to work in a textile mill!"

"Pick me!"

The first few farmers approached the soldiers. They haggled for a while, gesticulating, and then an official, holding a leather briefcase on which he had spread out some papers, said something. The farmers nodded. The official then distributed some documents among them and motioned to a soldier, who turned to face the crowd that had gathered by the gate and started picking out people from the front row.

"State your name," the official shouted at the first few who stepped forward.

"Maria Niessner."

"Noted."

A farmer pointed to one of the other robust women in the front row. The soldier pulled her out and steered her toward the official.

"Name."

"Charlotte Tomschik aus Gerspitz."

He wrote down the name on two separate documents and nodded. "Next!"

Many more women passed through the main gate, some with their children, and there were also two old men, one with his wife. The official, supervised by the Russian soldier, handed a sheaf of papers to the helper from Pohořelice and turned the group of Germans over to the farmer, who with the handle of his whip pointed to the first horse-drawn wagon. Then the next farmer stepped up to the Russian soldier.

It was thanks to him that Gerta, with Barbora clutched to her breast and her baby carriage collapsed in front of her, was now sitting in a horse-drawn cart, being jolted into the air each time one of the wagon wheels hit a pothole in the road. Beside her sat two young girls and two women, and opposite her, another young woman also with a baby carriage. Following them came the rest of their negotiated group, escorted by three volunteers from Pohořelice, and behind them another large group was already coming into view. They were heading south along the main road in the direction of the Austrian border, passing Mušov, where once, before the war, she had been on a day trip with her parents and Friedrich. And now, here she was on a glorious Saturday afternoon in June, and the sight of such serenity made Gerta want to cry.

VIII

Old Mrs. Zipfelová, as she now called herself, having added the Czech "ová" suffix, was a kindhearted and decent woman. She, too, had been through a lot, since they had taken away her only son to who knew where, leaving her alone with her daughter-in-law, Ida, to fend for themselves in her little cottage. While it was true that these were uncertain times, she was a Czechoslovak citizen who belonged to the Austrian minority, but having committed no crimes, had nothing to fear. On the contrary. Her son was a doctor who, before being called to the front, had done much to contribute to the advancement of the village and had saved the lives of a good many Czech and Austrian children, which all the parents still remembered very well. Zipfelová, on the other hand, since her husband had died, had never done anything more than to stay at home and tend to her cottage. It was a miracle that she'd managed to support her son in his studies. She never harmed a living soul, gave the village the gift of a doctor, and spoke Czech as readily as German, as had always been the custom in Bergen, these days Perná, since the old Austro-Hungarian days of *K.K.—Kaiserlich und Königlich*. She announced this right from her doorstep, as the anxious young women with babes in their arms were still jumping down from the cart and lining up with their backs against the wooden planks of the wagon, listening uneasily to her German speech. Everything she said was then repeated to them once more by Hubert Šenk, the man who had driven them there, and who let them know that they were in the hands of an old-time resident of Perná, who, in spite of her German name—"You mean Austrian," she corrected him—was a well-respected citizen. He furthermore told them that they should go inside, get some sleep, have some food, and be ready to start work the next day.

Ida stared at the women as if they were apparitions. In truth, the sight of them was anything but pleasant to Zipfelová. Ten women, a few with smelly, crying children; ten disheveled, haggard, exhausted, and starving women. One girl, barely grown up, had a swollen cheek, a split lip, and a missing tooth, as became apparent the first time she opened her mouth to speak. They had nothing. Most of them had arrived with only their children and the scant clothing they had on, nothing more. Two of them had baby carriages, their sole possessions. Ida was staring at them, and had Zipfelová not given her a nudge to move her along, she would have gone on gaping at them in dismay. That was just the way she was. Listless, sluggish as a phonograph that hadn't been fully wound up, that was little Iduška Měníková from the last house in the field by the road to the village of Bavory. Hard to say what Helmut had seen in her—probably her youth. Once he got back from his studies and had hung out his shingle as a doctor, he could have had his pick. Over the next ten years, while he was hard at work, they were all making eyes at him: Jitka from the Šenk household, Maria-Rosa, the daughter of Dr. Renner from Dolní Dunajovice, and finally even the widow of

Josef Theron, who had fallen off his horse and broken his neck. Nothing doing. He had waited for this tadpole to grow up. Granted, she was pretty; one had to allow that much. It was just too bad that they hadn't had any children. Helmut had been conscripted right after the wedding.

"You'd best have them all bathe, Mrs. Zipfelová, and wash their clothes, or better yet, burn them, and give them something fresh, something of yours or something the Heinzes left behind. You should have seen that camp. It was awful, one big pesthouse, raging with typhoid fever and dysentery. You don't want that coming into your house. Bathe and wash. And tomorrow morning have them ready for me at six o'clock. I need to head back and help deliver the rest. So long, Ida; see you later."

Hubert Šenk was a good man. He looked after the village and his farm, just as his old granddad once had done. It was said that good genes always skipped a generation. His father had more or less worked the farm as if it were simply a job, not a life. In the end, he drank himself to death, which was just as well as he had actually done Hubert a favor.

"All right, go ahead and take your clothes off," said Zipfelová, turning to them once Hubert and his horse-drawn wagon had gone.

Some of the women sat down on the ground; others kept on standing with their children in their arms, looking around. One finally asked for water, and the others immediately joined in.

"Get them some water, Ida. We're not going to have anyone dying of thirst around here," said Zipfelová. "Ida will get you some water, and in the meantime, all of you get undressed. It's a nice day; you won't get cold before your clothes have a chance to dry, and if need be, Ida will let you borrow something of ours."

One by one, the women started to undress. Gerta sat down cross-legged and unlaced her sturdy hiking shoes. The soles of her feet were on fire, and her ankles were swollen. She hadn't taken off her shoes in almost five days, not from the moment that their convoy had set out from Brno. She had been afraid of losing them, because on this kind of journey, good shoes were priceless. Ida emerged from the doorway of the house, carrying a pitcher. She advanced a few more steps into the courtyard, set the pitcher down under the water pump, and started pumping. As soon as the women heard the sound of water, they abandoned their efforts at undressing and removing their shoes, leaped to their feet, and ran over to her. Those who got there first fell to their knees and held out their hands, trying to catch the liquid. They didn't even wait for their cupped hands to fill up before they greedily gulped, then held their hands out again to catch more drops. Some even pushed the heads of their children directly under the flow. Ida wasn't prepared for this. Startled, she jumped back, and with no one pumping, the flow of water slowly tapered off. The girl with the split lip, whom Gerta remembered from the camp, straightened up and took over pumping in Ida's place.

"Wait, I'll get cups," Ida said, and turned back to run inside the house, coming out again moments later with several mugs.

"Here you are, go on, take," she said, passing them out to the women, who, reaching for them eagerly, filled them and drank.

After a while, the episode was over. Each of the women, their faces glistening, still fearing a shortage, took away cups filled with water. Gerta brought hers straight back to Barbora. She dipped in the tips of her finally clean fingers and held them to Barbora's lips. Barbora at once began to suck on them so greedily and desperately that Gerta's eyes again filled with tears. Supporting her little head, she dribbled a bit of water right into Barbora's tiny mouth. At long last, their thirst was sated.

Ida then brought out petticoats and blouses so that they would have something to change into while they washed their clothes and waited for them to dry. She then offered them her own bedroom and a small room at the top of the stairs. Scrubbed and fed, each of them looked for a place to lie down and go to sleep. Gerta lay down at the edge of a bed near the baby carriage in which nestled Barbora, bathed and freshly swaddled. She herself felt clean and, having eaten two slices of bread and plenty of soup, so full that her stomach hurt. Lying back-to-back with her to keep herself warm was the girl with the knocked-out front tooth.

"Teresa Bayer," she introduced herself in German. "My mother, Erna, about whom I was asking back at the camp, well, I found her, out by the fence. A sight I wouldn't wish on anyone," she said before they both fell asleep.

IX

Starting on the second day following their arrival in Perná, the new residents of Zipfelová's house got up with her just before five o'clock every morning. One of them tended the geese and the chickens, as well as a pig that the two Zipfelová women had kept all through the war, until the night at the end of August when a few Russian soldiers, drunk from the *Dožínky* harvest festival, shot it and cut the animal up right in its sty. Luckily, they hadn't broken into the house that time, as the women, who by then had finally recovered some sense of dignity, would have been hard-pressed to get away. All ten women were employed on Hubert Šenk's farm, where they had to show up for work every day at six o'clock in the morning. Hubert Šenk lived alone with his aging mother, having grown up without his father, his older brother having enlisted and then fallen somewhere on the front lines, and his sister having married and moved to the village of Bavory. The Šenks owned the fields that lay in the direction of Bavory, two large vineyards, and a farmstead with pigs as well as a herd of cows that grazed in a meadow adjacent to the farm buildings. A few days later, the women also began to work on a German farm that had been allocated to Šenk by the National Committee in Břeclav. It had previously belonged to the Knitz family, and they had been among the first to flee. This meant that the ten women were working in all the fields as well as on both farms, on top of which they were rushing back and forth to milk a herd of cows that had wandered into the vineyards out of nowhere. These animals hadn't been milked in so long that their udders had become engorged and they were bellowing with pain. They yielded so much milk that it was barely possible to collect it all. There was enough to supply the whole village of Perná, and Hubert Šenk even had some delivered to the camp in Pohořelice, where people were still hungry and dysentery continued to rage. Although Perná had been a village where, for decades, Austrians, Germans, and Czechs had lived peacefully side by side, these days, as Gerta made the rounds distributing at first pails of milk and cream, and then later sour milk, the reaction she got from the remaining Germans was a curt rebuff and a refusal, either out of disdain or fear, to accept the Czech milk. If only they knew what it meant to be hungry, thought Gerta to herself, but looking around at the cottages with their rambling gardens, she imagined that on such properties it was probably always possible to find enough to eat.

During the month of June, several of the remaining German families disappeared overnight. Some had lived here for generations and had deep roots in Perná through land they owned and through longtime neighborly ties. Others were Germans who had ended up here because of the war. Supposedly, it had started right after the Russian soldiers arrived. Thereafter, night after night, someone would be fleeing across the Austrian border, going ahead to get things ready for the rest of the family, preparing a place for them to resettle. Over the course of June, they would make regular trips back and forth by night, so that by morning they had managed to cart off bundles of their belongings in duffel bags while their mothers or wives pretended for a few more days that there was nothing unusual going on. After the initial euphoria, however, the Russian soldiers came back under the steely hand of their command and spent fewer nights drinking in the wine cellars around Perná, and were instead posted on regular sentry patrol. By the time Gerta had been working on the farm for two weeks, nightly shoot-outs in the area were routine for the sentries. Gerta never found out how many locals the Russians caught or how many they shot. She had no access to any information. At most, she would overhear something from Zipfelová, who, forgetting that some of the German girls spoke and understood Czech, would tell Ida the latest news. For example, that on the village square in Dolní Dunajovice, they had lynched Kurt Knitz, who was on his way home from the war, oblivious that his family had long since fled.

Overhearing this, Gerta thought of Friedrich. What could have happened to him? Had he been captured and killed on the eastern front? Had he found himself at the end of the war on the western front? Or had he ended up somewhere in Germany? She had no idea. Her father had tried to find out and had sent letters, to him as well as to the authorities. Since November there had been no reply, not from Friedrich and not from the authorities. Gerta found herself thinking about her father. Had he fallen victim to the bombing of Brno, or was he now in some forced labor camp, like all of the other German men still fit for work who had remained in the city? She had heard the rumors again and again, first on Mendel Square when they had rounded them all up, and later during the march from Brno to Pohořelice. Countless women would speak about how their brother, husband, or father had been taken away to a camp in Klajdovka, Kounic College, or Maloměřice. When her father hadn't come home after the night of liberation, it had occurred to her that he might have ended up in one of those places. And that at least he would have to atone for the wartime misdeeds he had committed in Brno by working off his guilt, which Gerta felt served him right. The days had gone so fast, especially once Jaroslav Stránský, the minister of justice, and President Edvard Beneš had returned from exile, that between having to report daily to her rubble-clearing work—which involved finding a place to leave Barbora and then searching for her again to pick her up afterward—and the endless scrounging around for food, there had been no time to look for him. Besides, why would she have gone looking, when she was relieved not to have him around? And furthermore, the main priority was to take care of Barbora and herself.

By now it seemed obvious what would happen to them—they would either be expelled, or they would be killed. That was the word going around Perná, and although no one had attacked her personally, she could read in the faces of the locals that, as far as they were concerned, she was here for one purpose only, and that was to do work, and that eventually her case would need to be dealt with as well.

One day on the way to the vineyard, with the perpetual question of what would become of them running again through her head, she suddenly heard a man's voice coming from the field. He was calling for help so softly that it was almost inaudible. Overhead, swallows were frenziedly flying about, circling above the road along which she was walking with Johanna, one of the other German women who now resided at Mrs. Zipfelová's. Gerta had first looked up at them and then at the sky, to see whether their swooping flight might be a harbinger of rain. She thought she must have imagined the voice. Or that it was her own inner voice calling out for help in German. But then she heard it again, and then again for a third time. She grabbed Johanna by the elbow, stopped short, and then they both heard it with unmistakable clarity—someone was calling for help.

It sounded quiet and desperate. Holding each other by the hand, they retraced their steps back down the road along which they had come. Again they heard it: *"Hilfe."* They stepped off the road into the ditch beyond which the field began, where the uniform border of the grain strip had been disturbed by a few broken stalks, flattened to the ground. Deeper into the field, the stalks straightened up again, but there were still obvious signs of someone having carelessly walked through them.

"Is anyone there?" Gerta called out in both German and Czech.

"Hilfe," answered the voice from not too far ahead of them.

"Let's not go there; it can only mean trouble," said Johanna, grabbing Gerta by the elbow and holding her back. "What will you do if it's a German?"

"I don't know." Gerta shrugged her shoulders. She was scared.

"It could be a trap. By the farmers, to see if they can trust us. Or it could be a returnee, you know, someone who has come back for his things or to get revenge. Neither would be good for us."

Gerta knew this. What if it was some fascist Nazi? What would they do with him?

"Hilfe, I'm wounded!"

Gerta turned to look back at Johanna, whose apprehension was written all over her face. With pursed lips, she was shaking her head no and backing away.

"Wait, we can't just walk away."

"What if he's lying there ready to shoot us?"

"I won't shoot; please help me; I'm bleeding. I need a doctor."

"We can't just leave."

Johanna shut her eyes and shook her head.

"You're crazy, and you're taking chances. We have children."

"If you want to leave, then go," replied Gerta.

Johanna was silent for a moment and then said, "You go first. I'll help you."

Gerta forged on, pushing aside the stalks of grain. She came upon a flattened hollow in which, right in front of her, lay a man. He was on his back with one hand holding the left side of his lower abdomen. His shirt was soaked with blood.

"Help me," he whispered when he saw them standing over him.

A short distance away, they saw a weapon, a hat, and a duffel bag. He didn't seem to be a soldier. He could have been a bit over fifty, his body slight and withered.

"How can we help you? There's no doctor in Perná. But Hubert Šenk could bring you to one. We work for him."

The man grimaced and vehemently shook his head.

"Not Šenk."

Gerta looked helplessly at Johanna.

"So how can we help you?"

"Get me the doctor from Dunajovice."

"We can't go to Dunajovice; we're not allowed. We're here to work." He groaned.

"If someone doesn't help you, you'll die here."

"I need Dr. Renner from Dunajovice."

Gerta shook her head. That was more of a risk than she could afford to take for him. She noticed that Johanna heaved a sigh of relief at her firm refusal.

"We can't go there; it's too much of a risk. We're being watched, and our children are with Mrs. Zipfelová."

"Then at least give me some water."

Gerta pulled a bottle out of the knapsack in which they carried their tools, as well as food and water for the whole day. She uncorked it and was about to raise the man's head and give him a drink. The man, however, propped himself up on the elbow of the arm with the hand that was clutching his side, and with his other hand made a grab for the bottle. Gerta was surprised to see he had that much strength left. He snatched the bottle and drank from it in great gulps. Then he sank back to the ground.

"Now leave."

"We can't. We have to find a way to help you. Without help, you're going to die here."

"So go to Dunajovice."

"Impossible. I'm going back to get Mrs. Zipfelová. She might have a better idea of what to do."

"Don't you dare," the man groaned in alarm. "Don't go anywhere."

"I have to. We're not about to just leave you here to die."

The man made a sudden lunge in the direction of the firearm. Gerta and Johanna both screamed and ran for the road. They raced back to the village.

"You left your knapsack and bottle there," Johanna shouted after her.

Gerta kept on running. They didn't stop until they reached the first few cottages of the village.

"Now what?" She turned, out of breath, to Johanna.

"You left your knapsack and bottle there," Johanna repeated.

"I know. So what now?"

"If someone finds your things there, they'll think we helped him. Šenk is going to ask you what happened to your knapsack."

Gerta hid her face in the palms of her hands, then let them slide down her forehead to her chin. She stood there frozen, her hands covering her mouth and her eyes fixed on Johanna.

"If we tell anyone, they'll probably kill him. Or he wouldn't be so scared."

"Maybe he was exaggerating."

"I don't think so, not these days. They shoot people all the time."

"You have to tell someone."

Gerta shrugged her shoulders.

"You have to tell someone, or if you won't, I will. Everyone knows we were together, and I'm not about to put my children in danger. I'm going to look for Mrs. Zipfelová."

Johanna took off down the street, ran across the square, and kept running until she got to old Zipfelová's house. Only there did Gerta finally catch up to her. Ida was sweeping the courtyard.

"Not her . . . Wait for Zipfelka. You'd best tell her first. She's more understanding."

Johanna shrugged her shoulders.

"We have to tell someone before they find that knapsack. Ida?"

Ida looked up and blinked in alarm.

"How come you're not at Hubert's? Did he send you?"

Gerta shook her head.

"Something happened. Could we speak with Mrs. Zipfelová?" blurted out Johanna.

"What happened?" asked Ida, scrutinizing them both with suspicion, surprised.

"Something unpleasant, Ida. Someone's in very bad shape."

"Who? Hubert? Old Mrs. Šenková?"

"No, not them. Someone out in a field. He needs help."

"Who? Come on, out with it. What's going on?"

"We found someone lying in a field," answered Johanna, her relief as she said it palpable. "He's lying out there in a field, shot in the stomach. He's bleeding. He called out to us, and we went off the road and found him. Gerta left her knapsack and water bottle there."

"Who is it? What does he look like?"

Gerta kept silent. Not even Johanna said a word.

"Is he German?"

Both nodded.

"Is he from around here?"

"He asked for Dr. Renner from Dunajovice."

"Renner? That's strange."

"He didn't want us to give him away. He was afraid of Šenk and even of Mrs. Zipfelová."

"Of my mother-in-law? That can't be. Who would be afraid of her?"

"A German from this area?"

Ida finally moved toward them. She lifted her broom off the ground, walked right up to them, and, taking Johanna by the hand, motioned for them to step inside. In the kitchen, the children were sitting around the table while old Zipfelová busied herself by the stove.

"Mama!" Johanna's children called out, and rushed over to the women in the doorway. Gerta made for the baby carriage by the window in which lay Barbora.

"Ida, what's going on here?"

"They found a wounded man in a field, Mother. What should we do? It's a German."

Zipfelová leaned back against the wall.

"That's all we needed. Helmut was the only doctor in this village."

"They say he asked for Dr. Renner and didn't want anybody else to know, not you, not even Šenk. Who could it be?"

"My God! What did he look like?" Zipfelová addressed the two young women.

"He looked like he could be about fifty, slight. Skinny. German."

"Who could it be?" muttered Zipfelová under her breath. "Last week in Dunajovice they lynched Kurt Knitz. Germans are being lynched. This is all we needed."

"We have to call Dr. Renner. That's who he wanted to treat him."

"Wonderful. Word will get out, and next thing you know, they'll be saying we're helping the fascists escape. That's far too risky for me, not to mention for you. How badly off was he?"

"He was shot through the stomach, somewhere here." Gerta pointed to her side.

"Hmm. Through his intestines. That's not good."

"His shirt was soaked with blood. He must've been there since last night."

"In that case, by now he would already have bled to death."

"He could still move. He wanted water."

"Hmm." Zipfelová shook her head and paced back and forth to the window.

126

"Maybe we should just let him be and leave him to his fate. Just as if you'd never found him. Because if we go get Dr. Renner now, Renner will either save him, in which case we'd have helped someone we weren't supposed to help, or he'll be beyond all help, and we'd only have drawn attention to ourselves for no reason, and that's the last thing you all need. Or you can just tell everything to Hubert Šenk, because in the end, he's the one responsible for you."

"We have to tell someone. Gerta left Šenk's knapsack there."

"Jesus Christ, silly girl. Well, now there's no point in trying to hide it."

Zipfelová paced around the kitchen, rapped her knuckles on the table, rapped them on the windowsill, then came back and rapped them on the table again.

"How on earth could you have left it there?"

"He reached for his weapon."

"Good God, an armed German lying in a field. We have to report this to Šenk and to the administrative commissioner—that would be Schmidt. He's just been appointed in Břeclav," said Zipfelová nervously.

Gerta glanced tentatively over at Johanna. It wasn't sounding good; that much she could sense. But at least Ida and Zipfelová could vouch for them that they hadn't helped anyone. Now that she was cradling Barbora in her arms, she felt she would give anything in the world for the certainty of knowing that no one would ever harm the two of them again.

"Would you come with me to find Šenk?" she whispered.

"We're going right now, before it's too late. Ida, keep an eye on these children. I'm going with them to look for Šenk."

X

A single shot was all it took. Gerta fell as if she had been cut down; her knees buckled. The sky closed in over her, the swallows disappeared into blackness and silence. Nothing. Then she heard Johanna screaming beside her. She was sobbing and shouting something into her ear, lying right next to her. Excruciating grief penetrated to the marrow of Gerta's bones; it was tangible. It set the tips of her fingers tingling. She began to feel them again and started tapping them against the dusty earth beneath her, then swept her arms up and buried her head in them. She didn't want to hear Johanna's cries. The cries were too much on top of the burden of a guilty conscience, which would now weigh them both down for all eternity. Forevermore she would live with the knowledge that they were responsible for the death of a person who had asked them for help. Forevermore she would envision her hand with its extended finger pointing to the place in the grain field. The Russian soldiers picking their way carefully through the green waves of grain, closing in from two sides on the spot where he lay. Standing on the road, Commissioner Schmidt and Šenk, wearing his wide-brimmed country hat. The shot rang out before they even bothered to take a good look at him. And obviously he must have still been alive, or they wouldn't have shot him. A heated discussion in rapid, convoluted Russian then followed.

"Šenk, they want you to go have a look" was the first intelligible sentence Gerta made out.

The sound of heavy boots on the hard, dusty road, the crunch of pebbles. The swish of shoes moving through the lush, green stalks of grain, waving left, waving right, parting and coming back together behind a person's back, swaying in unison. Like sea waves, but with a different sound.

Gerta still kept her eyes closed. Beside her, Johanna had calmed down a bit; by now she was only sobbing into Gerta's already drenched sleeve. Meanwhile, from the field came the sound of Russian and Czech voices, a medley of shouting and arguing.

"It's definitely not one of the Knitzes; I knew them all. But it could be someone from Dunajovice, seeing as he was asking for Renner. If only those idiots hadn't blasted his face off. How am I supposed to recognize him like this?"

"Hubert, there was no time to aim; you saw for yourself."

"But this is a gruesome massacre. Who's supposed to look at it?"

"Listen up, pal. The gruesome massacre happened on the front lines. You don't know what you're talking about. Here you had a Werewolf lying in your field, and you're complaining about the intervention. If you've got any sense at all, for God's sake, shut up."

"Who's going to clean this up? Just look at him."

"You got ten women off the transport, so don't go grumbling that you're shorthanded. Let the ones who found him deal with it."

"Yeah, right, those two," said Šenk, and he must have turned to look their way because the wind carried his voice over more distinctly. "First, someone has to revive them. He does have to be removed, though, we can't bury him here; we'll be plowing soon."

"Jesus Christ, so take him to the cemetery."

"The cemetery in Perná? Are you crazy? The locals will have you lynched! You know it damn well yourself. And besides, you haven't even identified who he is yet, so you'd better do that first, or have one of your commandos do it. He might just turn out to be someone from Dunajovice. He was after something around here. Maybe you'll find the answer in his duffel."

"Open the bag!" Schmidt ordered the Russian soldiers.

A moment of silence.

"And throw that hat over his face. Jesus, who's supposed to look at that?"

"There's an SA uniform in his duffel, Commissioner."

"There you go; he probably held up some poor devil and stole his civilian clothes. I bet nobody offered them to him for free. Wonder where he was headed, seeing as he felt the need to keep his uniform."

"Jesus, I bet he's local anyway. Why else would he have been afraid of me?"

"What do I know? Maybe the women didn't understand him correctly. Let's bring him in for an autopsy, or better yet, take him straight to Pohořelice. Have you heard what they've been digging up over there? Seems they were burying three hundred people a day. Dysentery and typhoid fever. And old age. People who didn't survive the trek. We'll just toss this one on the pile."

Hubert Šenk said nothing. Gerta hoped that at the very least he shook his head. Her own head wouldn't stop spinning.

XI

One week later, Gerta was marched into the village pub that had been converted into the temporary local administrative headquarters and was presented to Commissioner Josef Schmidt. He had requisitioned her from working in the fields to working in the office as administrative support to help record and catalog confiscated properties seized by the National Land Trust. Šenk remembered from that very first day that she had gone to a commercial academy and that her Czech was as good as her German. He couldn't refuse Schmidt's request, especially after Schmidt had assigned two night watchmen to his fields, realizing they had become a border-crossing corridor for men sneaking back to see their families—Nazi Werewolves, and who knew what other devils. They hadn't been able to identify that shot German, so there was no way of knowing what had brought him to these parts. In any case, it was better to stay on Josef Schmidt's good side; that much Šenk knew from his boyhood days, when they used to tussle behind the schoolhouse. So he sent him the Schnirch girl, who seemed reliable and above all smart. Hopefully someone like her wouldn't annoy Schmidt and wouldn't end up being blown to bits by his Russian goons.

Gerta waited outside the door until two men, who up to then had been inside talking to Schmidt in loud voices, came out. They walked right past her, having shut the door behind them, and a few moments later she knocked and went inside. In the former main dining room of the Perná pub, there were four wooden tables pushed together with the commissioner's paperwork spread out across them. On the tables behind him were reams of documents, boxes of papers, and office supplies. There was also a firearm.

"I'm assuming there's no need for me to explain in what state of affairs things were left here by the former German mayor, am I right? His office was the little house that burned down just off the square. I'm starting from scratch."

Gerta glanced up at the high ceiling of the pub, decorated with a border of wine-themed motifs typical of the region.

"Hell knows how long I'll be here or who'll come after me, but it makes no difference. We have to start somewhere and end up with some kind of a list. And we've got to start right away. We're already behind. By now we'll have a hell of a time figuring out who took off with what. Here, come sit in this chair."

Gerta approached the table and sat down opposite Commissioner Schmidt.

"Can you understand everything I'm saying? They told me you speak Czech."

"I speak Czech and German. My mother was Czech; my father was a Brno German. I went to Czech elementary school and German secondary school."

"What a shitty case. One hell of a way to be born. The worst part about it is that it wouldn't have been a problem if it weren't for the times we're living in. Excuse my language. It's just that I feel for your situation. You're still young. Bet there aren't that many skeletons in your closet yet, right?"

Gerta shrugged. It would depend on how one viewed her involvement in the *Winterhilfswerk*. And being young meant nothing. She knew girls her own age who deserved to find themselves in her current situation, if only for the zeal with which they had cheered on the *Wehrmacht* officers during the military exhibition parades. She thought of the exquisite Anne-Marie, waving from her car, seated between her father and the fair-haired SS captain, in a motorcade of gleaming black automobiles with swastikas on their sides, driving through Adolf-Hitler-Platz.

"I'm German, too, but my family has lived in Perná for generations, and no one around here would dare to challenge me."

Gerta looked him over. Had he been in the war? Had he already returned? If he had been conscripted, how come he was already home? Questions raced through Gerta's mind. What could there be in his past, when here he was at thirty-five, sitting behind a desk, tall, mustached, looking a little like the German actor Willy Birgel, a ladies' man.

"Well, the main thing is you know how to type, and you're good at shorthand and all this administrative stuff. Have a look at these papers. Some I found around town; the rest I got from the parish office. See if you can figure out a way to put them in some kind of order. Then you can show me what you've done. What you need to concentrate on first are the Perná resident records, understand? Especially the Germans who are still here and any new arrivals. And put aside any papers that don't state a date of death, which you should be able to find in the parish documents. Everyone here is baptized. Where there's no date of death, those papers need to be put into some kind of pile. Those are the people most likely to be missing. And you might as well start a box for the claimants. From what I hear, the first ones have already shown up and are waiting by the church. I'm going to go over there now. Get to work, and I'll see about finding us a different space. Supposedly, the landlord telegraphed his wife from Prague to say he's back from forced labor in Germany and in good shape, and expects to show up here in a few days."

Gerta nodded and surveyed the stacks of papers on the tables.

Meanwhile, the commissioner placed a Russian military cap on his head and with long strides in his gleaming boots, made for the door. At that moment, Gerta could have sworn they were her father's legs, marching around the Rathausplatz in his shiny black boots.

The record keeping was an arduous task. Over the next several days, Gerta made the rounds of the village, counting houses and the number of occupants living inside each one. She wasn't surprised to find that half of them didn't want to let her in. Some Czechs didn't want to let her in because she was a German pig; others, who were Germans, because they had something to hide. Schmidt was annoyed. At first, he thought he would go around with her from door to door, but then he came up with a better solution. He got her a search warrant, assigned her one of the Russian soldiers, and thus by order of the Russian military command in Břeclav, she was authorized to enter every household in Perná. Gerta preferred to avoid doing so; she was afraid she might see something that she would rather not see at all. Instead, on the threshold of every house, she would ask for a head count of how many family members were currently living there, how many had died during the war, and how many had not yet returned. And she would ask for a rough estimate of their property. Commissioner Schmidt was satisfied.

One week later, he moved them into a house formerly occupied by the village trustee Müller and his family, who had arrived in Perná at the outset of the war and had moved into the impounded Rosenbaum property, loudly proclaiming, "Blood and Soil." They had thought of themselves as local lords, living in the largest house on the square, right next to the church, and then in early April they vanished, leaving not even a colander behind. It was an attractive building and would make for a pleasant workspace, provided none of the Rosenbaums returned. Schmidt assigned Gerta a small room accessible directly from the entryway behind the front door, and took the room on the opposite right-hand side to use as his office. The sheds in the courtyard and the remaining rooms then provided ample space for the storage of confiscated property. Schmidt brought in wagonloads daily, assisted by several Russian soldiers who had been allocated to him from Břeclav.

First to be cleaned out was the Heinz household, where no amount of knocking had gotten Gerta inside, as the family had long since fled. Next came whatever the Pfeifers had left behind. For them, Zipfelová didn't have a single nice word. In the rooms of the Rosenbaum manor house, armoires, bedsteads, and dressers began to pile up. The Heinzes had left behind elegant china and dozens of books, a sheepskin rug, and even a mink coat, which Gerta had never seen before. In the barn, sacks of grain, potatoes, and walnuts were piled one on top of another, and the Rosenbaum wine cellar, just outside the village, was lined with casks of wine that had been boarded up so well that not even the Russian soldiers had managed to break into them. The chickens, ducks, and geese kept by the Heinzes, as well as the rabbits that the Pfeifers hadn't taken along, were set loose in a penned-off section of the courtyard. Two of the Heinzes' dogs were tearing around the village. Schmidt had Gerta write it all up and create a file for each family, itemizing everything.

Josef Schmidt was in demand around the clock. Gerta came in shortly after six in the morning, when all of Perná was just beginning to stir, and he was already waiting for her. When she left to the sound of the bells of the Angelus to go home, he would still be at his desk. Every day, homeowners and farmers like Hamza or Charoust went to see him with specific requests. Gerta had to document which objects Schmidt transferred over from the National Trust and to whom. It was hard to say based on what or whose authority.

Hubert Šenk was given an additional large tract of land that ran alongside the one he already owned going toward Bavory. This was because turning it over to him to cultivate made the most sense. The Charousts were given a field going toward Dunajovice that had been part of the Heinz property, and Schmidt's Czech brother-in-law got the rest. Gerta would never have discovered this if it hadn't been for a sloppily inserted piece of paper that she noticed in a folder intended for the Land Registry office in Břeclav.

And then there were the newcomers. Where they came from was anybody's guess. Toward the end of June, two packed-up families with their eiderdowns tossed over a hay wagon pulled up in front of the Rosenbaum manor, currently the local administrative headquarters. Not even Schmidt knew a thing about them. They were asking about vacant houses. Schmidt, looking flustered, walked off, made a phone call, returned, walked off again. Following him went the hay wagon, women in kerchiefs, men in rubber boots and jackets. When he got back late that afternoon, just before the Angelus, he told Gerta to start a new file and log the transfer of the Pfeifer house, including the field, to the Jech family from Hrozenkov. By the end of that week, Gerta had filled out five more such new files.

XII

From the beginning of July, she no longer needed to bring Barbora with her to the administrative headquarters. She was able to leave her at home with Zipfelová and the other children, as did all the women who worked in the fields. Old Zipfelová kept an eye on them as they played, either outside in the garden or inside the house; she fed Barbora gruel and even seemed to enjoy doing so. Helmut and Ida hadn't managed to give her grandchildren, so these children would have to suffice.

Schmidt, as soon as Gerta was no longer tied down to Barbora and the office, wanted her to accompany him everywhere. She went with him to inspect properties and catalog everything right inside the homes, since he had discovered that objects were pilfered by the time the Russian soldiers managed to get around to moving them to the Rosenbaum manor. She accompanied him out to the fields to make sure the newcomers were working the correct tracts of land, waving as she went by Johanna and Ula, hard at work on Šenk's land, feeling at the same time awkward about being better off than they were. She went around keeping notes, fetching items from the office, making phone calls, coming back with news. And suddenly she was amazed to realize that she started to feel like a person again. A person who was needed and whose work was appreciated. Schmidt appreciated her. It didn't take long before she noticed that he sought out her presence even when it wasn't needed.

Toward the end of July, when it was time to start harvesting, it was necessary to make a trip to Mikulov for equipment. In the prewar years, as far back as Zipfelka could remember, the small farmers of Perná would do the cutting and harvesting themselves, hiring some of the villagers to help. Even Zipfelka and Ida would lend a hand each year. Only the families with large farms like the Šenks, the Pfeifers, the Heinzes, the Krumpschmieds, and once in a while the Hrazdíras, would borrow farming equipment from Věstonice after the harvesting there was done. This year, Josef Schmidt decided to borrow harvesting machines from the district administrative commission in Mikulov, where they'd taken most of the confiscated farming equipment that had belonged to various Germans from the surrounding villages. All of Perná would bring in the harvest together. This was because so many families had disappeared that it would have been hard for the villagers and the German women from the Pohořelice camp to harvest all of the formerly German fields on their own.

Schmidt dictated to Gerta requests for tractors, combines, plowshares, and trailers, but the half-written request for additional German workers he had her discard. Instead, he dictated a new one in which he simply requested a harvest brigade, and a second one, in which he invited Czech citizens to come and take over the formerly German Perná farmsteads.

As he dictated, Gerta looked up at him in surprise.

"There's no way to stop it," he said. "Just last week there were six. And last night, more relatives of the Jechs showed up. You'll start a new file for them today and transfer the lower Gottfried house over to them. From now on, this is how it's going to be, and it's only right. New Czechs will replace the old Germans. Guilty or not."

Gerta shook her head and said, "New Czechs, possibly even guilty, will replace the old Germans, possibly not even guilty? And it's only right? And you're not afraid?"

Now it was Schmidt's turn to look up from his papers in surprise and narrow his eyes suspiciously. "What do you mean?"

"You're also German."

Schmidt looked puzzled.

"No one here would dare come after me. We've been landowners for generations, and everyone knows that's all we've ever cared about. I'm the first Schmidt to have gotten mixed up with politics. And it's only because I'm trying to bring some order back to this village."

"I heard the Krumpschmieds were also on the Czech side."

"Bullshit. In that case their three sons wouldn't have enlisted. And all three of them did enlist; not a single one joined the resistance. It all adds up to the same thing, to protest but then quietly go along or doggedly pursue a career. You know shit about how things work in these parts, so stop speculating and do what I tell you. And keep in mind that I was in the resistance."

Gerta dropped her gaze back to the papers she was holding. She should steer clear of such conversations. After all, she was still just a German, whom nobody would miss if she were suddenly to disappear across the border with a transport. In spite of this, she quietly said, "And will that matter to the ones who'll be showing up here, wanting German homesteads?"

Schmidt fell silent. The vein at his temple bulged, and the fine tips of his mustache quivered.

"Don't you ever say such things again! I've got as many Czechs as I have Germans in my family, understand? And we've worked the land here for over a hundred years. Just go to the cemetery and have a look at the Schmidt gravestones! You can see how far back the dates go."

His voice was cold, and Gerta bent even lower over the typewriter. She fixed her eyes on the slightly protruding *g* and *h* keys, her gaze darting between them. For some time now, she had sensed that Schmidt was holding on to his position only with the help of the Russian soldiers who fell directly under his command. Even so, the old-timers as well as the newcomers were treating him with less and less respect.

The Hrazdíras had plowed right over the dividing line between their fields and the Heinz fields without his permission. The Krupas had taken over a neighboring vineyard and informed him only when he came around to check on things at the onset of the harvest. Hubert Šenk had witnessed this and didn't say a word, and Gerta noticed that even he was beginning to look down on Schmidt. The newly arrived Jechs, still that very first week, had moved out of the modest Pfeifer house and commandeered two houses behind the church, one with its German occupants, the Hammer family, whom they relegated to a single room, still in residence. They kept the Pfeifer croplands, however, as well as the contents of the abandoned homestead and considered it all to be their own. When Herr Hammer, the German master of the house, appeared at the administrative headquarters to file a complaint, Jech came barging into the office and beat him up right in front of Schmidt's desk, kicking him even after he was down on the floor. Observing from the doorway, Gerta watched Schmidt trying to restrain Jech up until the moment that Jech turned on him and shouted, "Aren't you German too?" Schmidt froze, leaving Hammer to lie on the floor and Jech to carry on about being entitled to property that had belonged to some mangy Germans, and that he intended to fix it up. When Jech left, Schmidt walked out of the office as well, so as not to have to look his neighbor in the eye. It was Gerta who helped Hammer back to his feet and wiped the blood from his broken nose.

"What a shitty time," Hammer said, but then took no further action and just waited, with all seven members of his family, his young children included, to see if they would be reassigned to a smaller house or put on the next transport across the border.

Gerta observed Schmidt as he delivered his reports to the district administrative commission. She didn't understand Russian but saw how, after these phone calls, more and more often, Schmidt's features would harden. Then he would step out into the courtyard and have a cigarette, summoning Gerta only afterward to do some more work. She sensed his fear, that he was struggling, but that somewhere deep inside, he knew it was useless. More and more people were making him feel it, both those to whom he was assigning new property and, even more so, those to whom he wasn't assigning new property.

On the threshold to the administrative headquarters they heard the stomping of feet, then someone stepping inside and pounding on the open door, calling out Schmidt's name.

"What is it?" answered Schmidt from Gerta's office.

Hubert Šenk strode into the room and said, "They want to take away my German women."

"What do you mean?" asked Schmidt in surprise.

"That Georgian doctor, who's here with the soldiers, he stopped in at Zipfelová's and told her that all of the German workers and German residents would be put on a transport. He said he heard it from Mikulov. They're going to take them to Drasenhofen."

"Are you kidding? Who's going to do the harvesting?"

"Nobody told you anything?"

"No order came down. So far, there's only been talk about armbands and about patrols to keep all Germans under watch. And about property. Nothing about transports."

"As I said, that Georgian doctor just gave Zipfelka the news. He's going around with the ordinance to all the villagers who are housing workers."

Josef Schmidt looked over at Gerta and then back at Šenk.

"Well, that's simply not acceptable. There'd be no one left to do the harvesting. You can't rely on the newcomers; they don't know shit about what to do. And only about one-third of the old-timers are left, so they can't go off with a transport; there wouldn't be anyone left to do the work."

"Exactly."

Schmidt, who had been holding a sheaf of papers, set them down on the table in front of Gerta and motioned for Šenk to follow him into his office. They left the door ajar.

"We've just written up a request for a harvest brigade. One from Brno has already arrived in Dunajovice. Schnirchová will send it now and will follow up by telephone. In a week's time, you can count on having about twenty people. At least, that's what they said in Dunajovice."

"All right, but who knows what we're going to get. Most likely they'll be Czechs with no incentive to work hard." Šenk shook his head.

"Hmm. That's true."

"And what about in Pohořelice, is there anyone left?"

"Just the ones in the ground. They buried half of them and shipped the other half across the border. They say a couple hundred sick ones are still lying around in the field near Drasenhofen. The only other Germans left around here are the villagers and small farmers, but we already know what we can expect from them; sooner or later they're going to disappear. The harvest brigade is still the best option."

"So what are you saying? Fine, let them go ahead and send us whoever they want. I'll train them, though I won't expect them to do good work. But as far as my German women go, the ones who are here now, they're not going on any transport. On that I insist. They don't cause any trouble; they have kids, so they don't dare, and they're happy to get a bit of food. I need them," Šenk added softly.

Schmidt stood up from his desk and walked over to the shelf where he kept written appeals from the district administrative commission. He thumbed through them, then went over to the telephone and dialed a number. He waited a long time for a connection.

He made the call with his back toward Šenk and Gerta, who was straining to hear from her office across the hallway. She did not want to leave Perná. They hadn't deported her across the border a month ago, and wild horses couldn't drag her across now, nor in the future. She would not let herself be expelled from here. She would return to Brno and claim the apartment in which she had grown up and which had belonged to her family. She might find her father or Friedrich. She might even find Janinka, and once all this was over, she might even look for Karel. She was not about to leave. This was her home, hers and Barbora's. Who knew what would be waiting in Austria or Germany, and where was she even supposed to go? Should she plant herself on some street in Poysdorf or in front of St. Stephen's Cathedral in Vienna? Absurd. They would let her stay in Perná as long as she was useful, and that she was useful and worth keeping, by now, they surely already knew. And eventually she would go back home.

"We'll issue them papers saying they're indispensable. For now, they'll stay put, and after the harvest and the vintage, we'll see," she overheard Schmidt saying in the next room.

"You have such papers?"

"We just need to write down their names and their former places of residence, keep one copy here, and send the original to the district office, and they'll stay here, watched over by the farmers to whom they'll be assigned for work, and under the supervision of the local administrative headquarters. When they come in from the fields tonight, bring them right to me."

"Mine are all the women from Zipfelka's. But I'm sure Hrazdíra is going to want to keep his as well; he has about ten. Same goes for Krupa and Hanák. The rest I don't know."

"Gerta will notify them all. No need to worry about that. Bring all your women here this evening, and we'll write it up."

Šenk put on the wide-brimmed hat that up to that moment he'd been holding in his hand. He tipped it and said, "Well then, until tonight."

On his way out, he stopped in the doorway to Gerta's office.

"We'll say you're indispensable as well, what do you think?"

Gerta gratefully nodded her head.

"Thought so," Šenk said before walking out the door.

XIII

When Teresa, wearing only her nightgown tied across her narrow shoulders with a piece of twine, stretched out comfortably across the whole bed, it looked as though there couldn't possibly be any room left for Gerta or Ula, who night after night slept sandwiched on either side of her. Teresa would go through the same ritual every night as Gerta put Barbora to sleep and Ula her Dorla, who at the age of ten had no interest in sleeping, and instead would lie awake straining her ears, trying to catch snippets of the adult conversation. In the meantime, Teresa on the mattress would spread out her arms and legs as far as her nightgown allowed, then abruptly sit up and reach forward, grabbing the tips of her toes. They would hear the loud cracking of vertebrae run up her spine, as if someone were snapping dry twigs. In the small room, the three adults in the shared bed, with one child on the floor and the other in the baby carriage by the window, had become a tight-knit family.

"Don't you want to think it over some more?"

"Not even maybe."

"You're crazy, girl. What are you thinking?" Ula shook her head. "As if you haven't already jumped through enough hoops in your life, silly goose."

"This will be the last one, and it'll be the one that saves me, silly goose."

Gerta and Ula looked at one another. They had no faith in Teresa's notions, but then again, they didn't have much faith in their own either. Heads or tails, who could know how it would all turn out?

"I'm young, I'm pretty, and when I'm rich again, I'll get a new tooth. And rich I will be. In Vienna, where everyone has egg on their face, I won't stand out as that German bitch, whom anyone can use to lean their bicycle on or outright screw. There, I'll be one of thousands who may not have a place to lay their head, but whose past is nobody's business. A new beginning waits for me there, don't you get it? And if not in Vienna, then maybe in America."

"You're courageous, foolish one, but you might end up on the street, where nobody's going to pick you up because, like you said, you'll be one of thousands. Has that ever occurred to you?"

"I'm not afraid to work. And now that the war is over, there's plenty of work to be done. Why wouldn't someone hire me? Over there, no one's going to care whether I'm this or that kind of German, or if I'm an Austrian country girl. And the tooth makes it clear that I've suffered, so why should anyone start poking around, trying to find out if my father was or wasn't a Nazi? I'll become invisible. I'll vanish in the crowd of other Germans. I won't stick out like a black sheep. And I'll start over. I'm all alone anyway, so why stay here, to slave away just for a bit of food, when our future here is as uncertain as it will be over there?"

"Because if you take a look around, although we're slaving away just for a bit of food, it means we're needed here, which means nothing's going to happen to us. And we have everything. Food, a roof over our heads, and people who treat us pretty decently."

"Fine, but for how much longer? Until you're done harvesting. And what's going to happen in the fall, when you'll just be extra mouths to feed because there'll be no more work for you?"

Ula shook her head. "You're really silly. There's always going to be work to do around here. You can see for yourself how many empty houses there are, and fields with no one to work them."

Gerta looked up from Barbora, who was happily gurgling at her breast. "Well, not exactly. People are coming over from Hrozenkov. Supposedly they've been told that they'll be given German properties in exchange for their work on behalf of the Czech state. Today, Schmidt had me send a letter over to the district office offering up German homesteads. He says someone has to take care of them, and it looks like it's going to be people from Hrozenkov or families from around here. But we're still going to be needed; Šenk was clear about that even tonight. He said the newcomers won't know a thing about farming."

"We're always going to be needed. Look at us; we're like workhorses— we work ourselves to the bone just to get some food, and we're grateful to be given a place to sleep, us and our kids. We don't complain. They know exactly what they've got going here. Why would they want to get rid of us?" added Ula.

"Because there might come a time when even the Czechs will want a racially pure nation. Just for revenge," Teresa ventured wryly.

"I don't believe that. The Americans and Russians would never allow it, right?" Ula turned to Gerta, who just shrugged her shoulders.

"I don't know, but then again, those soldiers might not be here forever either. For now, they're keeping an eye on things, but once the Czechs are back on their feet, what's left for them to do here? They'll probably go home, right?"

"Right, and the next thing will be pogroms against any Germans who are left, you'll see," Teresa declared with conviction. "And then it will look like it did this morning, when we were on our way to the fields and they caught that Hammer fellow, who had tried to take his family across the border in the night. By morning, those new Jech folks were still chasing him around the village, and when he ran past us, his eye was dangling down his cheek. I almost puked."

"That was disgusting. Mercifully, the children didn't see it," said Ula.

"I saw it, Mommy," piped up Dorla from the nest of linens and burlap bags under the bed.

"You should be asleep, Dorla, not listening," Ula said anxiously toward the floor.

Dorla mumbled something and turned over.

"I don't understand why they didn't just let them go. They wanted to put them on the next transport anyway, so why couldn't they just let them cross the border in the middle of the night? Those Russians and those Jechs are out for blood; it has nothing to do with the law."

"It has to do with property. They can't let them leave in the middle of the night with valuables. They want them skinned to the bone and put bare-assed on the transport, with only the clothes on their backs. Same as with us a month ago. And then they'll divvy up what's left among themselves."

"They'd just as soon kill all of them for their money."

"And that's exactly why I don't want to stay here anymore. You see for yourselves. And there's no guarantee that it's going to change."

Teresa was determined to leave with the earliest transport that Šenk would allow her to join. On the day when they'd all been at the administrative headquarters, he had asked each of them if they wanted to stay in Czechoslovakia or if they preferred to leave. At first, the women all looked at each other in a quandary, nervous at being given a choice. Then the first to respond were the women who still had family somewhere in the country or a husband in one of the Brno labor camps. Next to speak up were the women with children, who for the time being felt safe in Perná. Only Teresa and one other girl mustered the courage to ask to be deported.

Šenk shrugged his shoulders and said that in that case, only after the harvest, meaning after the grape harvest, which meant at the earliest in the fall. Staring down at the tips of their shoes, they simply nodded and were then the last to dictate the personal information that Šenk asked of them and that Gerta typed up on two sheets of stationery with a piece of carbon paper inserted between them.

"Maria Schrammek aus Brünn, Wiener Straße achtundsiebzig," said Maria, to whom Šenk had pointed first among those who wanted to stay.

Before Gerta even had a chance to touch the keys of the typewriter, Šenk asked, "Can you speak Czech?"

"A little," said Maria, "but not very well."

"No matter, you'll learn. Gerta, on that paper write down *Marie Šrámková.*"

"No, I Maria Schrammek," Maria corrected him in broken Czech.

"Do you know what the name Schrammek is going to mean for your kids if you stay here? Do you realize that you're staying in Czechoslovakia? After a war that was started by the Germans?"

Maria kept on shaking her head.

"These days it's better to have a Czech name, Maria. He's looking out for you." Antonia gave her a nudge with her elbow.

Maria stood silently and hung her head.

"Does she get it or not?" asked Šenk, whose German was minimal.

"Write down *Šrámková*, and *Marie*, the Czech way, not *Maria*. It will spare her a lot of trouble."

Gerta looked from Maria to Šenk, and finally to Schmidt, who was addressing her.

"But what about her husband? He won't have the same last name."

"I don't have husband, dead in war," said Maria.

"So you see, you agree. Now, let's not hold things up. Write down *Šrámková*, and you, Marie, give us the names of your children."

"Just my son. Johann Schrammek, he's eight years old."

"Write down *Jan Šrámek*. Next." Šenk motioned to the woman standing next to her.

"Susanne Bauer."

"Keep *Susanne*; it sounds French. Write down *Susanne Bauerová*. Children?"

"Two girls, Hilde *und* Henriette."

"You see, also French," said Šenk, turning toward Gerta. "Write down *Hilde* and *Henriette Bauerová*. Ages?"

"Eight and six."

"Next," said Schmidt.

Johanna Polivka gave her name and her children's names in German. "Johanna Polivka, two children, Anni and Rudi, both four."

"Don't you speak Czech?"

"I do."

"So speak Czech. I don't want to hear any more German around here, understood?"

"I understand. But I insist on keeping the name Polivka."

"Good God, why? Don't you understand the situation?"

"I do. But my husband's name is Polivka, so my name is Polivka too. I will not change my husband's name."

"Fine, your problem, if you insist. Write down *Polivka*, if that's what she wants."

Gerta typed Johanna's surname without the Czech ending even for Anna and Rudi.

"Next."

Gerta recorded the names of all the others, most of them with Czech endings: *Hermína Herzigová, Ulrika Pipalová, Antonie Ainingerová, Edeltraud Ressová*, along with the names of their children, and then *Teresa Bayer* and *Rosalie Schwarz*, who were eager to get to Austria as soon as possible, and finally *Gertruda Schnirchová*. She didn't care. She wasn't hung up on any family traditions, and who knew where these forms, typed up by her, a German, and supervised by the German Schmidt, would end up. Someday, when someone somewhere asked for her name, by saying *Gerta*, she would give herself away just the same, and whether at that moment she would use Schnirch or Schnirchová, circumstances alone would determine.

"And once again I repeat: Speak in Czech. Understand?" said Šenk. "And get yourselves back to Zipfelová's. By now, she's already waiting."

The group of women turned toward the door. Schmidt let them pass, and once Šenk had gone out, he let another group into the office, the ten women who worked for Hrazdíra.

It was dark by the time Gerta could go home. Schmidt offered to accompany her because of the Russian soldiers, who from time to time would break into one of the wine cellars, on top of which there were the defecting Germans, so it was advisable to take precautions. When they turned off the village square and headed down the sloping street, passing darkened houses and gardens in which dogs barked, it occurred to Gerta that Schmidt might be even more dangerous to her than the Russian sentries or Nazi Werewolves. His proximity between the fenced-in gardens steeped in darkness made her uneasy. What if he was planning to reassert his dwindling authority specifically by using her, someone who had no hope of ever experiencing justice? It wouldn't be the first time that she had served such a purpose. Schmidt walked slowly, so she slowed down too. He spoke about the machinery they had to make arrangements to borrow, about the Jechs and the additional new arrivals that he was expecting, and he spoke about the Russians in Břeclav and Mikulov. When they arrived at Zipfelová's house, he wished her a good evening, made an about-face, and disappeared into the night. Startled, she turned to look after him. This was the last thing she had expected.

She passed quickly through the courtyard, stepped inside the front door, locked it behind her, and announced her return to Zipfelová, who was still sitting up in the kitchen with Ida. Then she raced up the stairs and into the small room where Ula, Dorla, and Teresa were sitting on the edge of the bed waiting for her, Teresa rocking the sleeping Barbora in her arms.

XIV

And then the day came.

A convoy of cars arrived from Mikulov and pulled up in front of the administrative headquarters. Out jumped a band of Russian soldiers accompanied by Schmidt. They marched into his office and stayed there for a whole hour. A few of the soldiers stayed outside, loitering around the threshold under the scorching heat of the midday sun, making friendly small talk and smoking with some of their Perná-stationed comrades. From time to time, one would walk over and tap flirtatiously on the window of Gerta's office. She would immediately bend lower over her desk and appear to plunge herself deeper into her work.

Once they left, Schmidt retreated back into his office and didn't summon Gerta for the rest of the day.

That same day, she personally transferred a formerly German property to two families that had shown up from Moravian Wallachia, and without waiting for anyone's orders, ran over to inform Šenk that the combine harvester with the thresher would be arriving from Mikulov the next day. On her own, she made the decision to send the original copies of the forms exempting indispensable persons from the transports back to Mikulov with the Russian soldiers, and on her own locked her office and the front door after herself, not knowing if behind the locked door of Schmidt's office anyone was still inside. There had been no answer to her knocking.

The following day, when she arrived at the office, Schmidt was already waiting for her. In front of the Rosenbaum house stood a buggy hitched up to a team of mares. Next to it stood Schmidt holding a whip, with which he motioned to Gerta to get up onto the box seat. Gerta wordlessly climbed up. Schmidt walked around to the other side of the horses, jumped up beside her, cracked his whip, and the horses set off.

"Where are we going?"

"To Mikulov."

"For the machines?"

"For the machines."

The road through the fields smelled of sweet clover. The air was damp with morning dew that was slowly evaporating in the cool sunrise. In the distance, there unfurled a bright yellow strip of rapeseed, cultivated by the residents of Dunajovice, and all around them swayed ripe stalks of barley with kernels like seed pearls clustered around each spike. Zipfelová had lent Gerta her shawl for the morning walks to the office, and now she was glad to be able to pull it closer around her shoulders and wrap the ends around her hands. The buggy jolted along the dirt road toward Klentnice, past the Pálava woods and around the Stolová hora mountain, as the sun rose at their backs.

In Mikulov, she waited for a long time alone in one of the rooms at the district administrative commission. In the hallway on the other side of the doors, she heard the sounds of passing footsteps in clunking work boots, the brisk tip-tap of boots, and the diminutive clicking of women's high heels taking hurried steps. After an hour and a half, the doors opened, and Schmidt walked in, accompanied by a short, thickset man with a protruding paunch. His eyes instantly and unerringly went to Gerta's armband marked with a large *N*.

"This is who's helping you?"

"She's off the very first Brno transport; we recruited about sixty of them for work. But even so, they can't handle it; most of them are women like her; some even have kids."

"Yup, it's just one of those things."

"About another thirty would do it."

"Yup."

"Come on."

Gerta stood up from the bench by the window and walked across the room to the door. The thickset man turned on his heel and led the way out through the door into the hallway, then locked the door behind them. The whole time, he kept rubbing his chin, his low-voiced mumbling punctuated with the occasional distinctly pronounced *yup*.

"Yup. That wouldn't work; we need 'em ourselves. Still, maybe them machines, we've got a few we confiscated back in April. Y'know, they didn't all take off on tractors. Although you wouldn't believe it, them sons of bitches, how they rob. And they're still out there, murdering people. Just two days ago, Stránský, the farmer who's got that strip of a field right by the border, he never came home. Went out harvestin' with a borrowed tractor and trailer, him and his son stayed out till evenin', managed to clear half the field, and then the bastards shot 'em. Left 'em lyin' there. We didn't find 'em till mornin'. His widow had us out there all night lookin' for 'em, 'cause it was obvious somethin' wasn't right. They shot 'em through the head, not leavin' a trace of tractor or trailer behind. Poof, across the border."

Schmidt listened closely, nodding.

"Yup. And a few Sundays ago, we had one lyin' around right here. The Russians finished 'im off. They keep on tryin'. And then them old-timers go bringin' their families 'cross the border, haulin' as much as they can away with 'em. We need reinforcements 'round here. At least now we've got them Financial Guards along the border and all them Russians, plus about twenty or so National Guard, so shouldn't even a mouse be able to slip through. 'Course if they get sloshed, they'll still get out, and when it comes to them Russians, well, who're we kiddin'?"

Schmidt nodded.

"But more often than not, they're scramblin' to get back in here rather than tryin' to get out there, over to Austria. That field hospital near Drasenhofen, just over the border, it's a nightmare. Ain't nothin' to drink, nothin' to eat, they're lyin' all over the meadow, dyin' by the dozens, 'specially them old geezers, the ones who managed to hobble that far, yup. Here we've got some six thousand Germans left, mostly sick 'uns. They're holdin' up the workers, the caregivers, and they eat like horses. But they've got prospects. The ones who make it through the dysentery, doctor says takes 'bout ten days, they've got a future here, yup. They can move in with relatives around these parts, bust their asses, and manage to get by somehow. But them ones on the Austrian side? You tell me, sir, how're they gonna make a livin'? There's gonna be a famine over there, unless they croak before they even make it that far. It's not like over there it'll just be the ones expelled from 'round here, y'know."

"So who do you have working for you right now?" Schmidt asked, still nodding.

"Germans, yup, them who can. But we've got them new folks from the heartlands comin' to settle 'round here every day, gold diggers, y'know, but so what. We give 'em houses that've been abandoned, farms, first come first settled. So them's already workin', too, even them whose houses are still bein' used as pest houses, 'n' then we keep on askin' 'em to send us them harvest brigades from Brno."

"Us too. But so far nothing. How many times have you asked already?"

"Well, a few times, y'know."

"And?"

"Like I said, so far nothin'. But it's clear why. The young'uns are all workin' as guards in them camps that're still crawlin' with German men, and the women are either in hidin' or scattered all over southern Moravia. Y'know yourself how many they chased out here. And y'know how many of 'em croaked of typhoid fever or dysentery too. Plain and simple, you're gonna have a hard time findin' workers 'round here. They're all either already in use or too sick. And there ain't gonna be no more slave labor comin' out of Brno."

"But why don't they send us some students? Some volunteers?"

"Yup, those they're sendin', at least they're tryin'. But it's slow goin', y'know. First come the towns near Brno. They say they're young folks, y'know. They've already got some in places like Modřice, Hrušovany, and they're movin' south, supposedly in groups of twenty. Should be our turn soon."

"In Perná, we'd need at least those twenty."

"Yup, so then you've gotta request it from the main office, y'know. Give the main office in Brno a call. They've gotta help ya out, and they will, 'cause after all, it's 'bout the harvest and the money, y'know."

Schmidt stood rapping his palm with a sheet of paper rolled up into a tube.

"Yup, I'll be sayin' goodbye, then. Y'all go see Franta. He'll show you the machines and get you three guys to drive 'em over. Gimme a call when you're ready to give 'em back, after you've figured out your workforce. But make it as quick as possible; I've got other villages waitin'. Oh, and go easy with the gasoline. Y'know yourself how hard it is to get yer hands on any these days. Economize—it's in yer own best interest!"

"Thank you. I'll let you know how things go."

The man held out his hand over his paunch, extending it a little toward Schmidt, who shook it and turned to leave. Gerta followed him.

Once outside, they walked around to the rear of the building and entered a courtyard. Inside the sheds and scattered all over the yard were several tractors, seeding machines, combine harvesters, and two threshing machines, while along the edges lay moldboard plows, and piled up in a heap underneath a pergola were dozens of plow points, scythes, sickles, pitchforks, hoes, stacked metal pails, tubs, and barrels.

Schmidt left Gerta by the gate and stepped inside a door next to one of the sheds. He reemerged shortly with a man who was glancing over Schmidt's rolled-up piece of paper. Together they threaded their way back through the tractors in the yard and disappeared behind a set of barn doors. Gerta leaned back against the wall, felt the crumbling grout under her fingertips, and raised her face to the morning sun. If at this very moment everything else ceased to exist, everything except the sun on her roughened skin, she would feel content. Everything else, even Barbora. Through her closed eyes, she would continue to look up at the sun's bright rays that seemed to come closer and closer in golden, crimson, and indigo circles, only to disappear behind the rims of her eyelids into pitch blackness. Nothing more. But then came the roar of an engine being revved up, and from the direction opposite to where Gerta, still blinded by the flood of sunlight, was standing, a tractor emerged from the barn doors. Schmidt, standing out front, shook hands with a man in a hat and then made his way back toward Gerta. He was just as morose as when she had first seen him that morning.

"Let's go," was all he said, and before long, they were heading back to Perná along the same road by which they had come.

The tractor with the plow attachment and the two combines were to arrive in Perná by way of the main road that led to Brno.

Gerta was silent, as was Schmidt. She was grateful that he brought her along, even though he hadn't needed her. She knew he couldn't have left her alone in the office, but he easily could have told Zipfelka to send her along with the other women to Šenk's for the day. Instead, he took her along for a quiet drive on a fine August morning.

"I consider you to be a smart woman," he said abruptly as they were passing the village of Klentnice.

Gerta turned to him in surprise.

"Which is why I'm going to give you a piece of advice."

Gerta kept her eyes focused on his nose and tightly compressed lips. What could be going through his head?

"Do you have any idea what's in store for you here?"

"No idea," she replied with an uncertain shrug of her shoulders. When Schmidt didn't continue speaking, she added, "But maybe things will get better. I want to go home, back to Brno. We have an apartment there."

"Damn sure you no longer do."

"I don't know. It's possible that my father is already back from the labor camp. They couldn't have kept him for too long; he's not young anymore."

"Nobody cares about that. You can be dead sure that by now you've got some deserving little Czech family living in your apartment. Or that your neighbor's grabbed it."

"You don't know that. And if, until things settle down, I could still stay here for a while with Barbora, at Zipfelová's . . . and help out. After the transports, once it's clear who's staying and who's a Czech, then hopefully things will get better, right? I haven't done anything wrong, so they're going to have to show some understanding for my situation."

"That's a naive idea." Schmidt shook his head indignantly. "But even so, I still consider you to be a smart woman who'll understand when I tell her that things are going to get worse for the Germans here. You see, every one of them is going to have to pay, even Germans who were in the resistance, do you understand?"

Was it possible that what she had predicted, and what not long ago he had still reprimanded her for, would come to pass?

"You mean even like you?"

"Even like me. And now, I'll give you that piece of advice. If you're not a complete numbskull and if you're prepared to give even a tiny bit of consideration to your daughter's future, you'll pack up your things. Tonight, after the women at Zipfelová's are asleep, you'll come to the Bavory crossroads, do you understand?"

"You want me to run away?"

"It's the only way to salvage any belongings and maybe even our skins."

"You want to run away too?"

"There's no other way. And if you're reasonable, and I think you are, then tonight at one o'clock, an hour past midnight, you'll be there."

Up ahead on the horizon, the steeple of the Perná church and the roofs of the houses on the low hill behind it came into view. Schmidt fell silent. What he was suggesting seemed to her to make the least sense of all. That she, with such a small child, should leave now, when the worst, as it seemed to her, was finally over? Those marauding gangs of Zbrojovka Arms Factory boys and that hell of a camp in Pohořelice? Why should she leave just now? She would go home, back to her own apartment or to some other apartment, to which she would surely be entitled. She, the daughter of a Czech mother, wasn't about to be intimidated by some unconfirmed reports or by the scorn of a few newcomers. She would stay through the winter to help with the harvest, do the work for which the locals were shorthanded these days—she was, after all, hardworking—and then she would leave for Brno, for home.

"I'm going to go back to Brno."

Schmidt snorted and slapped the reins against the horses' backs. The buggy lurched forward, and the horses picked up their pace.

"Stubborn," Schmidt muttered, and didn't say another word until they were back at the threshold of the administrative headquarters.

XV

"Just hold on; someone will show up."

"Yeah, but I'm thirsty."

"We didn't come here just to sit around, did we?"

"Easy does it, you'll work plenty hard; you'll be glad you had a moment to sit."

"Hey, look, he's got cigarettes and isn't offering."

"Let me have a cigarette, too, and don't worry, I've got some in my knapsack; you'll get it back."

"Don't tell me he's going to be a cheapskate, huh?"

"Who was thirsty? I've still got some water from Brno. But it's warm."

"Need a match?"

"Oh yeah, thanks. I can't believe I didn't pack any."

"Hey, look, another van. There's going to be a whole crowd of us here."

"You think they're from Brno too?"

"What do you mean, *too*? I'm not."

"I thought we were all from Brno, where else, right?"

"I'm from Jihlava."

"Now we're from Brno, but not that long ago we would've still said Frývaldov."

"The border region, huh? So how come you're not helping out over there? They must be shorthanded, too, aren't they?"

"He doesn't want to go back. We've got nobody left there."

"Do you smoke? Jesus, who's got cigarettes? Let me have one, too, or I'm going to go nuts."

"Boy, is it hot."

"Wasn't somebody supposed to be waiting for us here?"

"Hey, buddy, don't you want to take that off? You don't want to be standing around here all decked out, 'cause who knows how long it'll be before they come get us."

"Where do you think they'll put us up?"

"So, I'm actually from Moravian Wallachia. I was only working in Brno during the war, and then my folks called me and told me to check out the situation here, get the lay of the land. I hear they're giving away homesteads; first to grab one, gets one."

"I thought you were here for the harvest brigade, aren't you?"

"That's how it's always been. Some slave away; others take away."

"What do you think they'll have us doing? Personally, I don't know how to do very much, especially if it's complicated."

"They'll teach you."

"What matters is teamwork, right? Together we'll manage. The most important thing is to bring in the harvest."

"Oh no, she finished off my water."

"You look like you could be a Hubač from Jundrov; you've got the same eyes and that nose. Are you related? No? Well, I just wondered, seeing as they disappeared during the war, thought you might know something."

"C'mon, it's like you're in some hick town; are you related to so-and-so or so-and-so, as if everyone's supposed to know who you mean."

"It just so happens, sir, that I found my cousin in that car; look, right over here. I hadn't heard from her all through the war."

"And why are you here, ma'am? I thought only students were supposed to come, seeing as they've got time on their hands now. Wasn't that what they said? Járo, isn't that right?"

"I'm sick of just sitting here. I'm going to go ask around, or we'll be here till the cows come home."

"Good morning."

"Hi."

"Good morning, hello. There's no one here to meet you?"

"Hello."

"My God, there are so many of you."

"You've got a nice bunch of us here."

"Hey, young folks, how come you're just sitting around?"

"No one's opening up?"

"They dropped us off here and said this was the administrative headquarters. But there's no one here."

"So we're just waiting."

"How come no one's letting you in? Where the hell are they? Yesterday they were crying to the district administrative commission, and now today the ground's swallowed them up?"

"Could they be somewhere in the fields?"

"They might be out in the fields."

"The administrative commissioner? Nah. Maybe just running around someplace."

"That tall guy from Brno went over to that building to ask."

"Tell you what. Why don't you all get out of the car, that's right, and take your knapsacks. Listen up. I have to leave you here, right, that's clear, I need to get back, but tell you what—I'll drive around the village and track 'em down for you. The commissioner's name is Schmidt, got it?"

"He's German?"

"Well, yeah, he's German, but he was in the resistance or something. He speaks Czech."

"The commissioner here is German, huh?"

"Járo, you think we're going to have to put up with some German giving us orders around here? That's still allowed?"

"Hey, new guys, anyone got any water?"

"Come on now, kids, get your knapsacks out and pile 'em up. You can't leave 'em in the car; I've got to head back, I already told you."

"Hey, man, watch it, that was my foot!"

"Kamila, is that really you? I don't believe it. They said back in March your house got hit? Is it true? And everyone's all right?"

"Please, kids, settle down for just another minute. As I was saying, I'm going to take a spin around and look for Schmidt. You just wait here and save your strength for the work ahead; you're going to need it. Schmidt is a skinny guy, angular with dark hair and a mustache, always wears boots; you can't miss him. And he's got a pretty little German girl always running around with him. One of them will tell you what to do. For now, just wait here."

"Do you know if there's a water pump around here?"

"Nope, sorry, don't know; I'm from Mikulov. Just dropping you off here."

"I'm going to go sit by that church over there."

"All right, kids, do well and see ya."

"So long!"

"Where the hell is that Schmidt? Doesn't he know he's getting his harvest brigade today?"

Gerta was nearing the Rosenbaum manor, pulling a cart loaded with two bags of walnuts. Just the day before, Schmidt had instructed her to pull them out of the storeroom where they kept property confiscated from the Heinz estate, and to bring them over this morning. All around the locked front door of the administrative headquarters, harvest workers were either sitting or standing, their haversacks, knapsacks, and blankets strewn all over the place. The girls were lying on the grass with their pants rolled up, sunning themselves; a few of the boys were smoking on the doorstep. One was trying to peer through the window into the darkened office.

Gerta walked up to the door.

"Good morning. Know where we might find Commissioner Schmidt?"

"Good day. The commissioner's not here?"

"We've been banging away, but we can't get anyone to come to the door. Neither him, nor some German girl who's supposed to be helping out around here."

"Gerta Schnirch, good morning."

"It's you?"

"Yes."

"And where's the commissioner?"

"He's not here? That's strange. Maybe he's with the machines. They delivered them yesterday from Mikulov."

"They brought us here from Mikulov, because supposedly you're short of harvest help."

"Really? We were just there yesterday, and they told us they were short of help themselves."

"We arrived by train from Brno this morning. They told us they were all set and drove us here in a truck."

"I see."

"So where's this Schmidt?"

Gerta didn't know. She hadn't seen him yet that morning. She parked the cart by the front door.

"Just wait here a moment. I'll run up to Schmidt's farm and see if he's there. Or if he's with the machines."

She turned her back on the group and took off toward the church, continuing along a gravel path that went up over the crest of the hill and then veered to the right. She grabbed the handle of the sturdy gate leading into the courtyard, opened the pass door, and stepped through. The courtyard was neat, swept. The doors to the pigsties were all closed, the door to the barn and the door to the shed on the right as well. There was neither a dog, nor a hen, nor a goose, nor even a feather to be seen in the entire spacious yard. Empty. Silent. Gerta entered the swept courtyard and made her way toward the house. She pounded on the door. No sound came from inside. She reached for the handle. The door wasn't locked, so she opened it and stepped into a dark hallway that led her all the way to the kitchen. Although she had never been here before, she could tell that something felt different. In the room before her there was neither a table, nor a chair, nor a single shelf along the wall, just black smudges indicating where they had been and pale circles where plates had hung. All that remained in the kitchen were the curtains and the flowers in the pots behind the windows. And in the center of the immaculately swept room stood a coatrack, from which dangled a pair of tattered canvas shoes tied together by their shoelaces, slowly twisting in the draft. Nothing more was left of the Schmidts.

Gerta slowly made her way through the whole compound.

There wasn't a stick of furniture left in any of the rooms. Not a single item. The sun-drenched courtyard was still. Gerta opened up pigsty after pigsty. All were empty. The rabbit hutches, empty. The chicken coop, empty. The shed, empty. The water in the rain barrel under the gutter emptied, the rain barrel empty. Silence. The only sound coming from a distance was the clucking of a neighbor's chickens.

A tabby cat soundlessly padded across the courtyard. It narrowed its eyes and looked around. When it saw Gerta, it paused for a moment, then quietly continued.

"So you're the only one they left behind. You must've been out on the prowl last night, right?" Gerta laughed and squatted down. The cat, startled by her movement, froze, then scampered off and disappeared behind a wooden shed.

Gerta wondered how Schmidt had managed to pull it off. Could he have talked his Russians into helping him? He and his wife alone couldn't possibly have managed to load up everything, let alone in a single night, and so meticulously, packing it all away without a trace and whisking it off the premises, leaving not even a wisp of straw behind. With what could he have bribed them? Or had they done it on a lark? Or were they at this very moment lying drunk in Schmidt's wine cellar? Come to think of it, she hadn't yet seen a single one of them around the village that morning.

Gerta reemerged from the courtyard, shut the gate behind her, and set off for Zipfelová's. Whom else would she tell?

XVI

"Well, one can't just say it like that." Zipfelová stood, shaking her head, her arms folded on her chest. "Yes, he was local, the whole family, for generations, it's true. But where he disappeared to during the war and what he was up to before showing up here again so early in May, nobody knows. Where did that story about him being in the resistance come from, anyway?"

"Hell knows," said Šenk.

"I heard it from Hilda Schmidt. She said he was in the *RW*, the *Republikanische Wehr*. That's what those German anti-fascists called themselves after they escaped from Mikulov," said Ida.

"He could've made his wife spread that story around. But not the village men, and not the Russian unit in Břeclav. Come to think of it, he showed up with that wave of Russians, didn't he? Didn't they all seem to know him already, before they made him commissioner?" speculated Zipfelová.

"Please, they just gave it to the first person who asked. Not because they thought he'd earned it. After all, those Russians had no idea about who did what," Šenk said, shaking his head.

Ida was sitting at the table in the kitchen. She'd been the one to tell Gerta to fetch Hubert Šenk from his fields. Her gaze alternated between him, pacing around the kitchen, arms crossed, and old Zipfelová, who was leaning back against the stove.

"Schnirchová, please sit down. Why are you standing there so awkwardly in the doorway?" Ida said irritably.

"I was just thinking that maybe I should get back to work."

"You mean to the office? You're useless there now anyway without Schmidt to give you orders."

"But the harvest brigade is waiting."

Hubert Šenk stopped short. "What harvest brigade?"

"A group of people arrived, they said for the harvest brigade, from Mikulov."

"But weren't they short themselves over there?"

"They were. But supposedly Brno sent over so many people that they ended up driving some over here."

"How many are there?"

"About thirty."

"Well, isn't that grand," declared Šenk, his lips spreading into a broad smile. The corners of his mouth turned up, and his eyes crinkled. His face beamed.

Ida couldn't take her eyes off him. Gerta dropped hers.

"Well now, you hurry on back, so they don't leave. Or better yet, I'll come, too, and bring them back to my farm, before the Hrazdíras or the Krupas get their hands on them."

"And what about Schmidt?" Zipfelová raised her voice and called after Šenk.

"What about him? It's not like the commissioner's the most important thing around here."

"Someone's got to be in charge, or else those newcomers will clean us out. Those Jech folks just brought in another bunch of relatives, did you hear?"

"I know, but, Auntie, the harvest just started, in case you hadn't noticed. I've got enough on my own plate to worry about, let alone start worrying about others. Let them take their share, as long as they're fair."

"It's a question of what all they're going to take."

"Well, hopefully it won't be too bad," piped up Ida, the tips of her fingers smoothing the tablecloth.

"I'm going to get the brigaders; harvesting comes first. Schnirchová can take over for Schmidt. Listen to me, if you bungle things or take advantage, I'll have it out with you face-to-face, you understand?"

Gerta nodded. "And what should I do?"

"Wouldn't she be more useful in the fields?" Ida asked Šenk.

"No, somebody's got to watch over the Rosenbaum place. Remember, there's property from several households stored there. Make sure nothing gets stolen. Schnirchová, keep on top of those records, like you've been doing. Be sure you just lend things out, especially machines and equipment, and keep an eye on who takes what, even if it's for the brigaders. That'll be one big mess now. First, you're going to help me get them housed, and then you'll work on the lending and the monitoring.

And whether it's day or night, if anyone tries anything, you sound the alarm, is that clear? And also, call Brno, from where they sent us these folks, and report Schmidt missing. And report it to Mikulov as well, as soon as possible. They might still catch him at the border."

"Catch him?" Ida raised her eyebrows.

"Catch him. Chances are he didn't just take off for no reason."

"Probably not, leaving in the middle of the night like that. He might even have been an undercover Gestapo. Maybe when that delegation came over the other day from Mikulov, he got wind they were onto him."

"Had that been the case, Auntie, they would've shot him on the spot. Let it be, and don't let your imagination run away with you. Who knows how things really were. After all, you know yourself he wasn't a bad fellow."

"Was, wasn't. Up until when? The last time I really talked to him was still before the war. And the war changed a lot of people. Schmidt wouldn't have been the only one."

"Oh well." Šenk shrugged his shoulders, put his hat back on his head, and motioned to Gerta with his finger.

"See you tonight, Auntie, at *U Otrubů*. They've started serving wine on tap again. I'll let a few more neighbors know. So long, Ida. Schnirchová, let's go."

XVII

It was not that difficult. One actually just needed to concentrate a little, grit one's teeth or, on the contrary, yell out loud, aim, pull the trigger, once, twice, and then check to see if it worked. And then repeat the same steps—again and again, until the deed was done. To kill a person was terribly easy; even she could do it, of that she was certain, which was how she knew that anyone could do it. Not only Jech, for whom it was nothing new. If Barbora hadn't started crying, if Jech and his two cronies hadn't shouted so much, if the shelf Jech bumped into hadn't come crashing down, it all would have happened quietly, with only terse commands, barked orders, and the gunshot itself, and Gerta, still perfectly calm, would have crumpled to the floor, almost as if nothing had happened, as if she had just suffered a fainting spell. That was of course if there was no pain. But even if there was pain, Gerta knew it would only last an instant, a brief moment, after which long-desired peace, silence, and resignation would follow. Resignation, at long last, and a weightless head, through which the agonizing, unbearable trains of thought would finally stop racing. She would be at peace. At last, exactly what for years now—excruciatingly long years—she had been wishing for.

It was the Georgian doctor who saved both of their lives. He came rushing in, moments after Barbora started screaming as if she were being skewered alive, in a cradle that Gerta had pulled out earlier from among the confiscated German items stored in the Rosenbaum barn. It was hard to say what woke her—the perpetrators, after all, stole into the house quietly, and given the not exactly pampered circumstances in which she was growing up, she didn't startle easily. But the moment the latch on the door clicked, she started from her peaceful sleep that tinged her cheeks pink, and suddenly, it was as if something in her snapped. As if she had received a warning. Something from within or something from above. Some voice from heaven, perhaps that of the Perná Virgin Mary of the wayside shrine beyond the village, to whom Gerta surely would have prayed had she and God not gone their separate ways during the war. She turned her back on him only after he had left her in the lurch so many times—through the endless nights during which he allowed her father to do to her whatever he pleased, or the day she had been expelled from the city, or in the Pohořelice camp. No, never again did she want to hear another word about God. But perhaps with Barbora it was different. Perhaps those two hadn't parted in anger, because otherwise there was no explanation for why her screaming ripped through the room as soon as Jech and his sidekicks opened the door. How could she have sensed it? Her own Barbora, her very own child, to whom she now owed her life. To her and to Dr. Karachielashvili, whom she never would have expected to appear. He must have been very close by, perhaps right in front of the building or on the village square. That diminutive Georgian doctor with his slight shoulders and shrewlike nose, who spoke perfect High German and on one of the long, pale fingers of his exquisite, aristocratic hands wore a large signet ring. She knew she had won him over when she didn't take offense at his comments, claiming that in the Czech lands, the Czechs and the Germans were equally uneducated, since they knew nothing about his country. His condescending words didn't bother her at all. Contrary to his expectations, she straightened up from the pump where she was washing Barbora's diapers with a stub of grimy soap—that being all there was—swept a few stray wisps of hair away from her forehead with her wet, chilled hand, and proceeded to tell him all he ever could have wished to hear. He just stared at her, this German washerwoman, or whatever he imagined she was, as if she were an apparition. She described in detail where Georgia was situated, the location of Tbilisi, and the course of the Terek River. Having grown up on books by Lidia Charskaya, she knew it all perfectly, just as she knew, from having read Neumann, about the rebellion by the princes Karachielashvili, which she referenced in passing when she asked him about his own background, noting that he bore the same name. And with that, she wrapped him around her finger. From then on, the slight Georgian doctor—whom all the Russian soldiers in the village obeyed to the letter, as at one time or another he had helped get each one of them out of some scrape—instructed them to bring her gifts: bacon, eggs, brine-fermented pickles, a pot of lard, fish. And it was also this Georgian doctor who stormed into the office where she and Barbora were spending the night, keeping watch, just as the drunken Jech with his brother-in-law and nephew were trying to pry open the desk drawers in search of the keys to the barn that held property confiscated from the Perná Germans. And then a shot rang out that had drowned out Barbora's bawling. The bullet lodged in the wall above Gerta's raised arms. Barbora briefly fell silent and then started to bawl again. Then Jech began to shout, and next, Dr. Karachielashvili burst in with two soldiers, who struck the intruders from behind, knocking them down, and then rolled around, tussling with them on the floor. Meanwhile, Gerta grabbed her child, ran for the door, and raced back to Zipfelová's, away from the Jechs, away from her own death, clutching Barbora whose cries were still piercing the otherwise peaceful Perná night.

XVIII

A few days later, a new administrative commissioner arrived in Perná.

Josef Kratina from Brno-Líšeň was typically suburban and a bureaucrat. He arrived with just a small, greasy leather briefcase with straps, wearing a shabby suit and a shirt with a rumpled collar. Across it fell a fringe of stringy, untrimmed hair, which grew in a semicircle around a spreading bald spot. He smelled of sweat and musty old rags. In the office, he settled himself behind the desk, clucked his tongue, placed his hands down on the table in front of him, and proceeded to look around at the walls, into the corners, and at the floorboards. From time to time, he picked up one of the objects that sat in front of him on the table, weighing it in his hand and examining it from all sides. The crystal ashtray that had been confiscated from the Heinzes. The flowerpot that served as a pencil holder. He opened the drawer. Clucked.

Then he called for Gerta.

She came in with papers that needed his signature. He signed her clumsy report for the district administrative commission without even reading it and seemed prepared to sign anything Gerta put in front of him. He appeared to be completely indifferent. Before he went out to take a look around and inspect the grounds, he asked just one question: "This all belonged to Jews?"

Gerta nodded.

That evening, they were all sitting around in front of the house. Some sat on the ground; Zipfelová and Ida sat on a bench, watching the older children as they ran around chasing the dog and then disappeared after it into the orchard behind the house.

Ida was crocheting a collar. Zipfelová was just sitting there, resting her hands in her lap and observing the women seated around her. Some were holding a child. Gerta was rocking Barbora. Edeltraud was jiggling a baby carriage, one hand pushing it back and forth as the other rested on her hip, and Johanna was peeling potatoes for tomorrow's lunch.

"But Hubert Šenk needs twice that many, and he deserves them, too, not like those newcomers," Ida was saying to Zipfelová.

"Sure he does. But what's to be done? Those new folks will grab as many as they want. And who's going to go after them to tell them they have to give them back?"

"They shouldn't have been allowed to take them in the first place," retorted Ida, and shot Gerta an accusing glare.

"Oh, come on now, as if she were to blame," countered Zipfelová, throwing back her head.

"No one even asked me," Gerta said. "By the time Šenk got there, half of them had already been divided up. The Hrazdíras had already been there, and by noon, those new Jechs had theirs picked out as well."

"Had you spoken up right away, before starting in about that Schmidt business, Šenk wouldn't have been stuck here and could've gone right over and picked out the six men he needed. Not that they know anything, but at least they can pull their weight, right, Johanna?"

Johanna nodded.

"I'm glad we finally got some help. Those two from Brno are handy. Šenk still drives the wagon, but the older one knows how to drive that borrowed tractor, too, so they can spell each other."

"We didn't get any help for the vineyard," Ula said.

Gerta looked at her with pity. Every day she listened to Teresa groaning as she twisted and turned, trying to stretch out her back. She and Johanna would take turns working on her, cracking her vertebrae one by one, trying to relieve her pain. Even now she was lying stretched out across the empty bed in the little room upstairs, no doubt silently praying for the one-hundredth time for her stay in Perná to end. She often described to them how she imagined herself living in Vienna, all the things she would do, and how cleverly she would support herself. To their amazement, she didn't seem the least bit worried about the idea of leaving, come fall, for Vienna, a city already overcrowded and straining under the influx of new arrivals. Gerta, on the other hand, before falling asleep, thought of nothing else but returning to Brno as soon as she had the chance. She suspected it would have to wait until after *Dožínky*, the harvest festival. Most likely even later, because although by then the bulk of the work would be done, it still wouldn't be the right time for her to move. Though several months had already passed since the war ended, it was taking time for emotions to settle. The Perná villagers and farmers were only now beginning to treat the young German women, who had come from Brno through Pohořelice, as if they were human beings, although occasionally it would still happen that they permitted themselves liberties, which under any other circumstances would have been unthinkable. Just the previous week, for instance, Ula had come running back from the vineyard all beaten up. And it was only thanks to Dr. Karachielashvili that Gerta escaped from the drunken Jechs. If they had killed her, no one would have done a thing. That was how it was these days. And although at old Zipfelová's they had practically everything they needed—a roof over their heads, enough to eat and drink, and someone to look after their children—beyond Zipfelová's gate, they couldn't expect to be shown any respect. Whether dealing with the old-timers in the village or the newcomers, they were all too often met by either outright contempt or scornful disdain. Some of the farmers beat their German women; others acted with more decency, like Hubert Šenk for instance, whose behavior under these circumstances could almost be called gallant.

On the day that Ula had dragged her black-and-blue self back from the vineyard, Zipfelová slit a chicken's throat, and by the time Ula, sobbing in her room and squatting over a basin as she splashed herself with cold water to wash between her legs, calmed down, a hearty broth was ready. Zipfelová wouldn't leave Ula alone until she finished off three full servings and then made her drink a cup of lemon balm tea infused with poppy seeds, before sending her to bed. Afterward, at the administrative headquarters, Gerta witnessed how, filled with indignation, Zipfelová took the new commissioner to task, outraged to see him shrug his shoulders with indifference at the grievances she spewed at him. *Punish those criminals from Wallachia who are spreading out all over the village and attacking exhausted women. Don't give them any more property so that they leave, the riffraff. Post a public notice stating that anyone found guilty of a crime won't get even a thatched-roof hovel in this village, let alone a proper building.* The commissioner kept on shrugging his shoulders and cutting her off in annoyance. He hated a fuss and didn't want to be bothered by anybody. Zipfelová left but took a minute to sit down on the bench in front of the church—the callousness of that petty bureaucrat from Líšeň had left her short of breath. Her legs were trembling, and her heart was pounding, as if she had just been running for her life.

On the following day, as Gerta prepared the reports for the district administrative commission, she slipped a short declaration among the papers that the absentminded Kratina signed without paying it the slightest attention: *Let it be known that whoever is caught or found guilty of inflicting bodily harm on any resident, whether a Czech or a German, will not be given, and nor will his family, any of the confiscated property designated for redistribution. The war is over.* The next day, the declaration hung on the door of the administrative headquarters, the door of the church, and the door of the general store that a family from Hrozenkov had opened up in lower Perná.

Ida stuck her crochet hook into a ball of yarn and tucked both into a canvas bag.

"There's guitar playing over at the Schmidt farmstead today."

Zipfelka looked at her in surprise.

"So?"

Ida stood up and brushed a nonexistent speck of dust off her skirt.

"The brigade workers are going to be playing guitar and making a campfire. They invited me to come, so I'm going over to have a look."

"Now, at night?"

"Campfires usually are lit at night."

Zipfelová looked down at her wrinkled hands folded in her lap.

"It's still not safe to go walking around this village alone after dark."

Gerta noticed that Ida's cheeks were becoming flushed.

"Don't worry, Mother. You'll see; I'll get back just fine."

Zipfelová nodded.

"Is someone going to accompany you?" she said, giving Ida a sharp glance.

Ida kept her eyes cast down, brushed the last nonexistent speck off her striped skirt, repeated, "Don't worry, you'll see, I'll get back just fine," and disappeared into the house. In a moment, she reemerged with a knitted shawl thrown over her shoulders, sped past the group of women, called out, "Till later!" and slipped out through the wooden gate.

"So soon after the war," remarked Zipfelová bitterly. She closed her eyes, and in the evening afterglow, her deeply furrowed face seemed to fall, her jaw twitched a few times, her chin sank in disappointment, and a tear rolled down her cheek.

"How am I supposed to stop her, girls?" she said, opening her eyes abruptly and looking over at the women seated around her as they looked awkwardly back and forth at each other.

"You can't keep young people dressed in black forever," Johanna said consolingly.

Zipfelová nodded.

"Someday she's going to want a family too," ventured Ula, giving a little embarrassed cough, because she didn't know to what extent Zipfelová considered her son's death to be a real possibility.

Zipfelová once again hid her dark pupils behind her closed eyelids.

"And most likely neither Helmut nor I will be around to see it," she said quietly.

XIX

"You know, they don't pamper them much; you can be sure of that. It's not like they deserve it anyway, right?"

Gerta was sitting at the desk in her office, leaning back against the hard wooden chair, her hands folded in her lap. On the tabletop sat a demijohn of red wine that Hanák, Kratina's replacement, had brought up from the cellar, into which, over time, she and Schmidt had transferred all that was left of the inventory from the German wine cellars that hadn't yet been reallocated. All too often by the time they arrived, they were too late; the wine cellars had been looted and drunk dry by the Russian soldiers, and every morning following a rowdy night, for the remainder of June and July, the two of them would walk around together to see which one had been hit this time. By early August, however, they had managed to stow what was left of the inventory in the cool and musty wine cellar at the back of the garden of the Rosenbaum house. This wine cellar had been one of the first places Hanák discovered as he made his preliminary rounds of the unfamiliar village of Perná.

He had arrived the day after the departure of Kratina, who had left with two truckloads of confiscated furniture, porcelain, Mrs. Pfeifer's furs, kegs of wine, and bags of grain. Even the bag of walnuts from which Gerta used to nibble had disappeared from her office. The confiscated property that had accumulated in the Rosenbaum barn had dwindled. Most important, the valuables earmarked for either the National Recovery Fund or the district office were gone.

"Well now, that means everything's already there," chuckled Hanák the next day as Gerta described to him in consternation all the things that, according to her records, were missing.

"Should I report it somewhere?"

Hanák, who immediately made himself at home in Schmidt's office, chuckled again.

"You mean like to Mikulov? Or maybe directly to Brno? You'll just get Kratina picking up on the other end. Or someone exactly like him. Woman, you are naive."

Gerta stood as if frozen to the ground.

"All the porcelain has disappeared. And the furs. Several bags of . . ."

"Disappeared? Have you read about what happened to the Jews?"

Gerta hadn't read anything in several months. Not since the day that Beneš came to Brno. From then on, decrees were the only printed material she had laid eyes on.

"They disappeared up chimneys! And how many of them! And how much of their money disappeared! What do a few teacups matter, woman?"

Gerta leaned against the doorframe.

"I kept exact records here on Commissioner Schmidt's orders."

"So then, just cross those things out, all right? With a note saying they were transferred to some guy named Kratina from Brno. That way it's documented, should anyone ever bother to check. Do you even realize, woman, that there's been a war? And what kinds of things go on during a war? Now tell me, who the hell's going to care about a few teacups?"

"Obviously I realize that, sir. If there hadn't been a war, I wouldn't be here; I'd be back in my apartment in Brno."

"Well, there you are. But you had it coming. You're German."

"I never hurt anyone. And my mother was Czech."

"But old Papa was German, right? And did Papa have a clean conscience?"

"That I couldn't say, sir. But I have a clean conscience."

"But see, that could never work. The two groups have to be separated. You can't count on someone who resents the young Czechoslovak state to be committed to making that Czechoslovak state strong, right? Where would we end up? Right back where we started, isn't that so? In this, Beneš speaks God's honest truth."

Gerta didn't know what to say to this. Was Beneš's honest truth what she had seen scrawled on the walls during her last few days in Brno—*Germans out!*—or was it by now something different? Zipfelová didn't have a radio, and Gerta had no way of getting hold of a newspaper, if any even came to Perná.

"What's more, you need to work off everything you managed to squirrel away around here. We're not talking small potatoes, right? Just think of all that disappeared down your German craws. Paintings and jewels from Prague—there was just something in the paper about that—and all the things you stole from us, the amount of stuff you hauled out of Brno. And then there's all the stuff individuals hauled away for themselves. You should shut up! And work hard! Work hard, and be grateful that we let you live, do you understand?"

An icy chill spread through Gerta. She was beginning to hate this little man with red spider veins in his face. He was treating her like she was a die-hard Nazi. As if she had stashed something away, as if she owed gratitude for having been beaten, raped, and enslaved, just because she had never harmed anyone.

"I never harmed anyone."

Hanák slammed the palm of his hand down on the table.

"Every German did, every single one is guilty, you hear me, woman? The Germans were the ones who celebrated the occupation of Czechoslovakia, all of them. I don't know of a single one who didn't. Then under the Protectorate, they all rolled around, happy as pigs in shit, and lined their pockets. And every Czechoslovak had to suffer for it, you understand? So now every German has to pay the price. Afterward they can clear out and leave us alone to live in peace in our little Republic. Now, you go downstairs and bring me a demijohn, one that hasn't been opened, you hear; bring it to me sealed. And then the rest of the papers."

Gerta turned around and walked out of the office, forcing herself to remain silent. What point was there in arguing with this self-absorbed midget of a man with boozy eyes? She felt herself choking with help-lessness and rage.

"You know, they don't pamper them much; you can be sure of that. It's not like they deserve it anyway, right?"

Gerta was once again sitting at the desk in her office, leaning back against the hard wooden chair, her hands folded in her lap. She had been observing Hanák for several days now, listening to him talk and bringing him demijohns from the cellar. In the morning, when he first came in, he would be melancholy and subdued; a few times he even called her his little Gertitschka. By noon, with his first cup of wine, his courage began to swell, and he would start railing against all things

German. By nightfall, he was seething with hatred and ready to pick a fight. Then he would start to nod off at his desk, and twice now already Gerta had needed to help him get back to the room at the rear of the Rosenbaum house, which he had taken over as his own.

By the following week, he was calling her Gertitschka even in the afternoons, and a few days later, it became the norm for him to bring his work to her office, over to her desk, where he would sit across from her, setting the demijohn down between them. Other than the occasional deep sigh about being a lonely old man, however, he contented himself with just the demijohn and hours of blather, talking Gerta's ear off because she was the only person obliged to listen to him. As for the other villagers, he barely even had a chance to get to know them.

"You know, they don't pamper them much; you can be sure of that. It's not like they deserve it anyway, right?" he was repeating one afternoon as he described the current situation in Brno, his assignment before coming to Perná.

"There's a camp like that in Maloměřice, another one in Klajdovka, and one in Kounic College, and who knows where else. That's where they are, and they have to work like dogs. And the reason the Czechs don't pamper them much is because they're pissed as hell about everything they had to put up with during the war.

"From the rumors one hears, it's basically slave labor for hire. And they don't have to send them back in good shape. In fact, it's preferable if they don't. Teach the bastards a lesson.

"I saw them doing clearing work. They're paying their dues, that's for sure. If someone's working too slow, he gets a beating. One look, and it's clear just how they're doing. I wouldn't give them a scrap of food myself. Them pigs. Them Germans."

Gerta, her hands folded in her lap, listened in resignation.

"Gertitschka, do you have someone there?"

She looked up and shrugged her shoulders.

"You don't know? Or you do?"

"I think my father's there."

"Do you know where?"

"Before they expelled me from Brno, he was in Kounic College. At least I think he was."

"There you go."

He nodded and reached for the round, heavy, wicker-encased demijohn, picked it up by its neck, and refilled his cup from it with visible difficulty.

"You want some?"

Gerta shook her head, so he raised a glass to himself.

"The reason he's there is because he deserves to be there. That we're not even going to discuss. You can go ahead and feel sorry for him. But keep it to yourself."

It had never occurred to Gerta to grieve for him. Or to feel sorry for him. Because her father, in fact, was fully guilty, and she herself believed that he deserved to be punished, if not for his shady apartment dealings and his fraternizing with Hitlerites, then for what he had done to her. He deserved it. But what had happened to Friedrich?

"I also have a brother, but I don't even know if he made it back from the war."

"Well, that's how it is in almost every family. Everyone lost someone in the war," he said, shrugging indifferently.

From behind the door came the sound of voices and hurried footsteps, and almost immediately a pounding on the door. Hanák leaped up from the table, knocking over his chair. Into the room burst two of the Brno harvest brigaders, a young woman and a young man.

"Jech, up at the vineyard. Jech killed Führeder," the young man blurted into the room. He was blinking as his eyes tried to adjust to the darkness of the office, while the girl beside him just stared inside, wide-eyed and panting, flushed from having run so fast, her scarf having slipped down from her hair to her shoulders.

"He killed him, shot him . . . right in the vineyard." The young man spoke in gasps, propping his hands on his hips and bending slightly forward to breathe more easily. "He's lying there. We've come for you."

"What do you mean, 'killed him'?" Hanák said.

"Shot him. Hurry!"

"Why didn't they take his gun away after . . . after he aimed it at Schnirchová?"

"Fired it," Gerta corrected him.

"Why does he still have it?"

"For safety, naturally," replied Gerta sarcastically. "Kratina wasn't about to take it away from him, and you never gave the order."

"Christ Almighty."

Hanák clapped his small, round hat down on his head. It matched the suit he had arrived in, but not the checkered shirt tucked into his worn overalls that he had taken to wearing since the second day of his stay in Perná. He raced out the door but stopped short before heading in the right direction, and, perplexed, turned back to the harvest brigaders.

"Which way is it exactly?"

Since arriving, he hadn't ventured farther than the Rosenbaum property and its immediate surroundings. He hadn't gone beyond the church, and Gerta brought him his food. The brigaders pointed to the road leading up to the church and took off to run ahead.

Somewhere close to the middle of a row of the half-cleared vineyard that stretched toward Bavory stood a tight huddle of people, and others were crouching down or sitting around. No one was working. Two women at the edge of the group were sobbing loudly; two others sat side by side, a short way off.

"What in the world happened here?" Hanák called out loudly into the midst of the standing group, trying to get the attention of these unfamiliar people.

"I'm the new administrative commissioner. What's happened here?"

"He had him cut down the whole vineyard."

"You mean this dead man here?" Hanák pointed to the frail body of an old man, who lay on the loamy soil among grapevine stems and leaves, his arms flung out to the sides and his face covered by a hat.

"Over the years, he cultivated the best varieties around here by far. He'd even won medals for that wine of his, Mr. Commissioner," said a sad old man who was standing over the dead body, holding his hat in his hand.

"Did anyone call a doctor?" Hanák looked around at the group of bystanders.

"What for?"

"To get some first aid, huh?"

"But, Mr. Commissioner, he got a bullet through his head. Why would you need a doctor?" queried the old man in surprise.

"He was German," piped up a woman who looked to be in her forties, and whom Hanák, as he'd forced his way through the crowd, pushed out of the circle that had formed around the body. Now he looked over at her.

"My name is Růžková, Mr. Commissioner. This dead man here, he was Mr. Führeder, the best vintner in these parts, far and wide. Before the Great War, he was purveyor to the lords of the House of Dietrichstein, that's how well-known he was. He was the best of them all, except for Mr. Krumpschmied here. He's also an expert in every sense of the word, isn't that so, Mr. Krumpschmied? You've also gotten plenty of medals."

"Yes, yes," the old man said. "We had our fair share of rivalry, Führeder and I. But that wine of his, I couldn't touch it. Something so fine, with just a hint of blackberry. After all, he spent his whole life working on it. He managed to cross Traminer with Müller Thurgau; that's a blend you won't find anywhere else. Only here in Perná, in Führeder's vineyard. That's why he got those medals, poor soul."

"So, can someone explain to me why he's lying here dead now?"

"He couldn't tear himself away from his vines, couldn't bear to leave them behind. He would have died without them, you understand? So he decided to die with them," answered Krumpschmied, and then added, nodding, almost as an afterthought, "And do you know, the idea has occurred to me too? That I would take my vines with me to the grave. That row you see there, which stretches all the way down to below St. Anna's, it's all planted with cuttings from Greece. My son brought them back for me before the war. Just wait until you see the grapes they yield, big, reddish gold and sweet, much sweeter than the local varieties. And yet they grow under the same sun. I was also thinking I might take them with me to my grave."

"For heaven's sake, Mr. Krumpschmied, please don't talk like that," said Růžková, covering her mouth with her scarf and giving a sob.

"What would the grape harvest be like without you, for God's sake," a skinny, sinewy man standing beside her said.

"Mr. Krumpschmied, you'll survive this, and your vines will too. Nobody is going to want to deport an expert like you. You're not going to have to go anywhere. It makes no difference that you're German; everyone around here knows that you never cared about politics. They won't make you leave, and as soon as things settle down, you'll get your vineyard back, you'll see."

"Oh no," said Krumpschmied with a bitter smile, "I'm never going to make wine again. The new owners have already moved us out into the shed. Now my wife and I are just waiting to see when they'll send us away on the next transport. They've already told us it's going to happen. But they said I didn't need to worry about my wine and wanted me to tell them how to go about making it. They said that if I told them, they'd take care of it. And that if I didn't tell them, they'd plant an apple orchard. Or cherries. Here! On this piece of earth, kissed by God, that produces wine like Führeder's. This soil, rich with loess from the Pálava Hills. Madmen."

Růžková lowered her head and began to sob into her scarf.

"What's going to become of Járinka Führederová now? Who's going to tell her what happened? It'll be the death of her."

"It's going to kill her, that's for sure," one of the other women agreed.

"And who's this Jech, the one who shot him?"

"He's new around here, sir. He came to take over one homestead, and now he and his family have at least three."

"Well, they're entitled to them."

"They took over the Führeder property as well. They own these vineyards now. And they were keeping the Führeders locked up in a storeroom, demanding that they tell them how to make good wine. Führeder finally told them that this was the time to cut it all down, to let it finish drying out on the ground."

"So? Then why did he shoot him?"

Růžková stopped in mid-sob; the skinny man turned his entire body toward the commissioner; and old Krumpschmied snickered. "*Na ja*, have you ever heard of anyone cutting down a fifteen-year-old grapevine?"

Hanák blinked in consternation. "What?"

"He told them to cut down all the vines. He said that was how one made wine, you understand? He destroyed his best vines, Führeder did, to keep them out of the hands of those criminals from who knows where."

"In that case, he's one hell of a saboteur!" snapped Hanák sharply. "He's a saboteur, and people like him deserve a bullet!"

"Deserve it?" Růžková turned to him in astonishment. "For being driven out of a vineyard in which he had spent the past sixty years of his life breaking his back, working?"

"How is he a saboteur? He liquidated his own vineyard, which he had every right to do, since it would have been destroyed anyway in the hands of those godless people. You think the Jechs have a clue about wine? They know shit."

"What are you saying, his own vineyard? Germans no longer have the right to own property, or haven't you heard the news yet? Do you mean to tell me, all of you, that you haven't read about what happened at Potsdam? Not a single grape in this vineyard belonged to Führeder anymore, understand? He destroyed property that now belongs to the fledgling Czechoslovak state, and that makes him a saboteur!"

Krumpschmied kept his head down and nodded. Růžková started sobbing again and covered her face with her handkerchief.

"Man, you don't get it at all." The sinewy man shook his head.

A murmur of dissenting voices rose up from the crowd around Hanák.

"He should have put up a monument to honor Führeder for all the work he spent his life doing around here, and not have driven him out, let alone kill him."

"You can say what you want. As far as the law is concerned, that man didn't own a thing, and that makes him a saboteur."

From behind the group came the clattering sound of a wagon, and several people turned around to look.

"Here comes Šenk," said a woman, sitting by the hedgerow.

Hanák turned to look as well. "Who's that?"

"That's Hubert Šenk. He owns the neighboring fields," said Gerta.

"Good, at least he can cart the German off. He can't stay out here in the sun."

Šenk jumped down from the box seat and advanced toward the group. The others cleared a path for him as he slowly walked all the way up to Führeder's body, sprawled on the ground, and took off his hat.

"I'm the new administrative commissioner, Hanák."

"Šenk." The farmer introduced himself, nodding. "I'm glad you're here. Something has to be done about this. These newcomers can't just get away with it."

"Have you lost your mind too? Or haven't you read the paper since the war ended? Or listened to the radio?"

"I've read it, and so what?"

"So what would you like to do about it? He was killed for good reason. He was a saboteur."

Šenk bent down over Führeder's body and remained like that for a while, holding his rumpled hat in his hand. Then he turned to Hanák and said, "You're going to report this. They can't act this way around here. This is murder."

"Murder? What in God's name do you mean?" retorted Hanák, vigorously shaking his head. "This was, I repeat, sabotage. Sabotage by a German. And even if there hadn't been a reason, this dead man here's a German, and you'd better realize that, sir."

Šenk stepped right up to the shorter Hanák and said, "This murder, sir, you're going to report it. And if you in your official capacity don't, then I will. I'll file it as a complaint. This is the murder of an upstanding Perná vintner. That's who Führeder was. That he happened to be a German doesn't mean shit."

The blood rushed to Hanák's face. He turned crimson with suppressed rage.

"What happened here, sir, was the execution of a sentence against a saboteur. Retribution for treachery carried out in a vineyard that belongs to the Jechs, understand? As administrative commissioner, I am not going to report any murder."

"No record of a property transfer has been submitted to the Land Registry office yet," Gerta said softly. "Since the Jechs came to the village, they've already moved three times. They haven't decided yet which house they want."

"It's possible that these vineyards, according to some piece of paper signed God knows where and by God knows whom, someone who hasn't the slightest idea about Perná, no longer belonged to Führeder," said Šenk. "But as you've just heard, they don't yet belong to Jech either. So now tell me, by what right did Jech shoot him?"

Hanák's chin trembled with fury.

"I repeat," he blurted with utmost self-restraint, "I will not report any murder. I'm happy to sign a transfer of property over to a Czech. But the only good German is a dead German. Have I made myself clear, sir?"

Hanák then turned on his heel, rammed on his hat, and set off down the farm lane back toward the village.

"Schnirchová!" he called out.

Gerta looked anxiously over at Šenk.

"Go on, I'll deal with Jech myself," he said, at which Gerta quickly set off to catch up to Hanák.

XX

The cool, twilight air found them all once again bending over the stubble field, just as on the day before. The children, who that evening also needed to help, were there, as were Ida and Zipfelová, who was doing her gathering along the edges of the field while keeping an eye on Gerta's Barbora, Edeltraud's Katty, as well as on Anni and Rudi.

They continued bending down until the last rays of sun disappeared. Only after it was too dark to see did Zipfelová call out to them, and they came wandering back from the far corners of the field, their knotted kerchiefs filled with stalks of grain, the golden heads packed with kernels. At the sight of eleven full kerchiefs, Zipfelová's eyes lit up. Even in the dusk, they could see how pleased she was.

"One more time tomorrow, while there's still something left to gather. And then we'll be set for winter," she said, picking up little Anni who had finally given in to sleep, having waited as long as she could for the pickers to be done.

By the wayside shrine at the edge of the field, still a good ten minutes' walk from Perná, Zipfelová stopped.

"Please, everyone, stop, wait a moment. Johanna, come back!"

The women gathered around her.

"Here, take her for a moment," Zipfelová said, handing off Anni to Johanna, although she was already holding Rudi, also fast asleep, in her arms. Teresa darted over and took the little girl into her own arms.

"Ida, let me have a handful," she said, turning toward Ida, who was standing right behind her with a full kerchief. Zipfelová reached inside and pulled out a handful of stalks. She stepped over to the edge of the road, toward the wayside shrine.

"This is for the Virgin Mary. May she bless our farmers and vintners, especially Hubert Šenk, and may she bless these fields again for next year, and may she also bring us a good harvest. And this handful here is for Járinka Führederová and her husband. May the earth rest lightly on them."

She reached over and tucked two handfuls of grain into the niche where a statue of the Virgin Mary once must have stood. She crossed herself, took a few steps backward, and rejoined the small group of women.

"Let's go," she said, turning back in the direction of Perná.

"That wayside shrine, just so you know, was built by my husband's great-grandfather, also a Zipfel," she started to tell them after she'd gone a few more steps.

"He had it built to give thanks to the Virgin Mary for having survived a winter's night coming back this way from Horní Věstonice. In our family, it was said that it was in that very spot that the devil and his minions jumped out at him and tried to take him away, because he'd been out carousing. It was only his praying to the Virgin that supposedly saved him. These days, it may just sound like a silly story to you, but back then, he really spent half of his savings to build that shrine. The cross you see on top, he had it forged in Brno, and a well-known wood carver there made the statue. And then every Sunday, for the rest of his life, he would come here to light a candle."

One of the girls in the back laughed. "All for having been out carousing?"

"Supposedly he was the town drunk; that's what my late husband used to say. He, thank God, was spared. In that family, one never had to go too far for a shot glass. Luckily, they weren't vintners. I'm not sure how he would have managed if they'd had a wine cellar. Things might have ended up the same way as they did at the Šenks'."

Ida, walking two steps behind her, loudly clucked her tongue. Zipfelová grew quiet, and for a while they all walked in silence.

"But I'll always swear by that wayside shrine. Every year, on my Helmut's birthday, we would go there to light a candle, because it was right there, in that very spot, that I begged the Virgin Mary and was granted my only child. Every time I passed there, I would plead with her. And then, one summer day, it was there that my late husband and I received her blessing."

She laughed softly as she welcomed back this memory from long ago.

"And the Heinzes, the ones who had the farm down at the other end of Perná, by the road to Dunajovice, they would all gather here after the *Dožínky* harvest festival, and the whole family would ask the Virgin Mary to grant them a good crop and peace on the farm. And then, as if by a miracle, they were the ones who were spared by the great fire that I still remember from when I was a child. The entire farm next to them burned to the ground. Back then, people named the Lindovs lived there, and they ended up burned to a crisp, along with all their buildings and livestock too. There wasn't a trace left of them. Same thing with the cottage on the other side of the Heinzes, but there at least no one died. And the Heinz place, not even a spark touched it, just imagine. That's why they go there, or at least they used to, and the villagers would go with them. That's when the idea caught on, right after that big fire, that the Virgin Mary of the wayside shrine can help. And after they were done praying, Mrs. Heinzová would always give out angel wings. No other woman in the village made them as well as she did. Last year, we all still went, and now this year, who knows where the Heinzes ended up. They were such good people."

The small group of women was slowly approaching the first houses of Perná. They walked wearily, at an unhurried pace. In the first few courtyards, the dogs had already picked up their scent and started to bark. If Gerta had not given up on prayer, she would have gone to see the Virgin Mary of the wayside shrine every day to plead with her to return her former life. Her life before the war, when everything was still in order. And if that weren't possible, then at least for a future life of peace in their Brno apartment, but without her father. She would live there by herself, with only Barbora and all the things she loved. Her mother's set of little cups decorated with flowers, the long curtains in the dining room, where they used to have lunch. The peculiar flower stand with its assortment of wire hooks for hanging flowerpots—her parents had brought it back from some exhibition, and it had always fascinated her as a child. The carpet in her bedroom that received her feet every morning as she climbed out of her toasty bed. Every day she would have gone to see the Virgin Mary, to plead for the return of her home with its tranquility and the soft and steady ticking of the pendulum clock. If only she could, she would go and spend hour upon hour praying there. But she couldn't. Neither God nor the Virgin Mary had helped her, not even when she had most needed their help. Never again would she need them as much as she had needed them back then. And so she had shut the door on both of them.

By the time they finally got back to the small bedroom, it was already pitch dark, so they lit the single candle given to them when they first arrived in Perná. So far, they hadn't needed to light it often.

"It's all coming to an end. Soon it will be time for *Dožínky*, the harvest festival," said Ula, tucking the quilt around Dorla at the foot of the bed and giving her a goodnight kiss.

"It is for all of you, but I've still got a stretch to go," sighed Teresa, who worked in the vineyards.

"Nothing's coming to an end. There'll be plenty to do around here in the winter too. Some of the women will leave, and you, if they end up not letting you go, might get moved over to the animals. Šenk has plenty of them, and his mother is old."

"Why wouldn't they let me go once the season is over? And besides, Ida might be taking care of the animals by then, don't you think?" Teresa sniggered, and took the opportunity to quickly stretch out across the whole bed again, spreading her arms and legs wide, which she could only do before Ula and Gerta climbed in on either side.

"Did you notice how we'd barely come in, and she was already running back out?" whispered Ula softly, so that ten-year-old Dorla wouldn't overhear.

"I did. And I also noticed that she took off before Zipfelka got back to the kitchen. I'll bet she didn't tell her again," said Teresa, making a catty grimace.

"Then she'll lock her out of the room again, won't she?"

"And Ida will end up sleeping in the kitchen again," chuckled Gerta, who had already found her there once, fast asleep with her head resting on the tabletop.

"Or maybe not, maybe they'll finally wipe the slate clean and she'll stay over at Šenk's. Wouldn't that be something?"

"Zipfelová would have a heart attack!"

"Don't exaggerate. She's not blind; it wouldn't come as a big surprise."

"I say by Christmas, Ida's moved in."

"First, they need to have Helmut declared dead, and Zipfelová's not about to do that. Not before a full year has passed. And even then, it may be too soon for her."

"What if Ida were to have him declared dead? Even though the process, especially getting the court to issue the declaration, can take a while. But still, if the younger one puts it in motion, Zipfelová can say whatever she wants. It won't make a difference."

Gerta looked at Ula in surprise. "How do you know all this?"

"She could also find somebody who was on the front lines with him and might be able to attest to his death. The testimony of a fellow soldier is the most convincing argument. Ida could be free before the year is over."

Teresa and Gerta were silent.

"My husband is a lawyer," Ula then said softly. "I used to work in his office and helped him prepare his cases. That was before we had Dorla and Adi. If only he could see what's become of us now."

Ula turned away and buried her face deep inside the mattress. She wouldn't cry in front of Dorla, who was always straining to listen in on their conversations before falling asleep. From the day she had come back from the vineyard and slept through the rest of that afternoon, that night, and the following day, she no longer cried. Gerta and Teresa had tried in vain to get her to talk to them about what had happened so that they could console her. She refused to say a word about it; she would only cover her face and remain stubbornly silent. She wanted to wipe that day out of her mind completely, as if it had never happened.

"But you can't," Teresa whispered to her, once Dorla's breathing had finally become regular. "When they did it to me, it was twice in a row, each one held me for the other, as if I were an object. That was near Ledce. They dragged me into the woods. All I could do was bite the hand they were shoving into my face. To get back at me, they beat me until I was black and blue all over, no mercy, even in my stomach. I howled like an animal. And my mom, who was trying to wait for me, walking as slowly as she could so that I could still catch up to her in the convoy, then told me, 'Go on and cry, dear girl, go on and cry. Let it all come out and wash away. Go ahead and cry, and with time, it will seem as if it never even happened. But if you don't cry, you'll bury it deep inside you and never be rid of it.' That's what she told me. Poor woman, if only she'd known that two days later, I wouldn't be giving it a second thought anymore, that instead, I'd be crying over her."

Ula said nothing. She didn't cry; she didn't complain. She was living for a future in which she saw herself reunited with her husband, and tried to present the stay at Zipfelová's to Dorla as a summer holiday spent with Granny. How did she manage to do it? Gerta privately wondered. She herself had become skin and bones during the march; her milk had dried up, and the sound of Barbora's crying would often set her on edge. By now, old Zipfelová knew how to handle Barbora better than she did. It was only toward the end of the summer that Gerta finally managed to calm her inner shaking and started sleeping more peacefully and eating better.

"So shouldn't someone tell Ida?" asked Teresa.

"Tell her what?"

"That she can have Helmut declared dead and stop having to meet Hubert in secret? I mean, after all, shouldn't someone tell her that she's entitled to a happy life?"

"I'm certainly not about to tell her," Ula said. "Let her handle her life on her own. I'm not going to tell her, for starters, because of how she treats us. If it weren't for old Zipfelová keeping an eye on her, that hand of hers would be pretty quick, the charming little Ida. I can't tell you how often I've seen it in her eyes, how much she'd love to slap me."

"Well, there you go, at least she'd get out of here quicker," quipped Teresa.

"Zipfelová would end up in her grave sooner, and then who knows what would happen to us. You'd go to the Krupas; I'd go to the Hrazdíras; and the Jechs would get the rest of us. No way am I saying a word. She can figure it out for herself, if Hubert Šenk is worth it to her."

"I'd be happy for Šenk," said Gerta. "He worships the ground she walks on. He's a grown man; by now, he deserves to have a good wife at home. He sits around in the evenings all alone with his mother. I kind of feel sorry for him."

"Supposedly, he looks after her all by himself. She can barely even walk, at least according to Zipfelová."

"He really could use having a woman around to help him. It's high time for Ida to get herself over there."

Ula shook her head.

"To each her own. She can fend for herself. But it won't be easy for her. That case is going to take years. And the longer she waits, the longer it will drag on, especially if that Helmut of hers was an Austrian citizen," replied Ula spitefully, turning over onto her other side.

"Enough of this now, Gerta," she added. "Let's go to sleep."

Teresa looked at Gerta, shrugged her shoulders, and turned onto her side in such a way that her body curved around Ula's back and buttocks. Gerta undressed down to her slip, tossed her work skirt over the handlebar of Barbora's carriage, and blew out the candle. In the darkness, she slipped into bed alongside Teresa, also adjusting herself to conform to the curves of her back, her hips, and the crook of her knees. She draped her arm over Teresa's waist and felt her hand. She placed the palm of her hand over the back of Teresa's, and their warm, sweaty fingers intertwined.

XXI

For the first time since leaving Brno, Gerta felt almost happy. Her thoughts were no longer constantly turning back to her father or to Friedrich, not even to flashbacks from the march, nor was she being plagued by fears of the future. At least not for the moment. After many long months, she was finally carefree and delighting in every minute of this day.

Inside the church, she stood next to Johanna and her two four-year-old know-it-alls, who were constantly searching for something on the floor. Barbora was fastened to her chest with a large white cheesecloth, which Ida had lent her for today's occasion. Ulrika, Dorla, and Teresa stood behind her, leaning back against the wall of the church and inhaling the scent of incense, which they hadn't smelled in such a long time. Up until today, they hadn't been allowed inside the church. The Perná residents wouldn't tolerate it. Gerta didn't mind; she no longer needed any church or any God, but she was happy for Teresa. She saw that behind the cheerful facade that Teresa put up night after night for Ula, who was sinking ever deeper into her own world out of which at times not even Dorla could pull her, beneath the brave countenance, she was struggling and hurting, torn between wanting to forgive and wanting to take revenge on those who had done this to her, and perhaps even on herself. Her greasy strands of hair were plastered to her scalp and pulled back into a matted bun at the nape of her neck. Gerta never saw her bathe or rinse her hair with the chamomile extract that Zipfelová prepared every two weeks in a large pot on the stove. She observed the positive smile on her now-healed lips—with which she would try to cheer up Ula—and at the same time the neglected outward appearance in which she showed not the slightest interest. *She's going to rot away,* Gerta thought all too often as she breathed in the pungent, sour smell of Teresa's sweat before falling asleep.

But right now, she was standing at the *Dožínky* harvest mass, inhaling the familiar scents that she and her mother used to look forward to every Sunday. The collective singing of the villagers, which on this day included the Germans as well as the Czechs, the old-timers as well as the newcomers, and even the harvest brigaders from Brno, filled her with happiness. Absurd as that was, given the circumstances. Yet when she looked around at the faces of Marie, Hermína, Johanna, and the others, she saw that they, too, were smiling.

The priest ended the mass. Everyone made the sign of the cross, and people began to get up from the pews. Gerta along with the other German girls waited until everyone else left, and only then, under Zipfelová's supervision, did they peel themselves away from the back wall of the church and walk out into the sun, still warm on this last Sunday in August. In front of the church, the crowd assembled for the *Dožínky* procession.

Everyone was visibly excited by the commotion, which for the past five wartime years the residents of Perná had only been able to enjoy in the form of a memory. This was the first time since the war ended that the *Dožínky* harvest festival was again taking place, albeit with a new cast of characters. For the past two weeks, Ida, who was involved with the preparations, had been going every other evening to meetings at the pub, and it was her doing that the German women were allowed to take part in the festivities. This was certainly not out of any sense of sympathy, but rather because she didn't want to be stuck at home with old Zipfelová keeping an eye on them. Instead, she had managed to arrange for them to take part in the parade, so that she herself wouldn't have to miss out on participating. The women were grateful to her just the same. It was an opportunity for them to feel like human beings again. Not the kind no one respected, who had no rights, who were only good for working, and whom everyone wanted to get rid of—but human beings entitled to enjoy the fruits of their labors.

The procession lined up behind two festooned wagons. On the previous day, Ida, Gerta, Teresa, the women from the Hrazdíras, and all the children had helped to decorate them. They had wound stalks of grain and flowers, which they had picked in the meadows that morning, around the slats of the hay wagon and had decorated the scythes and sickles that would be carried in the procession as well.

On this day, the musicians began to line up behind the wagons, followed by the residents of Perná, two by two, some like Ida wearing festive traditional costumes, others in their work clothes, because those were all they had. The new landowners stood off to either side of the procession; they didn't know what to do as they weren't familiar with the custom. Only one family from Kyjov, wearing more elaborate traditional costumes with different embroidery from that of the locals, got in line toward the end of the procession and tried to fit in among the Perná folk. The mother, wearing a sizable headdress, nudged her children along ahead of her like a mother hen, clucked something over her shoulder to her husband, who was tamping down his pipe and patiently waiting, and threw friendly smiles around at her new neighbors who smiled back at her. What a beautiful day, thought Gerta, standing off to the side and waiting to see where Zipfelová would position them.

An old man and an old woman, the village elders, took their place in front of the two decorated wagons and presented the people of Perná with the *Dožínky* harvest wreath. It was braided out of twelve long, slender sprigs, bound with stalks of grain and wildflowers, like the festooned wagons, and further embellished with red poppies. After they made their speech and after the priest blessed the wreath and this year's harvest, they led off the procession, the two wagons drawn by Šenk's and Hrazdíra's mares behind them, followed by young men riding on bedecked horses and young women in festive traditional dress. Then the music began.

The moment Johanna's children heard the cheerful trills of the violins floating up the street, they began to dance in a comical way and to hum along, until Zipfelová and the other women bringing up the rear of the procession, both German and non-German, all had to laugh.

The elders led the procession toward Šenk's farm, which stood at the end of the road leading from the church to the lower meadows. The previous week in the pub, Šenk had been unanimously chosen as the farmer of the year and was to be presented with the *Dožínky* harvest wreath. He certainly must have been expecting it, as his was the largest farm in Perná and everyone, including the newly arrived settlers, respected him. Supposedly, at least according to Ida, people were already whispering about why there was still an outsider in the position of commissioner when Šenk could easily become the mayor—after all, the war was over now, things had calmed down, so everything could go back to normal. The last mayor before the war, the Rosenbaums' eldest son, hadn't yet returned, and it was possible that no one from that family would ever return. That was the rumor going around, based on what people heard about Dachau, from where the last bit of news about the Rosenbaums had come.

The procession, accompanied by the strains of a clarinet and violins, arrived in front of the Šenk farm gates, where a double bass and cimbalom were already waiting. Gerta felt overwhelmed and very emotional as she thought of the various processions in which she had been swept up over the last three months. When the music finished playing, the elder couple knocked on Šenk's farm gate. It immediately swung wide open, and there stood Hubert Šenk, dressed in traditional garb, wearing tall boots and black breeches with embroidered seams, a white shirt with embroidered wide sleeves that hung loose around his wrists, a black waistcoat, and a hat lavishly decorated with a nosegay and a sweeping feather. His slightly stooped mother accompanied him through the gate with tiny shuffling steps.

As soon as Šenk appeared, a cheer went up. All around, hats sailed into the air, along with posies that the women had up to then been holding. The elder couple waved their arms around, trying to quiet the crowd, but it was only at the first strike of the tiny hammers on the cimbalom that the noise finally abated. The elder couple then delivered words of thanks on behalf of the village to the farmer and with a bow, presented him with the richly decorated *Dožínky* harvest crown. From where she stood at the tail end of the procession, Gerta couldn't hear a word. All she and the other women could do was to try to catch a glimpse from the slightly raised vantage point of the street that sloped down from the church on the hill toward the farm, into whose courtyard Šenk, with a wave of his arm, invited everyone to enter. The men positioned the cimbalom so that it could be heard in the courtyard as well as in the street, where many remained because the yard couldn't hold everyone. Gerta and the other women sat down with old Zipfelová by the side of the road and waited in the midday sun to see what would happen next. In the courtyard, cups were being passed around, and wine was poured into them from demijohns. People were laughing, their words rising through the sultry air along with the strains of music and the whinnying of the horses that gave off a heavy, summer smell, which blended with the fragrance of grain and flowers. Couples were dancing the Moravian *skočná* as children were running among them, chasing dogs. The moment was full of beauty, harmony, and joy, and the war would have seemed a thing of the distant past if not for those fifty or so women sitting by the side of the road, wearing white armbands emblazoned with the black letter *N*, chatting quietly just now among themselves in German.

By early evening, Zipfelová's German women were sitting around a table in the corner of a room at the village inn. Gerta sat between Ula and Johanna, holding Barbora, who was looking around at everything. With a corner of the cheesecloth swaddling Barbora, Gerta dabbed at the dribble on her daughter's chin and laughed into the little eyes, wide open with curiosity as they took in everything around them. Zipfelová sat at the head of the table, keeping a close watch on Ida, who was flitting about on the dance floor and all around the pub. She seemed to be everywhere.

"Helmut married a flirt," she would mutter from time to time, "a real flirt."

Ula, who since the incident in August had felt the closest to Zipfelová, took her by the hand.

"She's young. Look at the other young girls; one of them is always with her. She just wants to have a bit of fun."

"But she forgets that she's married."

"That's only because she's young. Just give her time. You'll see how she'll change if . . ." Ula stopped midsentence, then whispered, "When Helmut comes back."

Zipfelová nodded in silence. She herself no longer knew whether she should say *if* or *when*.

The women sat closely huddled beside her on a bench in front of which the children were playing. Every so often, the little group of German children would be separated by the skittering village children, who were playing a game of tag among the standing and dancing adults, until finally the two groups blended together.

"At least the war didn't take away their freedom." Zipfelová nodded with a smile to Johanna, who was anxiously looking on as Anni and Rudi joined a group of the youngest ones.

"As long as nobody else minds."

"The village women aren't unkind; they wouldn't do them any harm. But just to be safe, don't let them out of your sight; you never know—some drunk might swipe at them. We'll be going soon anyhow. Šenk said to stay for the toast, but then we'll go home. All the same, Hanák and Jech might give him some trouble, since Germans aren't supposed to take part in any celebrations."

Johanna nodded and kept a close watch over Anni and Rudi.

When the music stopped playing, Šenk, at the table across from them, stood up. The other local farmers did as well. The sound of chatter in the room died down until it stopped altogether, with all eyes fixed on Šenk.

"Here's to wrapping up this year's harvest! And here's to a successful one next year. May it be abundant, and may we have the manpower and equipment necessary to bring it in. Because we're going to do it! So here's to our health, and to the health of all the hardworking newcomers, and to the health of the harvest brigade. And also, even though it's not allowed, to the health of my women, who worked hard day after day. It's also in large part thanks to them that our harvest is put away."

And before clinking his glass, full of dark red wine, to the glasses that the other farmers were holding out to him, he gestured with it to all sides, to the brigaders from Brno, who started clapping and whistling and stomping their feet; to the residents of Perná, who raised their own glasses back to him; and even to his and the other German women who were sitting in the corner.

Gerta quickly looked down at Barbora and tried not to take his words too much to heart. He had addressed them as if they were living beings. It really seemed as if that night, for the residents of Perná, they weren't just hunched over backs crawling around the fields and the vineyards, but people, people who had done their part in ensuring the survival of the village for the coming year. But this was mainly because everyone in the room was slightly tipsy, and a sense of satisfaction, whether due to the work they had accomplished or to their newly acquired properties, was written all over their faces. By tomorrow, Gerta thought to herself, it would all be different again. The ice-cold, loathing looks of the Perná women, barked orders the only words to reach their ears, the occasional vulgar jeer on the street—it would all return. To protect herself, she would continue to stay close to Hanák or Šenk or Zipfelová, so as not to get assaulted like Ula or the two women from Krupa's who were recently beaten up coming in from the fields alone one evening.

Gerta took one more look around the room. She saw the obdurate faces of the Jechs, whose numerous family members were sitting around, defiantly leaning on their elbows over pints of beer, having participated in neither the dancing, nor in conversations with others, nor having shown any reaction to the farmer's toast. *Not long ago they shot at me,* thought Gerta to herself. Johanna, seated beside her, suddenly leaped up when Anni and Rudi slipped out through the inn's doors with the other children.

"Mrs. Zipfelová," Johanna gasped, and Zipfelová took off after them immediately.

"I don't blame you," said Gerta, "You don't want someone like Jech or those folks from Wallachia, or even some of the locals, to get their hands on them, if they realize they're German. I still remember how they threw a child into a field near Ledce."

Johanna winced, not taking her eyes off the door.

"Well exactly, that's precisely why. It's impossible to forget. How they couldn't care less that the child had nothing to do with anything. And those dead little bodies in that shed in Pohořelice, I'll never forget it."

Johanna anxiously watched the door.

Dr. Karachielashvili came over and sat down on a chair facing Gerta. She noticed him only after he was already seated.

"How are you?" he asked in German with a Viennese accent.

"I'm fine, thank you," answered Gerta softly, also in German.

"I hope that incident didn't affect her," he went on in Russian, bending down toward Barbora.

Gerta shook her head.

The Georgian doctor was silent.

Zipfelová reappeared in the doorway with Anni and Rudi in tow.

"We're being transferred to Mikulov, have you heard?"

"No."

"Next week the whole unit is leaving. The new commissioner is only keeping two guards here. And just for a short time."

"I see," Gerta said.

The doctor fell silent again and rubbed the bridge of his prominent nose.

"Do you like to dance?"

"Excuse me?" asked Gerta, surprised.

"I asked if you like to dance?"

"Me? No."

The last time she danced had been with Karel at her senior prom; they had been inseparable the whole night. She hadn't given a single dance to anyone else. Those were moments she would never forget.

"You don't like to dance? You don't say. Why, you look as if you were made for dancing," he said with a laugh.

Joker, Gerta thought to herself, and began to rock Barbora so vigorously in her arms that the tiny pupils in her white eyeballs looked up at her, startled.

"I was just thinking that we could have a little dance."

"You know, Doctor, please don't take this personally," Gerta said, not even giving a smile, "but I'm not allowed to dance; I'm not even supposed to be here. Surely you have to know that Germans aren't allowed in pubs or other similar public places? Let alone to dance. It's only thanks to Šenk that we were able to sit here awhile, although it's not particularly comfortable for any of us."

Gerta broke off and motioned her head to indicate the women nearby. Dr. Karachielashvili took a deep breath and seemed about to say something.

"And even if I could dance, I still wouldn't. First of all, I don't know any of the music they're playing or how to dance to it, and secondly, I don't want to. I'm in no mood for dancing. Let me stay sitting. I'm fine right here."

Dr. Karachielashvili looked disappointed.

"You don't want to relax even just a little?"

"Relax?" She gave an ironic little laugh.

"Yes, just unwind a bit."

Gerta looked at him in disbelief. "Doctor, don't you realize that we're here to be punished? That we're barely tolerated? That we should be glad that, back in Pohořelice, they didn't just kill all of us right away? Or that I should be glad that in the office a few weeks ago I wasn't shot? I can't relax. Until I feel like a human being again, I can't pretend, not even for a moment, that I'm happy and feel like dancing. Can you understand that?"

Dr. Karachielashvili shrugged. "That depends on your attitude. It's possible that you might have quite a decent future here if you stay, and if the local people get used to you. If only you'd seen how those who crossed the border in Drasenhofen fared. Or what happened to the ones who stayed in Pohořelice. Compared to them, you have a future."

"Unless some drunk shoots me. Or rapes me, like Ula. Or stabs me, like what happened to the two from Krupa's."

"Well, yes," said the doctor, "the war's still not entirely over. But notice how people don't want to think about it anymore." The doctor looked around. "Now they want to think about the future, about bringing in the harvest, about having enough to eat in the winter, about things being back in order, the fact that next year they'll be able to sow and not have to worry about a battlefront coming through and trampling their crops. Make sense? Now it's time for living. Life is demanding its turn, and it will sweep you along. People are sick of killing. What they want now is to keep house and tend their land."

"We'll see," said Gerta before turning to Johanna, who was holding on to both of her children with all of her might.

Dr. Karachielashvili stood up, pushed in his chair, gave a slight nod, and moved away.

"What's the matter with you?" Johanna hissed at her in Czech. "If he were to take you under his wing, you'd have it made. Don't squander your good fortune—remember you're single!"

But Gerta just obstinately bent lower over Barbora.

"Gertrude Schnirchová, is that you?" a young woman wearing overalls and a black scarf, its hem embroidered in yellow, called out to Gerta moments later as she and the other German women were obediently making their way down the steps behind Zipfelová, leaving the village inn.

Gerta tried to remember from where she recognized that smiling face with its wide, full lips and dimpled cheeks.

"It's me, Jana Tvrdoňová from Sterngasse. We used to live in the same building, remember?"

All at once her image surfaced in Gerta's memory. *A blonde girl, straight out of* Das Deutsche Mädel *magazine, with soft curls framing her doll-like face, is descending the stairs, swinging her bag in which empty milk bottles are clinking, and says hi to Gerta who is just locking the door to their apartment.*

"Oh," said Gerta softly.

"So they kicked you out too? I can't believe it. Did they know your mother was Czech?"

Gerta shrugged.

"Why, that's just awful, that's what it is," said Jana, turning to a boy of about the same age who was standing next to her, a glass of beer in his hand.

"She's a German, right?" he asked quietly.

"Gerta, they wrote about it in *Rovnost*, right after you all left. They said that on our street alone, fifteen families were moved out—truly terrible. But they wrote that it had been a mistake, a misunderstanding, that those guys from the Zbrojovka factory had misunderstood. They were the ones who organized it all, you know?"

Gerta stopped and shifted Barbora to her other arm. The other women who resided with old Mrs. Zipfelová were all going by them.

"So what exactly did they write?" asked Gerta.

"They wrote that it was a mistake, that they shouldn't have driven you all out like that. That they took it to mean expulsion, but that wasn't exactly how it was meant, something along those lines. That what they should've done instead was to move you out of the city temporarily, you know, so that then you could have come back. And then the Red Cross would have resettled you in Germany."

"All of us?" asked Gerta, shaking her head.

Jana, taken aback, paused and shrugged. The corners of her mouth slightly drooping, she looked around for the boy.

"I don't know, probably not all of you. Some were allowed to stay, like the Bürgers, for example; they didn't have to go. Or the Böhringers, but then again, everyone knew they were anti-fascists."

Gerta nodded.

"You know, you probably wouldn't have had to go either, since your mom was Czech, right? They were just writing about it in *Rovnost*, saying the whole thing was totally disorganized—no one bothered to look left or right; they just made the decision to expel, and that was it. They chalked it up to that expression, *When felling a forest, splinters will fly*. I'm just really sorry that you ended up out here."

"Jana, can you tell me what things are like now? Do you think I could come home, now that they're writing about it and calling it a mistake?"

Jana uneasily slipped her hands into her pockets.

"Home where? You mean to Sterngasse? I mean, it's called Hvězdová now."

"What was it they wrote in the paper? When are we going to be allowed to go back?" Gerta pressed on.

"Well, they didn't write about that. I mean, they did write that it was a mistake. But have you heard that Germans no longer have the right to own property? I would think that someone would have told you."

Gerta looked around nervously for the other women, who were disappearing two by two into the darkness of the gardens in front of the houses.

"Nobody here has told us anything. You know we're only here to work. So, do you have any idea what's going to happen now? When are we going to be allowed to go back home, since the papers called it a mistake?"

Jana shook her head. "So far, they haven't written anything about that, at least not in June or July, anyway. But I don't know. I have a feeling that it's not going to be possible. Someone else is already living in your apartment. You know, these days in Brno, it's a bit like musical chairs."

Gerta's heart skipped a beat.

"Someone's living in our apartment? What about our things?"

"No clue. They're probably still there, unless they were given away. I really don't know. But there's a family living in your place, supposedly some disabled war veteran or something. I'm not sure."

"And what about Friedrich? Did Friedrich come home?"

"Gerta, I have no idea. Right now, there's so much going on. I haven't seen Friedrich, but my mom said that she heard from someone that your dad stayed in Brno. Supposedly he's in Kounic College. Do you know what's there?"

Gerta was momentarily taken aback, but then nodded.

"Schnirchová!" echoed just then down the street from the direction in which Zipfelová's group of women had gone. "Schnirchová, hurry up!"

Jana may still have been awkwardly mumbling something else, but Gerta didn't wait to hear. Placing her hand over Barbora's little head, she set off running after the group of women, trying at the same time to stifle the tears that were stinging her eyes, and to force down the sob that was choking her throat. And then Barbora began to cry.

XXII

"Bastards, crooks, that's what they are. They harm decent people, just for the fun of it. Bandits, my God, who would have expected this? From our saviors? They're murderers, not saviors," fumed Zipfelová, taking chunks of meat from the hands of the Dunajovice butcher who was out in the front yard with her.

In the kitchen, Gerta and Ula were also portioning out parts of the shot pig, cutting away tendons and separating the fat from the skin, straightening out the intestines the way the butcher had shown them earlier, simmering them to make tripe sausage and blood sausage. On the wide griddle sat pots of bubbling hot water in which knuckles were being boiled, and at a table behind them stood Ida, preparing the meat mixture for the headcheese.

"Russian sons of bitches, let them be gone already," she muttered, seething with hatred as she worked the meat mixture with her bare hand, her arm elbow deep in the metal bucket. "All they do is slack off and drink. Let them go where they're needed, or let them go home, not stay here abusing other people's women. Let them go home."

"Mama, look, Jan made me all dirty!" Dorla called out in German, bursting into the kitchen.

"Get out! *Raus!*" Ida shouted at once from behind the table. "Into the garden, you hear me? And speak Czech!"

Ula wiped off her soiled hand and pointed Dorla, who didn't understand Czech, back in the direction of the door, giving her a look that left no room for any objections. The girl backed out and quietly shut the door behind her.

"When are we finally going to have some peace around here again, for God's sake? Who's supposed to live in a house like this?" hissed Ida, her unmistakable tone of reproach clearly directed toward Gerta and Ula.

They kept their heads down and didn't react, just doggedly went on trimming one piece of meat after another.

"Ida, quick, the basin for the innards!" Zipfelová called from the courtyard, startling all three of them.

Ida grudgingly grabbed the metal basin and hurried out to where Zipfelová and the butcher were waiting. Gerta and Ula looked at each other wearily. Exhausted after a sleepless night, they'd been on their feet since daybreak, running around the shot pig. This was the first chance they'd had to take a break. Gerta leaned back against the tiled stove and slipped her palms beneath her sore lower back.

"Can you imagine what would have happened if they'd come inside the house?" she remarked.

Ula just shook her head and dropped her eyes back to the pail. She had barely spoken all morning and kept turning her face away, as if she didn't want to see any of what was happening around her.

"I'd be curious to know where Dr. Karachielashvili was last night, to have let them go on a rampage like this," continued Gerta quietly. "Where Hanák was is obvious—he was under the table before we even got up to leave. But what about the guards? They're always strutting around with those red sashes, scaring everyone, but yesterday there were none to be seen anywhere. Drunks, all of them."

Ula remained silent. She went on listlessly trimming the meat, tossing the cleaned pieces into a large stoneware pot at her feet.

Gerta thought for a moment about how she might draw Ula out of her morose thoughts, where, since the middle of August, she seemed to be spending more and more time, but nothing came to her. Who knew what this nighttime scene with the drunken Russians might have evoked for her, and what Gerta might trigger by reminding her of it. She decided instead to stop talking. She was afraid of unlocking Ula's dark and secret place.

"Schnirchová, Jesus Christ, what are you standing around like that for? Come out and help us carry," Ida, mightily annoyed, shouted through the door, upon which Ula and Gerta quickly ran outside. On top of the board on which the butcher from Dunajovice had dismembered the pig, all that was left now were a few heaps of meat and bones. Strewn underneath the board were scraps that the dog had caught wind of, while the innards had been piled into a large pot and several cast-iron buckets.

"Such a shame," lamented Zipfelka.

"Bring that inside," Ida directed as she herself bent down to pick up the pot.

"Look out, young lady; don't strain yourself, now," said the butcher, grinning at Ida as he packed his knives, hooks, and dainty saws into a canvas case.

When Gerta and Ula bent down to reach for the buckets, he said nothing. Zipfelová followed them inside, bringing up the rear.

"Such a shame," she repeated morosely as she counted the dishes lined up in the kitchen, and before she went out again, she turned back to them with more orders: "Ida, put together a care package for the butcher. You two, don't just stand there. Start carving up the meat, let's go, so that we're done cutting it up by nightfall!"

Gerta and Ula obediently reached for their knives, while Ida reluctantly spread a linen dishcloth out on the table and wrapped a few chunks of meat up in it.

"That should do him, don't you think?" she asked without looking up, and went on to prepare a second portion of lean meat. She then slipped the second package discreetly into the pocket of her soiled apron and hurried out into the yard.

When Zipfelová came back to the kitchen a little bit later, she went right over to the table and started straightening out the casings and stuffing the blood sausage.

"Don't worry, girls. You'll get some, too, and so will your little ones. We'll eat it all, and whatever we can't eat, we'll give away. What else are we going to do with it? Unless that black-market woman comes by, then we could barter in exchange for shoe vouchers or some fabric. But who knows when she'll come around again. She's been gone for half the summer."

Gerta and Ula were silent, each bending over her work.

"Unless I try to sell some of it to that little shop those new folks from Wallachia opened up. But who's going to go buy it, when everyone here has enough of their own, for heaven's sake. Except for maybe that Hanák. Or those damn Russians, the devil take them!"

It was only then that she paused and looked around. "What's happened to Ida?"

Gerta and Ula uneasily glanced up from their pots.

"Where's she gotten herself tied up now? Ida!" Zipfelka called out with a sense of foreboding toward the door, but there was no answer. One look through the window and they could all see that the yard was empty and the gate to the road ajar. Coming on top of the shot pig, Ida's disappearance that day was the last straw for old Zipfelová. Devastated, she sank down on a chair.

"I bet she's gone to see that Šenk, hasn't she?" She sighed. "Silly goose, running over there in broad daylight. What are the neighbors going to think? He was asking for a beating, Mr. Hero. Yes, it's a shame about Führeder. Nobody's happy about what happened. Why, old Führederová and I were classmates, back in the days of the kaiser. We went to elementary school in Dunajovice together. I feel bad about it, too, but what can you do? After all, old Führeder had no business destroying his best vineyard like that. He must've known he'd never get away with it—after all, he's been a German citizen his whole life! Then he goes and commits an act of sabotage like that. It's madness. And at this time! If he'd been even a little bit responsible, he never would've done it to Járinka. Poor woman, it's on him that she hanged herself, not on Jech. And how could Šenk have been stupid enough to go provoking him like that? And they were both drunk, the pigs. He deserved that beating, it's not as if he didn't, and because of our Ida, too, that young ninny. He's always turning on the charm with her, silly goose. I'm sure she went to look after him!"

At those last words, Zipfelová hid her wrinkled face in her hands and began to sob, until her whole scarf-covered head was shaking, and neither Gerta nor Ula knew what to do for her.

XXIII

Pride. Over the past several months, it was what the others had buried. Crawling around in the fields, toiling away at whatever they were told to do, grateful for a crust of bread—talking in the evenings only about the next day's work. They had gone mad. Their lives had gone missing. Their personal interests, desires, aspirations, the things that brought them happiness, were all gone. All that was left now were hollow husks that only thought about the work and what was to eat. For how much longer? How many more times would that question be asked? And the future, that was something no one ever talked about anymore. At the beginning, she would still hear "When I get back to Brno," or "After I leave," or "When all this is over." What did she hear now? Talk about harvesting potatoes and rapeseed; that it was better to kneel on a piece of sackcloth than to bend over, which made the back pain worse; or how many rows so-and-so had done today; and how lucky they were to be working for Šenk and not for Krupa, where you got slapped if you didn't bring in enough. Or she simply wasn't hearing anything, because the conversation was in Czech, which neither she nor Dorla understood.

Ula couldn't take any more. Every day felt like an iron ball and chain shackled to her feet, her wrists, her neck—by now she was dragging around dozens of them, one for each day. The weight forced her to buckle lower to the ground, fasten her gaze on the coarse brown earth. How many times had she already said to herself that it would be better to be lying beneath it, free of her suffering, her anxiety for the future, her fears over Adolf and Adi? The other day in the kitchen with Gerta, carving up the meat, the urge to turn the knife on herself must have come over her more than a hundred times. She couldn't take her eyes off it, mesmerized by the sharp point and the razorlike blade that would effortlessly glide through her stomach. And rid her of those thoughts, sever her from that foul-smelling, filthy body that had penetrated her in the field behind Perná, practically ripping her arms out of their sockets, so roughly had it pinned her down. And the kicks, those were the worst. The long, sharp blade would at once put an end to her sleepless nights, the stifled rage over the humiliation, and the maelstrom in her mind that she couldn't stop that kept her tossing back and forth between longing to forget and longing for revenge. And it would put an end to the loathing of her body, which would cease to exist. But there would still be Dorla. Dorla abandoned and alone among strangers in a country where she no longer belonged. She would stay behind, not quite eleven years old, and could end up just like her mother, Ula—after all, during those nights between Brno and Perná, she had seen plenty of such cases. And Adolf and Adi would also stay behind, somewhere in Brno, where right now they were laboring, but one day they would be released and would come looking for them—either here or across the border. What would her Adolf say if he were to find out that she had given up and left Dorla alone in the world? He would curse her. He would never understand.

Adolf, her strong, resolute Adolf, who always knew what to do. She could always lean on him. He made her feel secure—at his side she could safely close her eyes and let life blithely run its course. Because Adolf knew how to guide her through everything, first her alone, and later her and their children—in a state of prosperity and well-being, toward happiness. The years spent beside him had been pure and perfect joy. To tend to him, accompany him every day to his law office; to make a home for him; to give him Adi, at whose birth she saw him moved to tears for the first time; to give him Dorla, with whom he fell in love at first sight; to go on excursions together in their new car; to attend balls and socialize with the notables of Brno; to wear new dresses and jewelry and sparkle on his arm, beautiful and beloved. Sheer happiness. How proud she had been alongside him, proud of him, whose counsel was sought out even by Judex and Schwabe—how many Sunday afternoons had they spent on the terrace of Judex's villa near the botanical garden— and proud of herself for having borne him two beautiful children, so perfectly pure, that even the mothers of their Aryan playmates were envious. Proud of their lavish apartment and of the invitations they received. They went to the opera every time von Neurath was in Brno and always received an exclusive invitation to join the Judexes in their private salon. That had been happiness.

How was it possible that it all slipped away so easily? Merely a few months of convincing themselves and reassuring each other among friends that everything would be all right, that it was all just a tactic—the Führer's tactic—and that all would be well again. How could they have been so shortsighted? If only they had left in time, if they had packed up their things and been gone already by February, or by March, like the Freilichs, the Riedls, the Schrimmpels, and so many others—then she wouldn't be here today, with neither her Adolf nor her Adi, about whom she hadn't heard any news for five months now. If only Adolf hadn't been so stubborn back then and had been willing to give up his practice; after all, he easily could have reopened it somewhere else, perhaps in Regensburg, where they had relatives. How could he have even imagined that, under the circumstances, he could have kept on practicing? But no, he had believed, he had gone on believing—blindly believing—and Ula in turn had believed him. It never would have occurred to her that her Adolf, prudent and self-confident as he was, to whom the most sensitive cases were entrusted—over which he then often pored late into the night, sitting in their salon, smoking and explaining to her every possible angle— might have been wrong. Her very own Adolf. And yet he had been wrong, and she had been forced to humiliate herself, naturally to no avail, not only for his sake, but also for her Adi, her not-quite-sixteen-year-old son—her boy whose future had been so bright. A part of her died when she saw them line him up and march him away from the assembly place in a double line, striking him in the back with a weapon to shove him forward when he turned to wave at her one last time. It didn't help that she kneeled, begged, wept, offered jewelry that she had hidden—they tore it out of her hands and pushed her roughly to the ground, saying that she had stolen it from the Jews anyway. That was when she had gotten her first kick, which for a long time she couldn't let go. But by now, she had lost count of them. The same went for the punches, the slaps, the yanked hair, everything but the rapes. Those she still counted. Yet what was all that compared to the hunger and the deadly thirst, when between Rajhrad and Pohořelice she and Dorla drank nothing for almost two whole days? What was it compared to the fatigue and depletion that laid them low in the barns near Pohořelice? Compared to watching children die, and old women, who could no longer move? Disgusting. How could her Adolf have allowed her and Dorla to go through such hell? And how was it actually going to end? During those early days in May, she would still bring both of them, Adi and Adolf, at least the little bit that she managed to scrape together by working and begging. During those three visits, she could only glimpse both of them through a gap in a concrete wall topped with barbed wire, which the guards allowed them to approach in order to accept a few slices of bread. To see how Adolf looked back then had shaken her. Gaunt, haggard, with large circles under his eyes, his hands raw, and wearing clothes that once upon a time she wouldn't have allowed a maid to use even for rags. But it served him right, as he alone was responsible for himself and for the decision he made when he insisted they stay. But what about her Adi, why him? The moment she saw him with a swollen, bloody contusion over his eye and welts and bruises all over his body, over which he wasn't even wearing a shirt, she thought the feeling of helplessness would drive her insane. She was a disappointment to herself, both as a mother and as a wife, who hadn't sensed that Adolf was making the wrong decision. And now she was paying the price and, once again, just waiting to see what would come next.

But all this came to an end that moment in the kitchen, when, as she was carving up the pig, she decided not to turn the knife on herself. At that moment, her time of bondage ended, that period of waiting and feeling grateful just to be alive. At that moment, she made a decision, and did so with a conviction that she hadn't felt in years. She decided that she and Dorla would leave, as soon as possible. Leave this country where they no longer had a future, regardless of what Adolf might think. This country in which they had no rights, no property, and whose language they didn't speak. If they ended up having anything left here at all, Adolf could sue to recover the damages later; he was a capable lawyer. But given the memories she now associated with this country, Ula no longer wished to live here. This country, which for years they had helped to make flourish, had taken everything from her and had almost driven her to the point of turning a knife against her own body. She had to get away, across the border, either to Austria or to Regensburg, where she would wait for Adi and Adolf. Because here, in this country where they were driving her away with a whip, it was no longer possible for her to stay.

She confided in Teresa one evening at dusk as they were rounding up the poultry in the farmyard. Teresa stopped short, taken aback. Now? As soon as possible. Two women from Krupa's, and the two of them with Dorla. The hardest work was behind them. The potato and rapeseed harvests were almost done. Ida had already snappishly remarked several times that soon they'd have to go work in the brickyard as there would be no more work left to do in the fields. And now that they were no longer needed, people were becoming more hostile. Extra mouths to feed. "Away, away," hissed Ula as Teresa's face turned ashen.

They were all scared, even the two women from Krupa's, who had sent word through the grapevine to the German women at Šenk's. One of them used to let that old Russian, who was here with Karachielashvili, come see her—in a few days he'd be heading to Mikulov for good. He was willing to hide them under a tarp in the back of the truck and take them across the border, one piece of jewelry per person, or a bit of what he was getting from that woman at Krupa's. There was no other way to escape now; it was only possible with the help of a Czech or a Russian. Apparently, now the borders were closed and strictly guarded; one could only get into Austria illegally because the country couldn't take in any more refugees. That was what the Russian had said. But Ula, Dorla, and those two women from Krupa's needed to get away from here at all costs. Ula still had a few rings knotted in a handkerchief under the straw mattress—if Teresa wanted, she'd give her one, and then in Vienna, when times got better, she could pay her back.

Gerta suspected something. The past three nights, Ula and Teresa had been talking of nothing but Vienna. What was strange about it was that Ula had started to talk again. Teresa was always rambling on about either her back or about Vienna. But for the last several weeks, Ula had been silent, giving only curt answers, locked away inside her unhappiness. Dorla was the only person whom she would occasionally let in. Over the past few days, however, the words were gushing out of her like a waterfall. Words like *we must*, *when*, and *in Vienna*. Gerta anticipated something. And then one September night, she was awakened by a rustling. On the bed beside her sat Dorla, still half-asleep. Ula and Teresa were dressed, and each held a knotted bundle, presumably containing things that belonged to Zipfelová, because all three had arrived empty-handed. Ula was fumbling around beneath the straw mattress, and it was this movement that awakened Gerta.

She sat up. Teresa quietly came over, sat down beside her, hugged her, and gave her a kiss.

"You wouldn't want to come with us to Vienna, would you?" she asked.

Gerta shook her head. Her eyes filled with tears, and her throat got so tight that she could barely swallow.

"The Russians are taking us in their truck today. By morning, we'll be across the border."

Gerta nodded.

"I'll write to you as soon as I'm settled. Then you can come see me, anytime you want."

"Psst," hissed Ula, letting the straw mattress drop and taking Dorla's hand.

"We have to go now," she whispered, and came around the bed to Teresa and Gerta.

"I'm going to miss you terribly," whispered Gerta.

"Me too," said Teresa, her voice trembling as she hugged her tightly around her neck.

Ula leaned down and kissed Gerta on her hair.

"Farewell."

The sound of a dog's howl rose over the sleeping village. Then came another, and then yet another, all along the path down which Ula, Teresa, and Dorla were hurrying toward the crossroads beyond the village. There, a truck with Russian soldiers and two other German women curled up in the back under a tarp was already waiting.

XXIV

The first Christmas came and went. All of the women who still remained gathered in the small garret chamber. Very softly, so that no one would hear them, Gerta, Johanna, Hermína, Marie, and Edeltraud sang "*O*

Tannenbaum" and *"Stille Nacht."* They held each other's hands and placed dried fruits in each other's mouths. They went around in a circle, each passing to the one on her right. On the windowsill stood a vase with a few branches of spruce, filling the room with their scent. They were all on the verge of tears. Not one of them had received word from loved ones; not one of them knew what the future would bring. That night, Johanna's sobbing woke Gerta. Since the day Teresa and Ula had run away, the two of them had been sharing the garret room. Anni and Rudi slept under the bed, in the same place where Dorla used to sleep. Gerta took hold of her hand but said nothing. What could she say? She didn't know what would come next.

Behind the windowpanes, snowflakes fell through the darkness, enshrouding Perná in a blanket of white—that year the winter was harsh. Every day Gerta trod a path up the main street toward the church and the Rosenbaum homestead, which had now been converted from the administrative commission headquarters to the local National Committee. Every day, Hanák would be waiting for her in the kitchen, where she prepared his breakfast, and then together they went to his office, to work. Every day after the Angelus, she locked the front door and headed back to Zipfelová's cottage to rejoin the other women. Since November, their number had been reduced by half; some had disappeared while others had been transferred to the brickyard in Ratíškovice, just as Ida had predicted. With the decline in work came a decline in what little respect the residents of Perná showed them. Now they were only in the way. This was why no one went looking for Ula, or for Teresa, or for the many others who, during the months of September and October, had disappeared overnight—no one knew to where, and no one even knew if they had survived. Gerta, using a straight-edged ruler, simply crossed out the names of these Germans on the lists that the farmers would bring in for her to copy. She crossed off people who had been registered as workers and who had fled; old-timers who had vanished into thin air overnight, as well as those who had left on the first transport; and she noted those whose names were unknown, who had come to Perná that summer with neither papers nor relatives and had died there.

The parish office, which stood just three houses up from the Rosenbaum homestead, was where Gerta ended up spending many a winter afternoon. This was partly because of the district administrative commission index card catalog, which she was compiling using the parish book that Pastor Gmünd, an Austrian-born settler, gave her access to. But it was partly also because, since the death of Mrs. Führederová, the parish house duties had fallen to her. Finally, in November, this changed when Mrs. Hrazdírová, after losing her husband to old age, moved into the elder cottage on the Hrazdíra farm just steps away from the parish house. Her faith and zest for life still strong, she became the pastor's housekeeper. Even so, from time to time, Gerta gave her a hand with the cleaning.

How many dead had she and Gmünd counted by now? Nine women, who had arrived already sick with typhoid fever, and four children. They had picked up the infection in Pohořelice or maybe even in Ledce. Who could know what any of them had drunk along that miserable journey from Brno—they had already died back in June and July. She could no longer remember how many trips she and Schmidt made to that plundered pharmacy in Mikulov, or the military camp in Břeclav, before Dr. Karachielashvili finally succeeded in eradicating it. And then there were the dozen or so elderly people who had passed through Perná in early June on their way to Austria but didn't have the strength to go any farther.

A list of these unknowns, some of whom remained nameless because they didn't have any papers with them, still hung in Gmünd's kitchen, should anyone ever come to inquire. But who would come to inquire? Gerta privately wondered, thinking of all the solitary people marching in the column whose relatives had been irretrievably lost in the multitude of exiles. She recalled all the shouting and weeping at the crossroads beyond Mušov, where the mass of people, no longer supervised by Zbrojovka factory guards, flowed unchecked toward the Austrian border. Besides, how would it even be possible to find out the names of all those supine and suffering under the midday sun with no water, sick with dysentery or typhoid fever contracted in Pohořelice, dying like beasts? Nobody had helped them. On the outskirts of the villages she had occasionally seen a few soldiers or guards simply roll the dead bodies into the ditches along the roadsides and cover them with dirt in makeshift graves so shallow that dogs must have dug them back up in no time. Some of them, those who managed to drag themselves as far as Perná, had been lucky and now lay buried in paper bags along the cemetery wall. Some hadn't been so lucky and now lay in front of the wall. In this, Pastor Gmünd hadn't relented; those who had taken their own lives were to remain on the outside. And there had been more than a few of those, whose names had still needed to be crossed out during the summer. At the Krupas', it had been two women and a married couple. Supposedly everyone at the Krupas' knew what the latter two were planning; all they were missing was a rope. As soon as they got their hands on one, they hanged themselves, together, in Krupa's hayloft. And later on, there were a few more women who could no longer bear the rough treatment at the hands of the farmers. Finally, Gmünd ended up having to go over and have a talk with them. From among his flock, he allowed only a few to be buried in their family plots inside the village cemetery: Járinka Führederová, who had also hanged herself, and the Egerts, who, rather than waiting to be deported, had in their despair taken rat poison in advance of their transport. But not even they had anyone to nail together a coffin for them. So in the end, they, too, were laid to rest in paper bags.

Over the course of those months, Gerta witnessed very few happy endings. Josefína Reichertová was picked up by her sister and her brother-in-law. Antonia Ainingerová, along with her two children; Kristýna Kreuzová, who worked at the Krupas'; and Gabriela Etznerová, from the Lhotáks' were all allowed to return to Brno on the grounds of mistaken displacement, an appeal on behalf of which Gerta and Hanák had repeatedly telegraphed the Brno office of the Provincial National Committee until it was granted. One month later, in November, a letter arrived from Antonia, informing them of the dismal conditions they found in Brno upon their return. It had required Hanák's signature even though it had been addressed to Gerta, care of the district administrative commissioner's office. He stood over her as she read it, in turn nodding in agreement or smiling in amusement. Afterward, in her mind, Gerta went over it line by line, taking time with each sentence, as Antonia tried to answer the questions they had all been asking themselves during these past several months of isolation.

> *Dear Gerta, Johanna, Maria,*
> *and all my dear friends,*
> *I am writing to you in Czech, since my sister-in-law pointed out that letters in German, should they be intercepted, might not be delivered. For this reason, I'm relearning the language, which I haven't used in years. It's very hard and even harder for my children. But I'm sure you'll understand me. I'm writing to cheer you up, even though, I won't lie to you, things here are not the best. Brno is still very much in turmoil. New people are still arriving; they're either returning from the war or from concentration camps (those I'd rather not even write about), looking for a place to put down their roots. Even our house belongs to somebody else now, and although my Czech citizenship was ratified, and my Czech nationality confirmed, my children and I aren't going to get anything back, since, as you know, my husband was of German nationality, and as for the children, well, the German schools were closer. But I'm not about to complain, not*

while you, my dears, are still racking your brains over your own futures. This is also why I'm writing, so that you know what you'll be coming back to, should you wish and find a way to return. Brno is badly damaged; many buildings are demolished; many apartments are destroyed; and there's a shortage of space. And a shortage of work for those Germans who, for whatever reasons, remained in Brno. The only salaried jobs are for indispensable specialists. The rest of the German men work in labor camps, and if any of you have a loved one there, you should know that you have good cause to fear for them. I haven't been there, but my brother, with whom the children and I are living now, says the conditions are brutal. But what's encouraging is that it's no longer a matter of life or death in those camps. At least, what they say is that once they've worked them as hard as they can, they send them away from Brno with the Red Cross. For now, all the Germans remaining here have to wear armbands, like the ones we got in Perná, and they're not allowed to use the sidewalks or public transportation. More than once I've seen Germans being lynched, because the people of Brno still crave revenge. I'm living in Horní Heršpice now, Ober-Gerspitz, in case any of you want to come and find me once you get back. I'm helping my sister-in-law sew shirts and hope this way I can compensate them for the space my children and I are taking up. What will be next, I don't know. For all of you, I wish you as peaceful a time in Perná as possible. Hopefully the work is easing up, or maybe by now some of you have already left to join relatives in Austria or elsewhere. I wish you and your children the best of luck in your lives.

Antonia Ainingerová, Martin, and Rosa

As she read the letter to Johanna, Johanna began to cry. She was the one who most longed to return to Brno and to her husband, from whom she had been separated at the end of May, when he'd been taken away to the labor camp in Maloměřice. And what about Gerta, what did she actually want? She wanted to go home. She wanted her apartment, with its kitchen, and her mother inside it—her own bedroom, and the flowers they used to grow in the hallway. She wanted to believe that Friedrich would come home and that she would be reunited with Janinka. And with Karel. But their apartment was no longer hers. She couldn't go back to it. Nor could Friedrich, were he ever to return. Nor could her father, whom they would surely deport as soon as he had finished working off the mess he made in Brno. Gerta longed to go back to Brno where she felt at home, and she couldn't imagine going to live in some unfamiliar city full of strangers. But where in Brno would she go? And furthermore, now there was Barbora. Whom could she turn to? By the time she was expelled, it had already been a long time since she'd had any news of Janinka, and Karel could be anywhere. Not that he would help her, regardless; he certainly wouldn't have forgiven her yet. It was such a shame. They had grown so close, so incredibly and blissfully close. If only her father hadn't given her this gift of all gifts. She would never forget the expression on Karel's face when he realized why Gerta was growing fat.

So then why this great yearning to go back to Brno, when she had no idea where or even to whom she would turn? Gerta's eyes filled with tears. She looked down at herself, her hands with their withered skin, her skinny legs sticking out of the bulky shoes in which half a year ago she had arrived. Now she was nothing, just a body in the middle of an unfamiliar land. She was a nobody; she just worked here, as long as they allowed her to stay.

And as Gerta bent down to look at Barbora in her deep, infant's sleep, she realized that there was nothing she could do; there was no way she could fight back. She couldn't see a future. All she could see were the walls of the room where she was now sitting on the edge of the bed, all her strength gone. She was a human wreck who was grateful for a kind word from those who now owned her. Her and Barbora. And the worst of it? She felt indebted. Because unfathomable as it was, she felt that at Zipfelová's, nothing worse could ever happen to Barbora or to her. And if she could just let go of her expectations, reduce her needs to a bare minimum, stop concerning herself with how she had imagined her life would be, then perhaps she might even be happy here.

XXV

Toward dusk on Thursday, exactly three days after the New Year, Hubert Šenk stopped in to see Zipfelová. When he got to the cottage, he stomped the snow off his boots, brushed the snowflakes off his coat, then stepped inside, hung the coat up by the stove, and sank heavily down on the bench against the wall. He took off his hat and set it beside him.

"I've brought the paper," he said to old Zipfelová and to Ida, who welcomed him with a cup of chicory coffee in her hand.

"What does it say?" asked Ida.

"That the next transports are being delayed again. They don't have room for them in Germany," he said, motioning with his head toward the door behind which the German women had their room.

"What else does it say? What's going to happen now?" asked Ida.

"Maybe in the end, they're going to want them to stay right here?" Zipfelová narrowed her eyes pensively. "They must know that we don't have enough people to do the work."

"It says here that we do:

"*In total, approximately eight hundred thousand Germans have already left Czechoslovakia, and another seven hundred fifty thousand are to be deported to the Soviet occupation zone. Deportation to the American occupation zone has not yet been effectuated—it will be initiated as soon as Czechoslovakia meets the technical terms required by the Americans, namely that every German must carry an identity card. According to the plan, one hundred seventy-five thousand Germans will then be deported into this zone. Some one point six million Czechs have already relocated from the heartland to the border regions. This large number of Czechs offers a guarantee that the economic life of the border regions would not suffer catastrophic shortages even if the Germans were to leave all at once. According to the plan, however, the expulsion of the Germans is expected to take until July, so during this period, it will be possible to secure adequate replacements even for any German specialists.*

"I'd love to know where they came up with that," Šenk commented when he finished reading aloud from the paper. "*Wouldn't suffer catastrophic shortages?* They should take a look at Führeder's vineyard—*specialists*, they say," he muttered. "Or they should take a look at the Heinz fields. They always yielded such a big crop, and this year, there was barely half, and they didn't even manage to reap it in time. That's what those hacks should be looking at."

"May I have a look?" Ida leaned over the paper. "There, you see, they write about it too."

"What now?" Zipfelová asked tersely.

"About Hitler's son, haven't you heard?"

"And you heard it where?"

"Over the holidays, at the Krupas'. Mrs. Krupová was saying that Hitler had a son who escaped, and here they write about it. Listen," Ida said, taking the paper from Šenk.

"*From London. Special bulletin from the Reuters news agency correspondent in Nuremberg states: 'According to reports received, the Czechoslovak police have taken into custody a twelve-year-old boy in Bohemia who may be Hitler's son. Hitler's official photographer, Heinrich Hoffmann, when asked to identify the twelve-year-old boy whose photograph was found among Hitler's papers, answered that it was most likely Martin Bormann's son. Baldur von Schirach, who introduced Eva Braun to Hitler, claims that Eva Braun never had children of her own; she liked children, however, and often had her picture taken with Bormann's children.'*

"You see?" said Ida. "That's all we need, for that murderer to have had children."

"But they write that it was Bormann's son."

"But it's not certain. Supposedly, it's been written about in other places, not just the *Lidová demokracie* paper."

"And what do the Krupas read?"

"How should I know? *Slovo národa*? Or maybe she heard it on the radio. It must have been on the radio. They've been listening to it since the war."

"Well now"—Zipfelová shrugged—"as long as they can afford it. We were always used to minding our own business and our own animals first, and then that little bit of a field we have, and only then start worrying about others. To invest in a radio just for that, well, it never would have occurred to me or to my late husband. And Helmut never had time for it; he had people to take care of, as you know."

Ida turned and gave Šenk a wide-eyed look.

He cleared his throat. "All of us in the village know how much Helmut was needed. He would go wherever he was called."

Zipfelová gave him a hard look up and down.

"And he'll be needed again when he comes back," she declared, and turned her face to the wall above the kitchen stove.

Ida hung her head and stared down at the tabletop as silence filled the room. A heavy, awkward silence, during which tiny beads of sweat broke out at Ida's temples and Šenk's otherwise-steady hands trembled, making the pages of the newspaper rustle.

"So, what else do they write?" asked Zipfelová into the dead silence, her face still turned toward the stove tucked in the corner of the room next to the worktable.

Šenk lowered his head back to the paper. "Something about a Mr. Tylínek who died in Terezín."

"Hmm."

"And in Selly Oak, England, a twenty-one-year-old mother gave birth to a two-headed baby."

"What?" exclaimed Ida, horrified.

"*In the Selly Oak Hospital yesterday afternoon, the wife of an American soldier gave birth to a two-headed baby. At birth, the two-headed little girl weighed two point seven kilos. The attending doctors disclosed that the father of the child had returned to America back in July, and that the child had two heads on two necks, separated above the shoulders, and both were capable of drinking and crying, as each had a set of air passages and a pulse. The child will be x-rayed later today.*"

"That's horrible," gasped Ida. "Mother, can you imagine what would happen if I gave birth to a two-headed baby here in Perná?"

"Oh, hush," Zipfelová snapped back at her. "That doesn't happen to healthy women."

Ida shifted her feet underneath her chair. "But they do say things like that happen to older women, right? The ones who didn't manage to have their babies at the right time, when they were still young and full of strength, right?"

Zipfelová turned slowly toward her. "They do say that. Why?"

Ida just shrugged her shoulders.

"*It's extremely unlikely that the child will survive,*" Šenk read, finishing the article.

"Even if it did survive, what kind of a life would it have, poor little thing?" Ida said softly.

"And over the last half year, UNRRA has delivered four hundred thousand tons of goods worth approximately one hundred and fifty million dollars. My, my, my," Šenk said. "Listen to this.

"*The United Nations Relief and Rehabilitation Association, UNRRA for short, will carry on with its activities in Czechoslovakia in the year*

1946, in order to help the economy get back on track as quickly as possible. According to the plan, the UNRRA mission in Czechoslovakia will continue to import food, fuel, meat, breeding stock, cotton, and wool.

"I'd be really curious to know where all of that ended up. How many boxes did you say you got, Auntie?"

Zipfelová burst out laughing. "Well, seeing as back in August I still had a pig, I wouldn't have been eligible for one of their boxes, right? But the black-market woman stopped by with some things in the fall. Chocolate in particular. The children went wild for it, as you can imagine."

Šenk nodded and said, "It's mainly for the people in the cities."

"Oh well," Zipfelová said. "You may remember that woman who used to come around from Brno, always looking to barter for food, and how skinny she and her two girls had gotten. Why, they were worse off than we were out here in the country."

"That's for sure," Šenk said.

"You of all people have nothing to complain about."

"Do you hear me complaining?" he said, giving old Zipfelová a smile that spread a fan of hairline wrinkles around his blue eyes.

As for Ida's eyes, she couldn't take them off him.

"But one of those tractors that UNRRA is supposedly distributing would come in handy. There's one in Dunajovice. Then, come summer, we wouldn't have to go borrowing from Mikulov," he added.

"True, true," agreed Zipfelka, "but now, just to go back to it, seeing as we're all sitting here together like this. What are we going to do with them?"

Šenk cleared his throat. "I've been thinking it over for a long time."

He folded the newspaper into quarters and set it down with one side lined up along the edge of the table. Then he placed his clasped hands on top of it.

"I'm not going to send them away."

The tension in the room eased. Zipfelová let out a sigh of relief and smiled. Ida turned her gaze from Šenk to the old woman.

"I mean, not all of them," he continued. "The ones who want to go, for God's sake, let them go. I mean, any of those who are still here and haven't run away, but don't want to stay, we're not going to hold them back. But by now, they've had plenty of time to think it over, and if they still want to go, knowing that there's nothing good waiting out there for them, let them go. At least we'd be able to cross a few off."

"That'll be Edeltraud and Maria, those two for sure. And then a few of the ones who are in Ratíškovice now," said Ida.

"The ones over there will figure it out for themselves," said Šenk, "but for those who want to stay here, I'm going to vouch for them and say they're indispensable. After all, at the end of the day, I'm no brute."

Zipfelová advanced a few steps toward him and sat down on a chair by the table.

"You know, Hubert, I think you're doing the right thing. And although I know what went on in this Republic, and I myself have suffered the consequences with the loss of my own son, to say that women like Johanna or Hermína, or Ula or Teresa, or Gerta, are guilty—well, I don't think so. These here women are just as badly off as every other miserable wretch. Even worse. Now the war is over, and it took away from them, same as it took away from us, but for them it didn't bring any new hope. We at least can start to work on our properties now, and build ourselves back up. But for them, it's not over; they still have to work as punishment for things they didn't do. And they have absolutely no prospects. So to send them away, to some unknown place with small children on their hands, seems inhuman to me."

"That's because you've gotten used to having them around, Mother. I saw the way you cried when Ula, Dorla, and Teresa ran away. You don't want to lose those children."

Zipfelová looked at Ida reproachfully. "Don't forget, I don't have any others. But even so, I'd make peace with it. They're grown women;

they'll decide what's best for them. But notice that I talk about them as if they were people. To me, they've always been women with children too young to be blamed for anything, some had barely opened their eyes. But most of all, I treat them this way because of my faith, and that's something I'm not ashamed of. They're human beings just like we are. If they want to stay here where they feel at home, just like we do, they're welcome to stay. If they want to go, let them go."

"Human beings, yes," said Šenk. "According to the decrees, they may be human beings, but they're not citizens of this country, Auntie. You mustn't forget that. And until the Red Cross carts them away, they're supposed to be used for work, as we all know. And then the Republic needs to take advantage of those transports and get rid of them as soon as possible. That is to say, the ones who aren't specialists or indispensable. And a lot more of them are going to have to go than these Brno Germans, who are already half-expelled. The old-timers are going to have to go, too—the ones who haven't run away and are still waiting around, stuck in cramped rooms. Take the Krumpschmieds, for example. They'd certainly deserve to be allowed to stay here as specialists—after Führeder, where are you going to find a better vintner than Krumpschmied? And he was always an upstanding citizen. Yet, he may still have to go, because nobody's going to want to vouch for him. Much less so for our women, about whom we know nothing. What do we know about whose wives or daughters they were?"

"Even if one of them had been the wife of von Neurath himself, tell me what women like that, with young children, could possibly have done to be guilty?"

"Well, maybe just for providing the next generation of Aryans, Auntie."

"Oh, come on, enough of this nonsense. I was only joking—keep your feet on the ground. These here are ordinary women. If they weren't ordinary, they would've been gone long ago. They already would have flown the coop with all their loot. These are ordinary women who probably had no idea what was going on and stayed put at home, thinking that since they hadn't done anything to anyone, no one would do anything to them. But they were wrong, and now they're here. And to drive them even farther away, Hubert, well, that would be unchristian and shameful."

"That's exactly why I've decided to go and register them as indispensable. Tomorrow I'm taking them to see Hanák. Would you have another cup, Auntie?"

Ida leaped up, as if she'd been waiting this whole time for Šenk to ask, and made a beeline for the stove. She grabbed the hot pot with a dishcloth, brought it over, and poured the rest of the chicory coffee into his cup.

"I have to admit that I made the decision partly because I'm also human, and it really bothered me—the idea that it depended on me, whether they'd be put on a transport and sent across the border, ending up God knows where, and possibly victims of a fate I wouldn't wish on them, which here they might have been spared. Thank you, Ida. Besides, none of them have family over there, so they wouldn't have a place to live, and they wouldn't be able to find work. And then with those kids. Well, I didn't want it on my conscience. But it was also partly because I'm a practical farmer. For this reason, Auntie, I'd suggest that until they get their Czech citizenship, we leave things as they are. In exchange for their work, they'll get food and a roof over their heads. Right now, with those kids, that's the most important thing for them. And it will help me, too, because there's still plenty of work to do at my place."

"And what about housing?"

"I'll leave that to you, Auntie. Once the season begins, let's say starting February, I'd be able to help you. You don't have enough room for them here. Let's say they pair up, and the ones you don't have room for here can have a room at our farm. What do you say?"

Zipfelová looked relieved. No one was going to take away her little doves. It had almost killed her when she found out that Ula, Ula to whom she had devoted the most care, had skipped out, taking little Dorla with her. Who could really blame her? Who could blame a slave for wanting to be rid of her master? But how could Ula have thought that she, Zipfelová, would have tried to interfere, or wouldn't have let her leave? Was it possible that Ula had thought she might stand in her way? As a woman, she must have realized how Zipfelová felt about her. She thought of her as the daughter she never had. At the very least she, Ula, could have said goodbye. On the other hand, had she said goodbye, Zipfelová probably would have tried to discourage her from taking the risk. And then how could Ula have been certain that Ida wouldn't find out, and then from Ida, Hubert Šenk? Had Zipfelová found herself in the same situation, what would she have done? She would have held her tongue. The same as Ula. But still, she could have at least written a few words, gotten hold of some paper and a pencil, maybe from Gerta, and left her a farewell note. Never mind. In the end, Zipfelová knew they weren't her women. She didn't own them, and they weren't going to stay here forever. But those who just might want to stay forever she would help. She would help Gerta and Johanna; she would help Edeltraud and Maria; she would help Hermína, and should any of them wish to stay, they would be welcome. Her door was open to them, and there was enough work to do at Šenk's. In time, they could start to earn some money for it. She would look into that later on. And the little ones who called her Granny would also stay, and her cottage would be filled with humming and bustling—in place of a subdued, restrained serenity, there would be the cheerful prattle of children and women's chitchat. She would have something to live for until Helmut returned, and her life wouldn't be just about keeping the unhappy Ida in a cage.

"I agree. Even if Dr. Beneš and others might feel differently," said Zipfelová, pointing her index finger meaningfully up at the ceiling, as if toward heaven. "My feeling is that it's the right thing to do. We'll let them stay. The ones with the children can all stay with me. I've gotten used to keeping an eye on them during the day. The others, or anyone who wants to, can go to your place."

Šenk nodded.

"And one more thing."

Both of the younger faces turned to look at her.

"I'll go see Hanák and put in a request for the Krumpschmieds. They're indispensable to this village. After all, there's no better vintner around here now, isn't that so? I hope you'll support me."

Šenk smiled and gave a resolute, affirmative nod.

PART III

The City, "German-Free"

I

The sun sketched shadows on the wall of the opposite building, its oblique wintry rays crisscrossing the room. The windows had no curtains, draperies, or blinds; the piercing light poured in and ricocheted off the bare white walls. In the middle of the room stood a table with a worn tabletop, next to it a single chair with a flimsy back. Spread out on the table were all of their possessions. There wasn't much. A bundled comforter and several articles of clothing, either hand-me-downs that Gerta got from Ida, or things she'd managed to acquire over the past few years: two pairs of shoes, one for winter, one for summer, but not the rubber boots; those she'd left behind for Zipfelová—after all, what would she do with them in the city? And then Barbora's clothing: two little blouses, a pair of corduroy pants, a white shirt that had belonged to the little Lhoták girl, a picture book given to Barbora last Christmas. In addition, their scant toiletries, two loaves of bread, and a jar of lard that Zipfelová gave them to get them through the first few days, some silverware received as a gift, a purse with her identification papers, and a little bit of money. That was all they had.

In the empty apartment, every step, every audible movement, had its own distinct sound. Pushing the chair back from the table reverberated all the way to the ceiling. Every spoken word echoed against the peeling plaster of the walls and carried all the way back to the last room at the end of the hallway. Balls of dust and hair had accumulated in every corner. The walls of the three spacious rooms and the kitchen, to which scraps of torn wallpaper were still attached, suggested a well-to-do family. Who lived here before the war? Gerta wandered slowly from room to room and tried to remember. She was sure that the house next door was where Anička Goldová used to live, before she died on the sidewalk beneath her window. Even from the window of this room, her body with its contorted limbs must have been visible. On the street corner, which looked exactly as it had at the end of the war, fenced off and full of junk, used to stand Mr. Folla's newsstand, above which later a sign went up with the name "Konrad Kinkel." And just a little farther on, at the corner of Schöllergasse, now called Körnerova, was the house in which the Horns had lived. And then right across the street there used to be the fabric shop that had belonged to Mrs. Freibergová, the one whom Gerta had last seen with her daughter on the march of exiles. The daughter was just slightly older than Gerta, and they had been in middle school together. Even back then, she had been tough and mean, a perfect specimen of a League of German Girls *Mädel*. And among her schoolmates, she'd also been the one to pass around that rag, *Frauen Warte*, which described the proper way a German woman was supposed to dress and behave. Thinking back on it now, Gerta inwardly had to laugh. What an appalling fashion they had all rushed to emulate, herself included. She, too, had once worn a blouse embellished with Tyrolean embroidery, a dirndl, and white knee socks, of the kind that all Germans wore.

She remembered that they would often pass under the windows of this very house as they strolled up this street, then along Francouzská Street, all the way down to the park at Winterhollerplatz, today called 28 October Square, and then continue on to the Augarten, where they would promenade. Papa Friedrich with little Freddy in matching lederhosen. One bigger pair, with slightly longer trouser legs, and one smaller pair, with trouser legs that came just below Freddy's still-childish bottom, both wearing white woolen knee socks and sturdy hiking shoes, a white shirt and a hat. Two striding heroes, for whom a dazzling future lay ahead, and who one day would take part in ruling the world. And behind them came Gerta and her mother, the rearguard, treading upon soil already conquered by the braver and cleverer members of the regiment, happy and loyal subjects gazing with reverence and awe upon their mighty champions up ahead. Gerta remembered how back then she desperately longed to walk up front with them and be in the vanguard. So desperately, in fact, that she would forget about her mother. And it would then take her mother a long time before she was able to soothe the oppressive sense of blatant injustice that Gerta perceived in the white knee socks, which for some mystifying reason she didn't own. Had she owned a pair, she could have walked right up front alongside Friedrich and her father. Thinking back on it all now, Gerta found her mother's attempts to console her deeply moving. She remembered how on a day following one such walk, her mother had slipped her a little package at home containing a pair of blindingly white knee-high socks. Gerta pulled them on right away, wearing them until her father came home from the office that evening. When he saw her, he gave her mother a pat on the back, and a look of triumph spread over his face. That was when Gerta began to realize that her family had split into two camps. With that condescending smirk directed at her mother's downcast face, with which she was gazing lovingly at Gerta, eager to see her happy, he had given himself away. The white knee socks that she had so coveted and that were to have given her access to the world of her much-admired heroes suddenly began to burn her calves as if they had been knitted out of flames. At that moment, it dawned on her that the world of the elect would never include her mother. Gerta wore the knee socks just that once, and later that night cut a small hole into one of the heels, pulled the fabric apart as wide as she could, and watched with satisfaction as a run shot upward, leaving a wide unraveled line in its wake. Later on, when her mother sorrowfully asked Gerta if she wanted a new pair, Gerta said no. But that was all still before Gerta grasped that neither she nor her mother would ever be good enough for those two exalted Friedrichs. Then everything in their household changed, and Gerta could no longer remember their taking walks together. Except for that very last one, behind Mother's coffin.

Barbora jolted her out of her reverie, grabbing onto her thigh and rubbing her face into the coarse material of her skirt. If they were going to stay here tonight, she had to stanch the flow of memories flooding over her and get to work. She needed to seal the windows in at least one of the rooms, so that they would have a place to get settled and sleep without catching a cold. For now, that was all she was going to fix. Who knew how it would all still turn out. Karel might reappear tomorrow to tell her that, as a German, she wasn't entitled to an apartment after all—her case had simply been overlooked, and now she had to leave the Republic. And all of her efforts would have been wasted.

II

To get to Kuřim by train took almost a full hour. One hour to get there and one hour to get back. She should be grateful. Barbora had been accepted to a preschool, and Gerta had gotten a job. She had even been allocated the apartment. And she owed it all to Karel. Without his help, she wouldn't be leading this life. It was only the staggering salary deductions that not even he could do anything about. Plain and simple, Gerta Schnirch, now Schnirchová, was still German in nationality, even though Karel Němec of the Regional National Committee was looking out for her. Nevertheless, he apologized to her and kept running his fingers awkwardly through his short, wavy hair as he told her what her salary would be. She should have gone to work at the Zbrojovka

Arms Factory, as he had offered. There he could have had more of an influence, he said.

The Zbrojovka Arms Factory? The stupefied expression on her face implied that unless she had gone crazy, he surely had. The vision of a truck with the Zbrojovka logo on its side flashed through her mind, a group of juvenile boys jostling around in the back, dirty, dozing off, hungover, but still holding on to their weapons, their rifles erect, Medusa's enraged maw. With disgust she recalled individual faces, the pudgy one, who ordered her back to the marching column after the night in the barns near Pohořelice, or the one who had been shooting at the elderly Liebscher couple. She shuddered with revulsion as she thought of it. Shuddered at the mere idea of the factory, which, during the first month after the war, had coughed up so many pseudo-heroes, defenders of the homeland. Not one of them—if she remembered correctly, the subject had been hotly discussed all over Brno before the war ended—had undertaken to do a single thing. They had continued to work efficiently, going home to their mamas every night, and once a week receiving a very handsome paycheck. The salary they brought home from the Zbrojovka Arms Factory, where up to the very last minute they were busy assembling weapons piece by piece for the *Wehrmacht*, was more than anyone else in Brno earned. Klement Gottwald's appeals from Moscow calling for sabotage or a strike went unheeded; throughout all six years of the war, there hadn't been even a spark of resistance. Not one of them had lifted a finger, those heroes. They were all too busy licking the boots of their German bosses. And yet in the end, they got back at them for those premium paychecks, those generous food and cigarette rations, not to mention the company vacations that Zbrojovka employees were entitled to back then. Once the war was over, they paid them back good and proper. Once the purses of their German masters were empty, they wasted no time waging their own private little war. To a man, they wiped the collaborator's egg off their faces and, to cleanse their own consciences, made everyone bleed, and did so thoroughly, thought Gerta, so that everyone could see just who the Zbrojovka boys were. How could she go to work there now, among individuals in whose faces she might recognize the ones who shot at them, firing into the crowd of people as they were being expelled from the city? She couldn't forget how they beat the elderly to death when they could no longer walk, wrested from people anything they could grab, gold teeth, earrings, even their suitcases, leftover torsos of all they had once possessed. It wasn't yet that long ago. She refused to work at the Zbrojovka Arms Factory even if it meant that she would be locked up for social parasitism.

Karel looked embarrassed.

"It's not that easy to find you a job. I wanted you to do something that would be at your level. The Zbrojovka needs competent administrators."

Gerta had shaken her head in a flat refusal.

One month to the day after Barbora started attending the kindergarten behind the church in Zábrdovice, Gerta got on the train at the Židenice station and headed to Kuřim to start a job for unskilled laborers in a machine-tool factory. From that day on, every morning she made the long trek up through the town of Kuřim to the gate of the factory complex and punched in her time card exactly as the siren signaling the start of the workday went off.

She was assigned to a place next to a machine in Hall Nine, and her job, just like that of all the other women in overalls with red scarves tied around their heads, was to pick up a piece of metal and place it in a mold, piece after piece, time after time. The room droned with the noise of the machines and was lit by weak fluorescent-light tubes that stretched along the side walls of the cavernous space. At the wail of the siren signaling the end of each workday, she made her way to her locker, where affixed to the inside of the metal door was the first photograph she'd ever had taken of Barbora. Barbora at the age of five.

Day after day, Gerta picked her up, always the last child left in kindergarten, and Barbora would throw herself sobbing into her arms, while the kind teacher just sadly shook her head. But still, Gerta would tell herself, anything was better than having to look into the faces of those who amid shouts of "*Raus!*" had once chased her out of the city.

III

That short-lived period with Karel was the most beautiful time she had ever experienced in her life so far. Stolen bits of happiness, slivers of moments he would store up for her over the course of a day, flashes of bliss in his arms, all that had come back. She hadn't dared to hope it could ever happen again. But it did. And now almost two years had passed, two full and happy years since that sunny September day around noon, when she was getting ready to go out to the fields to help with the sowing of winter rye. She was just pulling the coarse material of her overalls up over her ankles when she heard Zipfelová calling for her from the yard. She quickly slipped into her still-warm rubber boots, threw a scarf over her shoulders, and ran outside. Squinting against the glare of the midday sun, she could barely make out the figure standing by the gate, so she brought her hand up to shade her forehead and peered again.

"Gerta, hurry up, now. Oh, there you are. You've got a visitor. He's from Brno."

"Thank you, Mrs. Zipfelová."

Gerta walked up to the stooped figure of old Zipfelová who was supporting herself on the picket fence. On the other side of it, on the grass, stood a gleaming blue car with the figure of a man leaning against it. Zipfelka straightened up from the fence and on her way back into the house gave Gerta a conspiratorial wink.

"What are you doing here?" said Gerta when she got to the fence. She leaned on it in the same spot where Zipfelová had stood and stayed put. Safely inside the yard behind the fence, a bird who had grown accustomed to its cage. He took notice.

"Are you going to stay behind that fence?"

Gerta gave a nervous laugh, shrugged, and slipped through the half-open gate to the outside. Karel held out his hand.

"It's nice to see you," he said, taking into both of his hands her right hand, which she had extended to him.

"Really?" A sarcastic smile flitted across Gerta's face.

"Really. Why, you're not happy to see me? After such a long time?"

"I never would've expected you."

Karel smiled and leaned back against the car.

"I look terrible, as you can see. All I do is work," she said, and with an apologetic gesture, indicated her work shirt and the overalls tucked inside her boots.

"I know. I expected as much."

Gerta felt pathetic, as pathetic as she had felt back then. Except even worse, because at that time she had at least been attractive. Now, she was standing here before him with a scarf over her shoulders in a work shirt and overalls, her rubber boots caked with mud and manure. A working machine that had long ago lost all traces of femininity. For the first time in five long years, she tried to see herself through another's eyes, and what she beheld was a disheveled woman from a cow barn, who woke up day after day, grateful for this demeaning job. A slave grown used to her shackles. A woman who might have been his wife. Who was he actually living with these days?

"You expected as much? How come?"

"I knew what you were doing. Shall we take a little walk?"

Gerta stood sheepishly fingering the ends of her scarf.

"I've got to get out to the field; they're waiting for me."

"We can go together. I can explain why you're late. They certainly won't mind if they hear it from me."

Gerta laughed out loud. "I'm not so sure about that."

She looked over at the gleaming car behind Karel, took in his elegant suit, and all of it together, along with the fact that he seemed surprisingly informed about her situation, was making her uncomfortable. She peeled herself away from the fence and set off alongside him in the direction of the most remote village houses. She kept quiet.

"Why did you stop working for the National Committee?" he asked abruptly.

She turned her head toward him and studied his profile. It hadn't changed, only hardened. She found him as attractive now as she had back then.

"I was classified as socially unreliable. After all, I'm still a German, right? Even though I'm a Czech citizen. Who knows what I might have committed in my official capacity." She laughed.

Her laughter sounded so unnatural, distorted. Even she was startled and fell silent. The bitterness settling deeper and deeper inside her could apparently break through even when she wasn't expecting it.

"How do you know that I used to work for the National Committee?"

Karel turned to face her. "Some papers you stenographed found their way into my hands. Speeches made by Šling and Životský, and even that atrocious transcription of Ďuriš's address."

Gerta burst out laughing again.

"Are you kidding? You call it an atrocious transcription? He's a gem, that minister of agriculture, Ďuriš. The ministry couldn't have picked a better speaker. They almost locked me up for that, in case you hadn't heard. That's when my social unreliability showed its true colors. After all, who but a displaced German woman would want to portray a Communist big shot in the worst possible light, right?"

Karel was nodding with an amused grin. "I heard, I heard. Supposedly, it was a big deal, and even the Ministry of Information came out to investigate."

"A full carload of them showed up and tried to put me away," Gerta affirmed sarcastically.

That late–Indian summer day two years ago came back to her. It was the first wine festival celebrating the Pálava grape harvest to be held at the foot of the ruins of the Orphan's Castle, where it was said that the Turners once also held their assemblies. The festival grounds were full of people. Children were milling among the adults who were sipping out of small wineglasses, blinded by the afternoon sun and deafened by the music blaring from the garland-festooned grandstand. Gerta was wearing new nylon stockings that she had recently received as a bonus for her lightning-fast transcriptions of speeches made by various political officials. She kept bending down to examine them, running her hand over their silky finish, unable to get enough of them. As if wearing them would allow her to step into a better time. Now, two years older, she couldn't help but laugh at her own naive expectations.

"I even made up a special symbol for that *yeah, right?* of his. He used it in every single sentence, and ended every sentence with it. His only coherent statement was when he turned Perná and its surroundings over to the folks from Moravian Hrozenkov and Halenkov as a thank-you for their efforts. The rest was all *yeah, right?*, and from the transcript, it was impossible to tell if he had actually said it or if I'd been trying to ridicule him. So they all showed up to check me out."

"But they couldn't find anything."

"They even brought along a stenographer from the Ministry of Information who confirmed that it was in the original transcript, and not just in the typed-up copy. And then he testified that he didn't believe that I had manipulated the speech, but that—and now get this—it was most likely an authentic transcript of the speech given by the minister of agriculture, who, furthermore, was commonly known as not the most, shall we say, gifted speaker."

They both laughed.

"I'm not sure why, but somehow it stuck to me after that, on top of the German thing. That Ďuriš business was tacked onto my file, which was marked *Not reliable for political assignments*, and then Hanák left, and when he did, so did I. The only option left for me here was to work in the fields."

The dry grass rustled under their feet. The air smelled of the wildflowers growing in the fields that had lain fallow that year. In the distance, the Pálava hills with the ruins of Děvičky Castle dominated the gently rolling landscape.

"How did those transcripts get into your hands?" asked Gerta.

"Through the Regional National Committee. I work for the Regional National Committee in Brno. I returned right after the war."

"I see."

"That's where I found out that they hadn't expelled you."

"But they had."

"Not out of the Republic."

"Not out of the Republic, but out of the city. Out of our home and out of my life. And that's how I've turned into what I am now. In the summer, I work out in the fields. Come winter, I'll be assigned back to the cow barns. They expelled me out of absolutely everything."

"Well, later on, that action was acknowledged to have been a mistake. You heard about that, right?"

"No one informed me, but I did hear about it. And then nothing more happened. Or did it? Is that why you're here?" She turned to him, cautiously expectant.

"I'm not sure what you mean. Everything is in order, at least officially speaking. The whole question of deportation was coordinated with the Red Cross, according to what was agreed on and signed at Potsdam, and it's been carried out more or less accordingly. The one mistake was that undisciplined action, but nobody could have prevented it after the war; it was the spirit of the time. You don't have to agree with what happened; after all, it was your skin. But from a global perspective, it was inevitable, even if it got off to a somewhat chaotic start."

"I don't know how much you know. But when it comes to what you refer to as 'the one mistake, that undisciplined action,' I was in the thick of it. And if everything is officially in order, then where, for example, is Helga? Or where is her child buried? Or what happened to the ones who ended up in Pohořelice, in that camp? Where are they buried? I remember them stacking dead bodies against a fence. I wouldn't call that everything being officially in order, would you? Some hundreds of people, if not thousands, didn't survive. And on that march, blindingly drunk teenage boys were shooting at us. I'm not sure one can simply call it a mistake, or just shrug one's shoulders and say it was done in the spirit of the time. I would have expected a little bit more."

"You're exaggerating. It wasn't that many, at most a hundred, maybe two hundred people. They died of dysentery. They obviously underestimated the sanitary conditions. Given how emotions were raging at the end of the war, my feeling is that it's a fairly negligible number. Podsedník conducted an inspection the very next day, and everything was quiet. It was just in Pohořelice that there were some sick people lying around."

"A hundred, maybe two hundred, who died of dysentery?" Gerta said, looking at Karel in surprise. "And what about the others? The ones by the road. There must have been at least fifty women they pulled out of that barn on the farm near Pohořelice, where those Romanian, or whatever soldiers they were, tore into us! How were those recorded? Also under 'dysentery'?"

Karel stopped short. "I'm so sorry. I didn't know about that. The official numbers, however—"

"Whoever wrote down the official numbers was probably not on the road walking from Brno to Austria that night and didn't stop in Pohořelice. I'm telling you what I saw, even though I can't give you an exact number. But thousands would definitely be more accurate than the hundred or so tallied up by some office clerk at his desk. I'll never forget those bodies. Back then, I almost kicked the bucket too."

Gerta was all worked up. They settled back into silence, walking slowly in the direction of Věstonice. From far away, they could hear the rumble of plowing tractors.

"Why did you come, Karel?" she said, breaking the silence.

For a moment, he didn't answer.

"I wanted to see how you were."

"So now you've seen what you wanted to see. Are you satisfied?"

"Would you like me to arrange for you to come back home?"

IV

Home. A city that barely resembled the one in which she used to live. Her home no longer existed. Her apartment belonged to someone else; her old street was missing entire buildings, not to mention residents. The shops she used to frequent had disappeared, as had their former owners. Of the old-time residents who used to live in her neighborhood, almost none were left. The few who remained no longer lived in their apartments. Caught up in the whirlwind of events, they took refuge among shabbier walls, because the best homes and apartments now belonged to the victors. The doorbell nameplates along Pressburger Straße, Schöllergasse, Köffillergasse, Sterngasse, Französische Straße, places that before and during the war she knew like the back of her hand, were either blank or bore the Czech names of new state-owned organizations. Apart from the Böhringers and the Bürgers, whom Jana Tvrdoňová had mentioned to her, and apart from Johanna, Antonia, and a few others whom she had met in southern Moravia, she didn't know of a single German Brno resident who remained. The change in Brno was palpable, and finally it was confirmed in print. Barely more than a thousand had stayed in the city, she read. A mere fraction of Brno's *Oberschicht*, the elite upper crust among whom, during the war, her father and Friedrich had proudly counted themselves.

"Everyone was there! There must have been some sixty thousand German hands saluting von Neurath. If only the two of you could appreciate the unity, the power of the Reich," her father had exclaimed back then in the hallway, just returned from a rally and all wound up, dazzled by the sheer volume of the crowd.

"Everyone. And so many fellow sympathizers! There must've been over a hundred thousand!" Friedrich made a gesture with his arms that seemed to indicate all of Adolf-Hitler-Platz before he and his father sequestered themselves in the dining room where they turned on the radio. Gerta always stayed at home with her mother; they simply didn't belong in that crowd.

And now, at the beginning of 1951, there were only some fifteen hundred of them left. Germans who hadn't turned themselves in, probably because they had no reason to feel ashamed, and who were so hung up on their heritage that they were prepared to suffer injustices for it and openly acknowledged their nationality even now. Like Johanna, for instance. But Gerta wasn't one of them, which was why, the year following her return to Brno, as she was filling out the endless pages of the first postwar census, she left blank the column where it said *other nationalities* and didn't count herself as German. She saw no reason not to take Karel's advice and checked off *nationality Czech* next to her and Barbora's names.

"Why would you want to complicate things? It's time to deal with reality and not make things harder for yourself. Besides, you always claimed you were a Czech. Like your mother. So go ahead and put it down," he'd said.

So Gerta did, although no one ever treated her like a Czech. Not during the war years in Brno, and not later in Perná, where she had been just a German, based on the first identity card she had been given that had already been filled out, no one having bothered to ask her any questions beforehand. On the *Residence Permit for Non-nationals*, which she had been granted in 1947, when an attempt had finally been made to differentiate between the last of those who were still to be deported and those who had been granted permission to stay in Perná, they had written *Gertruda Schnirchová, nationality German*, and the same for Barbora. In that way, once again, they emphasized to her that she didn't belong, and now here in Brno, it was no different, even though on her freshly issued identity card, her nationality was listed as Czech. Her first name would always give her away, even if it were to be followed by Němcová, as she would sometimes imagine with a certain sense of irony. At most, it might help Barbora. But as far as that was concerned, Gerta tried to make sure that not even her own last name could do her harm. It was largely because of her that she checked off *nationality Czech*, even though by now she no longer identified with it either. After those years in Perná, she felt stranded in a no-man's-land between nationalities, with a disjointed relationship to everything around her. Her world was confined to Karel and to Barbora, and to the walls of her new apartment, where politics couldn't harm her. At least for now, she said to herself, remembering how effortlessly the outside world had reached in behind the walls of her childhood bedroom back in 1945.

Barely over a thousand, she found herself repeating over and over, as she walked through the streets of Brno. Everywhere she went, she saw how the city had changed. The Germanic spirit was gone, along with the people, and could be detected only in details—on building facades, in the names of a few minor streets, in the Brno Hantec slang, or on the menu of their factory canteen. Pressburger Straße, now called Bratislavská, and its neighboring streets had, in the earliest days right after the war, quickly filled up with new Czech inhabitants. Now, six years later, a growing number of Roma were arriving from the surrounding regions and from Slovakia, gypsies who, whether they wanted it or not, were being resettled here as part of some crazy social plan. They were assigned to the yet again newly vacated apartments, which their short-term Czech tenants had fled for the new housing developments on the outskirts of town. But not everyone. Naturally, there were still some whom not even the postwar winds had managed to blow away.

One Sunday afternoon in May, she and Barbora were making their way down to the river. Walking along Sterngasse, which was now called Hvězdová, they passed right by the corner of the building in which Gerta had spent most of her life. She stopped under the plane trees that still spread their outstretched branches like a canopy over the small square. The square looked exactly the same as when she had last seen it, on that evening six years ago, when she had been forced to leave Brno. To this day, the buildings bore traces of the final years of the war. In the gray, dusty facades, there were still bullets embedded in the crumbling plaster, leaving behind tiny craters. Only the debris and rubble on one end of the square had long been cleared away. In its place sat an empty lot fenced off with barbed wire. The plot stretched halfway up the left side of Hvězdová and was now obviously being used as a garbage dump. Its uneven mounds were overgrown with tall grasses and lilac bushes, their fragrance these days filling the whole street, as well as with ash seedlings, whose tall, slim trunks were already shooting up. Their roots had forced their way undeterred even through the soil that was littered with shards of broken glass, old tires, and the metal frames of baby carriages and sofas whose outlines were disappearing beneath a sprawling tangle of morning glory vines.

Just as she was pointing out to Barbora where they used to live, the front door of the building opened, and a man wearing a long, loosely hanging, unbuttoned linen coat stepped out. He wore a hat and was carrying empty milk bottles in a yellow mesh bag. Gerta caught her breath. About to walk right past them was the caretaker, his indifferent gaze focused beyond her, on the side of the square with the empty lot. His glance fleetingly grazed past Gerta's face as he scanned the horizon from left to right, and then abruptly, in a horrified moment of recognition, he looked back at her. At once, he pulled his hat down lower over his forehead and quickened his step, disappearing behind her back, looking away in disgust toward the opposite side of the street. He pretended he hadn't seen her.

She felt like a louse. The memories of those last days in her apartment came flooding back to her: the unwashed bedclothes in his bedroom and the shallow, guttural grunts he emitted, signaling the end of each tawdry round of sex.

The new old Brno. The same city, and the same web of streets and memories connected to it. Except now it was *Deutschfrei*, German-free. Germans were no longer welcome. Not even those who were freshly minted as Czech nationals. For Gerta, Brno would never again feel warm and cozy, would never again be a place that felt like home.

V

He didn't know, but he could find out. In his position, it was possible. Her never-ending questions drove him to it, and as it turned out, the search for answers itself wasn't the hardest part. Keeping it from her was much harder. She didn't pressure him. She didn't even know that he had embarked on the quest. He hadn't promised her anything. At first, it was for no particular reason, just for himself that he tried to find out the truth. Had there been two hundred or a thousand? And what had happened to them?

He collected all the information he could find. He read the reports about the expulsion of the Brno Germans that had been written up by Louis Nissel and Willy Kapusta, the report from Pohořelice that had been presented on June 5 by the chief health officer, Dr. Julius

Mencl, and he spoke with Vladimír Matula, who had been chairman of the Central National Committee in Brno at the time. He was given access to everything: the minutes of the Central National Committee meetings, including private communications to Matula, even grievance letters in which civilians complained about the luxurious living and working conditions of Germans who even after the war refused to conduct themselves more modestly. He even sifted through the petitions from the Zbrojovka factory delegation led by Josef Kapoun, calling on Matula to expel the Germans, and Matula's letter to the National Security Guard issuing the order, a copy of which was also sent to Josef Babák, the chief of police. He had access to everything in terms of Brno's records. And the results as well.

During the last year of the war, there were reportedly 58,375 Germans living in the city, but how many of them disappeared during those final days of evacuation, when German defeat was imminent, nobody knew. Those who remained were assigned by decree to work in the labor camps on the outskirts of Brno; the rest were to be marched out of the city. Effective May 30, 1945, point of departure, the assembly place on Mendel Square. On the official National Security report, he found a note written in pencil, stating that due to the chaotic circumstances and the lack of any administrative apparatus, as well as due to the ongoing, uncontrolled transfer of the population, the data quantified in several of the paragraphs was being provided primarily for reference purposes. In the body of the report, it stated that on Mendel Square, 17,014 individuals were lined up into a marching column of exiles, mostly women, children, and people over the age of sixty, to which, as the group passed by Modřice and Heršpice, the National Security Guard added between two and two and a half thousand more individuals from the thirteenth police precinct, and finally another fifty from Líšeň. That same night, 853 men and boys fit for work were taken to the labor camp in Maloměřice, where they were thrown in with German prisoners of war and collaborators, of whom at the time there were approximately five thousand, dispersed among the various camps. Altogether, 575 individuals were declared unfit for deportation by a medical commission and were either left in St. Anne's University Hospital or permitted to remain in their homes. Of this total number, 1,226 individuals, on the basis of certified documents, were subsequently granted exemption from the so-called *Anti-German Measures* and were allowed to return to their homes. These were predominantly women and children from mixed marriages, and individuals who had been verified as having been anti-fascists. Karel personally recounted the results: 1,226.

He further determined that the march had been put into motion at ten o'clock at night and that the last members of the marching column left Mendel Square at five o'clock the next morning, all of them escorted by roughly three thousand Zbrojovka Arms Factory workers under the leadership of Josef Kapoun, and 125 men under the command of Staff Captain Bedřich Pokorný from the third military division. In the report submitted by the latter on June 2, 1945, he read that additional Germans being expelled from southern Moravia were integrated along the way into the column of expelled Brno Germans, so that the total number of expelled persons was estimated at about twenty-eight thousand, perhaps a few more. On the evening of June 1, the column, made up at this point of about one-third of the expelled Germans who hadn't yet crossed the border into Austria and were still marching, was stopped. Approximately seven thousand individuals ended up in the abandoned concentration camp near Pohořelice, of whom later fifteen hundred remained with farmers in Mušov, five hundred in Perná, six hundred in Věstonice, and eight hundred in Dunajovice, where they were given room and board and assigned to agricultural work, as per Ministry of the Interior orders.

Some of the notes suggested that three members of the march died along the way, victims of an unfortunate mishap during an uncoordinated discharge of warning shots. Subsequent deaths were recorded only in the Pohořelice camp, where some of the German refugees were sheltered in outbuildings beyond the town and succumbed either to dysentery or typhoid fever from having drunk contaminated water along the journey, or to marasmus senilis in cases of the elderly. There was no record of any other acts of violence, apart from the three accidental deaths, and no further documentation was available, because once the last of the refugees arrived in Pohořelice, the entire squadron of Zbrojovka workers returned to Brno. In time, some two thousand individuals followed them back, after it was proven that they had been expelled without justification, namely against the wording of Article 7.

To Karel, the official reports seemed plausible. Furthermore, he had already heard a thing or two about what had happened. From Podsedník, from Matula, and even from Otto Šling, who in the end criticized Zbrojovka for the organization's rash actions, something the arms factory leadership held against him for a long time. Back then, Germans simply could not be permitted to remain in Brno. Not while they were living in better apartments, holding better jobs, and eating from a limited food supply, even though the ration allowances had been immediately reversed during the earliest days of May. Brno couldn't afford to feed them back then as it was; there had been a proliferation of looting of German homes and murdering of German residents, and when they had tried to defend themselves, counterclaims had been filed against them. The Germans had to be removed from the city. At least for a time. Until first the international and then the local situations got sorted out, they needed to stay away. Preferably outside the city, somewhere in the countryside, supporting themselves in exchange for work. With any luck, if they wished, they would end up moving to Austria of their own accord. Agent Skalka, who was sitting in his office at the Central National Committee and had been a member of the Committee since the earliest postwar days, made broad gestures with his hands as he spoke, and it all seemed perfectly clear.

"And if every so often somebody would give them a kick, well, what would you have done, comrade, if you recognized people who'd knocked off your neighbor or, God forbid, a family member, huh? You know it yourself. After all, by then you were already back—those days you could practically cut the tension with a knife; that's how tangible it was. After six years of terror under Protectorate rule, those emotions needed an outlet, and they were supposed to flush away those years of humiliation. People were taking revenge for their own destroyed destinies, their own broken dreams. Naturally it was also a time for the riffraff. There were those who went on the rampage to improve their own prospects, or who saw an opportunity to get rich without worrying about consequences. During those first few days, it was hard to keep the mob in check. You witnessed it for yourself. Still, the important thing is that it happened. Just imagine if they'd stayed, and by now they'd be back to their scheming. Once was enough, wouldn't you say?"

Karel had been there, of course. But only as of the beginning of June, after returning from the Hostýn Mountains. He didn't know exactly when the Germans disappeared from Brno. And he hadn't paid attention. Anything to do with the past, with the Germans, he wanted out of his mind. Or he would have had to think about Gerta. He had other work to do; he was looking ahead. He joined the Regional National Committee and was a founding member of the Regional Committee of the Communist Party of Czechoslovakia, the KSČ, and back then, there had been so much to fight for. It was possible that, caught up in the middle of it all, he might have missed something, something that Gerta had experienced and that he had only been involved in from the other side.

When she talked about it, it was as if she were describing a completely different experience from the one that had found purchase in the consciousness of the rest of present-day Czech Brno. That one corresponded to the reports he read. And a thought occurred to him. He could compare those reports to what might still be found in Pohořelice.

He hadn't expected it, but they had sent him the complete *Register of Unusual Deaths for 1945*. Amazing, he thought to himself, the power of the proper rubber stamp. Also attached was a copy of the list of the interred that had been kept by the gravediggers Julius Hochman, Jan Kresa, and Jan Skala, who had been the ones to bury the bodies of the Germans from the Pohořelice camp in a field outside the town. They had divided them into five plots made up of thirty-four rows, in which 356 identified individuals and 97 individuals who remained unidentified had been buried. All told, a total of 453 people. Surprisingly, or perhaps unsurprisingly, that was already more than was reported in the classified files. More than the proverbial two hundred that seemed to be fixed in the mind of every witness who had ever talked about it. On the other hand, those who might have had something to say about it had already left Pohořelice on the day immediately following the expulsion.

Attached to the register was an original letter, in which it was noted that these records were acquired from the local gravediggers who had been charged with liquidating the bodies in the Pohořelice camp, now no longer patrolled by either the Revolutionary Guard or by soldiers, but left under the supervision of two doctors who had been dispatched from Brno. The last interments took place on July 18, 1945, after the camp had already been dissolved. The *Register of Unusual Deaths* also contained death certificates for the deceased. As Karel leafed through them, he noticed that they all listed the same cause of death. Dysentery. Dysentery and marasmus senilis, or progressive atrophy of the aged. Dysentery and marasmus senilis. Ten times over, twenty times over, four hundred times over. The death certificates were all the same. Even for women born in the 1920s. Even for children. *Dysentery and marasmus senilis*. What kind of nonsense was this? He requested the death registers from the nearby villages. They all looked the same; the only variation was in the number of identified and unidentified deceased. *Dysentery and marasmus senilis*.

"But you know, seeing as you're so interested, we've also got a few foreign documents on file, but you'll need permission, permission from up top," Skalka mentioned one day as Karel was returning some National Committee records from 1945 that he had borrowed.

"They're mostly in German; some are in English. They were sent over here in forty-seven. Seem to be reports from the other side," he added, peering at Karel over the rims of his thick glasses.

It took him almost two months to get his hands on those materials. Skalka brought him a folder with two pages of a typed translation, the original text of which remained in the archive.

"Here's all they gave me. As I was saying, it's highly confidential, but these are some excerpts, and from what I could see, taking a peek, it's a bunch of drivel. The guy is nuts. Same as when he was the deputy here."

Skalka handed Karel the excerpts from a *Petition to the General Secretary of the United Nations*, put forward by a delegation of Sudeten German Social Democrats in Great Britain, and written and signed by Wenzel Jaksch.

It was ludicrous. What kind of intelligence had he had, allowing him to write that fifty thousand people had been placed in concentration camps on the outskirts of the city? Where on earth had he gotten the information that along the way from Brno to "Pohořelce"—even the name of the town was misspelled—four thousand people died? Where had he found out that in the district of Muschelberg, which hadn't even been mentioned in any of the Brno reports, eight hundred had been buried? How could he maintain that another five thousand had been lying along the way or just on the other side of the border? Karel was stunned as he read the account.

In the vicinity of Brno alone, there were many mutilated corpses of people who had been for the most part either dragged, beaten, or tortured to death; or shot in the back of the head. Furthermore, thousands died in Pohořelice. According to very conservative estimates, approximately ten thousand people died during the march.

Karel found it absurd. During the last few days of the war, there hadn't even been fifty thousand left in Brno; a good half of them had disappeared across the border. After all, what reason did they have to stay? Indignant, he snapped the folder shut and gave it back to Skalka.

"Typical West. Pure garbage and misinterpretation," he said.

"What did I tell you? Not even worth having the whole thing translated, right? A little is enough to turn your stomach. But then again, what would you expect from a German, right?"

Karel thought the same. It had to be something like that. He didn't trust the West either. But Gerta? Could he trust her? When she woke up in the middle of the night, soaked in sweat, terrified that they had taken Barbora away from her, that they had taken him away from her, that they were again doing to her the same things they had done to her before? He wasn't sure. Maybe better not to. He himself knew the tricks memory could play on such experiences. He had his own share of nightmares from his days in the resistance with the partisans. Over time, memories like that, like it or not, had a tendency to become more exaggerated and fantastical.

It was only those death certificates—they didn't seem right. It occurred to him that he could request to have the death registers sent to him from the other side, from Austria.

VI

It was following a meeting one late afternoon that Pešek, the deputy chairman of the Regional National Committee, came over to him and put his arm around his shoulders.

"I've been hearing, comrade, that you're interested in the German expulsions."

Karel nodded.

"That wouldn't be because of your, er, shall we call her 'friend'?"

That he hadn't expected. He was under the impression that no one knew about him and Gerta. Taken aback, he shook his head.

"Well, comrade, should you have any questions, let's discuss them together. What exactly is it about that episode that you find so fascinating? By now, it's a closed chapter that's already been processed by history, isn't it? So what makes you want to revisit it?"

Karel wasn't prepared or in the mood to explain himself. But Pešek wasn't someone he could just dismiss.

"I'm interested in how the expulsion was carried out and what the death toll was. If it was ever clarified," he said.

"Are you looking for someone in particular, comrade?"

"No. No one in particular. I just find it interesting. As you recall, comrade, I wasn't yet back at the end of May. I was still in Hostýn. So . . . just to have a general idea."

Pešek, his hand still on Karel's shoulder, applied a gentle pressure and steered him in the direction of his office. They passed by the cubicle of the secretary who had gone for the day, and then Pešek opened the door for Karel and showed him in first. He motioned with his hand to a low settee, set his leather briefcase down at the foot of the coatrack, and sat down facing him.

"Cigarette?"

Karel gave a nod.

"It's like this, comrade. It landed on my desk the minute you asked for that Jaksch file. Interesting reading, right? The guy's crazy, right? A megalomaniac. And a miserable bastard too. Point is, he lies."

Karel struck a match, lit up, and sucked the smoke deep down into his lungs.

"I noticed the statistical figures weren't correct. Already just the number of German residents here during liberation."

"Exactly," Pešek said, nodding affirmatively, "and that holds true for almost everything in that report. Look here, comrade, as far as this business goes, you've already gotten yourself in pretty deep, wouldn't you say? What have you found out?"

For a moment, Karel was silent. Then he said, "It's a thorny subject, comrade. The reports paint a pretty clear picture: the situation in Brno was no longer tenable; the Czech civilian population was up in arms against the German one; there was looting, and there was murder. It was a turbulent time, as we all remember. I didn't get back here until close to the end, but no one had to explain to me what it was like—after all, I wasn't that far away."

Pešek listened, holding his cigarette straight up, the smoke rising higher and swirling around his head. "There's been quite a lot said, comrade, about your accomplishments."

"The expulsion of the Germans, at least for a time, was unavoidable. Already just because of the food shortage. And many other factors too. According to all the reports, it was carried out quickly and cleanly. The accounts don't hint at any complications. Up until the outbreaks of dysentery and typhoid fever in Pohořelice. That's what's so strange. I remember the first editorials to appear in the papers, in *Rovnost*, that condemned the march for being disorganized, chaotic, inhumane, and, above all, violent. Yet in all the reports I read, there wasn't even the slightest mention of that."

Pešek stared at him fixedly.

"And then the situation in Pohořelice. There's not much information in our archive about the number of deaths. It only goes through the first few days of June. It seems as if no one around here looked into it any further. But the death records in Pohořelice go all the way through the end of July. In the material we have here, there's not a word about how many of them there actually were. Just more marginal notes indicating that it was impossible to obtain exact figures. According to the Pohořelice register, which was never made public, the number was close to five hundred people, there alone."

"What did they send you from Mikulov?" asked Pešek deliberately.

Karel was surprised that he was aware of the request. Had they been monitoring him? Had someone reported him?

"They sent me the registers from Austria. I took the liberty of submitting an official request."

Karel placed his cigarette on the ashtray, opened the bag that sat by his feet, pulled out a notebook, and thumbed through it until he got to the page he was looking for.

"Listen to this, comrade. This whole business didn't end in Pohořelice. As people straggled on, they dragged that dysentery and typhoid fever with them. They were exhausted and dropped like flies into ditches along the roads, where in the end they were just covered up with a bit of dirt. In the local chronicles, from which they sent me excerpts, they occasionally list the numbers of deceased. Most of them without names, unless they had identification papers. In the field behind the Mikulov customs house, that last stretch before Drasenhofen, there were one hundred eighty-six. Back then, nobody even knew whose responsibility it was to bury them. Let's see, what else did they send me from Austria: Poysdorf, one hundred twenty-two buried; Steinebrunn, fifty-five; Wetzelsdorf, fifteen; Erdberg, eighty-two; Wilfersdorf, thirty-two buried; Mistelbach, one hundred sixty-five buried; Bad Pirawarth, fifteen; Stammersdorf, one hundred ten; Purkersdorf, one hundred eighty-five buried; Hollabrunn, sixty-nine buried. Obviously, one could go on counting from village to village. That's what they sent me from Austria. And let me tell you, the bureaucracy was a nightmare—it took forever."

With an amused smile, Pešek blew out a cloud of smoke and, turning to look out of the window, said, "Well, well, comrade, and you didn't find any of this in our reports, huh?"

Karel shook his head. "There are no sum totals listed anywhere. At least, not in the reports I was able to see. For that matter, when I finally did manage to get hold of something, and that was just for Pohořelice, the death certificates all looked exactly the same. It almost looked . . . manipulated."

Pešek gave a terse laugh. Karel had the feeling that it was the smug laughter of someone who knew more than he did.

"You know, comrade, not everybody's got a brain like yours. Out in the country, you get a lot of simple people."

"What do you mean, comrade?" asked Karel quietly.

"Comrade. You're one of us; it goes without saying that we trust you. But there are many others out there who need to be called into question. The reason you were able to get all that information is precisely because you have our trust. Your party profile is pristine. And furthermore, we need specialists, and if this subject is of interest to you, even though it's outside your purview, why not. As I said, comrade: you, we trust."

"Of course," replied Karel. After all, why wouldn't they?

Pešek settled himself deeper into his chair and crossed one leg over the other.

"Now, I'm going to tell you something. This German question is extremely, and I mean extremely, sensitive. I know that, and surely you know it, too, even though you weren't right here when it all happened. Still, you experienced Brno just after the war—why, you remember it well. That period demanded solutions. Another cigarette?"

Karel reached over. Although at first he hadn't felt like talking to Pešek, he now had the gratifying feeling that he was being brought into the inner circle of a conspiracy, which was what Pešek, his eyes still narrowed, seemed to be implying. *He's actually an agreeable person,* Karel thought, at the same time dismissing all those who went around spreading nasty rumors behind Pešek's back.

"There was no quick and elegant solution to be had," Pešek went on. "Not with a crowd of some twenty thousand people who owned property here and were scrambling to hold on to it. Some were entitled to it, and that was later acknowledged. But try to sort that out when you've got three thousand Zbrojovka men breathing down your neck, ready to jump into action. And I'll tell you, the only order they got was to carry out what was in the decree. All they were supposed to do was to march them out. As for how, that was up to Kapoun. But try to keep two packs like that under control. There were still plenty of weapons lying around. And plenty of schnapps, too, as became obvious. Comrade, seeing as you're to be trusted and already know a thing or two about what happened, I'll tell you this. Official reports are one thing. A necessity. Reality, it appears, is something a little bit different. You have to acknowledge that yourself; after all, you were in the resistance. Plans and their execution—sometimes they just don't add up. And that was also the case here. What exactly went on during that expulsion, only the head of each section knows. But one thing's for sure. Even if something did happen out there, nobody—I repeat, nobody—is ever to find out about it. Do you know why, comrade?"

Karel shook his head.

"Because at that time, it wasn't about individuals. It wasn't about some wounded German or even about an epidemic. Pohořelice was no tragedy compared to the havoc that they, the Nazis, wrought here over the course of those previous six years. It was about something else, comrade, something that you will surely appreciate. It was about our fledgling Republic. Do you understand?"

Pešek slowly leaned forward. He raised his eyebrows slightly and fixed Karel with an inquiring look.

"We couldn't permit ourselves any scandal. Absolutely none."

Karel was silent for a moment until he asked, "And those death certificates from Pohořelice?"

Pešek rocked back in his chair, steepled his fingers, and held them right up to his chin.

"Comrade, you're young and engaged. We need people like you now. And such people need to have a proper understanding of what they're dealing with. A lot of people died out there, and I can sincerely say to you, I am sorry. About the whole march and the epidemics that drove those miserable wretches into the ground. But there's nothing to be done about it; that was their destiny, and we all have one. Old dead people or sick dead people, that's what you had there. The examinations were carried out by competent doctors. Believe me."

Karel was rubbing his chin. This was about the Republic, first and foremost, he repeated to himself.

"As for this conversation, comrade, consider it confidential," came the sound of Pešek's voice again. "The only thing that's going to come out of it is a memo you're going to write me, letting me know that you're turning over those papers, the ones you got from Austria. And you're going to enclose the original documents with that memo, do you understand, and not make any copies. You're clever enough to know what to write, aren't you, comrade? Surely this isn't the first time that you've had to look at a problem from both sides, right? Recognize that this is about our reputation, which ranks even above that friend of yours. That is, if she was your motive for getting into all this."

Karel got nervous.

"For that matter, we're very pleased to know what close ties you have to the German minority. If anything were to happen, you know it would be up to you to intervene. The point is that since they've ended up staying, they have to blend in at any cost with the mainstream. Do you understand, comrade? That's what we're interested in seeing. To go back now and start poking around Pohořelice all over again, well, that's not going to help anyone anymore. I repeat, not anyone. We knew it back then, and we know it even today."

Karel ran his hand over his forehead, wiping off tiny beads of sweat.

"What are the official numbers?" he then asked quietly.

Pešek smiled, struck a match, and held it burning for a long time in front of his fresh cigarette.

"As I said, it's not going to help anyone anymore. So, we know that there are . . . How many did you say were buried there?"

"In Pohořelice, it seems there were about five hundred. I mean, that's how many death certificates there were with a diagnosis of disease, but . . ."

"So about five hundred, who died of dysentery, typhoid fever, and old age. That's it. And the ones on the other side of the border, those we don't care about anymore. And that's how it's going to stay. Understood, comrade?"

Karel nodded.

VII

Everything, everything goes. Slowly but surely. Bit by bit, we all move it along, collectively. Last year there had still been strikes leading up to Christmas. *Deprive the workers of their livelihood and they'll make mincemeat out of you.* Who wouldn't know that? Everyone had expected it, he thought. It surprised no one. What did surprise them was that it had come from the outside, that it had been reported in a radio broadcast from Paris. This they hadn't expected. But now that they were aware, they'd be that much more vigilant, knowing there were informers among them. Traitors. The Republic needed to protect itself. It was still in its infancy. Its people weren't yet prepared to accept collective thinking, to take responsibility for the common good. This was what Pešek had been trying to tell him, that there existed reasons why certain things needed to be kept secret. People weren't ready to hear them yet; they wouldn't understand. They were still afflicted by the war, unsettled, afraid to trust, and feathering their nests as best as they could. Their own nests. And who could blame them? When even the leaders had failed? Slánský and Clementis, or even Šling. He had evaporated like steam. They finally caught him in Prague, just as he was about to leave the country. A few years earlier, he had been the most powerful man in Moravia, Otto Schlesinger, postwar alias Otto Šling, the Communist Party's regional secretary in Brno. And what a clique was then uncovered in their wake. They were all part of it, mired in a swamp of greed— the speaker of the Regional National Committee, Svitavský; the head of the Culture and Propaganda Department, Kudílková-Blochová; and all their entourage. Pigs in the highest positions. Even he, Karel, had trusted them, so slyly had they masterminded everything. Before they were ratted out. Take Slánský, for example. Slánský's writings appeared on the shelves in bookshops just one week before the news broke. So who could blame the common men from the Zbrojovka Arms Factory, or from Zetor Tractors, or Královopolská Engineering, when they saw how unscrupulously the very individuals, to whose hands they had entrusted themselves, were ready to sell out to anti-nationalist elements? When they saw that there were arrests being made even within the ranks of State Security; that even those who were supposed to be the moral pillars of the nation were accepting bribes of twenty thousand crowns for taking reactionaries across the border? At a time like this, when food was still being rationed? Last Christmas, people had been putting gifts of food under each other's trees. A tin of sardines cost two hundred crowns; a ham, five hundred. And yet, the ones in whom they had placed their trust were cashing in tens of thousands from reactionaries and capitalist pigs.

Karel found it infuriating. If only the state apparatus weren't so full of weak individuals. If only he were surrounded not by these profit seekers but by people who respected the rules, people who could see beyond their own pockets and embraced the collective ideal, things could really move ahead. Significantly. But even though things were moving along, there were still plenty of those around who were without a conscience.

Or who, somewhere along their way up the ladder, had lost it. And all of this was happening now, just as things were changing for the better. Now, just as even Karel was finally beginning to get back some of what, over the past seven years, he had invested in the party.

It was true that the other day he and Gerta had shared a good laugh over the paper as they read excerpts from Jan Drda's latest novel. How did it go?

Comrades are dying, but the idea continues, alive, immortal! You'll see, your children will already be living in socialism. In the Soviet Union, they're opening new factories, new mines; they're building colossal dams and hydroelectric power plants. We must look to them, to the Soviets, to learn.

Gerta had laughed so hard at this dialogue between two milkmaids that tears had streamed down her face. It was true that such pathos generally did more harm than good to the common cause. Even Karel himself made fun of it a few times, although he would have preferred not to. In fact, he would have preferred that instead of paying attention to such cheerleaders, people would lend an ear to serious journalists who possessed a sense of moderation. Not those who, in a rush of exuberance or self-interest, tried to out-do one another, and in so doing devalued the very means intended to strengthen the socialist state. Karel knew moderation and respected the rules. He saw the direction in which things should be moving and what still needed to be done for Brno and for the Republic. For the past seven years, he had lived for the cause as no one else in his circle. Not even Josef and Radovan with whom he had run off to Hostýn toward the end of the war to join the Jan Žižka partisan brigade—not even they were still as engaged as Karel was. He understood why, naturally. If earlier on he had acquired a taste for shared evenings, for Sunday excursions, or for those brief moments when he stole away from meetings to be with Gerta, then perhaps by now he, too, might be less engaged. Perhaps. If toward the end of the war he hadn't found out that Gerta was pregnant, perhaps he never would have run away at all. If she hadn't gotten tangled up with whoever it was behind his back—God, how could she have done that to him?—he still would have been prepared to marry her after the war, on the spot if necessary, just so that she wouldn't have had to leave. And then everything would have been different. The truth was, he had never forgiven her. She had destroyed his future, which he had envisioned so clearly and which had made him so happy. She derailed him from the course he had charted for his life, in which she was to have played a major part. And the sudden upheaval she caused was also to blame for the situation in which they now found themselves. It had taken years for him to be able to trust anyone again. It would have been easy for him to find her through the district administration. And he easily could have intervened. Had he wanted to, by the fall, she could have been back home, on Sterngasse, that was to say Hvězdová—there would have been no need to reallocate their apartment. But for a long time, he found it impossible to forgive her for having someone else's child. The decision to bring her back he regarded merely as one of several options that might grant him some relief. That might bring back the light, which continued to emanate from their past, from a time when they were both barely twenty—a light he found himself craving to rekindle, to see if it might help him. So he gave it a try, without much enthusiasm and with minimal expectations. He gave it a try because at the time, he was prepared to try anything. And it worked. It worked so well that he had finally stopped obsessively scrutinizing Barbora's features and, after his committee meetings, he no longer went straight home.

VIII

Uncle Karel. Every time I say it, I feel like there's a butterfly fluttering in my throat. It's been like that from the beginning, since the first time I saw him. He was gorgeous, tall, and he came to pick me and Mom up in a big blue car, like I'd never seen before. He came and took the bundle that Granny Zipfelová had packed for us out of Mom's hand, put it in the trunk of the car, and when we were finally done saying goodbye to Granny, held the car door open for Mom—held it open for me, too— and had us sit on the soft seats inside that car and drove away with us, to a big city where I'd never been before, but that Mom had told me a lot about. She said it was big and beautiful and that lots of nice people lived there, but it must've changed or something, because I never saw anything beautiful there, just gray streets with big beaten-up buildings, not even a tree anywhere, and it smelled pretty bad. Even Mom looked disappointed. I guess she couldn't find those nice people she used to talk about, because the only person we ever seemed to see was Uncle Karel. I liked him a lot; I did, except at the beginning I was still kind of sad. A little bit because of the dumb kids in kindergarten, but mainly because of Granny Zipfelová—I missed her real bad. I had no idea we could exist without her, that it was even possible, since my whole life she'd been the head of our family. For as long as I can remember, we always did exactly what she said, me, Mom, Auntie Hermína, and before that, even all the other aunties who lived with us in the house, and all of their kids, who were like my brothers and sisters. That's how it was, Granny Zipfelová and Auntie Ida, who was always buzzing around and used to wear white petticoats under her skirt. They'd take care of us when our moms were at work. I remember our yard, where we all used to run around, me, Auntie Marie's Jan, Auntie Edeltraud's Katty, and Anni and Rudi who were Auntie Johanna's kids and had that funny last name, Polivka, which means *soup*. Back then, Auntie Hermína was still with us, and Auntie Teresa, too, with her knocked-out front tooth, but she left us pretty soon, same as Auntie Ula, whom the kids used to call "Antula," and Dorla, but actually them two I don't remember, Anni just told me about them. We were a really great family, I mean back when we were still all together, before Auntie Marie, Auntie Edeltraud, and Auntie Johanna with her kids all left, and I have to say I missed them real bad, too, especially Anni and Rudi. Maybe even worse than I missed Granny Zipfelová after Uncle Karel brought us to Brno. Yeah, I'd say definitely worse, because you couldn't do the kind of stuff we kids did together with Granny Zipfelová, and I still remember the things we did, because they were really funny. Like when we gave the chickens swimming lessons. I don't know what we were thinking. Nobody was watching us, because the yard was small, and there was really no place we could get hurt, so we did different things, even things that now seem totally dumb. Like with those chicks. Someone was saying that those little yellow chicks running around the courtyard were jealous of the baby geese because they knew how to swim, and they wanted to chase them around on the pond and stuff, but they didn't know how. Jan said that he already knew how to swim, and that we should help him teach them. But really, he had no clue; he was full of hot air when he said it back then. I don't remember us ever going to a pond. And I doubt Auntie Marie would have taken him on her own. Our moms did everything together. And I don't think they would have just taught Jan, when Anni and Rudi could easily have learned how to swim too. And besides, if my mom didn't know how to swim, I bet Auntie Marie didn't know how to either, and if she didn't know, then there was no way she could have taught Jan, right? But we taught the chicks anyway. We picked them up, one by one, and tossed them into the aluminum rain barrel that collected the water that came out of the gutter. Next to it was a pile of wooden boards. I remember climbing up that pile of boards, holding a little chick in my fist, and because I was clumsy, I kept having to lean on that fist for balance. So I'm not sure if it was already dead when I was holding it, or just when it went into the water, but at any rate, it didn't swim. It just sort of floated on the water but didn't move. I guess by the end, there were lots of limp little yellow chicks floating around on the surface of the water inside that barrel. Rudi still tried to get their claws to move, and I poked at them with a stick. The whole thing seemed a bit weird. I remember that when I'd poke them, some would go under and then pop back up. We were excited to see that some of them were already learning how to dive, but pretty soon they all sank to the bottom, and the fun was over. We stood around the barrel, looking at each other, totally confused. But the next day, when Granny Zipfelová was going around looking for them, the chicks showed up again, bloated and stinky on the surface of the water in that barrel, and me and Anni and Rudi and Jan got a terrible beating, which was how we figured out that we must have done something pretty stupid. It was my first beating ever, and Aunt Ida told us that the belt belonged to Uncle Helmut who'd disappeared—who had fallen on the front lines. I didn't know the first thing about it, but from then on, I was terrified of Uncle Helmut, because a beating with his belt hurt like hell; our butts stung for a good long time. I still remember it real well, because afterward, whenever I'd get it, I could pretty much predict for how long it was going to hurt. Uncle Helmut became a big bogeyman for me, although I never laid eyes on him. And maybe that's exactly why—the less I knew about him, the bigger and scarier he became. Aunt Ida and Granny Zipfelová both used to say he was a hero, but he must have also been pretty mean, to allow his belt to be used to give kids a beating. I can't even remember if Mom tried to comfort me that time, but most likely she just said something like those chicks belonged to Granny Zipfelová and Aunt Ida, and now they're dead, and that's why we got spanked. That's how I understood it, anyway, and she probably even agreed with it a little bit, but still, it hurt like hell, especially since no one felt sorry for us.

I caught a beating a few more times, that's for sure. Like when Anni and Rudi and me climbed up on the roof of the house and threw flowers down Granny Zipfelová's chimney to make her happy, or when we left the courtyard to go visit our moms in the fields and got lost on the road to Mikulov. But that time it wasn't Aunt Ida who gave us the beating; by then she'd moved in with Uncle Šenk on his farm, so it was Granny Zipfelová who used the belt on us one last time, and I think it gave her a lot less satisfaction than when Aunt Ida used to let us have it.

I may not remember that much, but I definitely know that we were a family and that I really liked it there. Even sleeping in the same room with the Polivkas, where there was just one big bed for the moms, and then blankets on the floor where Anni and Rudi and me used to sleep. I remember all the good smells and how there were so many things we could do, at least before Katty, Jan, and then in the end even the Polivkas left. Later on, we were just me, my mom, Auntie Hermína, and Granny Zipfelová. I was the last one left of all the kids and had only Granny's dogs to play with. Mom and Granny never let me go out to play with the village kids, not that they wanted to play with me anyway; the most they'd do was curse me out, calling me Hitler's bastard. If it hadn't been for me dreaming about leaving there and moving into a big apartment with a kitchen that would be twice the size of Granny's, with a round, removable inset sink, as well as a real toilet instead of Granny's latrine, and a bathroom, which I'd never seen in my life, then seriously, back then I'd have thought it was all over, that I'd spend the rest of my life alone with the dogs and never have any friends again. But those dreams kept me going the whole time, and then they even came true. Uncle Karel came to get us, and when we finally got settled in that apartment where he dropped us off, and that I'd always been dreaming about, we went to pay our very first visit, and it was to see the Polivkas. By some miracle, Mom had managed to track them down, and you can't imagine how unbelievably happy I was to see Anni and Rudi again. After that, I almost stopped feeling homesick, although to this day, I sometimes still close my eyes and imagine that I'm running through that sweet-smelling meadow behind the chapel in Perná, all the way to our cottage, where I push open the gate and call out for Granny Zipfelová at the top of my lungs.

IX

"Granny, Graaannnyyyy!" shouted Barbora as soon as she pushed open the gate in the picket fence.

The chickens scattered in all directions; the cottage and the courtyard looked deserted. The front door was closed, and the yard was quiet.

"Granny Zipfelová!" Barbora called out again, dashing for the door.

Almost at the same instant, Zipfelová appeared in the doorway. Barbora hurled herself into her arms.

"Easy, girl, easy, hold your horses; you can't rush at me like that; I'm an old lady," Zipfelová said with a laugh, hugging Barbora, who had locked her arms around her neck.

"Hello," called Gerta, shutting the gate behind her.

"Gerta, come on in, come on, what a happy surprise," said Zipfelová with a smile as they kissed one another on the cheeks.

Who could have imagined it back then, when Gerta had stood here for the very first time, famished and thirsty, pushing a baby carriage with Barbora in it?

On the threshold of the kitchen, Gerta stopped. It was as if she had stepped back in time to years before. Around the table again sat Johanna, Teresa, Ula with Dorla, Edeltraud, Maria, Hermína. On the floor about them, the children, and Ida and old Zipfelová.

"It's hard to believe it was real, isn't it?" Zipfelová said, still smiling as if she, too, were seeing the same thing as Gerta. "Remember how we barely fit? All the children, ten grown women, and the two of us, Ida and me? What a time, practically still the war."

"Of course I remember, Mrs. Zipfelová. It's impossible to forget. That and how good you were to all of us."

"Oh, come now, it's what any good Christian woman would have done. Why, you were all so skinny and exhausted, and those poor children. It was terrible. A disgrace is what it was. But enough about that.

Come on in and sit down—you, too, you little imp," she said, smiling at Barbora, who was bouncing around her.

"How've you been, Mrs. Zipfelová? I'm sorry I've been out of touch for so long."

"Don't be silly, girl. I knew starting a new life from scratch would be no bed of roses. I imagined you'd have other things on your mind than coming to visit an old lady. I've still got my Hermína here with me, and everything is the same. These days she works at the JZD, the farm cooperative. But tell me what you're up to."

"Granny, can I go to the garden?"

Zipfelová was just setting a third glass of water down on the table.

"Of course you can, my girl. You go right ahead and take a good look at everything."

Gerta gave Barbora a shake of her finger, just to be safe.

Zipfelová looked run-down. She was more stooped and brittle than when they last saw her a year and a half ago. She sat opposite Gerta, stirring her chicory coffee with a spoon.

"I don't even have anything to offer you. You'd be surprised, but we've got next to nothing around here."

"Please don't worry, Mrs. Zipfelová. I didn't come here to get fed." Gerta gave a laugh. "For that matter, it's the same for us. There's nothing in Brno either."

"No, dear girl, you don't understand. Here, we've really been left with next to nothing. Everything belongs to the JZD. We're not self-sufficient farmers anymore—a few chickens are all I have left. And there'll never be another thing from Šenk's ever again. Have you heard?"

Gerta leaned across the table. Zipfelová was looking at her quizzically.

"Heard what?"

"They sent Šenk to the mines, dear girl. Can you imagine?"

Gerta raised her eyebrows in astonishment. "To the mines?"

Zipfelová sadly nodded her head. "To Jáchymov, in the Ore Mountains. And they moved Ida and the child out to some state farm in Kostelec nad Orlicí. Do you know where that is?"

Gerta shook her head.

"All of us women went over there at six o'clock in the morning on the day they moved them out—her and her child, and his crippled old mother too. All they let them take were a few rags, a bed, a wardrobe, and their comforters. Nothing else. They drove away in a van. And on top of it, they had a guard from the National Security Corps, the SNB, standing over them, keeping watch the whole time."

Zipfelová began to weep. There had been times when she had wanted Ida out of her sight. It had taken years for her to accept that Šenk and Ida had decided to stop honoring her son's memory and had begun seeing each other even before Helmut had been officially declared dead. From what Gerta remembered, Ida had moved in with Šenk, bringing along just a few bags of clothing, a radiant smile, and rosy cheeks, her growing belly barely noticeable under her many-layered skirts. Zipfelová hadn't even come out to say goodbye. The following Sunday, they proclaimed their banns.

"Everything around here went downhill pretty quick after Jech became chairman of the cooperative. He was one of the first to turn his farm over to the JZD—you remember, the one he had no idea how to take care of, that had belonged to Führeder. Even the vineyards. Opportunist."

"Of course I remember. Hermína and I ended up taking care of his cows. The Führeders' niece, the one who married into the Kovář family, came over to show us how to milk them. I'll never forget the way she rubbed them between the ears and called them by their names and greeted them for Járinka Führederová. The cows would turn around to look at her, as if they understood. And then when Jech came in, they always got so nervous! He'd come marching through the barn, and the cows and us, we'd all start shaking."

"Even the animals were scared of him! Let alone the people!" Zipfelová exclaimed, raising her hand clutching a large handkerchief menacingly over the table.

"I was afraid of him. After all, he did try to shoot me. And then he ended up being the one who had me transferred over from the National Committee to the cows, remember?"

Zipfelová let her hand, now clenched into a fist, drop back to the table and resignedly nodded her head.

"He's got nothing on me; I'm just an old woman, but I'm afraid of him just the same. What a pig, showing up from God knows where. Dragging all his relatives with him. Why, half of Perná belongs to the Jechs now. And they all willingly joined the JZD, which makes sense. It was an easy way to unload everything they'd robbed and plundered for themselves over these past few years. If only you'd been here to see it! How many times did we—the Krupas, old Krumpschmied, and in the end even Šenk—shake our heads over what we saw them doing to the trellises? They had no idea how to take care of the vines, no clue about husbandry—it didn't matter if they were working a field or a farm. I get upset just thinking about it. And then, to top it off, that business with Šenk and Ida."

Zipfelová stood up and walked over to the window.

"At the beginning of the year, Jech started to make noise around the pub, blaming everything on the folks who didn't want to join the JZD. The shortage of meat, the shortage of fodder, the failure to meet quotas. They kept on having meetings at the pub, but by then it was mainly to bad-mouth Šenk, as well as the Krupas and the Lhotáks, the last of the private farmers. And then, did you hear about that tragedy in Babice, where three local party officials were shot dead? That was something. Jech wasted no time going around and blabbing about it. You could cut the air here with a knife. But Šenk still wouldn't budge. He even kept up with the delivery quotas. I don't know how they did it. I went over myself to help them a few times, not that I really felt like it. But

Ida kept on asking me, and then finally she even begged me, because she was afraid they wouldn't make the delivery. So in the end, I went over two or three times to give them a hand. They worked nonstop, in the fields, in the vineyards, around the animals. I felt sorry for them."

"But at least they still had their own place, and that had to be worth something, right?" said Gerta.

"Well, yes, but just for a few months. Then their cow barn caught fire, and word around the village was that Jech was behind it. It was awful. The cows were running frantically through the streets right up until the morning—the firemen showed up from Dunajovice, where they've got that volunteer fire brigade. But do you think anyone from Perná lifted a finger to help them? Not a soul. The pastor. He made the call to Dunajovice, to the firehouse. Everyone else was too scared."

"That's terrible."

"And then there were the quotas. More and more things started to go missing. It began with a few milk cans. Next it was chickens. Then the fire in the cow barn. Šenk called on the SNB to come and investigate why suddenly so many things were happening to them, all at once. And what do you think happened?"

Gerta shook her head.

"It started with them showing up in front of the chairman—in front of Jech—and it stopped right there. In the end, they put Šenk on probation, for slander and noncompliance with production quotas. He was lucky they didn't charge him with causing the accidents himself, as a way to get out of making the contributions."

"Poor Šenk. I can't even imagine him in that kind of a situation. Such a decent man. How did he take it? And Ida?"

"My dear girl, it was very hard on him, and it didn't go on for very long, you know. Then they took him away, and after that, well, I've only heard from Ida once. She wrote from that place, Kostelec, asking us to send her a few things, if they hadn't already been confiscated. And by then, of course, everything was already gone. And you know what else she wrote? That he got sixteen years. In Jáchymov, for high treason, for being the rich man of the village who had held up cooperative farming efforts. They lost everything. That's what finally put old Šenková in her grave, you can bet your life on it. She'd buried that drunk of a husband, lost a son in the war, and was herself a cripple. But it took this to kill her, sure as my name's Zipfelová—it took getting kicked out with nothing but a quilt on her back, like the lowliest servant. Off her own property, a good chunk of which had been her dowry, and off their own land, which her husband's father had worked, and his father, and his grandfather before him. For generations. Now tell me, what kind of justice is that?"

Zipfelová was dabbing her eyes with the large cotton handkerchief as she continued to stare out the window.

So that's how things had turned out for Ida. Beautiful, lovesick Ida, who, bitter at not having children of her own, had so often lashed out at theirs. Ida, who used to blush at the mere mention of Šenk's name. How long had her happiness lasted? One year? Two? How long before she once again lost a husband and, at the same time, her home?

"Ida used to like to think what a fine lady of the manor she'd make. Marrying into the grange. Remember the hurry she was in? I resented her for it back then, and I still do. Thinking what a fine missus she'd make. The wife of the farmer with the biggest farm in the whole village. And vineyards stretching all the way to Pavlov. She certainly got that one wrong, didn't she?"

Zipfelová turned away from the window and shuffled slowly back to the table, sinking down heavily on the chair.

"But this, I never would have wished it on her. If you'd only seen her when they were taking her away. With that child and crippled old Šenková. It would've brought tears to your eyes."

A heavy silence fell over the kitchen. Zipfelová looked from the table out into the garden. And then abruptly she said, "They drove out the Šenks and so many other neighbors. And see how it is now? Before the war, we all lived together here in harmony—every harvest festival, every wine festival, every Christmas, Sundays at church—we celebrated everything together. It didn't matter if you were Czech or Austrian or German. How many families like the Heinzes and the Führeders did we have around here? Maybe twenty? So now we've got twenty families who wandered in from God knows where, for whom our traditions are totally foreign, who have no relationship to this beautiful land, to this soil—you should walk around and have a look, see what they've done to Perná. Nothing matters to them. They stay holed up in their houses, the fellows in the pub, and out on the street nobody even says hello anymore."

Gerta put her hand over Zipfelová's.

"At least they can't do anything to me. I've got nothing left for them to take."

"Things will get better again, Mrs. Zipfelová, you'll see," said Gerta uneasily, trying to console her.

Zipfelová turned toward Gerta but seemed to look right through her.

"You remember the time they got into that fight, after Führeder got shot? How Jech beat up Šenk in the pub? Well, Šenk wouldn't leave it alone; he took it further. He took it to Mikulov, and maybe even all the way to Brno. It made no difference. Once the president announced amnesty for anyone who had assaulted a German or German property, either during the war or at any time up to the end of 1945, he had nothing more left on Jech. Remember how cocky Jech got? Because even though he'd committed murder, no one could touch him. That's where it started. And now this is where it's ended. Jech won. Šenk's in the mines; Ida and her child are all alone in some godforsaken place in the middle of nowhere, like two lost waifs; and old Šenková is dead from grief. The grange belongs to the JZD, and Jech's the chairman of both the agricultural cooperative and the local chapter of the National Committee. And he's setting his sights even higher, dear girl. He's already a member of the Regional Committee. Miserable bastard."

For a while they were silent.

"Forgive me, Gerta," Zipfelová said suddenly.

Gerta looked at her in surprise.

"Here I am going on about Šenk this and Jech that, and meanwhile your life must've changed something tremendous, am I right?"

Gerta awkwardly shrugged her shoulders. She took Zipfelová by the arm, and they went out into the garden to find Barbora, who was chasing the dog around the bushes.

"Oh, and before I forget," said Zipfelová as they were saying their goodbyes in the late afternoon. "You got a letter—here." She slipped a white envelope into Gerta's hand.

The edges of the asphalt road leading back to the bus stop were overgrown with grass, clusters of Carthusian pinks, and yellow shrubby cinquefoils; the early-evening air smelled of the neighboring fields and vineyards. The sun was setting behind Děvičky Castle, and the silhouette of the ruins offered an enchanting panorama. Gazing up at the patchy clouds in the sky and with Barbora dozing in her arms, she skirted the village and only out of the corner of her eye caught the twitch of curtains behind the window of one of the Jech houses.

X

Meine liebe Gerta, Johanna, Hermína,

all my dear friends, dear Frau Zipfel and Ida,
I greet you in a way that only my being here makes possible.

　　I'm writing to you, even though I'm not sure if all in Bergen is still as it was. Maybe some of you are already far away; maybe you're in Brünn; or maybe you're somewhere close by, here in Austria, trying to make a life for yourselves, as I am. Maybe in the end, everything turned out differently and this letter will never find you. In that case, I hope it will at least find you, Frau Zipfel, in the same cottage with the lovely garden from which I once fled without saying goodbye. I was never properly able to thank you for taking me in and for caring for me as you did, you and Ida. Please don't think I don't realize how lucky I was to have been placed with you and Hubert Šenk. I do realize it, and I thank you for everything. And I'm grateful to you even though I ran away, but that's another chapter, and I'm sure you understand that I simply had to do it, and the sooner the better. And today I have no regrets; on the contrary, I'm glad that I took my fate into my own hands, even though at the beginning it wasn't easy; that much I can tell you. I can also tell you that I'm still a stranger here, yes, even in this country where we all speak the same language and where so many of us came, filled with the hope of starting a new life. But even here it's "us" and "them," and we, the new-comers, will never be on equal footing with them. This curse has followed me from Brünn, and I'll never be free of it—perhaps it's my fate. But God didn't abandon me, and, thanks to that, in the end, I found Traude Fröhlich, of the Fröhlichs who used to live in Bergen, behind the church, and who takes this opportunity, joined by her whole family, to send you, dear Frau Zipfel, her warmest regards. Just so you know, there's a place on a hill here above Poysdorf from where you can see all the way to the Pálava Hills, and on a clear day, you can even make out Rassenstein castle. So many people show up every Sunday, week after week, to gaze toward those rows of vineyards in which I used to break my back bending over—you'd be surprised how hard it is to forget. The Fröhlichs, the Wlassaks, the Bergers, Frau Bürgermeister and her daughters, and others from Dunajovice, Věstonice, and one family from Pavlov, they all settled around here, within sight of their vineyards. They flattened out this hilltop and cleared a little area where they put a bench and planted a grapevine that climbs up behind it. And it's from here that I'm writing to you all, you whom I'd so love to see again sometime.

With sincere regards and thoughts of you,
Teresa Bayer
Renngasse 33-A, 1010 Wien
P.S. Dear Gerta, may I ask you a favor? Do you remember that fence in Pohořelice? Would you go and hang a little wreath there for me, in memory of my mother? Not a day goes by that I don't think about her and the final hours of her life. I hope someday I'll be able to repay you. Thank you. Teresa.
Poysdorf, September 27, 1951

My dearest, liebste Teresa,
Du kannst Dir nicht vorstellen—you can't imagine how happy I was to get your letter! And how close it came to never reaching me at all, so close. It took me a year and a half before I found the nerve to come back to a place that I'd left so full of fear, maybe even more fear than you had, back when you and Ula fled from here. Can you imagine, my dear Teresa, the dangers we faced in those years right after the war? Do you remember those days in the Pohořelice camp? I'm sure you do. It's impossible to forget, just like the nights that preceded them. But what

then went on afterward, after you were already gone, was a slow death, a long-drawn-out process of dying, and it almost did me in. Be grateful that you ran away, my dear Teresa—even though so far you haven't found your happiness, at least you still have a chance. Whereas we here don't. We here are condemned to rot, to be blamed forevermore for all the problems in this Republic. And, Teresa, not just us, not just all the Germans who stayed, not just me, a Czech with the wrong nationality, but even Barbora, Anni, and Rudi. Do you remember them? Barbora bundled up in burlap and Anni and Rudi, with their puppy eyes? That's what you used to say about them, remember? Teresa, they're all considered to be guilty too. It's a dead end from which there's no escape. And it's only thanks to Karel that I was able to take off old Zipfelová's filthy boots and get away from that cow barn, and that today I have a roof of my own over my head and a job, where they rob me of my wages. I would never have managed it on my own, by then I was already so dead inside. But that's a long story, Teresa, and mine isn't going to be any better or worse than yours. Are you still standing on that hilltop above Poysdorf? Are you still sitting on that bench and looking toward Perná? Don't do it, Teresa; don't mourn for something that stopped existing long ago. Hubert Šenk was sentenced to forced labor in the mines for not wanting to hand over his farm. Ida is living alone with their child someplace in the middle of nowhere, and in Perná there's practically no one left from the old days. And the same goes for Brno, just in case you've been missing those streets too. Don't be homesick. You wouldn't want to have stayed, believe me; everything has changed, and you'd be as unwelcome here as we are.

Instead of sitting on a bench overlooking Poysdorf, you'd be spending Sundays sitting with me and Johanna in Lužánky Park, watching our children chase each other around the grass, and that would be all you could do. Isolated, forever branded an enemy of the state. Classified as socially unreliable, just like Johanna and me, and just like someday our children will be. I know what it's like to long for home, Teresa, believe me. I, too, rejoiced when I thought I'd found it again. But all for nothing, Teresa, and it made my disappointment that much worse. Home isn't where one grows up; don't make the mistake of thinking that. Home is where they welcome you when you walk in the door. And that's something none of us here in Brno have experienced. It's downright outrageous, how differently it all turned out. There's another family now living in the apartment where I grew up. On the doorbell nameplate it says "Urban." They're occupying the room that was mine and Friedrich's. They're sleeping in our parents' bedroom, and if what people say is true, then they're eating off our porcelain plates, sitting at our table, and walking on our carpet. Teresa, we lost our home here the day they drove us out of the city, over the course of that night—remember the Feast of Corpus Christi? That's how it is. Be done with the past, and don't torture yourself with useless nostalgia. What you're suffering over is no longer here. Not even your mother has a grave here anymore; all around Pohořelice, far and wide, there's nothing. Not a single headstone, no memorial for all the people who died there during those days. I placed a small wreath as you asked by the fence where you last saw your mother. The building in which we spent the night is still standing; they haven't torn it down. It's still surrounded

*by the same rusted fence against which they stacked the
bodies. I put the wreath there and, for the second time in
my life, barely made it out of that place alive. The locals
still carry the war in their hearts, and there's so much
hatred, you can't even imagine. They called the SNB on
me—apparently honoring the memory of a dead German
is the same as declaring oneself a die-hard fascist. Teresa,
the people here have gone mad. Stay where you are, in
the free country of your dreams, and seek a new home.
I think that even if the locals are unfriendly, you'll have
better luck finding it there than if you were here. Even
though there you're treading on their soil, at least you're
treading on it as a human being. Not as a criminal or
a "Deutschak," as they've taken to calling us now, with
blood on your hands. Teresa, how much I'd love to see you
again someday. I really hope we have that chance. I send
you kisses and regards, also from Johanna, Anni, Rudi,
and Barbora.*

Deine Gerta
Brno, July 15, 1952

As she carefully licked the flap of the envelope and smoothed it
with her thumb, pressing down firmly and securing the corners, little
did she imagine the circumstances under which this letter, never delivered, would come back to her.

XI

*The Deutsche Wanderbühne, Prague's German traveling theater troupe,
has arrived in Brno.* Gerta couldn't believe her eyes as she read the
announcement in the *Rudé Právo* newspaper. Was it possible that some

were still trying to keep the German language and culture alive? Were there still people left who believed in their worth?

Goose bumps ran up her arms. How long now had she been trying to pretend that anything German had nothing to do with her? Eight years? Gerta read it again: *The Deutsche Wanderbühne, Prague's German traveling theater troupe, has arrived in Brno.* A theater company that performed in German. She hoped that Johanna wouldn't ask her to go with her to see a German play, which would serve to remind her again of her own German blood. That despised part of herself.

Gerta folded the newspaper into quarters and tucked it into the trash—it slipped in alongside a few empty cups like it was nothing, didn't even have to jostle for space. The German part of her no longer existed. Nor had it ever existed previously, in spite of her father's efforts. She had already paid the price for the big *D* that had been stamped on her ration coupons. A price higher than some could endure, and these days she was grateful to finally be able to put the German part of her identity behind her, and occasionally even forget it existed at all. Even if others around her couldn't. It was because of them that deductions were still being taken out of her paycheck and that the only work she could find was in a factory an hour away from her home. And then there was Barbora. Right from the start, it was obvious that the comrade teachers knew exactly whom they were dealing with. On the first day of elementary school, Barbora walked into the classroom with her big schoolbag across her whole back, glanced over her shoulder to give Gerta a big, trusting, partially toothless grin, and waved. But the enthusiasm didn't last long, and soon she was coming home from school in tears, each time with a different story about what her classmates had done to her that day. Where was this coming from? It wasn't until parents' night that Gerta realized what was happening, after hearing for herself the disdain with which the comrade teacher was evaluating Barbora's inability to distinguish similar-looking letters. This cow with her hair pulled back in a severe bun, standing on the teacher's podium and repeatedly tapping the palm of her hand with a pointer, like a dictator wielding an instrument of authority, was tyrannizing her daughter in front of the entire class. At the end of the first year, she advised Gerta to have Barbora transferred to a special school—or else she would have to repeat the grade. And that was what happened. In spite of Karel's efforts to intervene, the following year Barbora was stepping over the first-grade classroom threshold for a second time, and although Gerta suspected that her daughter hadn't been born with the sharpest mind, she knew for certain that she had been born with the wrong last name. An injustice passed down from father to daughter, from mother to daughter. But why Barbora, who hadn't even yet been born at that time? How long could human hatred persist? Gerta felt powerless. That she couldn't protect herself was one thing, though somehow, hell knew how, she'd always managed to get by. But now, she couldn't even protect Barbora, who looked up at her with her wide, uncomprehending, helpless child's eyes. All Gerta could do was to smother everything German inside them. That was all she could do, for herself as much as for Barbora. Banish it. Not to pass on a single drop of tainted blood, so as not to infect the other part of her. Avoid using the language that had brought Gerta so much grief—better not even to acknowledge its existence, let alone attend a performance by some German theater troupe. As if it hadn't occurred to the organizers that it was pointless, a useless battle that would only do harm to others, do harm to her, to Gerta. Best not to provoke anyone, to let things be, just as she and Antonia had done. Not congregate, not talk, not remember. For years now, Antonia had gone by the surname Ainingerová, as had Martin and Rosa. Only Johanna was foolish enough to believe that her husband was still out there somewhere, locked up, deported, and in her stubborn conviction had kept his name. Despite having seen what people were capable of doing. What they were capable of doing to her children. And now Gerta was aware of it, too, and so was Barbora. Even though Gerta had enrolled her in school as Schnirchová.

XII

The receiver in the Zábrdovice post office's telephone booth burned her hand like red-hot metal. Gerta had been holding it for a long time, unable to bring herself to insert the tip of her finger into the hole on the finger-wheel and dial the number. She felt the crumpled piece of paper with the hastily scribbled numerals in her pocket.

"Five. Four. Six, two, three," she dictated to herself aloud.

She dialed the last three numbers in rapid succession. Inside the receiver, she heard a clicking. Maybe the ringing on the other end would go on again to no avail, as it had that morning. Suddenly, on the other end of the line there was a clatter.

"Němcová," answered a terse voice.

Gerta kept quiet.

"Němcová, who's calling? Hello?"

"Hello, this is Gerta Schnirch," Gerta practically whispered. She hadn't expected such a harsh-sounding voice on the other end.

"Hello, what can I do for you?"

Gerta cleared her throat. "May I please speak with comrade Němec?"

On the other end of the telephone there was silence.

"What do you want from him?"

Gerta was prepared for this.

"I looked for him today at work, but unfortunately they told me they didn't know where comrade Němec was. I have an urgent work-related message for him."

The woman on the other end of the phone hissed, "Really?"

"Yes."

"Then go back and ask them again. They of all people know exactly where he is."

Gerta was silent.

"Or are you one of them?"

"Excuse me, one of whom?"

"Never mind. You wouldn't tell me anyway. What do you want from him?"

Gerta again cleared her throat. "It's confidential. It's information from the Zbrojovka Arms Factory."

"Zbrojovka, is it? In that case, trust me, Karel definitely won't need that information anymore. That's if he'll ever need anything again."

"What do you mean?" Gerta blurted out.

"Dear comrade, Karel isn't here. And he won't be . . ." The voice on the other end broke.

"Excuse me?"

From the other end came the sound of muffled sobs.

"Do you know when he'll be back at work?" asked Gerta, but the only response was the sound of a dial tone. Gerta remained standing inside the telephone booth with the receiver in her hand. Someone knocked on the glass door. She hung up the receiver, picked up her shopping bag off the floor, and stepped out.

A man was standing impatiently in front of the booth. "Finally."

Gerta turned her back on him.

How long had it been already? Fourteen days, three weeks? How long since she hadn't received a message, since she hadn't heard from him at all? Almost three weeks. This had never happened before. Never. He always came to see her with absolute regularity, two or three times a week; he would skip meetings and would come in the afternoons and stay overnight, always letting her know when she would see him next. Except now. And now it had been so long that she could no longer wait. So she made the call. It was the first time she had heard his wife's voice. And heard her crying. She was overcome by a sense of dread. She remembered how nervous Karel had been of late. How he couldn't concentrate on anything she said to him. He started showing up late and calling off their meetings. And in his sleep, he would cry out. And sob. It was the first time since the march to Pohořelice that she'd heard a man cry, and it was her Karel, waking up sobbing from terrible night-mares—like a child. On such nights, she would wrap herself around him and try to calm him. And then one day he didn't show up; he simply disappeared. Nobody knew where he was. Neither at work, nor at home. One day, she decided not to go to the factory, just so that she could sit on the square in front of the new state house and wait to see if Karel would appear, either going in or coming out. He didn't. And then things began to happen that attested to his absence. To his defini-tive absence from her life.

Something catastrophic must have occurred for the authorities to move the married Greek couple into their apartment.

They had shown up one day with their suitcases, a police escort, and an official holding some documents in his hand, before she even returned from work. They were all standing in front of the door, wait-ing, the suitcases piled against the wall. By the time she and Barbora got home, hungry and exhausted, she didn't have the energy to protest. They followed her into the apartment, removed their coats, and the official laid out the papers on the kitchen table.

"Mind you, now, comrade, no outbursts—three rooms for a sin-gle adult with one child, that's an outright crime against our People's Democracy. Do you have any idea how many disadvantaged people are out there without a roof over their head? We know all about the bour-geois lifestyle you were used to. Daddy was a loyal Henlein supporter, wasn't he? So, comrade, you should be glad this Republic has granted you asylum at all, and that you've even been allowed to stay here. You need to reciprocate a little; it's your civic duty. Besides, it's not like you have a choice. Sign right here, and then fraternal greetings, comrade! Honor work!"

Gerta bent down over the papers as if in a trance. She picked up the fountain pen and signed *Schnirch* in dark blue ink on the line to which the official was pointing. With an ironic smirk, he gave the paper a shake. His comrade said something that she couldn't understand to the couple; until now they had been standing by the kitchen door. They proceeded to enter the kitchen and set a pile of folded blankets down on the kitchen table in place of the papers. One of them was stamped *Eigentum der Stadt Berlin*. Property of the city of Berlin? This many years after the war? Gerta found herself wondering about it long after the front door of their apartment had closed behind the police officer and the official. In the kitchen, seated around the square table that Karel had once picked up somewhere, were now four people who were complete strangers to each other.

Gerta was exhausted.

So many changes in such a short amount of time, so very many. And Karel's absence played a pivotal role in all of it. As if a central bolt had fallen out and the world had begun to spin out of control, with no coordination, madly reeling as though at any moment it would explode. And at the center of it all was Gerta, caught in the vortex of this raging whirlpool, everything she'd managed to collect over the past few years falling away. Karel and their new home. A space refurbished with great care as a refuge for herself, for Barbora, and for Karel. A space in which something extraordinary had come to pass, something she thought had been lost to her forever, a place of privacy, where everyone who entered unquestionably also belonged. And now it was all in shambles. Her life with Karel, as well as her home. Once again, there wasn't room for her to breathe—for her to live her life. She fell into a state of apathy, unable to influence what was happening around her. She went on doing everything just as before. Each morning she dropped off Barbora at school, then took the train to work in Kuřim, left at the sound of the five o'clock whistle, and returned home with Barbora, always the last child to be picked up. In the meantime, the Agathonikiadis couple took over her bedroom, and the living room became Mr. Agathonikiadis's around-the-clock recreation room. Gerta had literally been moved into

Barbora's room without even a chance to grab the mattress off her own
bed. She was at the factory when the move took place. But she didn't
care. Without Karel, their home had lost all meaning for her anyway.
The home they'd fixed up together with their own hands, during those
evenings when Karel managed to slip away from his meetings. Karel,
who seemed to have been swallowed up by the earth and no longer
existed—not for her, and not even for his wife.

XIII

She had known it from the start. He couldn't be with her, at least not
in the way she would have wished. It was too late. She accepted it right
from the beginning, as soon as she found out, and never attempted to
change it. Not for almost three whole beautiful years. Neither had he,
as if any additional attempt might derail this hard-won return, this
fragile version of happiness they managed to keep locked away behind
the doors of the apartment on Köffillergasse, now Stará Street, where
he'd dropped her off one day back in 1950 with only a comforter and
the few things from Zipfelová.

So often she had wanted to. So many nights awake in bed, huddled
against his shoulder, her eyes staring into the darkness, so many times she
had wanted to liberate herself of this burden. But he never asked her, and
she didn't have the nerve to bring it up. What if doing so undermined
Barbora's opportunity? Her opportunity to have a man in her life who
over time might embrace her as a daughter, with unselfish, sincere affection. Even Gerta sometimes struggled. There was her all-encompassing
love for Barbora, and there was the voice that would ambush her from
within just when she least expected it. A ruthless, cruel voice that tied
everything to do with her daughter back to her bloodline. Even her
poor grades in school, even the fact that she still wasn't reading or writing properly. Even that she looked like Gerta. And like Gerta's mother

and like her father. That voice forced her to admit to herself how much it repulsed her. The resemblance. The gestures that Barbora only could have picked up from watching her. Gerta grappled with that voice, and this was another reason she feared revealing the truth.

And so every day she remained guilty, once again guilty. Early on, she often caught Karel scrutinizing Barbora as she chewed on her breakfast roll, her eyes still sticky with sleep dust. Delving into her features, his gaze only discerned Gerta as he continued staring at her so intently that he would forget to sip his weak tea, brewed from a single teaspoon of leaves in a small teapot they all shared. She would see him racking his brain, trying to unlock her secret, unearth who had destroyed his future. He came up with nothing. Nor did he ask. He would finish sipping his cup of tea as Gerta took Barbora into the bathroom to wash her face with cold water. Afterward, the two of them would head out into the dark morning while he stayed behind, never knowing when they would next all share such a morning together.

Gerta had gone along with it. There was no way to pick up where they had left off in the days of their youth. Those days had brought them together, and that was enough. And to bridge the gap of those seven years and pretend nothing had happened was something she didn't want to do. For Barbora's sake, but perhaps for her own sake too. She sensed what a fine line there was between love and loathing. She sensed it the first time he had touched her again. That time she had tried, as best as she could, to hold herself together, but still she couldn't relax. Like an ice floe that simply wouldn't thaw, simply wouldn't break down and dissolve into the ocean. That was how rigid, hard, and frozen she was. All she could do was close her eyes when he touched her, as, for that matter, she'd always done. There was no other way. Even though now it was no longer a necessity. For this reason, too, she wanted him to stay with his wife, this, and perhaps also because she was afraid of suddenly possessing too much happiness. Everything that she'd ever longed for. Gerta didn't think she could bear it. For far too long she'd been living without a future, relying only on herself, her perspective that of a single day, which she would muster all her strength to face. She no longer knew any other way. All vitality and longing had drained out of her long ago. She was no longer capable of desiring anything. Of blooming like a tree in springtime. She didn't want it. It scared her.

And besides, they never talked about it. Karel would show up and thaw out in their home like a snowflake on the lapel of a coat. The total opposite of the ice floe that Gerta carried within herself. He seemed happy and spent time with her often. There was no need for more. It had only been during these last few weeks that things changed. That he would leave in a hurry—if he showed up at all. Restless. Agitated. And scared.

"The revolution is devouring its own children," he had often repeated of late.

What revolution? Gerta had asked herself, curious, but also with a slight foreboding. Never before had she known such tranquility as what they'd been enjoying during these past few years.

"Sometimes things aren't what they appear to be," he had also said. Sadly, listlessly. Anxiously.

And then one day he didn't come, although he had promised he would and had said that he would spend the night. Gerta stayed up late into the evening, waiting. In vain. The next day, she went to work and called. The day after that, she called again from work. The fourth day, she waited in front of his office building—all in vain. Karel had disappeared, as if the waters of the Brno reservoir had closed over him, just as they had over the stones that on a recent Sunday she and Barbora had been skipping. Nobody knew a thing. Gerta was desperate. So much so that she decided to transgress her self-imposed boundary, trespass into forbidden terrain, and make the call to Brigita Němcová. She imagined an older woman with a well-kept complexion and an impeccable manicure approaching the receiver, the cultured daughter of a friend with whom Karel had spent time in Hostýn during the war. A charming, elegant woman to whom Karel was joined by marriage and through a relationship that had shattered into a thousand fragments of minor misunderstandings. At least that was how he spoke of it, the one and only time he ever mentioned her. Would the woman on the other end of the receiver know who was calling? Or was she too busy with her own life to have noticed Karel's nocturnal absences? Gerta didn't know. Her hand trembled as she dialed the number. It was trembling with fear of the unknown territory that she was about to enter. A territory into which she had never wanted to set foot. One that even in her thoughts she had sought to avoid, just as Karel had, in their idyllic home in which the outside world didn't exist. And then she had heard her—her voice and her sentences, which made it clear beyond the shadow of a doubt that the voice on the other end belonged to that other one. And then her tears, which confirmed to Gerta the worst of her fears. The system had swallowed up Karel, just as it had swallowed up Otto Šling, Svitavský, and Kudílková-Blochová, with whom he used to work—just as it had swallowed up Hubert Šenk and Ida, and just as it had once swallowed up her, cowering behind a baby carriage on a farmstead outside of Pohořelice. And if not gone forevermore to his wife, then most likely gone forevermore to Gerta. Because what could Gerta possibly mean to him if at home he had a wife who was weeping for him?

XIV

Compared to all the things that had gone on and were still going on around Gerta Schnirchová, this seemed a mere trifle. At least when it came to this, she wasn't caught in it alone. They were all caught in it, every person she met in the small independent shops, the women forced to find jobs and who now sat beside her on the assembly line, feeding heads of screws into an enormous press—even their former caretaker from Sterngasse, whom she had recently encountered on the street, was caught in it too. And Karel had been caught in it as well, except his blind faith in the system had left him completely oblivious. And back then, all Gerta had been able to think about was the happiness that had unexpectedly come her way. It had dawned on her only later, when she could no longer find any potatoes to buy for Barbora and when, eight years after the war, milk or butter was available only by using food coupons, provided there was milk or butter. Thinking back to those days now—when lightbulbs in shop windows illuminated a display of smoked sausages or fruit that no one could buy because one needed coupons for everything, and by the end of the month everyone was out—the whole charade was laughable. Or when she thought back to the flurry of advertisements that always popped up in the papers just before Christmas: *Have walnuts, will trade for lemons; will buy potatoes, or trade for onions and garlic; will buy sugar.* Terrible. Back then, even Zipfelová had written her, asking could she come to Perná and bring her some sugar, because their coupons had been revoked, and there were no independent shops in the village. In exchange, she had offered potatoes—what else—so Gerta made the trip, although with only a modest stash, since sugar had all but disappeared even from the Brno shops.

"If only they hadn't deported Ignác Pfeifer—he kept bees—at least we'd have had honey. But no, everything either went under, or someone came around after the war and walked off with it," Zipfelová had said back then, rubbing the paper packet of sugar between her fingers.

There was absolutely nothing, no food and no clothing, and on one meager salary, from which the state deducted an additional 20 percent for some national reconstruction fund, Gerta and Barbora just barely scraped by. She practically burst into tears of laughter one evening as, gathered in the kitchen around the radio Karel had once acquired for her, they were listening to a report about what things would cost once the currency reforms went into effect. Mrs. Athanaia looked at her in alarm; by now she had learned some Czech and could understand quite well, and therefore couldn't comprehend what about this catastrophic news was making Gerta laugh. Gerta couldn't explain it either. Maybe she was laughing because the situation in which she found herself was so absurd. There was no butter to be rationed, no sugar, no vegetables, not even potatoes, and hardly anyone could afford meat. The milk supply had run out. This despite the fact that earlier that spring they had already confiscated food coupons from all the misers in the countryside, whose stinginess was being blamed for the urban shortages, and then went on to confiscate them from the last of the self-employed—people just trying to avoid work—and finally even from pensioners who had held senior official positions prior to 1945. And from their widows. Gerta was surprised they hadn't confiscated them from citizens who had formerly been German nationals as well. They must have simply forgotten about them, or most likely it would come as part of the second wave, she thought to herself with bitter irony. And when, once a week, she permitted herself to buy a newspaper, what did she read? That all this was simply a side effect of a tremendous economic boom. That the standard of living was steadily improving, and people were happier. This was reported in all seriousness and made the front page under a banner headline. Meanwhile, in her neighborhood, they were no longer just turning off the electricity on Mondays, their main shut-off day, but also on Thursday afternoons, now designated as an additional *irregular delivery* day. This affected them all equally, regardless of whether it was her—that German bitch with the brat—or any of the Czechs around her. And if this latest stunt ended up wiping out the few Czech crowns she had managed to save, the hell with it. They had never amounted to much anyway, so doing without them wasn't going to be a big adjustment. In fact, in her household, the repercussions probably wouldn't have amounted to more than her outburst of bitter laughter by the radio receiver and Mrs. Athanaia's lamentations—if Zipfelová hadn't died.

That time, they all went to Perná together: Johanna, Antonia, and the children, Anni, Rudi, Martin, Rosa, and Barbora. And they stood around the grave with Hermína, who had organized the funeral, and Mrs. Krumpschmiedová, whose daughter-in-law had brought her. There was no one else.

"Before the war, the whole village would have been there. She would have had wreaths on her grave. From the Czechs and from the Germans. They would have carried her from the road all the way to the cemetery, taken her once around the field to let her have a last look at the Děvičky Castle ruins. There would have been a funeral procession, and there would have been music, even if she couldn't afford it anymore. Just out of neighborly sympathy. Because everyone around here liked her, back then."

Mrs. Krumpschmiedová's muffled German fell in shaky words that landed on top of the wooden table around which they once used to sit every day. Nothing inside Zipfelová's cottage had changed, except for the room that Hermína had moved herself into. There was a time when five haggard women had taken turns sleeping in it. Gerta looked around the old kitchen and down at the table, on which a frugal funeral feast had been laid out. Chicory coffee, bread with sweet curd cheese, and strawberries. When had she and Barbora last eaten strawberries? Such a luxury for city folk. Not since the last year that they had still been living with Zipfelová, of that she was certain.

"And the priest would have been there too. Our old priest, who left with all the villagers when they were exiled to Poysdorf, or wherever they ended up."

Mrs. Krumpschmiedová had her head bowed so low that it was almost touching the tabletop. At the back of her neck rose a hump that swayed in rhythm with the withered, hunched body that was continually shaking. She could barely make out any of the other women; their faces were above the horizon line beyond which her posture prevented her from seeing. From time to time, she would strain her eyes and try to raise her head to look at them, sitting around her stiff and upright, but then with a strained wheeze she would slump down again, letting her head sink back to her chest. She spoke only in German. After the war, she had never managed to learn Czech, not a single word. For Gerta, it was the first time that she had gone back to speaking in German for any sustained length of time. It felt strange. Unseemly. She had been the one to shoo the children out of the kitchen into the garden so that they wouldn't overhear them talking, and she would have preferred to run out with them. Zipfelová's old kitchen, suffused with memories and with the language that had been her undoing, felt so strange to her.

"She so wanted to have music. She kept a list of songs that she wanted to have played. These last two years, she would bring it up often, asking me which ones I thought were better. She kept changing them around."

Hermína's voice sounded choked up. How had their relationship changed over these past few years, since the two of them had begun living here together all by themselves? How attached had they grown to one another, once Zipfelová had lost all the children that she once took care of for her German girls, having already lost her own son and, in the end, even Ida?

"I blame myself for not having visited her more often. And when I did come to see her, I didn't even notice that she had death on her mind. She never said a word about funerals. She'd just talk about all the things that had been going on here over the past few years, you know? She seemed so spry, didn't she, Hermína?" said Johanna.

Hermína shrugged her shoulders.

"It's true. She was always keeping an eye on things, always interested in everything that was going on. When one of you visited, she'd tell you everything she knew. But then there were the nights when we sat here opposite one another, and the future was simply a blank. She knew Helmut wasn't coming back. After Ida ran away, something inside her broke, and she stopped waiting. Maybe she didn't want Helmut to find that just his old mother was still waiting for him, but his wife was gone. So somehow, she just pushed aside all thoughts of his return, and then realized that without them, there was nothing left for her to look forward to. The future was completely empty, and the only thing she could see waiting there for her was death. That's how she would talk about it."

Mrs. Krumpschmied's daughter-in-law brought a cup of water up to the old lady's lips and held it while she took a few sips. As she did, a dribble of water trickled down into the handkerchief held ready under her chin.

"She had it all planned out, down to the last detail, and that's also why this currency reform killed her. Whatever was left of her meager pension, she'd been putting it aside toward her funeral. And then overnight, she had nothing. Not even enough for a coffin, let alone for music or wreaths or the reception she so wanted to have at the parish house. Not enough for anything. Just barely enough for one of those paper bags left over from the war. She had the heart attack while she was looking at the newspaper, reading about the new prices."

Hermína paused.

"Come to think of it, you could say she was lucky. After all, by then she'd already started to accumulate debts. She was reading a paper that was ten days old; that's how long it took for it to get here. So the good Lord gave her a gift of an extra ten days. Ten beautiful, hot June days full of ripening strawberries and blooming lupines, which she'd always bring back in bunches from the fields. And beautiful early evenings sitting on the doorstep with the swallows and sparrows warbling and the smell of the garden."

They were silent. Mrs. Krumpschmiedová's head kept on nodding as she went on involuntarily shaking, and it looked as if she were agreeing with everything. In resignation.

"And the rabbits had babies. She still got to see the kits," added Hermína.

Johanna was dabbing the corners of her eyes with a handkerchief. Even Gerta felt teary.

"And what about Ida, why didn't she come?" asked Antonia.

Mrs. Krumpschmiedová stiffened the narrow, bony shoulders that hunched over her sunken chest, and tried to lift her head to see who had asked this question. But then her head fell again as the younger women all looked on with compassion.

"Hard to say. I wrote to her that same evening, the day I found Zipfelová. I had lit a candle for her. She was lying in the room next door. I had already gotten her ready." Hermína's voice cracked.

Antonia, who was sitting closest to her, placed a hand on her shoulder. Hermína was squinting and rubbing the bridge of her nose with her fingers so hard that it must have hurt.

"Hermína," Gerta said, but didn't know what more to add.

"So I wrote to her," Hermína went on, "but who knows if those few days were enough for the postal service to deliver it to her in that backwater. I tried to call the post office, but it was no use. They don't even have a post office there. The nearest one is in the next village where nobody had ever heard of her, small wonder. It's possible she never even got it."

"Has she ever been in touch? How is she?" asked Johanna.

Hermína nodded. "She wrote," she said, "but it wasn't good news. She can't get over to see Hubert. It takes almost a whole day to travel there—she has to go halfway across the whole Republic—and the one time she went, and even brought the child along, they wouldn't let her see him. She was only allowed to write him a letter, but up to the time she wrote us, she still hadn't received a single line back from him. That one time she tried to visit him, she spent the whole night at the bus stop and barely made it back to work on time."

"She's working on somebody else's farm? Who's taking care of the child?" asked Antonia.

"She didn't say. She probably brings it along—why, you yourselves know it's not impossible." Hermína shrugged her shoulders. "At least she's working—the address is the state farm in Kostelec nad Orlicí. Supposedly she goes in as a day worker, but they won't let her near the animals, because being a traitor who's an enemy of socialism, she might try to poison them. They just let her help with the most menial chores, so you can imagine how much she's getting paid for that. The only money she was allowed to take with her from here, she apparently spent on the trip to see Hubert. And it was a complete waste. At the beginning, since she wasn't registered there, she wasn't even getting any food coupons. And the people on the farm looked at her as if she were a criminal—never even offered her anything to eat. And right in the middle of it all, old Mrs. Šenková died. She's buried there in some cemetery behind the farm without even her name on the headstone. They just put her in a grave and covered her up. They told Ida she should be glad not to have had to do it herself. Imagine."

"Beasts," wheezed Mrs. Krumpschmiedová. "How are they any better than Hitler, hmm? They treat people exactly the same way. Worse, in fact! They liquidate and humiliate their fellow countrymen. Pigs."

The women looked over at the old German lady in surprise.

"Come now, Mama," exclaimed her dismayed daughter-in-law in Czech, having up until then remained silent. She obviously understood German very well.

My, my, how the tables have turned, thought Gerta to herself. Not that she ever would have wished ill upon Ida. Never. She had even rejoiced with her when she finally had a husband and a child of her own, nor had she, unlike Zipfelová, ever suspected her of being conniving. Still, she couldn't help but find something cynically amusing about this ironic twist of fate. Once, she and the women now seated around her had been the ones forced to work at tasks that they'd never done before, and Ida had been the one, at the beginning, to walk around with a stern expression, making sure they weren't getting away with anything.

And now suddenly, Gerta had a job in a factory; Johanna was working as a seamstress; Antonia was a saleswoman somewhere; Hermína worked on the JZD collective farm. And Ida? Ida was now paying her dues for no good reason, just as they, too, had once been forced to do. And not one of them had ever deserved it, nor did Ida.

"Bunch of swine, the ones at the top," Hermína spoke up. "But it's always the simple folk who end up bearing the brunt of it. Same as always, same as under Hitler, same as under Stalin. Let's not kid ourselves. Crooks will find their way to the trough wherever they are. One doesn't have to look very far, right, Mrs. Krumpschmiedová? The Jechs had it out for you right after the war, and now they have it out for the Šenks. And it's always about property. Whether German or Czech. And they always end up taking it away, just according to different rules. But at least these rules were adopted by the people, the ones who voted, anyway—isn't that so?"

Krumpshmiedová was listening to Hermína with her head bowed low as before. Only her shoulders with the hump in the middle shook harder. The sunken eyes in the midst of her wrinkled face reddened.

"Who could have imagined such a thing before the war? Life here was so good. Everyone took care of themselves, but we were still a community. What's happened to it all? Sometimes, when I get up in the morning, I still think it's all just a bad dream that I simply can't understand. They took everything from us, just because we were the wrong nationality, even though during the war we never harmed a soul. They barely let us stay in our own homes. And now all the money we saved up since the war—my son, my daughter-in-law, and I—it's completely worthless. Our neighbors, longtime neighbors, who stayed here, are being sent off to camps—for not wanting to hand over their hard-earned harvest to SNB agents who show up at their door with some shady quota collector. I'm too old for this world. How often have I wished, as Zipfelová used to say, that the Lord would already come and take me. May he grant me a peaceful death, and then just let my son arrange for me to be buried next to old Krumpschmied. No need for any music—no point in theatrics for an old lady. Let it just come already."

"Now, Mama," the daughter-in-law spoke again in Czech, putting her arms around the old woman's shoulders. "Richard and I keep telling you that everything's going to be all right again."

Gerta looked over at Hermína. She was sipping the rest of her chicory coffee that by now had grown cold.

"No, it won't," said Hermína, having set her cup down.

Mrs. Krumpschmiedová's daughter-in-law looked at her in alarm, and a shadow of displeasure flitted across her face.

"You know it yourself. As long as Jech's here—or as Zipfelová, poor soul, used to say, that whole Jech clan—things will never be all right. People who have no trouble taking down someone like Šenk can just as easily take down any one of us."

She looked around at the others—at Johanna, Antonia, and Gerta—then turned back and fixed her gaze on young Krumpschmiedová.

"I'm sure you still remember how the Šenk barn burned down, and how they never got the equipment they needed from the district to do their harvesting—even though an unused tractor and a trailer sat in Jech's co-op. Who do you think was behind that? And in court, it was Jech who testified; everyone around here knows it. And those walnuts, the sack of potatoes, and whatever else was presented as evidence of undeclared provisions, that could have been Šenk's, but what about those bags of wheat, when that year their wheat had been infected with blight? Their ruined crop had even been officially recognized, don't you remember? So tell me, where did those bags Jech was pointing to come from?"

The young woman shrugged her shoulders.

"Or the undeclared plots of land from which they supposedly had a secret harvest, as Ida wrote. Who could have possibly come up with such a notion? Hidden plots of land, here, where everyone can see into each other's backyard. And still they stuck it on him. That, and failing to meet quotas, and obstructing a superior method of farming," she concluded with a bitter laugh.

As they were saying goodbye at the gate, Gerta turned to Hermína and asked, "What's going to happen with you now?"

The children had dashed out into the street in front of the house and were carrying on, running in circles around Antonia and Johanna, who were saying goodbye to the two Krumpschmied women. The dog came out after them. Hermína called to it; it spun around and bounded back to her side in the yard.

"I don't know." She shrugged. "I expect the house and the garden will go to the National Committee. Zipfelová had no heirs. And the National Committee, that's Jech, as you know. Maybe he'll move someone in here. Or he might let me stay. After all, I do work in the co-op. In fact, I'm his best milker." She laughed. "Who knows?"

"If it doesn't work out, come live with us. Whether there are four or five of us makes no difference. In Brno, you'll find a job."

Hermína shook her head. "The city is not for me anymore," she said, casting a dreamy glance around the early-summer garden.

Fallen white blossoms covered the grass beneath the apple trees beyond the house; the peonies along the fence were bowing their full, crimson heads to the ground. Gerta smelled their heady fragrance all the way to the small wooden gate, where she and Hermína remained standing by themselves. The children and the other two women were already far up ahead along the way back to the bus stop.

XV

She distinctly remembered the strange fluttering like swarming ants in her lower abdomen the first time she sat opposite that man. It was almost a full year after Karel's disappearance. From time to time, she would still call his office to ask for him. Each time, a different girl answered the phone. The last one didn't even know that a Karel Němec had ever worked there.

And then that man intercepted her, riding the train with her all the way back to the Brno-Židenice station, where she got off as she did every day to pick up Barbora from the daycare center. He walked her all the way to the entrance and then asked if they might find a time to speak privately somewhere, under different circumstances than what the train ride had allowed. Gerta suspected at once that it might have something to do with Karel. Her every thought still circled back to him. She agreed.

They met a few days later, when she didn't need to pick up Barbora as early as usual because she had an art class. They sat down in the Friendship Restaurant—which, after coffeehouses had been banned as a bourgeois anachronism, sprung up in place of the former Bellevue Café—at a table covered by a soiled green tablecloth flecked with cigarette burns. The restaurant was completely empty except for two old women who were sitting next to the grimy windows looking out over the parklike Red Army Square, and who appeared to be spending their afternoon over watered-down coffee topped with whipped cream. The bored and sluggish staff didn't notice them for a good long while, so the man sitting across from her offered her a cigarette. Gerta declined with thanks and watched as a veil of smoke drifted past his face and swirled upward until it disappeared against the high ceiling. She was impatient, seeing as she'd been waiting such a long time to hear something. Anything. Some explanation, a scrap of news. Was he alive? Was he well? Where was he? The waiter casually sauntered over to their table and took their order while staring out into the sparse green of the park. As if the two of them didn't even exist.

She ordered a coffee, the man a cognac. Gerta raised her eyebrows in surprise, as did the waiter.

"We're out," was his answer.

Naturally, thought Gerta. What kind of demands was this man making, at a time when one couldn't even find a bottle of Moravian wine? And even if one could, the average person couldn't afford it. Had he forgotten he was living in the People's Democracy of Czechoslovakia? The socialist paradise?

"Then a Becherovka, please."

The waiter turned and left.

Gerta looked the man straight in the eyes. They were bluer than any she had ever seen. Almost transparent, sky blue—blue eyes, pure soul, she thought.

He smiled at her and said, "For courage, you make me nervous."

Is he flirting with me? Gerta wondered. The butterflies in the pit of her stomach intensified their fluttering. Not that she found him unpleasant. He was an attractive man, just a few years older than she was. Not that he would think so, given how worn-out Gerta looked. But it was uncomfortable for her to be in the presence of a man. Any man. Her world was reserved exclusively for Barbora. She didn't need anything: no new thrills, no surprises. If she hadn't assumed that this had something to do with Karel, she never would have agreed to meet with him. But now it was beginning to seem as if it might not have anything to do with Karel, but rather something to do with her. Could it really be that he was interested in her?

"Why did you invite me here?" she asked point-blank, her eyes fixed on the steaming cup of coffee that the waiter had just wordlessly set down before her.

The man seated opposite gave her a smile. "I see you don't waste any time."

Gerta didn't know what she should be waiting for.

"Did you want to tell me something? Something better not discussed on a train?"

The man hesitated.

"What if I just wanted to get to know you better?" he finally said.

So it was true, thought Gerta with a fright.

"Are you joking?"

"Why should I be?"

Gerta angrily shook her head. "It would have been polite of you to say so in advance. And not pretend you had some mysterious reason that required a confidential conversation."

"Don't get me wrong, now. I really do have something I'd like to tell you," he said with a slight smile as he leaned in toward her. "But it still doesn't mean that we can't mix business and pleasure and enjoy a cup of coffee together. And a Becherovka," he added, raising his glass in the gesture of a toast.

"What do you want to tell me?"

"I see you're impatient."

"In thirty minutes, I have to pick up my daughter; her drawing class will be over."

"I know."

Gerta slowly stirred her coffee with the spoon.

"Just so you know, you're a very appealing woman. I find you interesting. Even beyond the call of duty."

"What duty?"

"Official. Would you like to get right down to business, or would you prefer to enjoy your cup of coffee and a bit of small talk with someone who finds you attractive?"

"Don't joke with me, please. What business do you mean?"

"Fine. We'll get right down to it. I'm here to make you a certain offer."

"An offer?"

"Yes."

"What offer?"

"Well, perhaps there are some things that you might like to know about, and then there are some things that I, in turn, would like to know about."

"What things? What's this supposed to mean?"

"Nothing unusual. Simply an offer of cooperation."

"I don't understand," said Gerta, shaking her head, perplexed.

The man smiled and motioned to the waiter, who was sitting at the bar, looking over a spread-out newspaper. They had to wait a while before he noticed them.

"Another, please," ordered the man. "Anything else for you, Mrs. Schnirch?"

"Schnirchová. No, thank you."

"Schnirchová," repeated the man once the waiter had moved away. "That's right, you actually had the German version of your last name changed to make it Czech, isn't that so?"

"That's just the last name I have. Why?"

"I know, I know. We were talking about certain pieces of information. Has it never occurred to you, for example, to try and find out what happened to your father and to your brother?"

Gerta's heart began to pound.

"How do you know about my father and my brother?"

The man smiled. "As I was saying, I could share some information with you that you might find interesting. And there might even be some other information I could share with you. About Mr. Němec, for instance."

Gerta had felt this was coming. "What do you know about Karel?"

"Easy, easy," the man said with a nonchalant laugh.

In her agitation, Gerta knocked her spoon against the cup—the sound rang out through the room, and the two women by the window turned to look at her.

"Right, well, I could tell you the whereabouts of Mr. Němec."

"Is he all right?" Gerta leaned forward eagerly.

"I can tell we're going to work well together. But just a moment. I'll answer anything you ask me. But one step at a time. Do you know what I'd like from you in exchange?"

Gerta pulled back in suspicion.

"I'd like for us to meet from time to time after your work, just like this, for coffee. Maybe once every two months, maybe even less, whatever you wish. What do you say?"

Now Gerta understood. It had taken her a moment, overcome as she was by the prospect of finding out something about Karel. And about her father and her brother. But now the realization hit her, and she was absolutely certain of it.

"What do you want from me?"

"Exactly what I just told you. For us to meet from time to time. And have a chat about life. About life all around you."

"Why?"

"Because I find you attractive. And because you stayed in Brno and still get together with certain individuals who were also formerly German. And because you maintain certain foreign contacts."

"Foreign contacts? Me?" She looked at him in astonishment.

The man reached into his pocket and pulled out a white envelope. He put it down in front of Gerta and then, very slowly, swiveled it so that she could read the name of the addressee. It was her letter to Teresa.

"Teresa's letter!" Gerta cried out.

"Not so loud, please."

"Where did you get that? It's been so long since I mailed it." Gerta put her head in her hands. "So that's why she never answered."

"That's right. After all, you didn't exactly write very nice things. Complaining like that about the socialist state, about our People's Democracy!"

"You read the letter?"

"Of course."

"What are you?"

"You still don't know?"

Gerta narrowed her eyes down to two slits. Naturally, she already knew. What a fool she'd been, not to have asked herself back then, in front of the school, who this person calling himself Novák really was.

"I certainly do know."

"In that case, we're completely done with introductions. And now you certainly also know that in exchange for the information you could provide me, I could provide you with information about Mr. Němec. Or about your brother, which might also interest you."

Gerta made a face. If only he knew.

"So, what do you say? Do we have an agreement? I could also be helpful to you in other ways. Your daughter has her problems at school, am I right? Something could be done about that, too, you know? Or about those Greeks who got moved into your apartment."

Gerta shook her head in disbelief.

"Really, it could."

"You want me to pass on information about Teresa to you? But I never see her! She couldn't even write back to me because you confiscated that letter."

"That's not a problem—we can send it again. That is, in a slightly modified form."

"And what do you have to gain from it? Teresa's not a person you have any reason to be interested in."

"You never know," the man said with a shrug. "Besides, there are others we might be interested in."

"Like who?"

"Mrs. Johanna Polivka and her connections, your contacts in general with the German minority living in Brno."

"Excuse me, but what do you mean by Johanna's connections? The only person Johanna gets together with is me."

"Really?"

"Absolutely. It hasn't been easy for us to go on living here after the war. I imagine you can understand that, yes?"

"That's why you all stick together in that little group of yours, right?"

"That may be so, but I don't go visiting her. I'm not even teaching my daughter German. I don't want her to be tainted by her Germanness, as I've been."

"What a shame that you don't honor your traditions."

"Excuse me, what are you talking about? What do you want from me? There's nothing I can tell you. I don't have any contacts."

"But you could easily establish them. Show up at their gatherings and start attending regularly. It would be easy enough for you to gain their confidence, Mrs. Schnirchová. You're still spelling it with an *Sch*, right? Or is it with an *Š*?"

"It's *Miss*. You should know that seeing as you know everything about me."

"Of course, forgive me."

The man smiled faintly and ran his hand through his black hair. Almost the same way as Karel used to do. Karel. *That man knows about him*, she thought. How many nights had she lain awake with her eyes open—how many hours had she spent watching the shadows beneath the streetlights or staring into the dense, inscrutable darkness? What a relief it would be.

"You've gone mad," she said. "You want the impossible from me. I don't wish to join the ranks of some minority. I'm glad to be on my own. You obviously don't know as much about my German background as you let on. If you did, then most likely you never would have picked me. I'm the daughter of a Czech mother. Her name was Barbora Ručková, in case you forgot to read that part."

"And a German father, Friedrich Schnirch. And your nationality was German. And as a German family, you fraternized with many other Germans, some of whom stayed here in Brno. Or returned here, as in your case."

"That's possible, but I don't know anything about them," said Gerta, pulling a two-crown piece out of her change purse and putting it beside the unfinished cup of coffee.

"What's the hurry?" The man lifted his head and looked at her. "Slow down. I really think we could be useful to one another."

Gerta imagined Karel. His handsome shoulders. His chest, against which she used to love to lay her head. His broad smile that made one of his eyes crinkle more than the other, giving his face a quirky, lopsided look. And the map of wrinkles on his brow that stretched all the way to his temples. She imagined him with the certainty of knowing he was still alive. And that if he were to return, he would come find her. Or his wife, who had wept for him on the other end of the telephone. But he was alive.

"I think you've told me enough already. And I think it's already a lot more than I can tell you."

She stood up and swung her bag over her shoulder. "I think there's no point in my addressing you as Mr. Novák when I say goodbye, right?"

The man smiled at her. "You're sharp."

"Goodbye then," said Gerta.

He grabbed the hand with which she was still leaning on the table.

"I would prefer to say until next time. Because I'm sure we'll meet again," he said, nodding with a confident smile.

Gerta dashed out of the restaurant onto the street. The sky above Brno was already growing dark.

XVI

The earth was bare, hard, and trampled by the hooves of horses. They charged around in a frenzied whirling, pawing wildly at the air with their front legs, reined in by the female riders on their bare backs. Astride them sat beautiful, completely naked women gripping the sides of the horses with their powerful thighs, covered only by the flowing veils of their long black hair. Around them the dust was swirling;

they slashed at it with wild gestures and raucous whooping; they were terrifying. Suddenly, on the hilltop behind them appeared a group of men on horseback. Spiraling clouds of dust rose up behind them as they galloped down the hillside at breakneck speed toward the women. One could see them separating out, forming loose ranks, preparing to surround them, and not a single one of the women noticed. I wanted to shout them a warning, but my voice got caught in my throat, and no matter how hard I tried, all I could do was wheeze and rasp, and couldn't get even the slightest sound to come out. The men reached the foot of the mountain and were slowly mingling with the naked bodies of the warrior women. The first few swords rose high above the group and fell, then quickly rose again, the edges of the blades dripping with blood. Then one of the young women threw herself into the midst of the fray. I couldn't help it; I let my eyes follow her into the bloody turmoil. I saw her bend forward toward her horse's head, wrap herself around his neck, and bury her face in the twisted braids of his mane. She came bearing down swiftly on a man wearing a leather cuirass. In his hand, he wielded a sword with which he was slashing left and right, not even looking to see where it fell—human limbs were scattered on the ground. It was Achilles; I could see him clearly. His armor, forged for him by order of his sea-nymph mother, and his miraculous heel, which gleamed with a radiant light. I knew that no one could defeat Achilles. That not even this Amazon could change the course of destiny, which, after all, had been written by the gods of Olympus. I wanted to stop her, but it was too late—a dark cloud was descending over the fighting pair, and riding it was Athena, looking down at Achilles with concern. But by then, the young woman's chest was already soaked with blood from the wound that the invincible Achilles had inflicted with a strike of his sword. Her head tilted back as she let out a bloodcurdling scream; she flung her arms out to the earth and the sky and slipped backward off her horse. I could finally see her face, and even though

I'd suspected all along, it was only now that I knew. I was seized by a terrible fear.

"Mommy!" I screamed in sheer terror, as loudly as I could, and then I saw her face appear out of the darkness, right above my sweaty forehead.

Back then, it used to happen so often that Mom finally asked Auntie Athanaia not to tell me those stories of hers anymore. But I wheedled them out of her anyway. I had become so obsessed with them that I couldn't do without them. The steady ticking of the kitchen clock, the shallow breathing of Uncle Achilles coming from the next room, and the soft voice of Auntie Athanaia, who would cradle my head on her knees, stroke my hair, and tell me stories about the gods who lived in Greece on a mountain whose name sounded like the Olympics; about fearless warriors and beautiful maidens, who weren't afraid to stand up to them; about the sad fates of the children of the gods, like Orpheus and poor Eurydice; about Prometheus, who, as punishment for having given mankind fire, had to spend the rest of his life chained to a rock somewhere in Russia; or about brave Achilles, after whom Uncle had been named. Up until the moment when Mom would come home from work, Auntie Athanaia would manage to tell me lots of stories. But all that came much later, only after I was finally allowed to stay at home with her alone.

Early on, it didn't seem as if it would ever happen. Mom and I would hide out in our room and sit on the bed, waiting for Mrs. Athanaia to stop clattering around with the dishes in the kitchen. Back then, I couldn't understand why Mom had let herself be kicked out of our kitchen so easily—after all, it was our house. Except Mom didn't care. She would retreat into our bedroom, go over to the window, and stare out of it until it grew completely dark. Only then would she go into the kitchen to prepare some food, which we never ate at the kitchen table, but always sitting on our bed instead. Back then, I didn't understand why everything had changed so suddenly. But I had a feeling it had something to do with Uncle Karel, who wasn't coming to see us anymore. After he stopped coming around, everything went wrong. Mom stopped smiling. It was as if her lips no longer knew how, as if they'd forgotten how to stretch and turn up at the corners, letting her teeth show and laughter spill out. Maybe it started right around then, or maybe it had always been that way. I don't know anymore, but the only laughter I ever remember seeing cross my mom's face was a kind of spastic twitch, during which she would let out two *h* sounds in a row, and that would disappear as quickly as it had appeared. It was a strange, short laugh, as if she were afraid of being caught and punished, and she was quick to go right back to hiding again behind that unchanging, blank expression that refused to give away any hint of emotion.

For me, it actually came as a relief when my mom finally had enough. I don't remember anymore exactly when it happened, but one day she simply got up from the window and marched into the kitchen where Auntie Athanaia was preparing some food, and suddenly, without warning, lit into her. I'd stayed behind the door listening, surprised by Mom's yelling, by the pot crashing to the tiled floor, by the slamming of the cupboard door under the aluminum sink, and by the tears of Auntie Athanaia and the grumbling of Uncle Achilles, who probably hadn't understood a word. I have no idea how they came to an agreement, since not even Auntie Athanaia was speaking much Czech yet, but from then on there was peace. We stayed out of each other's way as much as we could, and everything was on a schedule—cooking, laundry, and even cleaning—and we all shared the living room. And if Uncle Achilles wanted to have a snooze, Auntie would lead him away to their bedroom.

And afterward, sometime later on, I remember Auntie Athanaia waiting for me when I got home from school with a warm pita spread with honey—no clue where she got it from, maybe those Greek girl-friends she talked about from time to time. By then I wasn't needing to go to after-school anymore, didn't have to wait there until after dark for

Mom. By then, we'd already become friends with Auntie Athanaia, me and Mom, who, at first, allowed her to come pick me up from school, and later on, when I was older, to wait for me at home with that freshly baked pita that Uncle Achilles and I were crazy about. But that was only on Wednesdays, and then on Sundays—not something one could have every day.

And it was all because of Lidice, the village the Nazis had razed during the Lidice massacre—the horror that I was always being bullied about, until Mom finally patched things up with Auntie Athanaia and let her look after me. At least Lidice was good for something. Lidice, and then the night I told her that Auntie Athanaia had shown me a photo of her little girl who had died somewhere in Žamberk, when after the end of the war she'd been sent out of Greece ahead of them, ahead of Auntie Athanaia and Uncle Achilles. Back then, I'd asked why they didn't have any more children—after all, most people had two or three. She looked terribly sad and just shook her head, saying, "*Nyet, moya smert, my death.*" Maybe that made Mom feel a bit sorry for her, and she stopped seeing her just as someone who had taken over our home. Then every once in a while, she'd even send me in to ask if they'd like some tea or bread with curd cheese. And then, for the first time, Auntie Athanaia baked pita even for us, and Mom and I both really liked it, and after that, we started to sit together and eat at the same table and offer each other food. And then once in a while, we'd even share a meal, and it went on like that, getting better and better, even though every so often the two of them would still get into each other's hair. I couldn't stand when that happened. Because, you see, by then I really liked Auntie Athanaia a lot, almost more than my other two aunties, Johanna and Antonia. And that was because she used to stroke my hair and tell me those amazing stories, and she also used to tell me about Greece—that it looked like paradise there, always sunny, and the sea always warm, with everyone swimming in it and laughing happily, and that people spent the evenings dancing together, not like here, where everyone was holed up by themselves at home. When she would tell me about it, I began to feel warm, too, as if I were also under that sun and by that sea, although I couldn't imagine what it looked like. Auntie Athanaia just called it *big, big water, beautiful*, and then my mom would call it water that was practically endless, and that covered half the world and was very salty.

Afterward, I tried to drink salty water, but I must have overdone it with the salt, because it wouldn't dissolve—it settled at the bottom of the cup and was so thick that when I tried to drink it, I felt salt crystals crunching between my teeth. And what's more, it practically made me throw up. Then that night, after all that, I still got a smack in the head. Mom was really mad, because I'd wasted half a bag of salt, and we already had barely enough money for anything. After that, I didn't long for the sea as much, even though Auntie Athanaia's stories still made me feel that wonderful warmth. There was no comparison to what I would have been going through at the same time at after-school. There, the other kids would have been cursing me out again, shoving me into a corner, and making me play Lidice, while the teacher pretended not to see a thing. But she saw perfectly well—I noticed that once, when I caught her looking toward our corner and watching. But she did nothing. The only time she did something was early on, in first grade, when she put me on her lap and made a fuss over the pictures I'd drawn. And at the same time, as if I were stupid, she asked me what my mother did, and did we speak German at home, and did we get together with other people who also spoke German. It was a good thing I never told her anything back then—stupid cow with her beehive hairdo, she wasn't even good at being two-faced. As punishment, she would then say to me in front of the other kids that I was in the school by mistake, and that I should have been sent to a special school long ago, because a fellow comrade teacher had told her that even in third grade I was still mixing up my letters. And that it was probably because Czech simply wasn't our language, meaning my mom's and mine. Back then, they obviously didn't know how to deal with kids who mixed up their letters, but basic human compassion should have been enough to stop a good teacher from talking like that. This comrade Brunclíková, though, had no such concerns, and who knows, maybe that was what first put the idea of Lidice into Aleš Kotečeks head. Whatever it was, it got everyone to chase me and play Torture, and naturally I was always the one who had to be tortured, because I had to atone for what we had done to the Czechs and the Jews. Back then, I had no idea what it was all about, and when I got home, Mom didn't explain anything to me. She just got really upset and became impossible to talk to, and the next day she came to school with me and went right to the headmistress. But whatever it was that she hoped to accomplish clearly didn't happen, because when she came after work to pick me up that evening, she didn't say a word, but she must have noticed, as I did, that Brunclíková did something with her lips that looked like she was spitting on the ground in front of us. It was only after we got home, and I was trying to explain it all at dinner, that Auntie Athanaia saved the day. She turned to my mom and begged her not to send me to after-school anymore, saying I could stay at home with her since, after all, she wasn't even working. And wonder of wonders, Mom nodded in agreement right away. I almost couldn't believe it, although I saw it with my own two eyes. From that moment on, we became something like a family. It's hard to believe, but we actually really liked each other and stopped feeling as though we were in each other's way. And that was how it stayed until the day Auntie Athanaia and Uncle Achilles packed up their things and went back to Greece, because they were finally allowed to go home.

XVII

On this particular day, Gerta didn't get off at the stop in Židenice but continued all the way to the Brno Central Station. In the late afternoon, she made her way up the Třída Vítězství, Victory Avenue, and across

Náměstí Svobody, Freedom Square—places she got to only rarely—searching for a suitable gift for Barbora, who was finally graduating from her place on the school bench, and with a vocational certificate no less, something Gerta hadn't even dared to hope for. Her Barbora was finally getting a diploma. After the ordeal of elementary school, after having to repeat two grades—following which Barbora still mixed up her letters when she read aloud—and after vocational school, which had required her to travel every day all the way to Letovice, forty-three kilometers away, her Barbora had really done it. She'd earned a vocational certificate and in July would be going to work at the porcelain factory. It had been a rough road with her, no doubt about it, but at least things hadn't turned out to be as much of a disappointment as they had for Anni and Rudi.

Barbora had never harbored any grand illusions about what she wanted to become. Fortunately, she at least liked to draw and had no greater ambition than to replicate designs from templates onto the smooth surfaces of porcelain cups. And to learn how to mix fusible pigments. And fortunately, no one was particularly interested in a vocational school in the small town of Letovice, which required a round-trip commute of more than an hour and a half each day because there were no boarding facilities.

Things had been much worse for Anni and Rudi, who had only started to learn Czech after the war. They both ended up having to repeat a grade, because apart from Johanna, nobody was willing to help them with a language that was only familiar to them from the jeering of other children. The comrade teachers took great pains to make the Czech language and their classroom experience as unpleasant as possible. Even later on, once Gerta was already back in Brno and would occasionally get together with Johanna, she would hear about all the homework they both had to contend with, and how desperately they struggled trying to learn two languages as similar as Czech and Russian at the same time—not to mention with every other subject, all taught in a language they didn't yet fully understand. Nevertheless, in the end, they finished primary school with honors, and proud Johanna was already envisioning her twins as students at the *Gymnasium*—or rather at the eleven-year school, which back then had taken the place of the *Gymnasium*—and after that, hopefully, even as students at the university. Nothing of the sort. In 1955, applicants of formerly German nationality were as a rule not accepted at such institutions. And Johanna couldn't find anyone willing to stand up for her children's right to have a future. With the greatest of difficulty, she finally managed to get them into a secondary school specializing in chemistry in Brno-Řečkovice, where they were grooming a new generation of workers for the Institute of Pure Chemicals that had recently opened in the sprawling Lachema complex. Did anybody care that Anni had wanted to study literature and Rudi engineering? Nobody. And that was even before they knew that neither of them would be allowed to study beyond secondary school. Rudi was drafted into the army right away and, as was to be expected, was dispatched to the most far-flung garrison in Slovak Košice; and Anni, after every one of her university applications had been rejected, was assigned to work at Lachema.

So, in the end, when it came to Barbora and her future, things weren't so dire after all. They had been fortunate in their misfortune, thought Gerta on that June day as she rode the tram back from the Brno Central Station. In her bag, she had several yards of green brocade; it had cost her a fortune, but Barbora had been wanting the fabric so badly for a dress. They would work on it together in the evenings, so that she'd have something nice to wear when that Jára of hers, who for a while now had been walking her home from school, asked her out. Gerta didn't particularly care for him. He struck her as a vapid type. True, he looked good in his turtleneck and jeans, for which he must have paid a pretty penny in the Tuzex shop, peering through his fringe of shaggy bangs, but his cool nonchalance vanished the moment she offered him food. The very first time, he had descended on the plate of kolach pastries like a swarm of locusts. When she next invited him for a Sunday lunch, she ended up putting one of her own slices of dumpling on his plate, concerned that six pieces hadn't been enough for him. Then for the rest of the afternoon, he lolled about on the kitchen sofa, not saying a word, the top button of his pants undone. He only mumbled in agreement or disagreement when Gerta asked him something as he sipped coffee with them, his distended stomach rising and falling in regular rhythm with his breathing—until he fell asleep.

At that point, Gerta looked over in surprise at Barbora, who just shrugged her shoulders and said, "He works on a construction site every day, you know, and moonlights too. I got myself a real workhorse."

And a real klutz, thought Gerta, watching him from the kitchen window as he pulled two more chunks of bread out of his bag while he waited downstairs for Barbora to finish getting ready to go out for the evening.

On the other hand, maybe he would be good to her, thought Gerta, and she'd keep him in line with those dumplings. And in the end, she was glad that Barbora had managed to find anyone at all. That she had found a way to escape these four walls, behind which Gerta had locked them both away. Unintentionally. She was happy for her, although every time she heard the front door close behind her, she felt an instant panic, and couldn't relax until ten o'clock, when she would hear the key rattling in the lock. But what mother wouldn't be worried about her daughter? she told herself, lost in thought about Barbora, the bag with the brocade at her feet, as she sat in the tram that had been stuck for a while now at the intersection in front of the Künstlerhaus gallery, waiting for a caravan of Tatra trucks full of cargo to go by. In the meantime, she glanced out of the window at a banner, fluttering in the summer-evening breeze. On it was a balloon, a round, bright red hot-air balloon rising over a green lawn. Gerta imagined herself in the wicker basket, floating above the pristine landscape of childish shapes and objects. "Kamil Lhoták Exhibition" read the inscription on the banner. Right then, she decided that on Sunday morning, she would come here with Barbora.

Balloons. Bicycles and motorcycles. A solitary, far-flung wooden fort on the outskirts of town. A world that seemed to have sprung out of a child's fantasy, but with every detail painstakingly rendered so as to seem realistic. They walked through the rooms and peered with fascination into the inner workings of another world. For the first time in a long while, she and Barbora shared a genuine sense of enthusiasm and an experience of pure joy. They went up the stairs into the main exhibition hall and made their way along the wall, moving from one painting to the next. And as always happened when in the presence of art, Gerta felt she was in the company not only of Barbora, but also of Janinka, with her fine flaxen hair and in her soiled skirt, the way she had looked in August 1944, the last time Gerta saw her, on top of a heap of rubble amid the bombed-out buildings on Pressburger Straße. She tried to look at the paintings through Janinka's eyes and wondered if she would have appreciated this technical world, rendered in such a romantically old-fashioned style, she who moved in a world of blazing colors and the most outlandish ornamentations. The world of a kaleidoscope. Or would she have stood in front of Lhoták's paintings the same way she had stood facing Gerta back then, with a blank, lifeless expression, her heels digging in and eyes staring right through her? The rubble had been crumbling beneath her feet, and the slight hand with pronounced veins had resisted Gerta's grasp as she tried to lead her down from the wreckage, back to solid ground. She wanted the doctor, scurrying among the wounded who had been dragged from the ruins of the buildings, to examine her, and was then going to take her back to their apartment and wait for her to calm down. The street was full of falling debris, ashes, and scorched scraps of paper. All around them echoed the continuous cries of the wounded and the voices of rescuers and relatives calling out to those who were missing. Not far off lay a person who was missing his leg from the knee down. He was gripping his thigh with both hands—blood was gushing from the stump. His face was a gaping mouth with enormous teeth that would momentarily clench together, only to open again in the next spasm of screaming. The sight made Gerta feel sick, but Janinka seemed oblivious to everything happening around her. She just stood there, shaking, looking down, staring at her tightly clenched fists. She couldn't remember for how long they remained huddled together in the midst of the chaos and mass of milling people before Gerta spotted a Red Cross vehicle and nurses in white caps who were helping to load up the wounded. She grabbed hold of Janinka and took off running toward them.

"Wait, please, have a look at her, examine her, please, check her. See if anything's the matter. Please," she called out to them. One of the nurses motioned her closer, and Gerta managed to prod Janinka toward her. But no sooner had the woman tried to touch her than Janinka doubled over and began furiously screaming and savagely, hysterically flailing her arms. Even Gerta recoiled in fright.

"Stop it, stop it," the nurse shouted at her as other people began to close in—a driver and a man with a Red Cross band on his arm. They grabbed Janinka around her waist and by her legs and carried her into the vehicle. All Gerta saw was Janinka's body stiffening in a spasm and then convulsively beginning to shake all over.

"Let me go with her," she shouted.

The nurse pushed her away from the narrow back footboard as she helped up a man with a bleeding wound on his forehead.

"The hospitals are overflowing. You can't come."

"Where are you taking her?" cried Gerta.

"To the Brothers of Charity. You can come by tomorrow. What's the girl's name?"

"Jana Hornová. Will you remember?"

"Yes, Hornová. Are you family?"

"No, but . . ."

"Tell her family to come by and ask for her tomorrow. At the Brothers, understand?"

Gerta nodded fervidly, her path obstructed by another pair of passing wounded, each helping to support the other. Then the vehicle drove off with Janinka in it.

It had taken Gerta over a week to track down Mrs. Hornová. On the first of September, Gerta spent the whole afternoon waiting in the passageway of their building, and when she saw Mrs. Hornová come in, she ran over to her, eager for news about Janinka's condition. At the sight of Gerta, Mrs. Hornová's face seemed to turn to stone. But that no longer deterred Gerta. She vividly remembered how, as the war progressed, the cordiality of her mother's longtime friend had gradually evaporated. "And who can blame her?" Gerta's mother used to say to Gerta, when Gerta couldn't understand why Janinka wasn't allowed to come over anymore.

"Is she better?" she cried out.

Mrs. Hornová, at that moment, was standing by the entrance to the passageway, and Gerta slowly advanced toward her.

"Is she better? Won't you please tell me?"

Janinka's mother just kept on standing there, staring at her with a stony expression. She looked Gerta's rotund figure up and down, her eyes narrowed to slits and her lips compressed into a hard, straight line.

"Please, Mrs. Hornová, how is Janinka?"

Mrs. Hornová made a few quick steps in her direction, moving simultaneously toward Gerta and toward the building's entrance. Gerta carefully stepped out of her way.

"She is dead," she said.

"What?"

"Janinka died. The day after the air raids."

Gerta stared at her in disbelief.

"Janinka is dead, do you hear me? She's dead because of people like you. Like your father, like your brother, like you. You disgusting, disgusting slut."

Gerta stepped back with a gasp.

"Don't you ever, ever come into my sight again, understand?"

With that, Mrs. Hornová spun around and disappeared behind the door. Gerta backed slowly away until she bumped into the wall of the passageway. Janinka, dead? Nonsense, she kept repeating to herself, still catching her breath. Nonsense. She couldn't be dead—she had seen her. Being lifted into the vehicle. In convulsions. But one didn't die from that. Gerta slumped down against the wall and dropped into a squat, keeping her knees apart, allowing her protruding belly to rest between them. Tears were streaming down her face. She wasn't sobbing. She wasn't even sure if she was crying. She was chased away from Janinka's doorstep once more, this time by both parents. They weren't about to tell her where Janinka was buried, Nazi slut that she was.

Since that time, since that unusually cool month of August of the next-to-last year of the war, Gerta thought of her friend whenever she was in the presence of art. And on that day, at the Kamil Lhoták exhibition, also. As she and Barbora were leaving the exhibit, she felt as though Janinka were right there with them, large as life. As if she were walking alongside her, quietly, as had always been her way. Then for a while, she seemed to recognize her in every woman they passed, even in that dark-haired lady with the teased updo and distinctive black eyeliner, who was being helped out of her luxurious fur coat by an older man in the museum cloakroom.

XVIII

Had she only imagined it, or had it really been her? It was distinctly possible that she'd only imagined it, as for that matter she so often did. Maybe the nightmares and hallucinations were coming back again. It would be nothing unusual, given the regularity with which they typically came on. She practically expected them by now. She, Jana Rozsývalová, had already grown used to them. The only thing she could never be sure of was the exact moment in which reality would change into delusion. She would be thinking that what she was hearing and seeing was the same as what others were experiencing, only to discover that she'd been locked up again because she'd been raving. Madness, how tender that word coming from Josef's lips had once sounded, just after the war, which they had lived through in that place together, each a victim of their time. These days, he would just brusquely rap on her bedroom door and slip medications he brought home from work into her mouth. He was good; he always knew what was wrong with her and how best to help her. Josef. Today, comrade Physician in Chief, Josef Rozsýval. And she, comrade Mrs. Physician in Chief, Jana Rozsývalová, housewife, who from time to time would go mad. Naturally, she wasn't officially a housewife—their socialist state, to which she and Josef were so devoted, would never tolerate such a bourgeois anachronism. But she did receive a disability pension; Josef had seen to that. So now, had she truly just imagined it, or had it really been her, Gerta Schnirch from Sterngasse? Was it even possible that it could have been her? Nonsense. She would have to tell Josef that the delusions seemed to be starting again.

After all, back then, her mother told her that Gerta had disappeared, along with her newborn child. She had disappeared, like most of the Brno Germans. She had even heard that she had died, at least according to the caretaker in her building. Just after the war. Just before she, Janinka, had been released.

It never occurred to her to question it and to go searching for her. Not after all that had happened. All because of the Germans. Even if she'd had the opportunity back then, she wouldn't have gone looking for Gerta. Because of her family: her father, a die-hard Nazi, and that brother of hers in his Hitler Youth uniform. He'd been wearing it the last time she'd seen him when he made her stand at attention behind their building and *Sieg Heil* while he groped between her thighs. Afterward, he had chased her all the way back home, the pig, Mr. Deutschland. Or had she made that up as well? No, certainly not, after all, the delusions hadn't started until after the war. Yes, definitely, not until after the war. Which had been brought on by the Germans, by people like Gerta and her family. Why had her mother ever let her be friends with that girl? Supposedly, Janinka's mother had once been close to Gerta's mother, whom Janinka could barely remember. Except what people used to say about her, that Schnirch kept her under lock and key, and would beat her with his belt for every Czech word she said—that much she did remember. But people would say anything.

Still, if it actually had been Gerta Schnirch, where would she have materialized from? Being German, she would have been expelled from the city, after all! Although if Janinka were to look around, she'd notice that a few Germans had remained. Indeed, even those like Morawczik, or these days rather comrade Moravčík, who was now a party member with Josef and accompanied him to meetings. Josef didn't remember him; he hadn't lived on Bratislavská Street back then, but Janinka remembered him very well. And, God knew, he was certainly no antifascist, as he had tried after the war to make everyone believe. He must have paid a pretty penny—how else would he ever have gotten his hands on a waiver?—but whatever, he'd still managed to turn his coat in time. But Gerta, how had she wheedled her way back here? That was, if that woman at the exhibition had really been her. She had looked old, very old. And that young woman with her, she could have been her daughter, that girl her mother had told her she had managed to get herself pregnant with toward the end of the war. Who knew whom she might have been willing to sleep with, just so she could stay in Brno. That was so typically German, to do whatever it took to maximize personal gain, stay put, and remain masters of everything, lapping up as much as they could for themselves, hanging on to property that they'd stolen from the Jews whom they'd murdered, those German monsters—if only there were a way to get back at them. Pay them back in kind, bastards that they were. Or at the very least, do back to them what they had done to her, Janinka. That was what she would wish on her, on Schnirchová, prancing around with her daughter at her side, as if nothing had happened. How was it that someone like her could have a child, whereas she, Jana Rozsývalová, wife of the physician in chief, couldn't? How was that possible? Because of them, those German butchers, who had poked around inside her and then left her, with only the scars on her thighs and a gutted womb to weep over. Tears started rolling down her cheeks.

Had it not been for Josef, she never would have made it to the end of the war. Her life would have been snuffed out by a higher-than-usual dose of sedatives. The Germans had done a thorough job of cleaning up after themselves before they fled. As it was, those last six months of the war hadn't been worth living anyway. She hadn't even been aware of being alive. It felt as if one morning she woke from a dream to find herself in a ward for the mentally ill. All she could remember were the laughing faces of some of the staff members, shouting that the war was over. And then all around her, the bodies, lying inert on beds or sitting moaning on the floor, wrecks of human beings. And Josef, seated by her, his head resting against the headboard of her bed, asleep. God, how glorious it had been back then to wake up, go back home, and have Josef. It never bothered him that they gouged her out as much as they had. The bastards. He moved in with her family, married her, joined the party along with her father, and from that time on, they'd led a good life. They were given a brand-new multigenerational home in the posh Jirásek quarter. And a company car. And Josef, the hospital errand boy, which he'd become after they shut down his department at the onset of the war, rose through the ranks to become physician in chief. And deputy chairman of the Regional Committee of the KSČ, the Communist Party of Czechoslovakia. But his wife hadn't borne him any children. And then a bitch like that, like that German woman long presumed dead, goes parading past her, putting her kid on display.

Or had it not been her? Was it starting up again? Was Janinka again seeing things that others weren't seeing? Maybe the image of Gerta only existed in her mind, and in reality, there had been no such person in the Künstlerhaus. And furthermore, what would she have been doing there, since, after all, she'd been expelled, and she was dead? And it served her right. Both of them, her brat as well.

XIX

She couldn't live the way Gerta did. She couldn't bear it personally, nor could she pretend in front of her children that everything was in perfect order. That the world was their oyster. That they had nothing to fear from it. Nothing at all. *Nichts.* And that she could let them leave the nest and carry on as if no one would try to do them any harm. She couldn't pretend that their ancestors, her parents and her parents' parents, and Gerhardt's parents as well, had all come from purely Czech roots. Besides, by now her children were too grown and too German to buy such a story. *Ihre Kinder waren Deutsche,* her children were German, plain and simple, and there was no way she could talk them into believing that they weren't. Or that nothing had happened. When the natural ease with which they were used to moving back and forth between Czech and German households had disappeared from their lives. When in the end, the Germans themselves had all disappeared, and for good. And when they personally witnessed the way in which they had all disappeared. She couldn't tell them stories, when back then they had both been marching the whole length of the way beside her—first to Pohořelice, and then on to Bergen, today Perná. Following that first night, Anni hadn't spoken for three whole weeks—ghastly, *schrecklich.* Anni knew perfectly well what had happened to all the Germans.

Nothing doing. Even had she wanted to, she lacked the ability to paint a prettier picture of the world around them. Maybe because she knew she couldn't fool them. Maybe because she didn't want to. *Vielleicht.* Maybe. And maybe, according to Gerta, because she didn't have enough strength to spare them the heavy burden that she herself carried around like a monkey on her back, *na ja.* Gerta had said this to her once, after they had put the children to sleep and had stayed sitting up together in her kitchen with its windows that looked out onto the courtyard balcony. Johanna had asked her for advice on how to carry on—she was tired of fumbling in the dark, always asking herself how best to guide her children's lives. With no Gerhardt, whom she'd really needed by her side in those days, to point them in the right direction, to help them make decisions. But he wasn't around. She was all alone, *ganz allein.* So she turned to Gerta, thinking that she, too, must be grappling with the question of how best to help Barbora deal with everything. Except that Gerta wasn't concerned. Not in the least. Gerta always knew right away how to handle anything. She had a precise gauge for assessing what was good or bad. This had always made Johanna envious—for her, making a decision had always been such a struggle, whether due to being afraid or overly speculative, she was simply incapable. And the same had held true back then, when she'd been grappling with the dilemma of whether, when it came to her children, it was better to let them blindly play the game of chance or reveal the world to them exactly as it was. Back then, Gerta told her that she could stay in her isolation if that was what she, Johanna, wanted. She could remain in perpetual mourning for Gerhardt, for dirndls and for Christmas *Stollen* filled with raisins, but if she kept her children locked away in that isolation with her, then it was purely out of cowardice, out of fear of being stuck in it all alone. That time, she, Johanna, had broken down in tears. If only it had been Gerhardt steadying her by the elbow, and not Gerta, who at that moment herself seemed embarrassed and upset. Had Gerta been right back then? Had she raised her children to honor their family traditions, their German heritage, respect their father, and stay away from the Czech world, just to avoid being left with it all by herself? She couldn't discern the truth; she felt as if she were blind. She knew that she could make things easier for them. If she were to impress upon them the need to be respectful toward all those Stalinist comrade teachers and comrade foremen in the rubber factory, where Rudi had taken a job to get away from chemistry. If she were to urge them to practice self-discipline and self-restraint. To think positively even about people who reviled them just because of their heritage. She knew that with enough willpower, she could force it upon them. But how could she encourage them to have a relationship with people who had expelled them and who had imprisoned their father, *nicht war*? She couldn't do it. Whatever the reason, whether out of cowardice or out of respect for their traditions, the thought of it made her feel sick inside. So she had raised them as Germans living undercover in a foreign country. This was how they talked about it among themselves at home. To the point that sometimes Johanna would even get frightened. After all, to this day, speaking German on the street was forbidden. If anything were ever to happen to her children now, she wouldn't survive it. And she would have only herself to blame for having cultivated their sense of otherness. She was especially concerned about Rudi. He had a temper and he was strong, and he carried her grief for his lost father within himself. She had seen him countless times try to step up and fill his father's shoes. In his desire to please her, he was willing to take on the impossible. In her darkest nightmares, she would see him caught up in a brawl because someone called him a "*Deutschak*," a derogatory term he couldn't stand. Johanna would then see them taking him away and would see herself standing behind a glass wall, through which neither her cries nor the pummeling of her fists could be heard. She would then wake up from such dreams in the room she shared with her two grown children, in whom she had been the one to keep the past alive. The past and their German heritage. Every Monday and Thursday they would review German together. She had written down all the poems she remembered from her childhood in a hardcover notebook, and this was what they used as study material. Instead of doing what Gerta advocated, which was to forget, as quickly as possible, the language that in this Republic brought them nothing but trouble. Gerta wanted her child to blend in. To stand solidly on her own two feet so that it wouldn't even occur to anyone to knock them out from underneath her—because Barbora herself would have no sense of why anybody should. Gerta had scrupulously hidden from her anything that had to do with her ancestry. And so far, it hadn't occurred to Barbora to ask questions. But for Johanna, this was unacceptable. She couldn't allow her children to forget their origins. To forget the German language. To bury, along with everything else, even Gerhardt himself. She didn't want them to blend in. She wanted them, on the contrary, to be fully aware of everything that was in any way connected to their lives. And to own it with pride. In honor of Gerhardt. So that one day when he returned, he would be proud of them. And he would praise her, Johanna, for how she raised his children. All alone and yet so brave. And independent. Johanna's eyes filled with tears as she imagined Gerhardt returning to her someday. A hundred times she had imagined the look on his face when he would first step into their one-room apartment off the courtyard balcony, and the twins would rush to embrace him and greet him in his mother tongue. In their mother tongue. *Auf Deutsch*, in German. And how he would then look at her when he realized that she had succeeded—she had preserved in them a faith in their values, in their society, and in their own German people.

Johanna and her children used to gather with the other Germans on Sundays, after church. It had taken her a while to get to them, but finally she had found them. One year after she and the children had returned. That had been in forty-eight, after almost a full year had passed during which she could finally stop living in constant fear of being expelled. At that point, she made the decision to leave the haven that Frau Zipfel had so unselfishly made available to them in Bergen.

Some of the other women made the same decision as well—each one for her own reasons. And some hadn't made the decision at all. For Johanna, there was no choice. As soon as it was possible, she had to try to find Gerhardt, who had stayed behind in some part of Kounic College. She set out for the unknown. To a city where she no longer had a roof over her head. Or a job. But she had no regrets, even though she hadn't yet managed to find him. This, however, was through no fault of her own, but rather because no one would give her access to any information. No one was willing to tell her anything. *Überhaupt nichts*, nothing. All the civil servants avoided her questions as if she were trying to unearth a state secret. The only certainty she had was that of her last memory of him. May 1945. Standing in front of a fence with barbed wire across the top, trying to catch a glimpse of Gerhardt during roll call in the Kounic College courtyard. And she had succeeded.

In her grief, she had received a great deal of sympathy from everyone in the German club, which technically wasn't allowed to exist as a club, because Germans were officially banned from congregating. Even the practice of their faith, which had brought them together, was forbidden to them. Or at the very least, strongly discouraged. But they couldn't eradicate her; she had succeeded in making her own inroads. Among people who had been left with nothing, and who no longer had anything to lose. And it was among these people that Johanna and her children found themselves toward the end of the 1948, back when Mass was still being celebrated at the Brothers of Charity on Wiener Straße, now known as Vídeňská Street. She would never be able to thank Father Augustus enough for all his support, which had helped to relieve her anguish. Or the Heissigs, the Grübers, the Mattls, and all the others with whom she would gather there. Their faith in shared traditions and in God carried her through all those years during which, without Gerhardt, she had become a mere shadow of herself. Now, at least she had their Sunday gatherings to look forward to.

Johanna didn't blame anyone for wanting to shed their former life. In the long run, it was probably better that way. *Vielleicht.* Maybe. She, however, couldn't do it, for the simple reason that she had chosen to continue living in the past. Attached to Gerhardt. And also because switching coats had always gone against her grain. She especially had no desire to switch out hers, brightly adorned by her faith, for Gerta's drab gray one, under which she was barely even visible. The truth was that in the end, regardless of their differing points of view, they were in the same boat. They had both learned to live in seclusion. Fearful of the world. There was just one small difference between them. Gerta's seclusion was absolute and final. She had locked herself away in it alone, to give Barbora the chance to live a life different from her own. The only person allowed to encroach on Gerta's seclusion was most likely Johanna, and perhaps Antonia and Hermína. Johanna's seclusion, on the other hand, although outwardly the same, was actually full of people. People who didn't pretend they weren't German. Who didn't pretend to have stopped living and breathing in harmony with God's world and their own conscience. Johanna's seclusion was full of others who bore their destiny alongside her and her children. And whenever she pictured their procession, bathed in heavenly light, led by the benevolent Father Augustus and his two altar boys, enveloped by the fragrance emanating from the softly clinking censers, she felt certain that for herself and for her children's futures, she had made the right decision.

XX

She arrived unexpectedly, appearing overnight, accompanied by Hermína. Suddenly, there she was, standing in the doorway with a big smile. The first thing Gerta noticed was the gleaming gold tooth in the upper row of incisors. It was just as conspicuous as the black hole it had replaced, and with which she remembered her.

"I decided to have the old days gilded," said Teresa, in German, with a laugh.

Gerta stood with her arms spread out between the wings of the door and couldn't budge. She stared at her as if she were an apparition, until finally even Hermína laughed as she stood next to Teresa, looking like her poor relative: thickset, wearing—although it was summer—a gray checkered fleece skirt and bulky gray stockings that covered her rotund calves, which in turn protruded from black felt, fleece-lined booties, one with a broken zipper on the instep. Teresa flung herself into Gerta's arms, and as if it were just yesterday, the familiar scent of Teresa's strawlike hair filled Gerta's nostrils, just as when she used to breathe it in, night after night, more than twenty years ago. A tear rolled from the corner of her eye down across her temple.

"No crying, girl." Teresa grabbed her by the shoulders. "You can cry after I leave. Now, we're going to celebrate! At nine o'clock tomorrow morning, I'm heading back. Not a minute later. So don't waste any time. Throw on something decent, and let's head out!"

Hermína shook her head, saying, "It's like she's thrown off her chains—the whole bus ride, she couldn't stop talking about how they confiscated her Tokaji at the border. Have you ever heard of such a thing? She was bringing us Tokaji wine! Supposedly so we could celebrate! And now she thinks she's going to run out and buy another bottle." Hermína twirled her finger next to her temple. "So at least I grabbed a slivovitz at home, and then she still insisted that I bring a small demijohn, too, the one young Krumpschmiedová gave me," she said, lifting her other hand in which she was holding a bulging mesh bag. "It's a Riesling, pure poetry. If she saw the empty shelves everywhere, she'd have a heart attack, don't you think?"

Gerta still couldn't utter a word.

"Get yourself dressed, and let's go," Teresa said, giving her another shake, and only then did Gerta move to let them pass into the entrance hall. She then rushed to feed the cats and pulled on a polyester dress with a matching scarf that she used to wear on Sundays to take walks by the river, so she wouldn't look so out of place next to chic Teresa. The way Hermína did. Teresa had changed. She had grown lovelier and softer, and now, dressed in a blazer and a knee-length red skirt of Diolen fabric that was narrow and fitted, not wide and pleated as was the current fashion in the Czechoslovak Socialist Republic, she looked as if she had stepped out of a magazine. So simply lovely, as if it were the most natural way for a woman to be. Gerta felt almost ashamed, both of herself and of Hermína—over the years, their femininity had completely withered away. Had the iron curtain really cast them to such opposite poles?

She wound the scarf she had folded into a sash around her head to hide her unstyled hair. She regretted how minimally she took care of herself. On the other hand, why bother?

"Where does Johanna live?" Hermína called to her from the other room in German.

"A few stops by tram, about twenty minutes on foot, whichever you'd like," said Gerta, coming out of her bedroom.

Teresa was sitting at the kitchen table. In front of her was a trim black handbag with fine, delicate handles. Gerta had never seen one like it before.

"Would you mind if we walked? It's been over twenty years since the last time I was here," said Teresa.

So they set off from Stará Street and took her down Bratislavská, past vacant lots, which, boarded off behind plywood panels plastered with layers of peeling cultural posters, all these many years later continued to be reminders of the August air raids during the last full year of the war. As they crossed the *Sady Osvobození*, or Liberation Gardens, which just a few years earlier had been obsequiously renamed Stalin's Gardens, Teresa surveyed the white building of the new Janáček Theater.

"Where is Zeman's coffeehouse?" she finally asked. "At the end of the war, it was still standing there."

"They tore it down. First, they let it fall apart, and then they tore it down. An example of the bourgeois individualism of the First Republic. The theater, on the other hand, is for everyone. So now we have a theater here."

"Well, maybe that's not so bad, right? That place was pretty expensive anyway, wasn't it?" ventured Hermína tentatively.

They went on, making their way slowly along the footpath and looking over at the newly constructed building. Above their heads swayed the branches of linden and hornbeam trees that were interspersed with rows of rustling silver birches. Their footsteps fell softly on the carpet of birch catkins and linden blossoms. Then the venerable trees in front of them parted, and into view came a monumental statue of a soldier victoriously holding a raised weapon in his hand, menacingly pointed in the direction of where the German House once stood.

"So they tore that down too?" asked Teresa, her eyes scanning the empty horizon of the Náměstí Rudé Armády, or Red Army Square. Gerta tried to see the square through Teresa's eyes, and it again appeared to her just as desolate as it had the first time, when she had seen it after the war.

Gerta nodded, saying, "Supposedly, they blew it up right after the war, the minute we were gone."

They ran across the street, over to the park. Slowly they walked around its perimeter, keeping to the edge of the grass. Right in the middle, exactly where the majestic brick German House with its high, neo-renaissance facade used to stand, was a circular concrete area with an empty basin for a fountain. There was no water spraying out of it, and clusters of dead leaves and litter rolled around on the bottom.

"Not that it's hard to understand why, but still, that building was gorgeous. This stubble field bears no comparison," said Teresa. "Did either of you ever go to the theater there?"

Hermína nodded. "I used to be in the amateur troupe. We put on shows like *The Blue Bird*. I'll never forget that, you know, all those people in the audience clapping. They'd stand up, and you'd step forward and back and then bow. It was wonderful. Although one did see some uniforms in the seats."

"You used to act?" Gerta said, turning to her in surprise.

"My mother would take me. She started going, and I went with her. First, I was a child actor in *The Magic Satchel*. And then I did Schiller. You should've seen me. I was fabulous!" she declared with a laugh.

"I believe it," said Teresa, grabbing Hermína by the arm.

They turned their backs on the park and continued past the churches of St. Thomas and St. James, then down along May 9 Street, where they could hear the clanging of the tram coming from the upper end of Česká Street.

"It all looks so strange here," said Teresa, glancing around at the flaking facades, the peeling lacquered display windows, and decrepit shop signs. "In Vienna, it's finally gone—it's been about ten years now. Right after the Declaration of Neutrality. There's no trace left of the war anymore. But here, it's as though it still has some breath left in it."

"Do you really think so?" Hermína asked incredulously.

"Yes," said Teresa, motioning to the other side of the street, where a partly collapsed wooden fence stretched along the right side of a block where, still during the war, a department store that boasted the first escalator in the Republic had stood.

"So tomorrow we'll have breakfast at the milk bar opposite the train station," said Gerta. "Then you'll see something really world-class. You're not going to find something like that anywhere else, not even in Vienna."

"What's a milk bar?" asked Hermína.

Gerta gave a short laugh. "You've never seen luxury like this. Counters filled with delicacies in a beautifully decorated hall, with tables and chairs on spider legs, just you wait. Barbora and I went right after it opened—we almost couldn't eat, we were so taken by how beautiful it was."

They crossed the Náměstí Svobody, and slowly made their way up Zámečnická Street toward the Rathausplatz, which after a brief interlude during which it was called the Dominikánské Náměstí, was given a most horrendous name, derided by all of Brno: Družby Národů—Friendship Among Nations Square. Once upon a time, Gerta had stood here with Barbora, then just a few months old, clasped tightly to her chest, listening in dismay to Beneš as he delivered his inflammatory speech. Had she known back then what lay ahead of her, would she have done anything differently?

They continued on, walking up the middle of the street, where, still during the war, tram tracks had run, past the boarded-up Church of St. Michael, through the narrow Dominikánská Street over to Šilinger Square, and from there up to Špilberk Castle. They let Teresa stand there for a while, observing her in silence as she leaned against the crumbling edge of the parapet and looked out over the city.

"It's almost as if it never happened," Teresa finally said, slipping between them and linking her arms with theirs, as together they made their way back down toward Úvoz Street. As they slowly descended toward Mendel Square, not one of them had the courage to break the silence. Overhead swayed streetlights suspended transversely across the roadway, coming on one after another as the darkness spread from the castle behind them through the city. When several streets later they rang a doorbell next to the name Polivka, there was a long pause during which nothing happened.

"She doesn't have a phone?" asked Teresa.

Gerta erupted in a short burst of laughter, and Hermína began to explain to Teresa how it was with telephones in Czechoslovakia. Where she lived, in Perná, there was one telephone at the firehouse and another one at the National Committee, and now there were plans to install a telephone booth in the soon-to-be post office.

"Well, here we're a little better off," said Gerta as she rang the doorbell again. "But even so, seriously, almost no one has a telephone at home.

There's a long wait to get a telephone unit. Then another long wait for them to hook it up. And finally, they'll only hook it up if they consider you to be politically reliable. And that's a category to which neither Johanna nor I belong. Let me run up and see if there's a light on in the apartment."

Gerta dashed up the stairs. On the second floor, a door off a courtyard balcony was just opening. In the doorway stood Johanna, wrapped in a pink nylon dressing gown. She stepped over to the balcony railing and looked down.

"Johanna! Teresa's here!" Gerta called up to her.

XXI

Teresa remembered a different Brno. The city of her childhood and adolescence, in which she knew every church, every park, and every tram intersection like the back of her hand. The city in which she had moved around her whole life, even during the second half, when she was already living in her new home. In her dreams and fantasies, she was always back in Brno. The street corners and the trees lining the sidewalks would seem as real as when she leaned against them before she had been expelled.

Teresa's Brno had served as the backdrop to her steps. Her father used to call it the pulsating city of grandiose visions. A city that had defeated Olomouc in asserting its dominion over Moravia and was in constant competition with Prague, as to which city was the real heart of the Republic. A city that would soon stand alongside Paris, Berlin, and London. It rushed forth in leaps and bounds to embrace the fledgling First Republic and the new Europe with its redrawn borders. So her father had said. Many times prior to and even during the war, she walked with him through the streets, and he taught her to look at them through his eyes—he had knowledge to share about everything, and because of him, she learned to understand their city.

But that was long ago, and now, as she stood once again on the hill in the courtyard of Špilberk Castle, with Hermína and Gerta at her back, looking down at all of Brno spreading out below her, she realized that she no longer understood the city, that she no longer belonged in it. This city for which she had yearned for over two decades, and to which she had compared everything. It was like being reunited with a sibling whom one hadn't seen for years. An awareness of the bond remained, but the mutual understanding had evaporated. Brno was no longer her city; it was no longer her home, and this realization was a bitter one.

Instead of the city with model streets and bustling squares that she had preserved in her memory, sprawling before her was a gray mass littered with mutilated buildings and ruins—a dusty conglomeration of residential blocks and new, space-devouring housing developments that spread defiantly up the sides of the Brno basin, which had once held the old town and its outskirts so cozily nestled between the bends of its two rivers. Such was the city that her father had once shown her from this very spot. His arm outstretched and his index finger extended and bobbing along the horizon, he had pointed out everything from features of the landscape to the most conspicuous buildings, and visions that only he, an initiate of the Association of Moravian Architects, was privy to and that he conjured for her with a dreamy look.

His index finger would proudly rest on the German House, the evangelical Red Church, and the *Turnhalle* Gymnastic Society building at the foot of the Špilberk hill; the German Theater, which had been among the first on the European continent to have electric lighting, with Edison himself designing the light installation; and the Industrial Workers Association Pension Fund building, which everyone in Brno called the *Bienenhaus*, or Beehive Building, because of the enormous bronze honeybee sitting on top of its cupola, the symbol of the fund, which as a child she always waved to when passing by. And then he would acerbically point out the blocks of the newest buildings: modern gray or white cubes strewn across the hillside of the Jirásek quarter, or the tall high-rises, the afternoon sun beating down on their glass windowpanes that shattered the light into a thousand blinding shards against which Teresa had to shield her eyes. He would frown the same way upon the Cyril and Methodius Savings Bank on the Zelný Trh market square; at the new Avion Hotel, supposedly built on the narrowest lot in Brno; at the new Moravian Bank on Náměstí Svobody; at the Convalaria apartment building with its shops and the Dorotík Café, completed already in time to usher in the Second Czechoslovak Republic; and even the Villa Tugendhat, which the famous architect Mies van der Rohe came to Brno to build. Not for him, let alone for any other acolyte of modern architecture, did her father have the time of day. Works like that, he liked to say, devoid of decoration, with no particular significance, could only have been built by a Czech without an ounce of taste, or by a Jew, greedily turning over every five-crown piece in the palm of his hand. Barbarians, he called them, all those who were in the other camp and who, in the years leading up to the war, were doing better than he was, better than all of them were, the German architects and builders whose company he kept.

Back then, he often came home from their meetings exasperated, because another lot had been snatched up by the Czechs with their purist tendencies, and because Brno, which for years had accommodated both architectural styles, suddenly had no room for buildings that honored the Germanic tradition. He resented them for having lumped him and his colleagues together, relegating them to a suddenly insignificant group of perceived fuddy-duddies, deprived of any power or influence. He resented them because, no sooner had the wind shifted than they started to rewrite history, and suddenly there was no more room for the names of the German architects and builders responsible for most of the city's public works. They now pretended that the Germans deserved no credit for the city's appearance. He was angry that their investment in municipal buildings, schools, and universities was being denied, that those who built the

City Courtyard, Bergler's Villa, the *Erste Brünner Maschinenfabrik*—the First Brno Engineering Factory, which had employed and been a source of livelihood for Czech and German workers alike—were now being forgotten. Even the fact that it had been the Germans who had given the Petrov Cathedral its spires, that, too, was forgotten. The First Republic, in all of its zeal, sought to remove anything German from the face of the city as if it were a carbuncle—and her father, with his visions and unfulfilled architectural dreams, along with it.

Through him, Teresa had experienced this atmosphere whipped into a frenzy of extreme nationalistic competitiveness. And then all at once, as if by the wave of a magic wand, it ended, and her father once again began to receive commissions from the city, starting with the completion of the Ringstraße extension and the grounds of the park and gardens beneath Petrov Hill. Over the course of those first two years, she saw him beaming, full of satisfaction and gratification, pleased that art had prevailed, making it possible for him to start building again. He lived for it, and on Sundays took her along to show her how a construction project was progressing. Later on, she would run over after school on her own, going either directly to his office or to the building sites themselves. Until the day he disappeared elsewhere, because once again he was not allowed to build, and had to leave, this time not just—as her mother's daily tears attested—for work, but for good.

How different Brno appeared to her now. As if it were still bearing witness to a calamity. The war had long been over, but the empty lots barricaded behind wooden boards covered with peeling posters didn't seem to suggest that the city had forgotten, even twenty years later. The streets of Brno were full of its traces, on the desolate corners of Bratislavská and Koliště, along the whole stretch of Dornych Street, and even in the heart of the city, where Římské Square, Kozí Street, and the empty public space behind the main train station stood bare. Only here and there odd structures had sprung up, which Gerta referred to as the spawn of the latest crop of graduates from night schools that produced working-class architects whose main instruction was in Marxism and Leninism. What Teresa was seeing during that summer visit in 1968 were the ruins of a bygone time. A battered gray corpse, riddled with holes, from whose gutted entrails protruded, skewerlike, the glass tower of the skyscraping Hotel Continental, in the place where the Šmálka housing development had once been—a shantytown where, unbeknownst to her parents, she had gone roaming a few times. She could see the unsightly sheet-metal market hall that had gone up on one side of the vegetable market, and the massive, looming, boxy buildings that disfigured the once-parklike Mendel Square. And the deserted train station that was to have been the hub of the European railway system. Looking down at all of the squandered opportunities from the crumbling, unmaintained ramparts of Špilberk Castle, she felt like crying.

Only one thing hadn't changed. The subconscious awareness of every Brno resident that was imprinted with an unwritten map of the city, one passed down from generation to generation, on which the Czech pathways sought to avoid intersecting with the German ones. *Human memory is short, but the Brno cliques have remained,* thought Teresa as she looked down from the northern side of the Špilberk at the hustle and bustle of the inner city. The Czech residents of Brno still avoided walking down Běhounská Street, or the Rennergasse, which was now completely deserted without a single pedestrian. Instead, they made their way along the parallel Česká Street, which had once been home to Czech shopkeepers, restaurateurs, newspaper offices, and the renowned bookshop founded by Joža Barvič, a Czech patriot from Moravian Wallachia, which had been the first Czech business of its kind in Brno. And even Red Army Square, formerly Adolf-Hitler-Platz, where the German House had stood, gaped empty, as if people were afraid to set foot in it. And almost as if it were being punished for its history, it hadn't been planted and remained empty and bare, with here and there just a few patches of dried-up grass, and that fountain basin in the middle without any water.

"Apparently that place isn't even worthy of a piece of carved stone. The statue of the kaiser that still stood there during the war got stashed away someplace. The two allegorical figures ended up under Petrov Hill in Denis Gardens Park, and the only thing left of Masaryk is the pedestal. Maybe what will end up staying is that pathetic cluster of statues they're planning to install—there was just a picture in the *Rudé Právo*. It's going to be called *Communists*. They say it's already in the works," Gerta had volunteered when she realized what Teresa was looking at.

Would she ever come back here, to this refurbished square, where she had once spent long afternoons in front of the German House? Would she ever see it again? Would she be permitted another trip back, and if so, would there be enough time? Teresa asked herself these questions with apprehension, and with uncertainty. Because not even she could say how much time she had left, nor could the doctors, who had found that viper in her intestines. A viper nesting in a lair deep inside her, a lair that, were it to be disturbed, would release a venom that would burn her from within. A tumor that wouldn't shrink and would now go on growing and become hardier until it was the size of a baby's head, and by then she would look pregnant. And then at some point, sooner or later, she would die, pumped full of morphine in the Viennese hospital where she'd been going for her medical checkups, usually escorted by the commiserating gaze of the doctors and nurses.

She sensed that she wouldn't be back and would spend the rest of her days nostalgically looking through old postcards of Brno, which she searched out in Viennese secondhand shops and hung up in ornate, gilded frames on the papered walls of her apartment. Postcards depicting Brno as it once was. *It's disappeared beneath the sediment of time and the oppression under which the people here live,* she said to herself as she strained to catch a glimpse of what was now only the slightest glimmer of her youth in these streets whose beauty seemed to have withered away.

XXII

"It wasn't easy. It was terrifying. I was just as scared then as I'd been on the way to Pohořelice. And then at the beginning in Bergen."

The hushed German permeated every corner of Johanna's cramped kitchen, as did the smoke from Gerta's Mars cigarettes, an indulgence that, since Barbora had moved out, she permitted herself at regular intervals at fixed times to be savored each day. Teresa was chain-smoking her own cigarettes, and Johanna, as the glasses added up, would occasionally reach over and help herself to one of her exotic Camels, a whiff of the capitalist West.

"On top of everything, it was terribly cold. Terribly. At first, we slept outside, because no one wanted to take us in. All of Drasenhofen—in front of which those Russians dumped us—all of Poysbrunn, Ottenthal, and Poysdorf, every single town was still full of those who had come across the border that summer. Some had stayed because by the time they'd arrived, they were already sick—dysentery and typhus were raging there all summer too. People brought it with them from Pohořelice, so they had to stay put; they didn't have the strength to go any farther. Especially the old people. You've never seen so many old people in one place as there were in the homes of those locals who, mercifully, had taken them in. Every single one of them asked me if I'd seen any of their relatives—either near the border or along the way. They were absolutely desperate—they'd lost entire families. Catastrophe. You know what was left for them to do? Nothing. For the ones who hadn't already died in June, on the way—remember those bodies lying around everywhere?— all they could do now was to die as soon as possible. For strangers, they were a burden. In all those border villages, there are masses of graves, even communal ones, where there's just a number on the headstone to show how many are buried there—people who'd already been picked up in June from the fields, where they died like dogs. I say it that way on purpose, because that's how the locals talked about it. They saw how the Russians and even the Czechs drove them as if they were livestock."

Teresa was still shaking her head in utter disbelief, even so many years later.

"Finally, on the third night in Wetzelsdorf, I slept under a roof again for the first time," Teresa continued. "Ula begged them because of Dorla, who already had a cold, and in the end, they let us all sleep on some hay up in the attic. In the morning, they gave us goat's milk and some bread, our first real food in two days. We didn't take much from Zipfelová, just a small jar of jam, for sugar and strength. They sent us to a cloister in Mistelbach, saying that it was a gathering place for refugees, and they would know what to do with us. We wanted to get to Vienna, but in the end, we agreed with Ula that it might be better to get our bearings first and go someplace where they were prepared for refugees. You know, we had no idea what to expect. We hadn't really thought it through. We just kept imagining that in no time we'd be in Vienna, either looking for work or at the Red Cross. We never imagined how terrible it would be there in October, so soon after the war. That there would be people everywhere, even worse off than we were. And that neither for them, nor for us, was there going to be any room anywhere. You know what they would say to us along the way? Not just the kids, but the adults, too, when we'd pass by and ask for shelter or food? They'd shout at us that we were scum, gypsies, or that now we finally had what we'd always wanted—and that it was our own damn fault, because of our insatiable *Heim ins Reich*. Or Nazi pigs—they'd shout that too. There was even one time when a man with a Red Cross badge came over with a camera and started filming us as we were helping to clear out the rubble from the cellar in Mistelbach, to make more room. When I asked him what he was filming, he said it was going to be a documentary film about how the Nazi wives now had to pay for what they'd brought about. You can't imagine how I felt when he told me that. Here, in this land I'd dreamed of, where I'd imagined that I'd find a new home. Ula held on to me that time—had she not been there, I think I might have even come back. Or I would've done something to myself, as so many others did—death was everywhere. If back then I'd been given a choice to live as a Nazi bitch with all of you and Zipfelová, with food and a place to sleep, or to live all alone with nothing in a foreign country, then I would've chosen to go back to Bergen. Had it not been for Ula. 'What were you expecting?' she'd ask me. 'Offers of ball gowns and dancing shoes on a gilded platter?' That's what she'd say as she'd stroke Dorla's feverish forehead while she lay on that pile of straw. We were still in Wetzelsdorf then. We had to wait almost a whole week before Dorla was strong enough to go on. I couldn't answer her. I hadn't really imagined anything specific. I just thought things in Austria would be better. But that would still take some time; we had to be patient—Ula would repeat that to me as well. Girls, Ula was incredibly brave."

Teresa paused, taking long, deliberate drags from her cigarette.

"From Wetzelsdorf to Mistelbach, it was only about an hour and a half on foot," she continued after a moment. "Up on the hill stood the cloister, also quite damaged during the war, but there was a home for the elderly and a hospital. In those days, when we got there, it was bursting at the seams. There was no room for us. They told us that their numbers were decreasing because old people were dying every day, but when we arrived, there were people lying everywhere—even in the hallways, in terrible condition. And inside the rooms, they had put down extra beds on the floors, in the basement, too, which was full of rubble, so they were constantly clearing all that out, stepping over the sick people lying on straw pallets all over the place. It was dreadful. Those days, I kept on crying in total disappointment; I couldn't help it. It would come over me uncontrollably, in the middle of the day when I'd be doing something like dicing potatoes in the kitchen, where they let us help out for a few days. Or at night, before falling asleep. But Ula kept us both going, Dorla and me. It was awful. And most of all, it made no sense for us to be in Mistelbach. With each passing day, we both felt worse and worse. Old people, sick people, no prospects, people dying every day. It was hitting us harder and harder, until finally it seemed entirely pointless to set out for Vienna, where we were told the conditions were the same, that they also looked upon refugees as Nazis who had fled the Protectorate, or as thieves, or even just as people who would give the locals competition. There was no room to cram us in. Austria was hopelessly overcrowded; people were hungry and full of hatred; and this was where Ula and I had wanted to start our new lives! It was in Mistelbach that we suddenly felt that the whole thing was stupid, such a bunch of nonsense that only a child could have believed it. Then Ula decided that she had to get to those relatives of hers in Řezno—Regensburg—as quickly as possible. So we moved on again, because she couldn't get there from Mistelbach, we had to get to Vienna. It must have taken all of her strength to convince me to keep going. In the meantime, she stashed away potatoes, one at a time—we would slip them under our skirts and hide them in small pouches that we'd made out of some rags. Raw potatoes and onions, anything we were able to swipe from the kitchen, where we were helping out. It was rotten of us, because nobody there had anything, and we were stealing in order to put away provisions, but we'd heard that people along the way were no longer willing to give out anything. After three months during which the flow of immigrants hadn't slowed down, they had practically nothing left for themselves—they didn't even feel sorry for us anymore, and when they saw us coming, they'd go inside and lock their doors. So we had no choice but to steal. We took what we could, hid it away, and then set off, once more, for Vienna. First, we went to Wolkersdorf, and from there to Floridsdorf, where there was a refugee camp."

Teresa fell silent, reached for the bottle that was sitting on the table, and poured herself another slivovitz.

"I don't know if we'd have been better off had we stayed in Mistelbach for the winter, or in some other small village in the country-side. Not that they would've wanted us, but where we ended up in Floridsdorf, the misery—if it's even possible—was even worse. The place was an old factory. It was falling apart, but probably not because of bombs, although there were holes in the roof and the windows were cracked—at first only the wind blew in, but soon, so did the snow. Winter came early that year. They sent us directly there—no way would they let us into central Vienna. So there we were, stranded in the middle of this horde. You'd sleep three across on wooden pallets, that was if you were lucky enough to grab a spot. People would even sleep on the floor, and many of them were sick. Not just with the shits that they'd brought with them from Mähren, but with hypothermia—they'd be taken to the hospital, but often it was too late. And everyone had lice. And everyone had the shits—again, there was dysentery all over the place, and they'd come around once a day with tin cans giving out soup, which was the only food you could get. A serving of watery vegetable soup, and seven ounces of bread per person, and whoever didn't have the shits yet, they'd get them from that watery soup, even if they were still healthy. And for that entire factory, where there were more than a thousand of us cooped up together, there were only three outdoor latrines. Do you know what that was like? Thoroughly disgusting. Blessed Bergen, blessed Zipfelová. From what I heard from some of the others, who'd also been sent to southern Moravia to work, not everyone was treated as well as we were. Not a night went by that we didn't pray and give thanks to Zipfelová for having taken such good care of us. Chances are that if it hadn't been for her, and we'd arrived as malnourished as some of the others, we wouldn't have lasted. You know, there wasn't a day that they didn't have to carry someone out, someone who didn't make it. And then Dorla caught it. She came down with those terrible shits and got a fever. The doctor there, who'd been expelled from Znojmo, came by and said that it didn't look good, and he had nothing to give her that could help. Then the next day, people from the Red Cross came back again to hand out more soup, and Ula latched on to them and insisted they take Dorla to a hospital. She was beside herself with despair, and that was probably why she ended up succeeding, because they wouldn't take just anyone. There was a Red Cross doctor who would visit the camp, and he allowed only the worst cases to be admitted. In the end, they loaded us into a truck, even Ula and me—because I wasn't about to let myself be separated from them for anything in the world—and drove us to a hospital in the center of Vienna. They kept Dorla there, and we expected them to assign us to some kind of work, and then, once Dorla got better, to send us right back to that same camp. To this day, I'm grateful to Dorla for waiting to get sick until early December, when we were just outside of Vienna, and to Ula, for managing to get us all on that truck. I can't imagine how we would have survived the winter in Floridsdorf. All we had to wear was just what we had on when we left Bergen—whatever the Red Cross brought in was useless to us. If you weren't fast enough, you got nothing, and fast was something Ula and I were not. It was only later that we got coats and shoes, when we were already in Vienna, from a charity."

Teresa lifted the glass of slivovitz to her nose, breathed in the aroma, and went on.

"Vienna was overcrowded. Beggars everywhere—I mean people like us—on the streets, in the parks, on benches, in collapsed buildings, people looking for work and for food or people who were completely out of it, lost, just standing around, waiting to see if someone would give them a handout. Nobody did; there was nothing left to eat in Vienna—there wasn't even enough for the residents themselves, let alone for the refugees. They couldn't feed us. Just from Brno alone there had been over ten thousand people who had come to Vienna along the Brünner Reichsstraße, the Imperial Road, and people were arriving from all over—from the Protectorate, from the Sudetenland, from Hungary—and Russians, the place was crawling with them. They were terrible too—don't think the women there were any better off than they were here, at the end of the war, in Brno—they were up to the same old tricks. On the other hand, later on . . . later on, it came in useful."

Teresa threw back the shot glass, and the slivovitz disappeared down her throat, past the even row of teeth in which the golden one gleamed.

"I have no problem telling you about it, because it's very possibly the only reason we survived. Without my Russian friend, by the end of that first winter, we might've already been pushing up daisies. Keep in mind, the Austrians were the only ones getting ration books, and what did that give them? One-third of what we were getting toward the end of the war—barely enough to survive. And the refugees? We got nothing. There simply was nothing to be had. You had to hope that you'd run into a Red Cross food truck to have a chance of getting any food at all—more of that watery soup, sometimes a runny *Eintopf* stew. Ula and I used to go over to the *Südbahnhof*, but if we got there late, we were out of luck. Still, in the end, we got lucky after all, because that's where my Russian spotted me. He could have helped himself to it for free had he waited to jump me somewhere in the dark. After all, it was the daily norm, as we all know. But instead, he offered us bread and lard, and then another time it was sugar, or dried fish. Who the hell knows where he got his hands on it all. But I for one didn't care. For three eggs, which he gave me one time, I would have done plenty more. By then, I no longer gave a damn about anything—nothing, except for that god-awful cold and that unbearable hunger. You turned into just a body that didn't think, made up of just a stomach that gnawed on you so badly that you couldn't sleep at night. Probably the only time I felt like myself was when we'd be standing in line for soup, or when we'd gotten hold of some potatoes that we'd cook in tin cans over a fire in the park, where together with some others, we'd burn benches, branches, or bits of timber—there was plenty of that all over the place. In the meantime, they found us some rooms in these small camps—really more like shelters for refugees who were allowed to stay in Vienna. They sent us to Postgasse Four, where later we also brought Dorla. First, though, Ula and I had to shave each other's heads that they then smeared with some foul-smelling, mercury-based delousing ointment, which they'd already applied to Dorla in the hospital. Then they gave us fresh, new clothing, after which we looked ghastly. It was so humiliating, that business with the hair, but we had no time to dwell on it. In any case, I couldn't understand that Russian of mine at all—I looked awful, but he kept coming back anyway, until one day he disappeared."

Teresa gave a faint smile.

"Ula tried several times to get a permit so that she could go on to Regensburg, which was in the American zone. Had she wanted to leave, though, she first would have had to go back into one of those detention camps outside Vienna, where neither of us wanted to go for anything in the world. After that, she finally gave it a rest for a while, and I was glad, because all through that first December and January, I don't know what I would have done in Vienna without her. I thought about going with her, thinking that it didn't really matter whether I was in Regensburg or Vienna, but truth be told, she never asked me. She imagined that once she got to her relatives, she would be reunited with her husband, and then they would either go back, or start over somehow. I'm not exactly sure. All I know is that I didn't figure into the equation, and probably all my yammering about Vienna had given her the sense that I was at peace with my future prospects. Well, back in Perná I had been, but that feeling disappeared into thin air like a puff of smoke the minute we crossed the border.

"For a while, everything stayed the same. She ended up leaving two years later, on one of the last transports, because it took forever before they finally gave her an *Ausweis* identity card, and the certificate of good health that the Americans required. Then, in forty-seven, she and Dorla packed up their things and left for Regensburg, and that was that. By then, I already had a job, if one could call it that, and earlier they'd already moved us into an apartment that belonged to a certain Frau Wojanczik who lived on Herringgasse. She had to turn her spare room over to us, and she wasn't happy about it, but back then, nobody was.

We were rabble, the dregs of society, women from who knew where, with who knew what for a past. At the same time, we were wondering about her past—she was such a crotchety old crone. She never spoke to us, just occasionally snapped at us when she didn't like something, and in the end, we were right. One day, we found her slumped over among burning candles with photographs of her sons in SS uniforms and Hitler, scattered all over the place. Poor Dorla was the one who found her, that's what bothered us the most, but after that, things got better. We reported it right away, so that we wouldn't be blamed, and instead of throwing us out, they moved in three sisters from Troppau—from Opava—along with their old mother. They took over that second room. I don't know how that old woman survived the journey, although they told us they'd been transported from Opava to Vienna in a cattle truck—they'd even been allowed to bring fifty kilos per person. But all along the way, the Czechs and the Russians picked through everything, so that by the time they got to Vienna, they were pretty much in the same boat as we were: empty-handed. Later on, we found out that one of them had lost a baby along the way, that her husband had fallen in the war, that their father had been sent to a labor camp near Ostrava, where they had good reason to be worried about him—they never heard from him again. Meanwhile, as for their grandparents, they hadn't even survived the journey from Opava. Of the entire family, there were just the four of them left, and it would have been only three if they hadn't stopped the eldest one from slitting her wrists with a broken piece of mirror. One would hear stories like that from just about everyone."

She poured herself another slivovitz.

"Let's have your glasses," she then said. With a shaky hand, she refilled all the shot glasses. "Then Ula and I found ourselves some work. Actually, up until the early fifties, when I got my proper citizenship, we refugees, by law, weren't allowed to be employed except as unskilled laborers. In the beginning, Ula and I helped with rubble clearing, just to get some food, and that went on for a while, right up through the summer of forty-six, when they brought me in to help in a hospital kitchen. Ula went to work in a factory just outside Vienna, where she commuted every day. Our pay was a joke, but at least it was something and it helped with the household, although most of it went to food anyway. The things we'd hear back then, you can't imagine. To the Austrians, I was just a Czech slut; even the stupidest cow in the hospital looked down on me. I didn't dare do a thing about it. I was supposed to be grateful that they'd even let me stay in Austria, taking food out of their mouths. That legendary Viennese heart of gold I'd heard so much about, well, I never found it. As for Ula, they used to call her a *Rucksackdeutsche*—a German tramp with a rucksack—which was pretty funny, seeing as back then we didn't even have any summer clothes yet, still just the winter ones that we'd gotten from a charity, let alone anything to put in a rucksack. I don't know what those people imagined we would do to them that made them hate us so much. But they couldn't stand us, and they made it very clear. Dorla got it from her classmates, and we got it from anyone whose path we crossed. My *Brünnerisches* German always gave me away, that soft accent of ours—I couldn't get their *Wienerisch* past my tongue. No sooner would I open my mouth than they could immediately tell I was Czech. They can tell to this day, and they act accordingly. You can't imagine the faces they make. In the meantime, though, I'd say that I've managed to make a few acquaintances among the Viennese Austrians. But the only people I can really call friends are the ones who came to Vienna because they were driven out of the Protectorate. Like Traude Fröhlich from Bergen, whom I ran into one day on an excursion up the Mühlberg, from where you can see as far as *Rassenstein* castle. They were also deported, as you probably remember. In spite of the fact that they'd been farmers in Bergen since Maria Theresa's time, and had headstones in the cemetery dating back that far to prove it. It didn't matter that they were never mixed up with politics; they were expelled, just like us, and now their farm belongs to Jech's son-in-law, some guy named Kocman."

"He turned it over to the JZD, too, right at the beginning, just like Jech. Now they just have that house behind the church with the garden that goes all the way down to the fishpond," said Hermína.

"It wasn't easy for Traude either. But at least she knew how to sew and embroider, so soon word got around that she could fix anything, even if she had nothing to work with. Today she's got her own Singer machine and sews at home and lives pretty well, even though it's all under-the-table. That's something that, to this day, we're still good enough for. Outwardly they hate us, yet if we can be useful to them, they overcome their distaste."

Teresa's face twisted into a grimace.

"Now, these past few years, there's been a lot of talk about integration, and how successful it's been. Nonsense! Although it's true that now we have the *Landsmannschaft*—a welfare and culture society for Germans born in the eastern part of what was formerly the Reich—so that's at least something. But otherwise, to this day, we're just the rabble that wandered in, and in terms of a pension, what do you think I'll get? Jack shit, because my pay is a joke, and it doesn't look as if it's going to get better anytime soon. Unless I marry well. But that's not so easy either, to meet someone there, when all the locals are trying so hard to avoid you. For them to accept me as an equal Austrian citizen, which on paper I've now been for a few years already, most likely I'll have to be dead. To this day, no one gives a damn about us, and they make it obvious, again and again. It can't be helped. People belong in their own country, and today I regret how it all turned out. I regret that I didn't stay here with you, although—hell—what more could I have expected here? I never even learned to speak Czech properly. So I don't know. Home is neither here nor there. Somehow, I just seem to be stuck between places and memories. Some life, wouldn't you say?"

She looked around at the others. Hermína was nodding off in a rocking chair in the corner of the tiny kitchen; Johanna, her head propped up on the tabletop and her eyelids drooping, was looking back and forth between Teresa and the empty demijohn; and Gerta was taking a drag on what was left of a smoldering cigarette butt.

"Girlfriend, had you stayed here, you wouldn't have done yourself any favors," Gerta finally said after a long pause, so softly as to be almost inaudible.

For a long time afterward, she kept on thinking back to Teresa's visit, heartened by the promise of next year—the wine harvest in Perná, when they planned to spend a whole week with Hermína at Zipfelová's house. But man proposes, God disposes. One night, shouting coming in through the window that opened onto the courtyard pulled her from her sleep. At first, she couldn't make out the words; still groggy, she threw a knitted shawl over her shoulders and went over to the window to look out. On the opposite balcony, a man was standing and shouting. Gradually all the lights in the apartment block started to come on, one by one, and from somewhere in the distance came a droning rumble.

"For fuck's sake, turn on your radiooooooooooos!" he was shouting over and over.

And as Gerta in her kitchen did just that, the empty room filled with the familiar voice of the radio announcer:

Yesterday, on August 20, 1968, at approximately twenty-three o'clock, the armies of the Union of Soviet Socialist Republics, the Polish People's Republic, the Hungarian People's Republic, and the Bulgarian People's Republic crossed the state borders of the Czechoslovak Socialist Republic. This happened without the knowledge of the president of the Republic, the chairman of the National Assembly, or the first secretary of the Central

Committee of the Communist Party of Czechoslovakia. The presidium of the Central Committee of the Communist Party of Czechoslovakia calls on all citizens of the Republic to remain calm and not resist the advancing armed forces, because the defense of our state borders is impossible at this time. The presidium of the Central Committee of the Communist Party of Czechoslovakia considers this act to be contrary to all principles of the relations between socialist countries, as well as a violation of the basic norms of international law.

XXIII

That day nobody did any work. Inside the manufacturing halls and in the administrative offices, time stood still. The few who even bothered to show up at the factory crowded into the administration building, where they sought out either friends or relatives who worked in one of the offices, and huddled around the wireless receiver. Even in her office, they were packed in like sardines, since half of the planning department had come down from Floor Five to see Jarka Humpolíková, whose husband worked up there. Jenda, sitting by the file cabinet, on top of which sat the receiver, was flipping between channels, hoping that when one stopped broadcasting the news, he'd pick it up on another. They were all as crestfallen as Zipfelová's chickens after a downpour. From time to time, they managed to shake it off, and then an intense discussion would erupt in the room, until Jenda found another broadcast, free of static interference.

The Soviet news agency TASS is not offering any commentary on this event. This is because there is nothing it can say. This intervention was ordered by neither the government, nor by parliament, nor by the Central Committee of the Communist

Party of Czechoslovakia. Naturally, some individual still could do so. Retroactively . . . but let's hope there is no such person to be found in Czechoslovakia. There is nothing more for us to do at this time except to say that any statements made by TASS are unsubstantiated, that in spite of all the tanks in the streets and all the planes in the sky, we can all remain calm. History will vindicate us. And in doing so will vindicate freedom, humanity, and socialism with a human face. Friends, you are listening to Czechoslovak Radio. We will continue to inform you about the developing situation as long as it remains in our power to do so.

That time, Gerta, standing behind them as they were all turned with their gazes fixed intently on the radio receiver, couldn't suppress a snicker. Jarka glanced up at her quizzically, then immediately dropped her eyes again, as if standing in front of her and the other listeners were not just a radio receiver but editor Jeroným Janíček himself. "History will vindicate us," he had said. Well now, that was something Gerta couldn't wait to see, just whom history would choose to vindicate. In case that naive man behind the microphone didn't know it, history had a way of vindicating the victors. And to suggest that now, on the brink of war with Russia, those Czechoslovak stuffed shirts would come rushing back to the city in late August, abandoning their ROH trade-union dachas, ready to storm the military warehouses and grab some weapons and confront their Red brethren—well, that was extremely, but *extremely*, optimistic. Gerta knew how it would end. The same way it had ended last time. Everyone would have a mouthful of what they were going to say, and then very quickly they'd fall in line and oblige their new masters. And afterward, they'd be more Catholic than the pope, heroes as submissive as lambs. She wondered what might be going on right now in the halls of the Zbrojovka Arms Factory. Were the same brave champions still sitting on the committees, the ones who back then had driven her out of the city shouting, *"Raus"*? By now, they certainly also had to know what was coming next. They surely remembered the same charade, except back then, it played itself out in brown. Now they'd have a chance to do it over, this time in red. Gerta felt herself making a face. Not one of these people here right now, not a single one of them, would do anything in the end. And as if to prove her right, no sooner had the three o'clock whistle gone off than the men sitting on the floor around the radio receiver slowly stood up, stretched out their arms, cracked their backs, and then quickly dispersed, each to their respective home. To make sure they got back in time to go swimming with their wives in Srpek Lake just outside the town while it was still sunny.

Gerta walked along the main street from the upper end of town down to the train station with Jarka and Jenda. On the Náměstí Osvobození, Liberation Square, people were standing around in small groups, looking at a monumental statue of a soldier holding a firearm raised victoriously in the air. His face had been smeared with blue paint. *And that,* thought Gerta to herself, *is just about the extent of what's going to happen here.*

"I always thought Kuřim was liberated by the Romanians, wasn't it?" said Jenda, turning to Jarka and shaking his head, perplexed.

"Yeah, by the Romanians," Jarka replied, shrugging her shoulders.

Later on in the train, Gerta's bottle of milk accidentally spilled on the floor, and the people around her made a fuss of crossing one leg over the other or, if they were standing, of taking a dramatic step backward, grimacing as if this were the worst possible thing to have happened that day. Gerta couldn't understand it. At the same time, already that morning at the Brno-Židenice train station, there had been two armored carriers and a tank, atop which sat a few young men smoking and looking down at several of their pluckier cohorts, who were collecting signatures. Otherwise nothing was happening. Could everyone have already forgotten the war? It hadn't been that long ago! Surely these

people around her couldn't keep on acting this way—as though getting
to the lake in time for a late-afternoon August swim or keeping spilled
milk from getting their shoes sticky took precedence over the tanks in
the streets and the fighter planes at the Brno-Tuřany Airport.

And yet, very possibly, they could, as Gerta discovered over the following months. People could act as though nothing had happened at
all, or they could act as if the whole thing had happened by invitation,
as they officially voted to do a few weeks later. And finally, they could
even act with complete indifference. A total lack of interest. Like, for
example, her own daughter.

The night that the news had come over the radio, Barbora had
already been moved out for a long time. She was living in one of the
new housing developments in Brno-Žebětín with that couch potato Jára
and little Blanka, and was completely indifferent to what was going on.
Gerta was all alone with her fears and her nightmares. She would wake
up from them in the middle of the night, drenched in sweat, convinced
that another war was about to break out. That, once again, she and others like her would be running downstairs to take cover in basements
and to pray that the worst thing to happen to them would be that they
crap in their pants.

Plagued by such misgivings, she visited Barbora throughout the
rest of that summer and fall. And in her fear, she spoke to her daughter
more openly than she ever had before—together they even laid bare all
the secrets that Gerta had at one time preferred to forget. The past no
longer lay as an obstacle between them. Through their conversations,
it had been reunited with the present, and Gerta hoped that now, from
the broader perspective of their family history, Barbora would understand her fears.

But Barbora ignored her, and not only her, but also their shared
past, which no longer held her curiosity with unanswered questions,
and even their present, which interested her even less than Jára's belch-
ing. She would just stare at Gerta with a totally blank expression, and

finally Jára ordered her and her political gibberish out of their kitchen. In that instant, it was as if a gaping rift had split open between them, across which Gerta could no longer see into her own daughter's soul. Into the mind beneath the once-teased hair, which these days fell limp and was tucked behind her ears—into the mind of her own flesh and blood, for whose sake over the past twenty years she hadn't given up.

Gerta returned home and went through the following months as if in a dream. Russian and Polish soldiers were encamped around the perimeter of the city. They took over the barracks on Šumavská Street, at the Brno-Tuřany Airport, and in Židenice. They became a part of the city, part of its population—suddenly one heard Russian even in the shops. Even in the factory. A new deputy director came in. And from there, the effect began to trickle down, lower and lower, until it found its way to her, right to her desk in her office, where next to her type-writer she cultivated Christmas cacti. In the windowless warehouse to which they transferred her, they no longer bloomed the following year. The cadre credentials of a Czechoslovak citizen of formerly German nationality—who to this day kept in touch with members of a closely monitored German minority and maintained suspicious relationships abroad—didn't suit the profile of a secretary in the personnel depart-ment, who had access to sensitive information that could be at risk of being misused. Gerta the spy, in the service of imperialism. But she didn't find it amusing. She ended up back in the warehouse, from where she had diligently worked her way from assembly line production to the planning department, all the way to the administration building. They had taken advantage of all her skills, even her German, which came in handy for processing orders from East Germany, as well as her stenog-raphy and her advanced typing speed. Over the course of all five years that she worked in the administrative office, there hadn't been a single complaint. Yet all it took was a slight shift in top-level management, and the factory caved in like a house of cards. And Gerta's card landed her deep in the bowels of the warehouse where, in 1970, she found herself alongside Lída Kořínková, who, when she wasn't drinking, was fast asleep. Alone, isolated from everyone, in a warehouse where nobody ever went. Alone at home, too, because nobody ever came there either.

When the war ended, Gerta felt that she hadn't deserved what had happened to her. That she hadn't been even remotely the cause of what people were taking revenge on her for. But as she sat in that warehouse over the winter of 1970, in her company-issued quilted vest, beneath a single lightbulb that flickered erratically by the ceiling, she felt that this time they were finally going to succeed in destroying her for good. Her world had imploded, and a profound emptiness flooded her very core. All she had left was time, which ticked away slowly, minute by minute, inside the cold warehouse. Early on after she'd been forced out of Brno, the pain had been physical. Her whole body ached, first from that nighttime march and later from working in the fields, and internally, from the degradation inflicted on her by that soldier. Yet there had always been a reason to go on fighting: Barbora. But what about now, in the face of yet another unmerited degradation? What was there left to fight for, now that Barbora had cut her out of her life? For this, Gerta had no answer.

PART IV

The Present Past

I

A storm was brewing. The bus was traveling along the causeway between the two newly created lakes that had replaced the village of Mušov and now spilled out below Perná. Through the window, Gerta watched the slender aspens, freshly planted along the shoreline, being buffeted by the wind. It threatened to pull them up, root balls and all, held them pinned to the ground, tossed about their juvenile crowns, and tore off their early-spring leaves, which went swirling in a wild frenzy over the surface of the lake.

The bus swerved in a gust of wind, and Gerta wouldn't have been surprised if, along this open stretch, it were swept off the road. They would be flung over the guardrail into the choppy waters of the adjacent lake, and as the cabin of the bus slowly filled with water, they would descend lower and lower toward the sunken houses of Mušov. Maybe they would land in front of the Felbers' mill or on the roof of the Freisens' farmhouse, which used to stand somewhere near here, by the crossroads from where the road then curved down toward the center of the village. When she closed her eyes, she could still see the farmyard jammed with the trucks and armored cars that had been parked there by the Russians and the Romanians during the first few days of liberation. She vividly remembered the small groups of soldiers leaning back against the bullet-riddled walls of the buildings and smoking, turning to look after them as they went by in Šenk's buggy, heading toward Perná. But that time, they'd been considerably farther down, judging by the position of St. Leonard's Church, whose walls and steeple still stood against the gray sky at her eye level, rising above the water's bleak surface. The whole village had been flooded as far as the hilltop with the church, which was now slowly falling into disrepair—like a mute witness—like an outcry of helplessness.

"You should have seen how the people fought against it," Hermína said, shaking her head disapprovingly. By then, Gerta was already sitting in Zipfelová's kitchen beside the blazing stove on which Hermína was heating up a kettle of water for tea. She had left Brno behind in all of its May Day frenzy. It had begun to festoon itself near the end of April with red and red-white-blue tricolor flags and was teeming with white paper peace doves that dangled in the windows of shops and apartments. They never hung in Gerta's street-facing windows. She refused to honor a nation that reminded them on a daily basis of their own weakness, nor would she honor those horrible days of liberation. Nor, for that matter, the Big Brothers of that nation, if only because of how one of them had treated her personally. Not that they were all like that, of course. Privately, on such occasions she would always in her mind thank Dr. Karachielashvili, whom she still remembered. But that was it—even throughout the fifties, when Barbora used to come home from school with a dove that she had painstakingly cut out of a quarter sheet of white paper and would beg Gerta, sobbing, to stick it in their window like all the other families did. Like comrade teacher said to do. Yet it wasn't true that all the other families did, and Gerta would then point out to Barbora other windows where the view wasn't marred by a dove. Not even in their building were all the windows decorated. Out of eight parties, barely half. In spite of the reminders that the caretakers posted on the hallway message boards in red block letters: *REMEMBER TO DECORATE YOUR WINDOWS!* Gerta hadn't forgotten, as she would emphasize to Mrs. Šedová when she ran into her on the stairs. Gerta didn't decorate on principle, and finally even Šedová made peace with there being only a single dove poised to fly from the Agathonikiadises' window. Back then, it had been Mrs. Athanaia who had given in to Barbora's pleas and put up the dove. To this day, Gerta wasn't sure if it had been out of gratitude to the Republic or purely out of her fondness for Barbora.

The storm had caught up to them right at the bus stop. By the time she ran all the way to Hermína's, she was soaked to the skin, right through to her *vasilka* undershirt.

"Here, have some linden tea. It's from that tree behind the little shrine where Zipfelová used to go every year to give thanks," said Hermína, handing her a large cup of hot tea with steeped leaves at the bottom.

"What happened to all those people?" asked Gerta, holding the brown earthenware cup in both hands.

"I'm not sure. I heard some of them got apartments in one of those new housing developments on the outskirts of Mikulov, and others probably moved in with relatives. Last year at the fair in Dunajovice, some people were saying they'd be moving into a state farm near there, where they'd put up some new units too. Everyone was griping about it, you know. They forced them all out with eviction notices, and there was nowhere for them to go and object. It was like trying to talk to a wall. Well, you can imagine, in this Republic, who can you turn to for anything when word comes from the top? No one. So they moved them out. I still remember all those trucks loaded up with beds, wardrobes, and comforters passing by Perná on the way to Mikulov. And then *basta*. They opened the floodgates, and two days later there was nothing left, just the two lakes and the church in the middle."

Gerta shook her head in dismay and said, "More expelled people. The idea of home means nothing in this Republic. They take homes away from people to punish them or just like that—for no reason. Because it came from the top. From some desk."

"Hopefully there'll be some advantages too," Hermína said. "They'd always had problems with the Dyje River. Don't you remember how often we used to have to go over there and help out when it flooded?"

"I do remember. But after all these years, I thought they finally had a handle on it, didn't they? They built those two mills and put in those basins along the banks. From what I remember, the people in Mušov weren't worried about it. And they had the biggest volunteer fire brigade by far."

"Well, maybe so. But what's done is done. And not everyone was that upset about it. Most of the people there had come from somewhere else too. After all, before the war, it was mostly Germans who lived there. Zipfelová used to say you couldn't get by without speaking German. And that the water had always caused problems. Remember what she used to say about marsh fever?"

"No."

"That the people in Mušov came down with it every year. They caught it from those three shallow fishponds that used to be on the village square near the statue of St. Florian. Supposedly, that came here all the way from Italy or someplace. Anyway, those ponds were a breeding ground for mosquitoes, and every summer, during the hottest days, just when there was the most work to be done in the fields, the whole village, one by one, would get sick with varying degrees of fever. Whoever had a fever every day would get over it the soonest and could go back to work after a few weeks. Some had a fever every other day, and the ones who had one every third day were the worst off of all. It would take them forever to get rid of it. That's why they ended up filling in those ponds on the village green with dirt. Afterward, supposedly, they finally had some peace."

Gerta shook her head skeptically.

"I'm selling it the way it was sold to me," Hermína said. "Every village around here has a story. And wherever there are still some locals left, the stories live on. Even if only behind closed doors, like here in Perná. Just you wait. If Herwiga Lhotákovic stops by tomorrow—she's from Dobré Pole and married into these parts—she can tell you what it was like to be in Mikulov with the Croats. It's not all that different from what we lived through ourselves. Because the Croats, you know, sided with the Germans."

Gerta pulled the blanket closer around her shoulders. "You really feel at home here now, don't you?" she then asked.

Hermína hesitated for a moment, before saying, "Yes. There's no other place where I feel at home. Not even in Brno, not since my mother died and then later my brother on the front lines. Those first few years, I somehow forgot about trying to find him, you probably remember. I was somehow, how should I put it . . ."

"Not yourself."

"Not myself, exactly. Same as all the rest of us who ended up here—after all, you know it as well as I do. Sort of homeless. No sense of direction."

"No drive."

"And then suddenly it dawned on me: Zipfelová was my home. She was such a good woman."

Hermína got up and went over to the window. Behind the glass windowpanes, the rain was coming down in ropes. They seemed to lash into the broken stems of the irises, their blooming heads lying on the drenched earth in surrender.

"She needed me as much as I needed her."

Gerta picked up the kettle and poured some more hot water over the linden leaves.

"When she died, I thought I'd have to start all over again. That I would have to move. Into the apartment block on the state farm that Jech was having built at the time. Or somewhere else entirely. But on the contrary. It was better for him to let me stay in an old and run-down place than to move me into the new housing he was preparing for the tractor drivers and for some other fellas. So he was the one to arrange it, and he made sure I could call this place home for good. So now this is my home. And finally, it's also in part because of the people. With the war long over, Zipfelová wouldn't let them send me away. So for the ones who came after I did, I was considered a local. To be perfectly honest, I'm actually grateful to Jech. I have a house, a job, and I have friends. And neighbors."

Quiet filled the room. Gerta wondered in silence if she could take Hermína at her word.

"Hermína, are you really happy?"

Hermína leaned back against the window ledge, folded her arms under her bosom, and said, "Yes."

"What did you actually do during the war?" Gerta then asked.

It was the first time she had ever asked anyone this question, which lurked in the back of everyone's mind, but which everyone, herself included, tried to ward off as much as possible, to avoid having to confront the past.

"I was a nurse. A registered nurse. I worked at St. Anne's University Hospital, on Annagrund Street. Right up until the end of the war. That night, they brought me to Mendelplatz straight from the hospital."

"Hermína, can you really be happy when you imagine that you could still be working in a hospital? That you could be living in Brno, going to and from work like any other respectable person? That you might have had a husband and kids, or that you could go out to the movies every week? And instead, here you are, mucking stalls and milking cows."

Hermína gave a short laugh. "There you're wrong, my dear. I don't muck stalls anymore. I don't even bed them. I'm a milkmaid. And now that they've introduced the milking machines, girlfriend, you can't even begin to imagine. You just scratch the cows behind the ears, pat them on the back, attach the milking cups, and then all you have to worry about are the tubes and the hoses—you just have to make sure nothing's blocked. It's great! Hanka Horáková was saying that the cows give less milk because they miss the human touch and don't get to know their farmer anymore. But I haven't noticed them being particularly stingy."

She stopped when she saw Gerta's quizzical look.

"What does it matter to me, whether I'm taking care of people or of animals? You know what it boiled down to? Survival. During all those years after the war, the one thing that mattered was to survive. And after a while, not just physically, but also on the inside. Not to die inside and to find something to grab on to. I grabbed on to this here kitchen and Zipfelka, and to all those women in the cow barn who accepted me as one of their own. You see, I found something here that I could hold on to. Whether I'm a nurse in a city hospital, or milking cows in some backwater where the foxes say goodnight, who cares. The main thing is I've got my own four walls and peace inside them."

"And that's exactly what I'm talking about," Gerta said after a while. "They really took absolutely everything from us. You're grateful for a pair of beat-up boots, and you don't even realize you stink of manure."

Hermína opened her eyes wide. "I stink?" she asked, sniffing at her shoulder, horrified.

"No." Gerta quickly shook her head. "I meant it figuratively. I mean, except for your hair, which retains the smell. What I'm trying to say is, I graduated with honors; I have a secondary school diploma; and I'd make an excellent accountant, if not something even better. I was good in math, and nowhere was it ever written that I wasn't supposed to finish business school. And in spite of that, I spent eight years working in a factory where I made wing drills. They took away our future as punishment for acts we never committed. And look at Johanna's twins. What have they done that they need to atone for?"

The blanket slipped off Gerta's shoulders as she abruptly leaned across the table, bringing her questioning look and wide-open eyes as close to Hermína as possible. She waited anxiously for her answer. As if Hermína could now exonerate them all from years of humiliation.

"But you see, there's a difference between us. A small one, but there is. Not that it solves anything or absolves anyone; you're right about that. Johanna's children are paying the price—and it's not fair. But not me. Don't put me into that mix anymore. I've barely paid any price at all because, in fact, they didn't take my future away. I was actually ready to walk away from it myself. You know, back then, times were rough. I wasn't interested, although by then I should've been. My brother had joined the *Wehrmacht*, although he hadn't wanted to, but that was mostly because he didn't want to go to war, not because he had anything against the *Wehrmacht*. I guess we were sort of . . . indifferent, that's the right word. And, of course, we shouldn't have been. When the war ended, I wanted to go away. My mother was dead, so was my brother, but I just stayed on, working. Again, indifferent. Sort of in slow motion. I didn't know where to go. Naturally, once they started bringing those men from Klajdovka or Maloměřice into the hospital, I knew that somehow I had to make a move, that I didn't want to stay there. Partly out of shame, but partly also because of what I was seeing. But again, I couldn't bring myself to move. I kept on going to and from work, just like you were saying, practically like any other respectable person. Until they grabbed me by the arm and marched me out to the Mendelplatz. My only regret is that I had none of my personal things with me—photographs, my mother's jewelry, the blouse she embroidered for me . . . just whatever I kept in my work locker. You know, I may not have the life I once thought I'd have, but on the other hand, I have more of a life now than I ever imagined would be possible after the war."

Gerta's eyes remained fixed on Hermína, but she slowly drew herself up and leaned back in the chair. This, too, was a fate, she thought to herself. Hermína had lost, but at the same time, she hadn't.

"And you know what? Back then, what I wanted most of all was to get away. More than anything else. And the only reason I couldn't do it was because I didn't know how or where. You know, I worked in the emergency room. I'd be running around, wearing that armband with the black *N*, and was one of the first people to talk to the men they were bringing in. And during those first few days, right after the war ended, there were so many. More than you can imagine, especially considering the war was over. And we weren't allowed to give out anything to the Germans—just water or bandages. No anesthetic, no pills, no medical supplies, just damp cloths. They'd be lying in the basement on mattresses right on the floor, side by side, and no doctor would treat them. We nurses knew they'd only been brought in to die as quickly as possible. You can't imagine what it was like to tell someone with a fractured skull, a broken pelvis, and contused kidneys just to be patient, that everything would be all right. There was someone named Venklarczik from Stiftgasse—I remember it as if it were today. They claimed he'd sold vegetables to the Gestapo. And then the Czechs in his building threw him out of a second-story window and dragged him up the street by his broken legs to make an example of him. Or all those mangled men, beaten black and blue, coming out of Kounic College, Jundrov, and Maloměřice. It would have made you weep to see it."

Gerta looked away. She stood up, keeping the blanket wrapped around her, pinned under her arms, and checked to see if her clothes hanging over the stove were still damp.

"Shall we have some more tea?" she then asked Hermína. She didn't want to hear any more about people who had been brought to the hospital from the labor camps. The proximity of her father's unknown fate caught her by surprise.

Hermína shifted herself away from the window ledge and began to prepare some fresh tea.

"So for me, all of this," she said, gesturing around the room with her hand, "is a kind of resolution. But I'm not blind. It's clear to me that they ruined it for us. But on the other hand, not only for us. For the Croats too. And for all the Šenks and the Idas. And all the priests like Father Anthony, who spent years in forced labor somewhere near Želiv before he was allowed to come back and start preaching in Moravia again. And do you know what you can do about it? *Summa summarum*, not much. Down here, at the bottom of the heap, you have no leverage. And yet there is something you can do. Don't let yourself be crushed underfoot, and be happy with what you have. With a nice and simple life that's so insignificant, it's not worth their while to destroy it all over again. Do you understand? That's what you can do."

Gerta envisioned her chair next to the metal table in the basement of the cold warehouse and found it hard to believe that Hermína meant it seriously.

II

If before going to sleep at night she prepared a sandwich and set out her clothes for the morning, she could save herself a good fifteen minutes. She figured that out right at the beginning, because no matter what, even after all these years of getting up early, she'd never been able to adjust to it. Not even when she was still working at the hospital. The night shift, from what she remembered, was still manageable—she would go to sleep just before dawn and get up while it was still daylight—but having to get up in the dark, in the very early morning, was something she never adjusted to. Her mother used to tell her that she had come into the world with the first rays of sunlight, so that every morning she needed to relive the moment of her birth. As long as it was still dark, she was still lifeless and lay in the deepest of sleep, but as soon as the sunlight tickled her eyelashes, her body would go into motion; it would come alive and start to function—she could practically hear the tiny nuts and bolts tinkling around inside her. Ah well, nothing doing. For almost thirty-five years now, she hadn't been awakened by the sun's first rays, not on Mondays through Saturdays, and not even on Sundays, since Mass was at eight. There was simply never a chance to catch up on sleep. But she wasn't about to complain—she, Hermína, never complained. About anything. Because she was in fact content. Yes, it was true that she didn't like to get up in the morning, but once she'd taken her first gulp of hot tea, and the warmth and sweetness started to spread down her throat into her stomach, she began to look forward even to the biting cold. To her very own biting cold in her very own village of Perná, where she had her very own cottage. She had ended up with everything, lock, stock, and barrel: the chickens, the rabbits, even the garden that produced those glorious, tall Marguerite daisies and, come fall, those honey-sweet Macs that kept all winter. And if she got everything ready the night before, all she had to do was throw on her shirt, overalls, and boots, tie a scarf around her head, toss the piece of buttered bread into her bag, and jump on her bike—purchased back in fifty-two when she'd finally managed to accumulate some savings—and she'd be at the cow barn by 4:00 a.m. sharp. And then what came next was in and of itself a heavenly feeling: to step inside that enormous barn, warm with the breath of the cows, and to exchange greetings with the other women who had already been there working since 3:00 a.m., and then with those who were coming in for the 4:00 a.m. milking. And to give each other an elbow in the rib with Herwiga Lhotákovic when it was particularly obvious that one of the other milkmaids had gotten up on the wrong side of the bed that day, or at the sight of the perpetually sour face of head milkmaid Mašková, who came over from Dunajovice every morning. Hermína had fallen in love with the work, and she'd fallen in love with the cows in her milking group, and even the women whom she saw morning after morning, all yawning into each other's faces before starting their shift. By then, the old manure would have already been cleared away by the women on the earlier shift, and since they'd put in conveyor belts and a fully automated milking system, it went fast—the wet straw and manure were carried away on those belts and dumped into a trailer outside the cow barn. All one needed to do was to shovel it on. After that, it was just a matter of bringing out clean straw in wheelbarrows and spreading the fresh bedding around with a pitchfork, saying a word or two to each cow in a soothing voice as if talking to a child, so that she wouldn't startle. By the time the milkmaids arrived, everything was already tidy. Then with feeding, it was just a matter of getting around a few wheelbarrows standing in the way full of either silage or clover, which would be tossed into the troughs, and the cows would go after it as though they hadn't eaten in weeks—such drama queens! She knew the routine well. It was the same each morning. She and Herwiga had two rows of twenty cows each, right across from each other, so they would work their way down the line together. Hermína always started off by walking around her group, saying hello to them and observing their moods as they munched away, swishing their tails. By now, after all these years, she could tell at a glance. Number One was an open book. If she looked up from the trough for a moment, it meant all was well—it was a greeting, a sign that she had noticed Hermína's presence. Worse was if she didn't budge and kept on scrounging around with her muzzle, hearing nothing and seeing nothing—that meant she wouldn't stand still for milking, and when Hermína was first assigned to her, would even kick. But back then, her girl was just a young heifer, still green. The slightest thing set her off. Whereas now that she'd had two calves, she had mellowed, and these days she was just a placid, old cow. She was the one Hermína cleaned up first for milking. She always stood right up front and kept herself clean, not like the others, whose hind legs were covered with manure that their tails would fling up onto their backs. When one of those was having a bad day, the dried cowpat would be crusted over so hard that bits of her hide and flesh would come off with the curry brush. Hermína would always say to them, "If you were smart, then you'd rock forward each time you dropped a cowpat—then you wouldn't end up covered in crap, and it wouldn't hurt so much." Because that, Hermína had noticed, was how Number One did it. Every time she took a crap, she rocked forward a little bit—it didn't take much—and the cowpat would drop onto the straw and miss her hind legs. And people said cows were stupid. Except that some of them really were stupid, and those were the ones who got all crapped up—and then Hermína would have to spend up to an extra ten minutes cleaning them off, so that sometimes she wouldn't even be finished by six o'clock in the morning. And then, while everyone else was already done with their snack, she'd just be pulling off her work gloves. They would all then have to move around her with their milk carts and milk cans, the aluminum clinking while she sat chewing on that piece of bread she'd brought from home, listening to Herwiga, who always waited for her. They had learned how to do the automated milking together. At first, they snickered at all the tubes and suction cups that looked like a four-legged spider, with that glass bottle in the middle that made her think of an IV bag until she realized what it was for. But they had stopped laughing pretty quickly—the minute they'd tried to attach the teat cups for the first time, the cows had balked, even though they had made a point of starting with the calmest ones. Rinse udder with water; turn on vacuum hose; attach left rear, right rear, left front, and right front teat cups; initiate suction; hold; insert hose into can; place can between legs; don't break the glass bottle; and keep the cow calm. The whole process must have taken them at least three times as long as it would have taken had they milked the teats by hand directly into a pail. It was true that their hands were less sore in the evenings, but their backs hurt just as much—and then, just the amount of time that was involved. The whole thing seemed radical. But eventually they got used to it, and in the end, it took them the same two hours to milk twenty cows as it had before. That was provided there was no mastitis. When that was the case, the milking process became a nerve-racking ordeal, and that had remained true to this day. Recently, Number Ten came down with it. Her whole udder became infected, and they put her on antibiotics. Afterward, Hermína expressed from two of the teats a thick, curdlike substance as the cow bellowed and spasmed in pain—she and Herwiga had been forced to hobble her hind legs because she kept on kicking, and their hands were practically shredded. She had managed to squeeze out almost a quart; there was blood in it, too, and the stench was foul. One would think not even the pigs would drink it, but they did, so they brought that curdled slop, along with a can of milk from the other two teats, over to the pigsty. At the time, two of her other cows had calves and were giving colostrum, so she added their surplus to the pail destined for the piggery, and for a while really only had seventeen cows to milk. Her output average dropped as a result, but what could she do? To see those calves, that was always amazing. Every time when they would finally come out, she would cry. The most recent one to calve had been Number Twelve. It had started in the evening, and Hermína had been working the night shift—the veterinarian was gone for the day, as was the manager, so it was all up to the women who were on duty, and they worked hard. Birthing a calf was no picnic. That one came out hooves first, so they tied a rope around them and pulled, trying to help. Number Twelve was thoroughly exhausted by the time the calf finally slid out and plopped down onto the straw beneath her, with the placenta and water bag coming out right after it—the latter burst while still in midair and splattered all over the women who were standing around, soaking them. But afterward, the sight made it all worthwhile. There was Number Twelve, drenched with sweat, her knees still shaky, licking the little one with her enormous, warm tongue as it slowly opened its eyes. Sublime. Now her Number Four was coming into heat—she was all jittery, and when Hermína spread the heifer's vagina, it was full of mucus, which let the inseminator know she was ripe for covering. They would let this one calve a second time.

Hermína liked the work, even though it was tedious. Not the work as such, obviously—she'd have been just as happy doing something else—but she liked the cows, and Herwiga, and her life here in Perná, where she'd dropped her roots and where, by now, almost no one remembered the circumstances under which she first arrived. Everything around her had settled down, and she finally had a sense of security. And that suited her. She was glad not to have stayed working in the hospital—in any hospital for that matter, even St. Anne's—because by the time the war was over, she could no longer bear to witness suffering. Maybe it was because of Uncle Kurt, her mother's brother, who had been in the *Volkssturm* toward the end of the war and whom she had seen there in late May. There was no way he had recognized her. His eyes were already glazed over, and he had looked right through her, but she recognized him. Even though it had already happened several times that, while working there, she'd been assigned to someone she knew, her uncle's face had seared itself into her mind just like the red circles left by the scorching hot plates that had been placed all over his body. His singed nipples weren't even discernible in the bloody pulp that was left of his chest. The same was true of his sex, where they had placed a fiery hot plate as well. As punishment for having been a Henleiner. Hermína had known it—they had all known it—but even so, she pitied him, because, apart from his pride in the Reich, the only other thing he probably ever did was raise his arm in a *Heil Hitler* salute on Adolf-Hitler-Platz. It was possible that during those final days, when members of the *Volkssturm* were setting up barricades in the streets and running around the city with hand grenades, fear got the better of him and he went overboard—who knew. She had seen all sorts of people lose their minds. Maybe he deserved some degree of punishment, but to such an extreme? Aunt Gudrun, who used to make the best *Eintopf* stew, had brought him over on a rickshaw, right from their house. They didn't even have a chance to haul him off to a labor camp; the neighbors in the building worked him over like this first. He died that same night. Amid the chaos and constant influx of newly wounded, for whom they had no room anywhere, she caught one last glimpse of Aunt Gudrun as she waved to her from the far end of a long hallway. By then she must have already known how things had gone with Uncle. Had she then, too, been expelled from Brno, or had she managed to slip away? Who knew. Hermína hadn't looked into it any further—over those next few days, she barely slept; there was simply no time. And shortly thereafter, she was already walking out of the city, caught in a tide along with hundreds of others like her—a beggar, with only her nurse's uniform and the handful of belongings from her locker. But she didn't complain—even though she could have, she didn't. It was only when she looked at Gerta that she felt regret for all they had been through. In her, Hermína saw what it meant to spend one's whole life at odds with the skin you were born into, tormented by thwarted ambitions. Cursing her life as it tossed her up and down—each time Gerta managed to dig herself out, someone would knock her back down, and for that, Hermína felt terribly sorry. For all of the random misfortunes in Gerta's life. There was one time Hermína had hoped it was all finally coming to an end, the time Gerta left Perná with that Karel of hers. The timing had been perfect. She'd just been thrown out of the National Committee. All she did was get up every day, pull on rubber boots, head over to the cow barns while it was still pitch dark, muck stalls, eat something, do the milking, clean up, go home, tend to Barbora, and sleep. She went through the motions like an automaton, completely mechanically. Anything that forced her to break out of that rhythm was cause for celebration. Naturally, Hermína already knew that for people like Gerta, it was better if they could switch off their thinking completely. If only she hadn't been born a German. If she had fled

Brno right at the beginning of May . . . but then again, to where? Or what if she had stayed in Pohořelice? Or run away with Teresa and Ula? Or had pulled herself together and gone back to Brno with Johanna? But at the same time, she needed to keep a roof over her head—after all, there was Barbora. Hermína never needed Gerta to explain any of this, nor had Gerta tried. Back then, she barely spoke at all. It was as if she had become frozen inside, incapable of doing anything that fell out of her daily routine. Up until the day that Karel showed up and lifted her out of it. He returned the blood to her veins, as Hermína could observe on the rare occasions when she visited. Before everything caved in on her again.

Hermína had observed it all—no one needed to explain anything to her, Gerta least of all. She understood perfectly well, and for Gerta and for all those other women, she felt sorry. But these days, Hermína no longer shared the aversion that Gerta and Johanna felt toward everything here. Because she had managed to start a new life, a fulfilling life. She knew the exact day it happened. It was when Hubert Šenk had said to them that if they wanted to keep on working, they could stay. At that point, she had settled down with Zipfelka for good and, not too long afterward, had been granted a wage and then citizenship. That had resolved everything for her. And not just for her, but also for Zipfelová, who had been afraid she would end up all alone. This way, they both ended up being content. And Hermína was content to this day, even though Zipfelová had now left her. Hermína was content and did not complain. Praise be to God.

III

Gerta, on the other hand, did complain, with good reason. She was living either in the basement of a warehouse or within the four walls of her apartment, and instead of enjoying her life, she was surviving it. In seclusion, keeping in touch with just a handful of others whose lives had been similarly afflicted. She, after all, saw clearly the injustices inflicted on them—and for what reason? Because they had been born into the wrong column. *Nationality German.* The past was still pursuing them, was ever present; even twenty-five years later it refused to set them free. Gerta was seeing it and living it, as were Johanna, Teresa, and even Hermína. They were all badly off. Teresa, lost in a city where she could never feel at home; Hermína, trying to convince herself that she was happy, working in a cow barn and living in a cottage that was about to collapse on her head; and Johanna and herself, meeting week after week for their walk in the park, growing increasingly older and more decrepit. And the ones she blamed for ruining her life were nowhere to be found. It had always been the hand of the executive arm that had toyed with her, the one not burdened by decision-making. The adolescent boys from the Zbrojovka Arms Factory, even Mrs. Panáčková from the personnel department, who had been the one to inform her that she was being transferred to the warehouse—none of them were individually to blame. They didn't make the decisions. And the ones who did were too high up for Gerta to reach. She had resigned herself to her discontent and grew more and more bitter, despondent, and lonely, without prospects and, ultimately, without Barbora. Now Johanna, on the other hand, hadn't resigned herself to anything. She was still fighting. She was battling furiously, and Gerta admired her for it—for her persistence, her relentless faith, and her ongoing hope that her Gerhardt was still out there somewhere and that when he finally came back, everything would be better. Johanna had never given up. Until the day they went to visit a man named Schweiger.

Johanna had written dozens of letters. She wrote to the authorities, to hospitals, to the Red Cross. If she got any answer at all, it was negative. She even wrote to the president but received no response. She had tried everything, and it took years for it to find its way to her, the crumpled piece of graph paper on which there was an address for this man Schweiger. She was practically beside herself with joy—now that she'd found a trace, there was no stopping her. She was bubbling over with exuberance and bubbling over at Gerta, dragging her along to the post office, falling into her arms once she got off the phone, and two days later insisting that she come with her to pay a visit to this Schweiger, on whom she'd forced herself. He hadn't been interested, she had said, but she refused to be put off. After all those years, it was the first concrete trace of Gerhardt that she had managed to track down, and she wasn't about to be dissuaded. Her life depended on it.

And he might even know something about her old man Schnirch, Johanna had said as she was leaving Gerta's that day to rush home and give the twins the news. Gerta didn't care. She didn't want to know anything more about her father than what she already knew. As far as she was concerned, he had disappeared from her life with the war, and what happened to him afterward was of no interest to her. In her mind, she'd buried him long ago, and the last thing she wanted was to find out that he might still be alive somewhere—possibly even living nearby. He or her brother. But she accompanied Johanna nonetheless. Who else was going to go with her if she didn't?

"Supposedly he was in the Kounic College camp until forty-six, and afterward they didn't deport him, who knows why. For whatever reason, he stayed. And he knows something about the men who were there—in there, and also in the Klajdovka camp, where they transferred him. It's impossible that he wouldn't know something. About Gerhardt and about your father," Johanna was saying just before she rang the doorbell to his apartment.

He was swaying back and forth in his rocking chair, and he smelled. He was quite old already and a little bit unsteady. On his head there remained just a few sparse, white strands of hair combed from right to left across his bald pate. He didn't look pleased to see them—Gerta took note of that right away. He must have already known why they had come. But Johanna was ecstatic. She thrust a box of chocolates and a mesh bag of oranges into his hands and eagerly settled herself on the sofa by his easy chair—there was no holding her back.

"Polivka," he said, at first in a slow, drawn-out way, after she had rattled off the reason for their visit.

"Polivka," he repeated once more, and then, with a sullen look on his face, slowly dropped his head, letting it sink below his shoulders. "It's possible he was there. You know, I'm old now. And I hardly knew everyone; you have to forgive me."

This took Johanna aback, but then she blurted out, "But of course you remember him. You worked with him in Hawiger's rubber factory! Why, he was your foreman. Tall, blond receding hairline, blue eyes. Don't tell me you don't remember him."

Schweiger tipped forward in his chair, his gaze fixed on the palms of his hands as they rested in his lap.

"Oh, that one," he then said.

"Yes, that one."

"He was a good foreman," said Schweiger. "He'd let us go even if we weren't on break. He was generous. And he didn't bark at us the way some of the others did. He was reasonable, he was."

"Well, so you see, he was there too," Johanna said. "The last time I saw him was in the Kounic College courtyard, you know, where they used to do roll call."

Schweiger was quiet for a moment, but then said, "So he was there too? You see, I don't even know."

Johanna looked dismayed. "But you do know. That's precisely why they sent me to you, because you know. Because you stayed, and because you know which men were transferred where, and which ones left on a transport."

Schweiger wheezed and gave a short-winded chuckle. "They left, did they?"

"Or maybe they stayed here. I don't know what happened to them."

"Well, yes, I guess some of them did leave, some did," he said, having settled back down.

"And Gerhardt?"

Schweiger shrugged, saying, "If he was there, it probably didn't bode too well for him. Same as for the rest of us, missus. Same as for me."

Schweiger grew quiet and rocked lightly in his chair. Johanna looked helplessly first at him and then over at Gerta. Was it possible that he really didn't remember anything, that he had nothing to tell her? Gerta was convinced that he was just desperately trying to avoid having to talk. Either to them, or about the camp, or most likely both.

But then he resumed on his own, rocking as he spoke. "Every morning and every evening, we had to line up to be counted. One evening, Polivka was supposedly still there, but the next morning he was missing."

Johanna stayed quiet for a while, waiting for him to go on. There was a long silence.

"And where did he go?" she finally asked.

"I don't know. Nobody knows. Who in that place was going to tell us? Please, it was a labor camp, ma'am. Everyone was glad to go unnoticed, or if noticed, at least not beaten. We tried not to draw any unnecessary attention to ourselves. That's why nobody ever asked about people who disappeared. Sometimes the men wouldn't even ask about their closest relatives; that's how scared they were. Who knows how I would have behaved if I'd had someone in there I was close to. But I didn't; in my family, there were always just girls. And all of them had gone—back then, I had no idea where—but I hoped they were hiding somewhere and that they knew where I was and would wait for me. But in the end, it all turned out very differently."

Johanna leaned forward so that she could see into his face.

"And you have absolutely no idea what could have happened? Why he wasn't there in the morning?" she asked slowly and deliberately.

"It's hard to say. It could've been anything, whatever they felt like. They could have shipped him off somewhere, but then after the war, he would have come back. Since he didn't come back, I'd say there's no longer any point in looking for him. He's no longer alive."

Gerta knew that everybody except for Johanna already believed that, herself included, but no one was allowed to voice it in her presence. On the contrary, Anni and Rudi had to honor his memory: everything he had ever done, the way he had been, and before going to sleep, they also had to say goodnight to him—to Papa Gerhardt, in the form of eight blurry photographs with dog-eared corners, tucked behind the glass of the kitchen cupboard. They had been handled so often that they had practically disintegrated into shreds of tattered, velvety fibers. Johanna had stuffed them under her blouse when they were being expelled from Brno, taking them with her all the way to Perná and then back home again. For as long as Gerta could remember, Gerhardt had always been talked about in the conditional tense, and anything related to him was firmly anchored in either the past or a future, whose outlines were always slightly blurred—perhaps so that when he reappeared, he could easily slip right back into them, start living with them again as though he had never left. Gerta found it a bit perverse, especially when she overheard the twins talking about their father as if he were about to come home from work at any moment, while at the same time they no longer remembered him. Barbora once told her that sometimes Anni and Rudi were scared of him, afraid that he might be living with them as a ghost, watching them—keeping an eye on everything they did. At times, Gerta felt like saying something to Johanna about this business of his legacy or living absence, or whatever it was that she'd managed to create at home—that she was taking it too far. But even the one time she'd made up her mind to do it, she couldn't find the nerve. To tell her she had to rid herself of the ballast of the past, because if Gerhardt was still alive, by now he would have certainly found her. And this man Schweiger had just said it out loud.

"What do you mean, 'he's no longer alive'? What could have happened to him, that he's no longer alive?" asked Johanna, dumbfounded.

"Anything is possible."

"Might you know, or might you remember, being that you say he's dead? Do you know how? Or why? That is, if he really is dead, if they didn't just send him away somewhere?" Gerta probed further, knowing this was a question Johanna would never ask.

"Oh, come on now. Sent him away, didn't send him. If they sent him anywhere, it would have been to Klajdovka, and there he would have died for sure. They had that man Kouřil there, and he was a brute. Especially to someone who'd survived the war in as good shape as Polivka had. They didn't send him anywhere, at least as far as I know."

"Not even on a transport?" peeped Johanna.

"Not as far as I know, no."

"So what do you actually know about him? Please!"

Schweiger's expression darkened, and he started to rock back and forth in agitation.

"Please, you have to understand. Everyone was afraid of drawing attention to themselves. Everyone was afraid of seeing anything. Or of asking anything. Not one of us who was there from the rubber factory asked about him."

Both women were silent.

"But it's possible, more than likely, he was hanged. Or shot."

"My God, why would they do that? What did he do?" Johanna cried out.

Schweiger pulled a folded handkerchief out of his pocket and dabbed his brow.

"He may have done nothing at all," he said after a moment of silence.

"Then why are you saying they hanged him?"

"I'm saying that I don't know, but it's possible."

"What do you mean?"

"He was simply one of those men—and there were a bunch of them—who didn't have to do a thing. Chance can be a big fat bitch. Or the reverse. Actually, speaking for myself, I'd say the reverse."

"I don't understand," Johanna said, shaking her head. "Can't you be more specific?"

"I can't. I don't talk about it."

"You don't talk about what?"

"You came here to ask me where Polivka ended up. And I'm telling you that I don't know. No one can know, and that's the answer. And as far as that other one, Schnirch, where he ended up," he said, nodding at Gerta, "I don't know that either."

"Yes, you do know. You suspect something; I can see it in your face," Johanna exclaimed, and it was obvious that if she didn't get any more information, she would burst into tears. "You suspect something, so you can't stop now. I can't leave here until I find out what it is, do you understand? This is about my husband. You don't have the right to take whatever it is you might know about him to your grave. Forgive me for speaking so bluntly. But I'm going to keep coming to see you until I find out what it is, understand?"

Schweiger rolled his eyes, inhaled deeply, then loudly blew out air through his bulbous, fleshy nose, but said nothing. Only his eyebrows seemed to sink deeper into his face, accentuating the furrows on his forehead.

"I don't talk about it, because I don't know how one says such things. It's that simple. And besides, I'm really not in the mood."

"I understand. But I'm not asking you about anything else except for what's mine to know. About my Gerhardt. Can you understand?"

Schweiger appeared to crumple in on himself—his shoulders slumped forward and sank lower, and he seemed to double over. Like a piece of paper that's been balled up and then squeezed hard once, twice, three times, to make sure it's nice and tight.

"Well, as you can imagine, different things went on there. Many men didn't survive. They were hanged or shot in the back of the head. Toward the end, they preferred doing it that way. It was quicker. For them, that is. Every imaginable offense was punishable that way."

He gave a dry swallow, and his Adam's apple bobbed up and down.

"Then other things happened that had nothing to do with any offense. Those made you lose your mind. And whoever went crazy was no longer useful as a worker—he just caused trouble, so they'd shoot him. It was that simple. But at least in that there was some logic. If one was careful not to go crazy, one could survive."

"What would make you lose your mind?" asked Gerta.

"Random chance. Just like that, no rules whatsoever. The ones who were on night-watch duty and couldn't have women drank, naturally. They drank like animals. And they placed bets. Why call them animals?" he said, more to himself. "You'd never see something like that in nature. In the natural world, logic and order prevail—you kill to eat and to survive. They drank like only men can drink, and they placed bets. During the night, someone would always go missing, and the next morning, it was better not to ask questions. Sometimes they woke people up and made them watch. Sometimes they went to sleep without even cleaning up the mess after themselves. So with some of the men, we knew what happened to them. Then there were others about whom we never found out."

"And about Gerhardt?"

"Probably, yes. There were rumors. But that time they didn't wake me, nor did I see anything. So who knows? They could have made a mistake."

"Please, tell me." Johanna grabbed his hand.

Schweiger curled himself up even tighter. His head hung low on his chest with only his chin jutting out, and he was staring down at the white blanket tossed over his knees. His hands were clasped together, fingers intertwined, and from time to time he lifted them and feebly let them fall, striking his thighs. A fall that seemed in keeping with a sense of helplessness that suddenly now, after years of his not having dared speak of it, was spilling out of him, as it should have back then. Johanna squeezed his hand.

"It's something you can't begin to imagine. Something you wouldn't even be able to think up. No normal person could. The helplessness, the inability to influence anything, to prevent anything. The knowledge that you're just a body to be toyed with. Nothing more. In order to survive and not to go crazy before it was my turn to be picked, I learned to switch myself off. I turned into exactly what they thought of us. I simply switched off. I watched, like they wanted us to, but saw nothing, and then I went to sleep and thought of nothing. Day after day, I did what they told me to, but I didn't give my body any conscious instructions, let alone think about what I was doing. All I consciously did was to fix my eyes inward on some imaginary black spot during the whole thing, as if I were somehow looking inside myself. I don't think I can do it anymore, but in the time it took me to rid myself of that habit, I grew old. You can see for yourselves what I look like now," he said in resignation, spreading his hands.

"And of the various things that used to go on there at night, one consisted of tying a naked man to a chair and setting it at the edge of the top step of a flight of stairs. They bet on red or black. They played cards next to him, and he knew what was coming, and those of us they dragged out to watch, we also knew what was coming. And what one of us had coming as well. Sometimes they didn't like to get their hands dirty. As you know, back then, whether it was one or a dozen Germans, nobody would miss them. Besides, the only reason we were there was for them to finish us off, anyway. Prisoners were slave labor, and if some Russian or some Czech in one of the camps wiped us out, nobody cared. No one really knew how many of us were in there to begin with, so they came up with those games. For the nights. They would have us line up, as I said. Then they set the one who was tied to the chair at the top of the stairs. Next, they held a pistol to the head of the other one and started to count. Nobody lasted past five. Everyone gave in, everyone pushed the chair down the stairs. Black meant he flew face forward, red that he flew backward, looking at the one who pushed him. Whoever couldn't bring himself to push would lose his mind. He'd shit himself right there, and they'd both end up dead. The head always took the brunt of it. Down below, they'd just sweep up the shit. And even better was when they tied him by his pecker. Then he'd fly backward, and the only thing slowing him down was this." He pointed to his crotch.

They could barely breathe.

"They said this could have happened to Polivka. But I didn't see it. I know nothing about it. Just that the next morning, he didn't show up. And then this rumor started to go around."

He let his hands fall into his lap once more, and this time he let them stay there. He unlaced his fingers and wiped his damp palms on the blanket.

"The worst part about it all was that it defied all logic. There were no rules, no way to influence anything. Only one thing was for sure. Somebody was going to get it. Now, can you imagine that your life is hanging only by a thread of random chance? No, you can't. Nobody can. Because it's impossible to live that way. It goes completely against nature, against common sense. And that's why so many lost their minds. Is this what you wanted to hear? Now you know. What did you expect? After all, we'd lost the war, and we were all Nazis, one the same as another. If you were German, you were a Nazi. It's true that some of them deserved it. But like this? No. And the worst of it was that even people who spent the whole war feeling ashamed of being German, and who had tried to do sabotage wherever they could, they ended up having to pay the price too. Hugo Zimmler, who also worked in the rubber factory, he was one of those. An anti-fascist, but you'd be surprised, he was out there slogging away just like everyone else. In the end, I think he did leave with a transport, once they'd closed down the camps. He was lucky to have survived. I was too. But some weren't that lucky."

Had Johanna, in the deepest recesses of her heart, ever conceded that Gerhardt might be dead, then it was strictly having died a hero's death. While fleeing as he was trying to get back to them, or in an uprising against some Czech brutes or Russian soldiers. Only his pride or his courage could have caused his death, nothing else. But that it had been the result of chance? The extended finger of some drunken camp guard who, now that the war was over, in addition to the back-breaking rubble-clearing work, wanted to make things for the Germans burn even hotter?

Gerta imagined that extended, wavering finger pointing at Gerhardt Polivka or at her father—that finger, which could have moved just as easily a few centimeters in the other direction. Then the lives of Johanna, Anni, and Rudi, and maybe even her own, might have unfolded entirely differently. Random chance, she thought to herself.

Johanna began to sob.

IV

With Mom it was never easy. I spent my whole childhood standing like a little suppliant in front of the hard, blank face with which she reacted to everything, no exceptions. It was the same face with which she reacted to my having to repeat the first and third grades, and then the same face again when I got my apprentice certificate and was hired as a draftswoman by the porcelain factory. Exactly the same. If I had to sum it up, I'd say that Mom was completely without feelings, really tough. And I'm not sure why, but most of all to me. Not that she wasn't good to me, she was, but for that other face of hers, I had my own private name. I used to call her the mean ice fairy, because a lot of the time, that's how she was to me. Because of small stuff. Sometimes it was because I hadn't followed her insanely pedantic rules—because I hadn't dusted, or neatly arranged my shoes in front of the threshold to the living room—and other times it was just because I'd asked her something about our family. Then she'd become really stiff and frosty, a total ice queen. But it was as if that iciness were reserved just for me. To other people, I mean the few that she used to see, she wasn't like that at all. Not even to the stupid cat, come to think of it—because when it came to that cat, completely different rules of love seemed to apply than applied to me. It was a sad little thing that the gypsies used to torture, the ones they resettled here out of their caravans, which they'd confiscated and burned. They moved them right onto our street and into apartments around the neighborhood that were supposedly cursed, Mom used to say, because no happiness had ever come to anyone who lived in them—not to the Jews, then later not to the Germans, and finally, after them, not even to the Czechs, who abandoned them to move into the new high-rises in the housing development—that was how Mom always used to explain it to me. The gypsies didn't seem to care that they were living in cursed apartments, or that these were fancy apartments right near the city center, because they built fires inside using the wood from the parquet floors, until one day a building on Bratislavská Street went up in flames and collapsed. Well, whatever, those gypsies had already poked out one of the cat's eyes and chopped off its tail before Mom jumped in and took it away from them. Supposedly they had tied its head to its front legs, and it was squirming so badly that it looked like it was about to strangle itself. And it definitely would have been better off, because what was left of it now was pretty gruesome. But Mom didn't see that and loved it—one could almost say more than she loved me. She smothered it with food, got all kinds of blankets for its bed, and always talked to it very slowly and softly, real soothing like. And sure enough, the cat started to respond to her—at first, it didn't react to anything at all, just cowered under the bench in the corner of the kitchen and peed. Once in a while, it would move a little way out of its favorite spot, always crouching, and would pee or crap, and then dash right back. Mom never yelled at it, even though the litterbox the cat was supposed to use was sitting right there. And that's saying a lot, knowing how pedantic Mom could be, which I did. But this business with the cat proved that it only applied to me. Sometimes, I felt I was cursed, as if I didn't deserve my mom's love. Then I would desperately wish for another person to love me, a dad. That's why I was so happy when Uncle Karel started hanging out with us, and later on, when the Agathonikiadises moved in.

From what I remember, Uncle Karel was all around awesome. The two or three years that he used to come around, he would take us out in the car for day trips and stuff like that. Or he'd take us to ride the carousel, when the carnies came to Brno, and one time we even went to the circus. There was a woman in a teeny white dress who walked on a tightrope with her arms held out to the sides, waving these two little paddles to keep her balance. I desperately wanted to be like her and told my mom, but she just rolled her eyes and gave Uncle a grin, and today I can understand why. If my little Blanka were to come up to me and tell me that she wanted to be a circus tightrope walker when she grew up, I'd probably roll my eyes too. For now, she's still little, but when she grows up, I know she's going to do something respectable—I dreamed about it—like being a saleswoman or something. You know, a decent job.

Uncle Karel, back in the days when he used to spend time with us, was practically like a god to me—obviously someone high and almighty. I think even my mom used to see him that way, although today I'm not so sure about that anymore. But still, as far as I was concerned, he was the only man I'd ever gotten to know, and he liked me, which I could tell from the way he always used to stare at me really intensely, without even blinking. I think I might have even had a little crush on him—just a childish one, obviously, because I knew he was my mom's. But I wanted a little piece of him, too, so I would try to doll myself up as best as I could. For example, at school in art class, they taught us how to take a napkin and fold it into a rose. So I took a bunch of napkins from the cafeteria, stuffed them into my tights, so that comrade teacher wouldn't see and start blabbing about me again, and then when I got home, I made myself lots of roses. I stuck them into my hair using sharp, black bobby pins, and felt I'd made myself really beautiful for Uncle Karel. Later on in the kitchen, they probably had a good laugh over me—it's very possible. To this day, I remember how those roses began to slide down my straight, wispy hair, and ended up dangling like pompoms on my forehead, until finally one plopped into my soup. When I looked up, afraid that Mom was going to ream me out, they were both beet red with puffed-out cheeks, which really pissed me off. Then that was it as far as being elegant and trying to look pretty for Uncle Karel. But I still went on thinking of him as my dad and used to tell my classmates about him, when they would ask me stupid questions like was my father German too. And then someone started to spread around that he wasn't my dad at all, but just Mom's lover, and that nobody would want to marry a stupid German cow like her anyway. And that I was a bastard. When I got home and told my mom, she got really mad, and made me say it again in front of Uncle Karel the next time he came over. And already back then, Uncle Karel proved he was almighty, because suddenly the kids in school weren't allowed to say those things anymore. Whenever the teacher would overhear something, she would tell them off, even though it was just for show. At home when I told my mom about it, she said that Uncle Karel had made a phone call and had really let comrade teacher have it. These days I have to wonder what he could've had on her—there must've been plenty, since he was in both the

District and Central Committees. That phone call to esteemed comrade teacher Brunclíková must've been a doozy.

Uncle Karel also lent us money for a tombstone, I remember. It was right after we'd moved back to Brno. We went to visit Grandma Ručková's grave, and that was where we made the discovery. That whole day was a big deal. It was the first time we'd ever gone there, and my mom said we had to get dressed up, which only meant that she dressed me in the same clothes as usual, the only ones I had, and put her scarf—the one Aunt Hermína gave her—over my coat, the point hanging down between my shoulder blades and a knot tied under my chin. The ends hung down over my chest, and I was really excited, feeling so fancy. That day we went by tram, and I remember it very well, because it was my first tram ride. I kept that ticket for ages. Mom tacked it up on the wall over my bed and said she was sure that I'd have a whole row of tickets up there soon. I loved that idea. Later on, I sort of got over it—sometimes Mom didn't have a nail, so some of the tickets got lost, and by then we used to take the *šalina*—the proper Brno slang word for tram—so often that the feeling of it being an adventure somehow went away. The one thing I can still remember very clearly is the big fight Mom and I had the first time I used the word "*šalina*" instead of "*elektrika*." I don't even know exactly when I brought that word home from school, where everybody used it a lot. Mom got all worked up, telling me I had no idea what I was saying, and did I even know what it meant. I had no clue. All I knew was that *šalina* was another word people in Brno used for the tram, and this sent her off the deep end. But then again, how was I supposed to know in second or third grade that it came from German? I was by far the only kid who was even slightly connected to anything German—although then I didn't even know it. Later on, Mom said that the people of Brno had ruined it all—any good thing that could have existed between them and the Germans. They'd expelled them all and then kept whatever suited them for themselves. Like, for example, that Hantec dialect people in Brno used, which gave me trouble, too, as if I didn't have enough problems already. They made fun of my language and my accent for almost the entire first two years, but I couldn't help it. I spoke the way Mom and Granny Zipfelová had taught me, so what was I supposed to do, right? I tried really hard to learn those words of theirs, but then I'd get in trouble at home, and Mom would yell at me. It was pretty awful. Like with that business of "*elektrika*" and "*šalina*," which the Czechs stole from the Germans, turning "*elektrische linie*" into "*šalina*." Get it? *E-lek-tri-š-e-li-nie* became *š-e-li-nie* became *š-a-li-nie*, which became "*šalina*." At home, I wasn't allowed to say that word; it had to be either "*elektrika*" or "*tramvaj*." Both were really embarrassing to use, because only old people said "*elektrika*," and nobody ever said "*tramvaj*." So at home, I would say "*tramvaj*," to get around using Mom's "*elektrika*," and outside, I would use words like "*šalina*," "*pajtl*" for pilfer, "*zoncna*" for sun, "*prigl*" for the Brno Reservoir, "*mózovat*" for mosey, and sometimes even "*krchov*" for cemetery, like normal people talked. And that brings us back to the cemetery. It was my very first time going by tram, and our first trip to visit the family plot, which was at the upper end of the cemetery, surrounded by trees that looked like tall, thin candles. Mom said they were called thujas—back then I called them *toothas*—and we strolled underneath them along a sandy path all the way to a low wall, where our family plot was supposed to be. Well, it was there, all right, but the headstone was cracked and lay knocked over by the wall. And the plaque was smeared with old paint that had partially washed away over the years, so what was left of the golden letters that I didn't yet know how to read was showing through again. Mom, when she saw it, burst into tears and said it was all because of our German name that was engraved there, and that it seemed we'd never be free of. Afterward, Auntie Johanna told her she should be glad the grave was still there at all—that the remains of our ancestors were still buried in that earth—because many other Germans hadn't been so lucky. Supposedly, Auntie Johanna couldn't find either her own family grave or the family grave of her missing uncle Polivka anymore—both had been in a small cemetery in Řečkovice, where the locals simply got rid of them because they had German names and they needed more room for Czech graves. And she said the same thing had happened to lots of other German families, that the tombs of their ancestors had been defaced and the graves destroyed. Supposedly, most of it happened right after the war, but it was still happening back then. For all I know, it's still happening now, although that time is long gone, and these days it's not the Germans people around here hate; it's the Russians—even though they're still quick to put down anything German too. Unless it's something really special, like the Parnas Fountain on Vegetable Market Square—nobody tore that down even though it was commissioned by Germans—and Trabant cars are a big hit these days. At any rate, Mom finally calmed down a bit, after Auntie Johanna, whom we'd stopped in to visit, had talked to her like that for a while. It was the first time I'd seen Anni and Rudi in three years, but it felt like not even a week had gone by. We hit it off again right away, and from then on, they were back to being like my brother and sister, even though they were a bit older and, by then, they were already really smart. They knew three languages—they had learned Czech, although it still sounded a little clunky; they were learning Russian at school; and at home they spoke German because Auntie Johanna didn't want them to forget the language their father spoke. She wanted them to be equally fluent in both mother tongues, so that they would be bona fide Czech citizens, as she put it. But according to what they said, they weren't that at all. At school, the other kids would make life hell for them, and they ended up having to repeat a grade, because their Czech wasn't good enough and they couldn't understand the assignments. Anni said she didn't really mind, because it gave her a chance to get away from that mean group of kids who always beat up on her after school. This way, they'd gotten into a better class, where even though none of the kids wanted to have anything to do with them, at least they weren't getting beaten up. Back when she told me all this,

I didn't have a clue about that game of Lidice yet—that was still waiting for me a few years down the road—but I thought it sounded pretty terrible. Luckily, we had each other, though, and that was good enough. Every Sunday, we'd go running around in Lužánky Park, or we'd go over to the Polivkas', or they would come over to us—sometimes the Ainingers came, too, and it was super. But again, back to the grave. In the beginning, my mom had no money at all, so Uncle Karel paid for lots of things, even that new tombstone that we went to pick out—and we chose a small one. It was made out of a cheap, gray marble with salt-and-pepper flecks, and had silver lettering, which was cheaper than gold. I mean, there was just one inscription. Mom had only Grandma Ručková's name engraved, and it didn't bother her at all that there were two other people lying under the same stone—her dad's parents, who had the same last name as we did: Schnirch. She also had my grandma's name written as Barbora Ručková, which, by the time she died, wasn't really her name anymore. Except that Mom really didn't like Grandpa Schnirch, who was a German, which might not have been so bad, but supposedly he was a Nazi. So she never talked about him, and I know practically nothing, except that she probably could never forgive him for being a die-hard Nazi, a mindset with which he'd also infected Mom's brother, Uncle Friedrich, who had disappeared someplace in Russia during the war. But Grandma, her she loved. Supposedly, she was very pretty, which she probably was, because Mom is pretty too. It's a shame that we don't have a picture of her—Mom had to leave every-thing behind when they drove her out of Sterngasse, where they used to live. So I don't even know what anyone in our family looked like, which I kind of would have liked to know, since I never got to meet any of them. Anyway, supposedly she was slim and pretty, and had a beauti-ful voice, and she and my mom loved each other very much. Sometimes I'm envious of them, because the kind of loving relationship the two of them had, well, my mom and I, we have nothing like it. But no point complaining, at least I've got Jára, whereas Mom . . . For a while, she had Uncle Karel, but now she has nobody. As far as I can remember, he stopped coming around to see us when I was in about third grade. Mom didn't know why and didn't talk to me much about it, so to this day I'm not exactly sure what happened. But it was pretty lousy, because little by little, things at school took a turn for the worse. First came the crap about my not being able to learn how to read and write properly, and then right after that came the Lidice game, and that was horrible. The long shadow of Uncle Karel that had protected us all those years had disappeared. He'd lost his power. That's when I'd start to wake up all sweaty in the middle of the night, because I had terrible nightmares about poor Uncle Karel. A group of big guys would be playing the game of Lidice with him, while a group of smaller guys would be marching all around him in a circle. They'd either be shouting at him, or they'd be looking at him, sweet as honey. Then after a while, Uncle Karel started to come into my dreams all gray, and skinny, and exhausted, with his teeth knocked out—he'd be working in some quarry. And then finally I stopped dreaming about him, because by then, I had other, more important things keeping my imagination busy, namely the stories Auntie Athanaia used to tell me. Uncle Achilles was all right, too, even though he was older and uglier than Uncle Karel—and above all, he didn't speak any Czech, only Greek, which of course I couldn't understand. So I only talked to him through Auntie Athanaia, who had learned to speak Czech pretty quickly. I grew really attached to her back then, maybe because living with Mom wasn't exactly easy. And I really needed someone who was genuinely nice, and that's what Auntie Athanaia was. When, after those five or six years, they finally went back home, I missed them terribly. It was immediately obvious that they'd been the ones who had made us feel like a family. When they left, that feeling of shared warmth went with them. Suddenly, everything felt so empty—no more little celebrations that up to then took place all year long, because according to Auntie Athanaia, there wasn't a month in which there wasn't something to celebrate. She said that's how it was in

Greece, that life was made up of little festivals and celebrations during which one mostly ate and drank wine. She always had a new surprise ready for us, like at Easter, when late at night all the lights were turned off and we sat, just by candlelight, eating Auntie's *magiritsa* soup. It was made from the insides of a little lamb that Auntie must have gotten hold of somehow through her Greek girlfriends in Brno, because according to Mom, you'd never find something like that in any of the butcher shops. Or she would organize a beautiful New Year's Day celebration, when we would all hold our breath, waiting to see who would get the piece of her *vasilopita* cake with the golden *fluri* coin, which would bring that person good luck for the whole year, as well as oodles of money.

Auntie Athanaia was a really neat lady, and she spent a lot of time playing with me and talking to me. She told me that back home, when she was little, they would put a bit of everything on a little altar, an *iconostasis*, but that later Uncle Achilles forbade it, because they were Communists, so she gave up the *iconostasis* out of love for him. Or she would show me how she used to dance the *kotchari* better than anyone in her village, or, come early March, she would tie a *Marti* ribbon around my wrist that I would then wear all spring until I saw the first swallow. I still remember it all as if it were just yesterday, and how she would talk to me and show me everything. It all comes back to me when I hear those two gorgeous girls who sing songs about Greece here in Brno—songs like "*Dále než slunce vstává*," "Beyond Where the Sun Rises"—Martha and Tena Elefteriadu, who only became popular after the Agathonikiadises left. Later, I wrote to them about the sisters. I even sent them a record but just got a postcard back, once or twice. But then again, I knew writing had never been Auntie Athanaia's thing. Same with me, for that matter. It took me years before I finally wrote to them for the first time, and then our contact kind of faded out again, which was too bad.

But maybe that's how it's supposed to be—people come; people go. And then not too long afterward, Jára came into my life, and it was obvious to everyone why I latched on to him the way I did. As soon as it was possible, I got out of that silent and dreary household of my mother's. I wanted to start my own family, because, as they say, the family is the foundation of the state, and the mother, the architect of society, right? And it feels good to have a purpose. Besides, I didn't know what else to do. One thing was for sure: there was no way I could stay stuck in that cold and empty apartment with Mom, trying to figure out if at any particular moment she liked me or didn't like me, or if she was or wasn't talking to me. Besides, we kept on seeing each other after I moved out, and it was actually better, because she didn't give me a stomachache every day, just once a week over the weekend, when she'd come to visit. And it could have gone on like that, nice and peaceful, and that whole business of kicking her out wouldn't have had to happen, if only she'd been reasonable. If she hadn't always been lighting into us in our own home—Jára called it emotionally blackmailing us— always coming at us with accusations. She would arrive and go stand by the open window, lighting one cigarette after another, even around the baby, talking, talking, talking, about all the things she never wanted to talk to me about before. And it was obvious that it was just her way of trying to still control me, because she'd always end those litanies of hers with some kind of veiled threat: Did I understand everything now, and was I grateful to her for having banned all traces of the past from my life? Back then, it had really upset me, and it had upset Jára even more. So then, after the Russians rolled in, and Mom started making one scene after another in our kitchen—calling us ignorant, asking if I'd understood anything of what she'd been telling me these past few months, because everything was about to repeat itself all over again— that's when it happened. He finally just kicked her out. And he was right to do it. She had no business carrying on in our house as if it were my fault that the Russians had marched in. It was as if someone flipped a switch in her brain, and not just once, but several times over. At first, she kept scaring us, saying that another war was about to break out. She even managed to find us gas masks, and then, when nothing happened, she started to ridicule the Czechs, calling them weak, incapable of taking action. Her attitude toward our own people was one of complete disrespect, as if they were just colored pawns in a Trouble game that were constantly being knocked back, never able to make it "home." She would talk about our nation with absolute contempt, as if she weren't a part of it. And this came after all those long-winded outbursts, in which she complained that the Czechs had driven her out, and that *they* had never accepted *her*! I would stare at her as if she'd lost her marbles. It was as if there were two completely different women living inside my mom. One was the wronged German woman, who had been driven out of her home, and the other was the superior German woman, who looked down at the Czechs living in her community with nothing but scorn. Both women were German. The Czech woman, the one she'd always identified with, seemed to have vanished.

She almost had a heart attack when Jára told her not to drag politics into our house—that we couldn't care less. That they could all do whatever they pleased, but that we were busy building a home and raising a child, and whether this, that, or the other one was in power made no difference to us. That we were simple people who liked to do simple things, and not dwell on politics in which we had no say anyway.

That time, she got up from the table as if she'd been stung, running out to catch the bus one hour earlier than usual. She must've gotten offended or something, just because we weren't interested in sticking our noses into that Russian business.

Her personality had always been a bit peculiar, and I always felt she used to take things out on me. But that she'd stop talking to me for years—that our communication would be reduced to a card on my birthday and another at Christmas—that I never expected. But that was exactly what happened. And little Blanka first had to grow up before she could bring us back together again.

V

He had given it a lot of thought, already long before he lay dying. But it was only on the day immediately prior, when he felt the end was imminent, that he called over his wife and asked her to bend down to him. He then proceeded to rasp into her ear everything that he wished to leave behind for posterity. It didn't seem to make that much of an impression on her. He had imagined the tears rolling down her cheeks in horror and disgust, but she had just patiently listened and nodded. At that moment, he saw that she was prepared to forgive him everything, if only he wouldn't die. She must have thought it was his fever talking; she was looking at him with such compassion—prepared for anything. But he felt that this would be the final moment of clarity, in which he could see the contours of the past and the present in sharp focus for one last time, before the fog in which he had been lost for days would descend again. So he took advantage of it and made her take out a pencil and some paper from the bedside drawer, so that she could write down what he was about to tell her. She did it while feigning a smile, for show as it were, as if she were humoring a child, so that it would stop pestering. Very deliberately she picked up the paper and pencil, put her ear once more to his lips, and prepared to listen. He started with Gerta. She had to be told about her existence, and he could see her recoil in alarm even before he had finished his sentence. But as he already knew, at that moment she was obviously ready to forgive him anything.

So he dictated to her Gerta's full name, her date of birth, and the street address where he had last left her. On March 23, when he had just tapped her on the shoulder, not wishing to say a more personal goodbye—such was the contempt he and his father had felt for her back then. Then he had set off, eager to test his mettle, excited to put on a uniform like everyone was back then, ready to fight for the Führer, for the Reich. He had joined up with his sights set on the front and on officer's stripes, so full of anticipation that he hadn't even noticed that his father was trembling in fear. Not until they were standing in front of the German House and he reached out to shake his father's hand for the last time. It was only then that he noticed it, along with the bloodshot eyes and the sniffling, to which he'd been oblivious the whole time they had been walking from Sterngasse. Most likely, at the time, he, Friedrich, had been the one doing all the talking. About his prospects, the future, the *Endsieg*, the ultimate victory. His father hadn't uttered a word. So he had said goodbye to him, and that was the last time he'd seen him—he, the son with the bright future, in which he was destined to return as a hero. For him, that was all that mattered. And that held true even much later, when he was actually at the front and receiving one promotion after another. He had come out of the Hitler Youth as a second-rank private, and from then it went like clockwork. Lance corporal, corporal, squad leader, sergeant—in Volhynia, for the village of Czech Malyn, that they burned and razed to the ground in July, he was promoted to staff sergeant—and later on, in the autumn of forty-three, after they had wiped out Michna-Sergejevka, he was made sergeant major. One year later, he became first lieutenant. But then it had come. It started with a tingling in his stomach, just as had happened at the very beginning. But back then, he had been a mere private, and in the display of excessive zeal that he had put on for his squad of soldiers, he had barely noticed it. Authority, that was what he had been focused on. So that not one of them would dare to make even a peep when he gave the order to fire. And so that not one of them would notice that even he was gagging on his own vomit, when the Jews would lay themselves down in the pit, their faces to the feet of those already dead, so that their bodies would take up the least amount of room. As far as that went, he was still doing all right. Some of the others had turned into drunken pigs—they couldn't even walk out of the barracks sober the next morning—and others simply went out of their minds. They no longer even went home on leave, because they couldn't look their wives in the eye. Not to mention that they would've been totally useless anyway, since after six months in the slaughterhouse, most of them discovered they could no longer get it up. He was no exception. But there were those who took it particularly hard. They solved it their own way. Over the course of one month, in their district of Rivne alone, there had been three or four. For the most part, they would shoot themselves right in the forehead, temple, or mouth. But that was simply a matter of *Weltanschauung*, one's worldview, he had told himself back then.

But soon the tingling in his stomach returned—it would come back again and again, increasingly intense and relentless. At some point after the business in Czech Malyn. The order came from above, issued directly to him because he spoke Czech and because that district fell under his jurisdiction. Who knew what made them choose this village. However, in doing so, they had also chosen him, and to this he wasn't indifferent. At least not afterward. Not that he wasn't used to that sort of thing. Except up to that point, he had always heard it a little bit differently. First, they were liquidating only Jews, and that was by necessity. More specifically, it was gratifying. They were cleansing the area and liberating the resident ethnic Germans, the *Volksdeutsche*, from parasites. They were dealing with the first order of business—safeguarding a living space for their own people, ensuring that the Reich had the potential to expand. To this day, he could still summon up that feeling of pride he experienced when their general sector of Volhynia-Podolia was officially declared *judenrein*, clear of Jews. Clean. Next, they liquidated the Banderites, the Soviet partisans, as well as the Polish partisans in the *Armia Krajowa*, the underground Home Army. And that was also by necessity; it was the cost of survival. There wasn't much to think about—either they would get to the partisans first, or the partisans would get to them. In those days, Ukraine was a jungle, and life there was a stake in a lottery game. Mainly because these partisans, unlike them, knew their way around the Volhynian and Podolian forests. And the villages had stood by them—even women and families took them into hiding, although the penalty for this was death. He had been called into service a few times on such occasions as well, but when he'd had to shoot these abettors, he'd turned a deaf ear. He couldn't understand what had happened, why in Malyn he hadn't been able to do the same. Maybe because of that cursed Czech language, which was why it had fallen to his unit in the first place. In total, 374 Volhynian Czechs, 26 Poles, and, in the Ukrainian part of Malyn, 132 Ukrainians burned. He didn't know why it hit him so hard, coming after Mlyniv, where the number of Jews had been 1,118; Sushybaba with 752; Kowel with 799; and those were just the ones that went directly through his hands. The numbers were exact, to a person; their administrative precision was beyond reproach. It must have been that cursed Czech language, coming through the barn doors even after they'd been nailed shut, and from the pigsties, into which they had crammed them in groups of twenty, twenty exactly, so that there was just enough room for them to stand, shoulder to shoulder. When moments before the order was given, he would hear pleas in Ukrainian like *Dajtě pomilovanije! Have mercy, please!* Or, *Help! Don't shoot!* It left him cold, as if he hadn't heard it. But that Czech language, after Malyn, he would hear it every night, every single night without exception. *Smilujte se! We're meeting the quotas! Why? Mercy!* He heard that every night. And meanwhile, earlier that day, he had still been chuckling about how seamlessly everything was proceeding, just as the *Kreislandwirt* had anticipated. When he and his unit had surrounded the village and summoned everyone back from the fields, they had shown up within twenty minutes. And, after all, who wouldn't have come, when it was allegedly just a matter of a document check, a routine inspection of the labor force in the village? Anyone who didn't show up would be putting his family at risk, so everyone came. They stood around on the village square like a herd of oxen, grouped together by family, and waited under the blazing July sun for an hour or two, until the entire population register had been examined, and each individual checked off, one by one. And then with a smile, cordially, since the inspection had gone well—no one had been missing, and according to the inventory list, everyone had met their *Wehrmacht* quotas—they began to separate them. The women from the children and from the men. Trusting, they didn't protest; after all, they had nothing to fear, as they were repeatedly reassured. They dispatched the men to retrieve foodstuffs and valuables from the houses and had them load everything onto hay wagons, which some soldiers then transported to Rivne. Next, they ushered them into a barn that was registered as belonging to a Václav Činka. They corralled all the women into a cow barn on a farm belonging to a Josef Dobrý—"*dobrý*" as in *good*—and he couldn't help but smirk as he noted the irony of it. *Good Coffin* was still going through his head when it began to burn. But then there came those cries in Czech. The screaming, the pleas directed to God, to them, to him—to Friedrich—and all in Czech. Until finally, a stillness set in, permeated by the repulsive, sickly sweet smell of charred flesh and acrid smoke that they left behind as they headed back toward Rivne. And then it began. Nights in which he heard the language of his mother—the common, vile Czech of his vile mother—until finally not even he could walk out in the morning without taking a swig of *samohonka*, the bootleg brandy that, back then, was used as currency in Ukrainian villages instead of money. A full half year, until orders came to advance on the next Czech village, Michna-Sergejevka.

He used to go there often in forty-three. It was a tidy village with a few farmsteads, smaller and poorer than Malyn, and the number of inhabitants corresponded exactly to the prescribed parameters: maximum one able-bodied man per three hectares. The village was practically empty, mostly women. There was a pub there he liked to frequent, their local bootleg rye brandy was among the best. A few times, Málek and Levandovský had even joined him. And it was with the two of them that it started, and then, once again, the problem had been dropped into his lap—who else's?—to solve. What exactly had made them pick Michna-Sergejevka, he didn't know. As if they hadn't been aware that no *Volksdeutsche* had ever lived there, not even before the war, in which case how could they have been murdered, as the justification for the order stated. Even today, he remembered the faces of the girls from the pub, could hear their voices and the soft intonation of their Czech, which after five generations had become mixed with some Ukrainian. Well, their skulls hadn't exploded any differently from the skulls of others who'd gotten a bullet in the back of their head. Even though he knew them.

They had been the first ones to come back into his mind when he had finally begun to remember. After thirty-three years, in 1977, when he found himself again looking at human torsos without limbs, vacant eyes staring unblinking at a ceiling, shapeless mounds of flesh that lay soaked in blood on the floor of the minibus. They had rolled down the cliff like ripe pears—only two had managed to claw their way out of the crushed metal box. The rest stayed inside until they had been able to cut them out, extracting them piece by piece—but that he had no longer seen; he had just imagined it. That was the moment in which his memory had come back, and the past fused with the present into one clear, lucid, and unadulterated whole, with full awareness of continuity. Suddenly, everything took on contours, and questions were answered in one fell swoop. After those girls from the pub resurfaced, their hair neatly combed the way Gerta used to wear hers, next came the nails, driven into the boards tacked across the barn doors in Czech Malyn; his off-post army apartment in Rivne; the kitchen in Sterngasse; the faces of his mother and father—all of it. Suddenly, it seemed as if everything lay in the palm of his hand. All he had to do was pick a memory, and it would start to play itself back to him, as if it were happening all over again with him as an active participant. After so many years. They thought he had gone into shock. And yet he was fully conscious, more than he had been for untold previous years. He had turned inward, immersed into himself, and had begun to sift through visions, sorting them and making sense of them, recapitulating and analyzing one after another, one by one, in the order in which they arose.

So this was why, after the war, he couldn't tolerate the thought of Czechoslovakia or the Czechs, who were busy building that nuthouse of theirs behind the iron curtain. Not even his son had been able to convince him in the mid-sixties to go to the Grand Prix—the mere sound of the name Brno was so disagreeable to him. This was why. This was the reason he had been so disillusioned after the war. He had never made peace with it. Never. And just now, it all came together, and he suddenly felt whole, as he hadn't felt for the past thirty years. No longer was he merely a returnee from the eastern front, whom they had sent back to the Reich with a gunshot wound in his head to die. No longer was he the Friedrich Schnirch who, apart from the name and diagnosis written on the chart at the foot of his bed, knew nothing about himself. At this moment, he was no longer just the one who, during the final days of the war, had gotten up and run away from the hospital so as not to have to confront the fears about which the other wounded men raved every night. In the confusion of those final days, just before the capitulation, he, Friedrich Schnirch, had disappeared, without a single recollection and without any papers. As had so many others.

All this he said to her, to his wife, who had been by his side throughout the rest of his life. He rasped it all into her ear, to the extent that his strained vocal cords would allow. She didn't even flinch. Not even when he was relieving himself of the burden of Czech Malyn and Michna-Sergejevka. She dutifully took down Gerta's address and all of the things he had wanted to say to Gerta these past several years but had never found the courage. Not even to find out if she had survived. Throughout the three long years that had been granted to him before his death, the question kept him awake at night, yet still he had done nothing. Because he wasn't sure. Would he be able to face her if she was alive? His own sister, the Gerta whom he had once so despised? He couldn't step out of the shadow of his own pride and reach out to her, only to hear that she and their mother, the martyrs, had been on the right side of the barricades. Because, in fact, they hadn't been in the right. They had not, and it was just an ironic twist of fate that had tipped the scales in favor of the wrong side. The side of the plebs. And the *Herrenvolk*, the master race, by unfortunate circumstance, found themselves forced back into the narrowest of confines, with no possibility of proving to Europe and the rest of the world the greatness of the idea. The idea of a clean Europe. Europe as a greater place, a realm for the *Übermensch*, for a Greater German Nation. One for which he had shed his blood and would shed it again. For men who strictly adhered to the principles of order and discipline, and for women dedicated to the concept of nationhood and a higher social interest—for the glory of a Greater German Reich. For the sake of Germany and for the sake of the Führer, who had sought to change the world for the better.

Such were his last thoughts. In his death throes, which lasted only a few hours, he saw the red flag with the swastika superimposed on a white background flying over a new, united Europe. It was glorious. Surrounded by flawless people in a free Germany, he ascended toward the gates of Valhalla. There, until the break of dawn, he cavorted with the Valkyries, all of whom looked like the exquisite Anne-Marie Judex, whose beautiful face had fallen out of his memory for over thirty years. He ate the apples of Iduna that would preserve his youth and grant him immortality until the twilight of the gods, after which an even better world would come—one in which men like him would be respected. Then he descended again, his soul filled with a sense of peace and well-being, conscious of his place in the clearly structured web of order, and he was content. And in such a state he also died. It happened during the night while his wife was breathing peacefully on the couch in the next room and the luminous, serene light of the full October moon flooded the apartment.

VI

Everything was changing again, by now for the umpteenth time in her life. It almost seemed like a farce, but this time a genuinely cheerful one, devoid of irony. Still, before allowing herself to fully believe, she wondered if the Czechs truly had it in them—the capacity to take their destiny into their own hands. But then she gave in to the euphoria, which, considering her age and her prevailing frame of mind, took even her by surprise. The explanation she offered herself was that her life was simply in need of a change. Since retiring, she had fallen into a state of lethargy and, little by little, had come to terms with the notion that the rest of her life would unfold as it had up to now, that nothing would ever change. The only time she still bothered to turn on the television was on Saturday evenings to watch *A Kettle of Color*, the East German variety show that usurped both existing channels as well as the minds of its viewers. She no longer had the strength to swim against the tide—now that she could no longer vent her disdain to Barbora, whom she saw so rarely, she had grown tired of taking an openly critical stance toward the rubbish they put on. Sometimes she would turn on that foolish Bohdálová, and when that got really kitschy, she just shook her head and that was all. What was the point, anyway? It didn't matter, not even the movie *The Ten Commandments* could save this nation. It could hardly compete with those TV variety shows and the brainwashing series of screenwriter Jaroslav Dietl: *The Tin Cavalry, The Man in Town Hall, The Woman Behind the Counter*, and countless others. Gerta had become resigned a long time ago, perhaps even before she retired, but now that she had practically no more contact with other people, even more so. She had stopped watching the news, since all they ever showed anyway were the Potemkin villages of the Eastern Bloc and the Sodom and Gomorrah of the West, and she no longer felt like getting worked up about it. She had stopped listening to the radio, and she had stopped reading the paper. She had cut herself off from the outside world and had sealed herself within her own four walls, where all she heard were the cat's mewing and the sounds of her housework. Once in a while, she would borrow a detective novel from the library, exchange a word or two with her neighbor, or stop in to see Johanna, and that was enough for her. In fact, over these past few years, she had been content, because she had finally become resigned to her situation.

And then came another revolution, this time one with no violence, and things took an unexpected twist. It wasn't immediate—by now she had become far too slow to be able to understand things right away. It took her at least the first full year before she began to process what this new era entailed, apart from getting rid of the Russians, who for the past twenty years had sprawled all over the place and whom she despised. By the time she realized it, a new president had already long been ensconced at Prague Castle; all the borders had been opened, and as Blanka had said, anyone who had a passport was free to go back and forth. And passports were being issued to everyone—no more special permissions, foreign-currency pledges, or exit stamps required. The distance between her and Teresa had just shrunk considerably, mused Gerta. Actually, though, only in terms of the travel from Vienna to here, to Brno. Because when it came to her, between her diabetes, which had caused her to gain so much weight over recent years, and her bouts of nausea, even just a trip to see Hermína had become a major under-taking for which it took her a long time to prepare. Still, it was only five stops by tram to the central bus station, then a forty-minute bus ride to Southern Moravia, then just the walk from the bus stop to the crossroads, and finally up to the church and back down into the village, all of which really took no effort at all. At least at one time it hadn't. Then the diabetes crept in—at first it seemed that the pills would do the trick, but then she was forced to switch to insulin, and now she was injecting herself twice a day, morning and evening. And she had lost all of her strength. How many times had she woken up in the middle of the night feeling nauseated, and if she hadn't had a sugar cube handy, who knew how things would have turned out. On the other hand, it was for this very reason that Barbora finally succeeded in getting her a telephone. And indeed, three years ago they hooked up a line for her and installed a phone. Then, up on the wall, she tacked the telephone numbers for the nearest emergency room, emergency medical services, Barbora's home and workplace, as well as the numbers for the company where Jára worked, and the post office in Perná. This last one she had gotten through the operator, and had then called Hermína on her birthday, for which to this day Hermína reproached her whenever they saw each other. But it was only for show, since they both knew how much it had meant to her. She had ordered her paged by the local radio station: Hermína Herzig. She'd had the post office call the local exchange and request that a public announcement be made asking Hermína to report to the Perná post office in half an hour. Gerta could imagine how Hermína's heart must have been pounding as she raced down the hill from the parish house to the nerve-racking peal of the glockenspiel that accompanied every public announcement in Perná, while the nosy neighbors stood by their cottage windows and watched from behind the curtains. She couldn't help feeling a smug sense of satisfaction when Hermína came on the line and announced her name in a trembling voice. "You crazy old girl," Hermína had said, heaving a deep sigh of relief once she'd recognized Gerta's laugh on the other end of the receiver. Although this act of folly had cost Gerta a fortune, the truth was that for her it had been the greatest excitement of the whole year. Actually, pretty sad, right? But since she'd gotten sick, nothing had been particularly cheerful. She had long since stopped going to see Barbora, and she didn't have the stomach to ask Jára if he could drive her over to Hermína's in that shiny new Lada of theirs. And so once a year, when the weather was good, either in the spring or in the fall, she would head out for a few days to Zipfelka's old cottage, which never changed.

But to go back to the telephone that she'd been given because of her diabetes—for her and for Barbora, it proved to be an absolute blessing. As a result, their relationship improved dramatically. Making a call was somehow less painful than making a visit. In the brief chats about Blanka, the weather, or even cooking, they could avoid all the topics that might trigger an allergic reaction in one or the other. It started out as an obligatory two or three minutes, which little by little they had gotten used to, but then soon Blanka began to call as well. Time and again the phone rang, and there Blanka would be on the other end, asking about this or that. Usually she needed help with her German assignments for an evening class she was taking. For her, Gerta was happy to remember. And then, from a certain point on, once Blanka was attending vocational school and could get around the city on her own, she would sometimes stop by and visit. And then, wonder of wonders, occasionally, if she had a six o'clock start in the morning or some special event in the evening, she would even sleep over, and Gerta's apartment began to come alive again. With Blanka's coming of age, life, movement, and color flowed back into Gerta's world. And to her great surprise, in the end, it was Blanka who gave her a reason to keep on living.

VII

Gerta didn't deny that it was her own fault that Barbora showed no interest in either her, personally, or their shared family history. Early on, Barbora had been interested, but Gerta's response had caused Barbora to put up a wall of self-protective indifference. It had happened when Barbora was still a child, endlessly asking questions about their family and about her father, which Gerta couldn't bring herself to answer.

Instead, she plunged their entire family history into a shroud of secrecy. Taboo. With Barbora, she never found a way to get the words out, and it was hard to say if that had been a mistake, or if in the end it had saved her from greater conflicts. From external ones, but even more important, from internal ones. Like those that Johanna's children had to contend with. With Blanka, on the other hand, it was different. Something had seeped through already back when she was little and Gerta started talking about the past—long before Jára had kicked her out of their home. By then, Barbora already knew practically everything, except, of course, her father's name. And Blanka grew up with this awareness and, to Gerta's amazement, to no detrimental effect. The passage of time, she came to realize, had swept it all away; it was now water under the bridge. For Blanka's generation, it had all happened so long ago that the events of back then seemed to have nothing to do with them. Young people like her viewed it purely as a tragedy lived through by their grandparents, and as children they no longer had to grapple with the issues foisted onto their parents. For these children, it was simply a matter of history, and not a burden.

Gerta came to this realization together with Johanna, who observed it in her own grandchildren. This even though in their home, they always made a point of emphasizing that they were a German family and that they identified with the German part of Brno. And yet, Johanna's grandchildren were Czech through and through, and it wasn't just because of Anni's husband or Rudi's Alenka. Even Anni and Rudi themselves, while always respectful of Johanna, had relaxed in their reverence for all things German. Or perhaps they had never taken it to heart to the same degree as Johanna, believing, at least according to Barbora, that it was better to feel at home here and not create additional, unnecessary problems for themselves. So they had adjusted, and now all their children, Blanka and the rest, no longer gave a second thought to the question of where and what was home. And this was why, coming from Blanka, it caught her so by surprise.

When she first heard about it, she thought she would have a heart attack. For a long time, she couldn't say a word, couldn't utter even a syllable, as if she had become frozen. Blanka, her eyes shining, was sitting across from her in her kitchen on Stará Street, expectant, most likely anticipating that Gerta would erupt in jubilation. But Gerta remained motionless and, little by little, Blanka's smile began to fade.

"You're not happy about it, Gran?" she finally asked, perplexed.

Happy was definitely not it. Astonished, perhaps—by such nonsense—by such foolishness. By this idea of apologizing to the expelled Germans, an idea cooked up by Blanka and her friends. As if she didn't know from Gerta herself that to fight for such a thing was pointless. No one would go along with it. The city officials in the town hall would sooner cut off a leg than allow such a statement to be publicly released.

"Such nonsense," Gerta said, shaking her head and trying to calm her wildly pounding heart.

Blanka in her disappointment was silent.

"Have another piece of *Stollen*," Gerta offered, and put the kettle on the stove, striking a match to the loudly hissing gas and only then realizing that she hadn't filled the kettle with water—the aluminum clinked against the faucet, and the water fizzled on the bottom. The flame around the burner flared. She stuck the whistling cap onto the kettle's spout and set it back on the burner.

"They'll never do it. It's pure nonsense."

"But, Gran, the moment is now! The time is finally ripe, and that's why they should do it now—if not now, then when? Why aren't you happy about it?"

"I would be happy about it. But first they'd really have to do it."

Blanka was silent.

"Until they actually do, I don't believe it. Nothing will come of it. All you're doing is baiting the wolves. When they get annoyed, they'll bite."

"You're such a pessimist, Gran."

Gerta shook her head and made a cynical face.

How long had it taken, before she finally became resigned to it? Her whole life—from the moment the war ended, as far back as she could remember. Her entire stay in Perná, during which she tirelessly tried to prove to everyone that none of it had been her fault and that she was as worthy as the rest of them. Pointless. And then again throughout the seventies, after the first wave of normalization swept her away and she felt those sharp fangs inside her, biting, shredding her insides, and not just figuratively, as that was when she'd had her first attack of gall-stones. It took a few more years before she'd finally been able to tally it all up, underscore it with a big fat line, pack up her things, and go off into retirement, burned out like a cinder after years of must-nots and imposed need-nots. Only then did she manage to make a clean break—tie everything up in a compact bundle, toss it behind her, and begin to enjoy having unstructured and uncontrolled time, during which no one derided or insulted her. Her pension was laughable, that was true—after twenty years of demotions and working for minimum wage, there was no place for money to come from, but she was free. For the price of having given up.

And now, here was Blanka, telling her that they had formed some kind of group, Youth for Intercultural Understanding or some such thing, and that they were seeking reconciliation with the past. Now, when Gerta had at long last found peace—when she finally felt ready to forget everything and let bygones be bygones.

But the third generation must have woken up or something, thought Gerta, because Blanka simply wouldn't let it go. Gerta resisted as much as she could. This time she was defending her hard-won peace, the four walls of her kitchen and bedroom, and she had no desire to let in a world that had slipped out of her grasp and no longer held any interest for her. But Blanka was poised to attack and overflowing with deter-mination and exuberance. And eventually also with disappointment at

Gerta's lack of enthusiasm for something that Blanka felt she was doing mainly for her grandmother's sake. Gerta saw her dismay. It stuck in her mind after Blanka left, along with some of what she had said. About reconciliation. Reconciliation with oneself and with the collective whole. And that it was not impossible. Again she saw the resolve with which Blanka stood up and said, whether with Gerta or without her, it was no longer possible to remain silent about these things. And if nothing else, then at least, she, Blanka, and others like her, were prepared to make an effort and try to set things right.

"And you think an apology would set them right? Those fifty long years when I was different from everyone else? You think I could forget? At a time in my life when memories are all I have left?" asked Gerta on the phone when Blanka called her the following day.

"That's the point, Gran. You don't have to forget. You just have to forgive. After they've offered you an apology. Publicly. You'll see how much better you'll feel. And what's more, the whole question will then be out in the open, fully exposed—just wait until you hear them say that a part of Brno belongs to the Germans too. Or that they expelled people who all through the war had been on the Czech side. Like you. And, Gran, in some other countries, there's even talk of reparations."

Gerta caught her breath. This was of interest to people abroad? To those on the other side, like Teresa? And they wanted not just an apology, but reparations? It sounded dizzying. An apology that would be substantiated by reparations? A rewriting of their destiny as the eternally guilty party, which would be noted around the world—words of apology that, after fifty years of inner turmoil, would soothe her soul and put an end to her perpetual lack of trust. An apology would mean the admission of guilt and repentance, the bowed heads of dogs whose muzzles, for fifty long years, had been snapping at her heels, chasing her down in her dreams, and confiscating everything she ever painstakingly acquired: her apartment, her work, her freedom. They would bow down before Gerta; before Hermína, who had become a milkmaid; before

Johanna, who in spite of her university degree had spent her whole life working as a seamstress; before Anni, who instead of studying literature was sanitizing test tubes at Lachema; and before Rudi, who instead of studying engineering had learned to be a car mechanic.

Blanka had sown a seed of hope inside her that germinated even in the barren soil of Gerta's fear of yet another disappointment. She resisted as fiercely as possible. But then, from a certain point onward, Gerta could think of nothing else.

VIII

They even invited Gerta. Johanna was there, as well as lots of people from their German culture club, including the parish priest and Antonia, joined by her children, whom Gerta hadn't seen in almost twenty years, as well as her second husband, whom none of them had laid eyes on since their wedding. There was Rudi, who had aged quite a bit over the years, and Anni with her husband, proudly gazing over at their son, the young doctor with his university degree. He was exuding self-confidence as he stood in a corner next to a baby carriage with his newly baptized infant, gesticulating with his hands, deep in animated conversation. Even Barbora and Jára came, because Blanka wouldn't have it any other way. They sat beside Gerta, and Gerta felt inwardly triumphant. All thanks to Blanka, who had brought them back around to her. All of a sudden, Barbora was interested. In Gerta, in others whose plight had been similar, and finally even in the German blood flowing through her own veins. About which it was best to keep quiet, Gerta thought to herself as Blanka placed her palm over her own two wrinkled hands that lay folded in her lap.

"So, are you curious?"

Gerta smiled. "I'm not sure. I'm a bit nervous."

"You, Gran?" Blanka beamed.

Maybe she felt nervous because it was her own life that was some-how about to be reconciled. Satisfied. *But let's not get ahead of ourselves,* she chided herself. Nothing had yet happened. And still might not hap-pen, given that the new, post-revolution town hall was full of people like Mr. Novák, whose real name was Mr. Rozrazil, and who had worked for State Security but was now a member of the Civic Forum. Mr. Novák, who had once dragged her out for a coffee at the Friendship Restaurant and afterward sought her out from time to time, always with the same questions. *Have you seen the folks from the German culture club? And how's Miss Teresa doing? Has she written?* She had written—back then, he was in a better position to answer that question than she was, since all the letters Teresa ever sent to her ended up on his desk. This became evident one year after the revolution. Suddenly, three letters arrived all at once, in yellowed envelopes that had obviously been opened and resealed. Recently enough that the paper still smelled of glue.

> *Meine liebe Gerta,*
> *How are you, my dear? Why haven't you been in touch? I heard what happened over there. How are you managing? Are the Russians still the same as they were back then? I wouldn't be able to stand the sight of them. My poor dear, I think of you so often. Whatever happens, don't let them get their dirty paws on you, not on you or Johanna or Hermína, living all by herself in Bergen. Please write, so I know you're okay.*
> *Thinking of you, Teresa*

And next:

> *We are pleased to announce that on September 27, 1970, Teresa Bayer and Jan Jelinek will enter into marriage . . .*

Gerta burst out laughing at the thought that she would be sending wedding congratulations twenty years after the fact. But better late than never, and at least she finally had some news about Teresa. Whom did she have to thank for reposting these letters? She didn't know. But she was as thrilled as if she had found Teresa all over again. Suddenly, she seemed so close. At long last, after all these years during which Teresa, Gerta realized, had never received a single word of news back from her. And then there was that third letter, which, once again, took everything away.

> Dear Frau Schnirch,
> Forgive me for the great delay with which I write to let you know of the death of my wife, Teresa Jelinek, born Bayer. It's only now that I'm getting around to putting her final affairs in order, among which was also her wish that you be informed of her passing and of her last thoughts.
> Jan Jelinek, Vienna, July 19, 1973

So Teresa was dead. Without ever having had the chance to say goodbye, the chance to exchange a few more words, the chance to go back to Pohořelice once more, to the place where Gerta would go from time to time to lay a wreath of flowers in memory of her mother. Teresa had been gone now for years, and Gerta never even had a chance to shed a tear for her. It was with a heavy heart that she shared the news with Johanna and Hermína, and then telephoned to tell Antonia. She felt as if she had been robbed of something. By someone.

That someone had been hiding behind that scab Novák's handsome face. It was obviously thanks to him that she hadn't received a single one of those letters in time. And now he was strutting around the Brno magistrate's office, posing for photographs and wearing a self-satisfied smirk. If they were going to make the appeal to him, Gerta thought to herself, or to someone like him, who had simply traded in his old coat for a new one so that the old regime could work hand in hand with the current one, then Blanka and her friends would never succeed.

Johanna snapped her out of her thoughts when she pulled up a chair beside her and dropped heavily onto it.

"So go on, read it. I could go on listening to it over and over again."

Barbora and Jára moved in closer, closing the circle around Blanka.

Blanka pulled a piece of paper folded over several times out of her blue jeans pocket, smoothed it, and held it up right in front of Gerta. For years now, Gerta had needed one pair of glasses for reading and another for distance, and all she could make out was a blurry, black-and-white rectangle.

"We sent it already on Wednesday, Gran. What I'm reading from here is a copy," she explained.

"*Honorable Mr. Mayor and Honorable Members of the Council of the City of Brno:*

On the thirtieth day of May of the year two thousand, fifty-five years will have passed since the forceful expulsion of the German residents of Brno. This so-called death march was not merely a spontaneous outburst of hatred accumulated over the years of German occupation, but a consciously planned action organized also in part by the political representatives of the city of Brno. The action was carried out on the basis of a decree issued by the National Committee for the Greater Brno area dated May 30, 1945, which ordered the assemblage, still on that same day, of all German women, children, and elderly persons. During that night and into the morning, they were then forced to start marching in the direction of the Austrian border. This procession, numbering some twenty to thirty-five thousand people and escorted by armed overseers, proceeded under the direst conditions to Pohořelice, from where the expellees later continued on. According to eyewitness accounts, many dropped dead right on the road from sheer exhaustion; others were beaten or shot to death. The overall number of victims of the

Brno expulsion is estimated to be from several hundred to one thousand people."

"There were that many of us?" Gerta said, lifting her head to look at Blanka.

"Don't you remember?" Johanna said, patting her on the shoulder.

"Please, how am I supposed to remember the number of people?"

"Well, after all, you know the procession dragged on for almost three days before everyone made it to Pohořelice. And then what about that camp? Don't you remember how many people kept on streaming in? Masses of people. There was no room for them to sit, let alone sleep—just remember."

"Well, it's true that we weren't just a handful; even Karel said that."

"We tried to get an exact number by examining the records from Pohořelice and from Austria, to see how many actually got there. In the end, all we could come up with was a rough estimate, also partly based on wartime and post-wartime statistics. But that should really be the task of some commission that could also verify everything. But hold on, that comes later."

Blanka looked back down at the piece of paper and read on:

"It is important to realize that this violent action was directed specifically against women, children, and the elderly, who made up the majority of the participants and the victims. The basis for this was that, according to the aforementioned decree, all German men between the ages of fourteen and sixty were required to remain temporarily in Brno to do forced labor. Among the expellees, there were also many Czechs and German anti-fascists. This act of retribution, however, only marginally affected those who had been active participants in the Nazi atrocities."

"That's very well written," noted Johanna, nodding her head affirmingly, "and you should add that it separated families that had managed to stay together all through the war. Ula was there, marching with just her daughter. Her husband and her son had been forced to stay behind somewhere. Who knows if they ever found each other. And same with us!"

Gerta nodded, turned back to Blanka, and gestured for her to go on.

"*The Germans were already expelled from Brno before August 2, 1945, when the terms for the deportation of German residents from territories belonging to Czechoslovakia were agreed upon at the Potsdam Conference; thus, the conference participants were presented with a fait accompli that was no longer possible to rectify. We are well aware of the incomparably more extensive crimes committed by the Nazi regime. At the same time, we realize that suffering is suffering, no matter who is the perpetrator and whenever it takes place. Even with the expulsion of Germans from Brno, the unacceptable principle of collective guilt was applied, and crimes were perpetrated against a group of residents purely on the basis of their ethnicity. In view of the fact that the application of such principles to this day leads to the perpetration of acts of cruelty in many parts of the world, we know the value of rejecting them outright. For this reason, we are turning to you to request that as the current representatives of the city of Brno, you declare that you categorically denounce these events, for which the political representatives of Brno at that time were responsible. We believe that an adequate way to deliver this declaration would be in the form of an apology to the expelled Germans of Brno, formally issued by the town hall. Why an apology, and what purpose would it serve today? This is not just a matter of a single symbolic act. An apology by the town hall of Brno, in our opinion, would serve rather as a means for delivering two important and timely messages. The first would be a message of reconciliation directed to those who were affected by the forceful expulsion. The second would be a message directed to us, today's residents of Brno, who for the most part have nothing to do with the expulsion that took place here fifty-five years ago. An apology does not imply a self-indictment, but rather a responsibility for the coexistence, today and in the future, of persons from the most diverse cultural and ethnic backgrounds. It offers the hope that as long as we cultivate an awareness of the unacceptability of the aforementioned crimes and are able to assume an open and honest attitude toward them rather than making them taboo, no such thing will ever be repeated.*

"Signed by the members of Youth for Intercultural Understanding and twenty-one prominent Brno citizens. What do you say to that, Gran?"

Gerta was struggling to catch her breath. She didn't have a heart attack back when Blanka first came to her with this idea, but she thought she might have one now. Just a tiny bit more, and she'd be in convulsions, falling off the chair, rolling on the carpet, clutching her chest, and giving up her ghost.

So.

This was how it sounded in writing. When it was written down on their behalf, for someone who would now have to deal with it because it could no longer be ignored. This was how it sounded to someone who realized what it must have been like. And that wasn't even taking into account what it had meant to stay here, stigmatized as a German. That would probably look good on paper too, she thought, looking around at everyone gathered there for the christening. Considering what it had done to them—all of them, not to mention others whom she didn't know and who had also stayed here after the war. And what it did to the ones who hadn't stayed—to Teresa and all the others unable to feel at home anywhere.

It sounds nice, she said to herself, *very nice.* It sounded like history holding its nose, finally ready, through the mouths of those whose fathers were running around on the sidewalks of Brno, to apologize. And what would it cost to apologize, anyway? This was a polite letter, a hand offered in reconciliation by those who had done nothing, by those who after the war had stayed, by those who had lived it all firsthand and now finally wanted to forget. All that was left to do was to accept it and, naturally, try to save face—but that could be done even while apologizing.

So.

It had to succeed, because it was the truth. This was what had happened, and by now, after all, it would be hard to deny it. And furthermore, there was no point. Today, these things could be admitted. It was a different time. And it would be a relief. A tremendous relief, because they would finally feel at home here, with nothing more to fear. And for those at the top, it would also be a relief—by atoning, they would be cleansing themselves of the sins of their fathers, as Johanna would say. Not that these would have been Gerta's words—after all, everyone knew where things stood between her and God. But she couldn't come up with a better metaphor. They had offered their hand, and now all that remained was for it to be accepted. And then they could all draw a big fat line under the whole episode. All of them. Those who had stayed as well as those who lived here as a matter of course. The two groups would merge. And the city would once again belong to everyone, as was only natural.

"Five, six, seven, eight, Hitler's little head of hate! Prague, Brno, Paris wail, let the villain rot in jail!" She heard the words rising up from the buzz at the table behind them, where children of various ages were scribbling on random scraps of paper with crayons.

This was their very own history, which had forced its way through generations of children to come full circle, and to which they themselves were now about to bring closure.

PART V

Solo for Barbora

I read it to her when she was already lying in a coma. The doctors were just waiting to take her off life support—they were waiting and waiting, because I wouldn't give my consent. Even though Jára tried to convince me that I was just prolonging her pain. I knew she was in pain. I knew she was suffering—they told me that they had given her morphine, that her body was so riddled with cancer that she basically had no chance. But when I saw that face of hers, so peaceful, lying back against the white pillows with dark blue stripes, blissful and serene as it had never been before, I just couldn't bring myself to do it. I couldn't get enough of the sight of my mom with this sweet, clear, gentle face. It was very rare that I ever saw her like this—and at those moments, I knew she was my mom, my mom who loved me. The warmhearted one, who smelled of that mixture of Vaseline from her screw-cap jars and her own sweat, the smell I loved so much as a kid. Come to think of it, that really had been her scent for her whole life. She never bought perfume. And the one I got her—it smelled like lily of the valley, came in a small rectangular bottle with a twist-off top, was made by Alpa, and back then all the women wore it . . . two or three drops at your throat were supposed to keep you smelling good all day—she gave away to Auntie Johanna. And she came right out and told me so. She said it wasn't for her, but it would be for Aunt Johanna. Come to think of it, I should've asked Anni if she ended up with it—that would've been kind of funny. My floating present, that everyone wanted to get rid of. But had Anni wanted to get rid of it, she would've definitely given it to me, who else. And I never got it.

I came every day to see my mother, to look at her lying there so calm and peaceful. I would sit with her the entire visiting time, and Jára would always be the last guy standing around in front of St. Anne's Hospital, waiting for me. I couldn't let go, because I felt that during this period, my mom and I were closer than we'd ever been. Except for maybe when we were still living with Granny Zipfelová, but after that, it wasn't until she was on her deathbed. That sounds like a terrible thing to say, but it's true. It was as if after all these years, I could finally really talk to her. She would listen to me with that devoted, peaceful expression on her face, which I'd practically forgotten existed. I told her about what I was doing, what I was thinking, what our home looked like these days, what had changed. And that Blanka had now permanently moved in with that boyfriend of hers, whom she met at the barn, horseback riding. I explained to her how it was with young people these days, that they weren't in such a rush to get married. Although for Blanka, it was slowly getting to be time. But these days, they do things differently. First, they travel somewhere together, now that it's possible—they feel each other out, check to see if they work as a couple, and if they don't work, they split up and leave no trace behind. Although a trace is exactly what Jára and I would wish for more than anything else. I'd so love to hold a baby in my arms again, look into those googly little eyes, staring past me into space, dab the drool off the tiny mouth. But that's not how things fly these days: first you travel, and only later do you plan a family. And that's how Blanka sees it as well, and Jára and I are supposed to keep our mouths shut. It's her life. As I said all this to my mom and she just lay there with her wispy white hair fanned out against the pillow, I felt she understood me. I felt that she, too, would have wanted to see her bloodline live on, felt how proud she'd be to see Blanka bring her another little girl, carrying on the family tradition. She would have no choice but to cry, just the way I was crying now. I bent down over her yellowed, blotchy hand that I'd been rubbing between my palms and sobbed with longing—for a baby, and for Blanka, too—a longing that had somehow gotten mixed up with something else, something that had to do with me and Mom and the baby and a profound love with which I wanted to shower them all. Something impossible to describe that came gushing out of me like a river, and I sobbed into my own hands and into hers until the nurse finally came and told me that visiting hours were over. So I left. And then the next day, I returned and told her a whole bunch more. About Jára. That we'd managed to get things back on track, and that now everything was just the way it had been before. I even told her about that Rozára of his. I mean, why keep it from my own mother? Especially now, when everything was pouring out of me and it felt so wonderful to be able to talk to her, why should I hold back? It wouldn't hurt her the way it hurt me when I found out, and Jára wouldn't need to feel embarrassed, because it wasn't as if she would be going around telling anyone. I told her how I'd found out about it. It was up at the weekend cottage that we bought in the Bohemian-Moravian Highlands, right on Zemkáč Pond—it's surrounded by forest and there's only room for cottages on one side, and that's where we have ours, and where the other Brno families that we've become friendly with have theirs. So that's where I found out. We were all gathered around the campfire again, grilling sausages wrapped in tin foil to put in rolls with ketchup and cheese, and people were drinking and talking. That night, Pepík came over to sit by me, and he told me that Jára had been meeting up with Rozára, who was always there on her own. Everyone knew her because she'd been coming alone for years—she was kind of a fixture there—and she'd been trying for years to snag someone. And apparently, she managed to snag my Jára; that's what Pepík told me that night. He told me as a friend, because he cared about me. At that moment, I didn't believe a word he said, but then I had to wait all through Sunday until the evening before I could see Jára, who had stayed in Brno, and ask him straight out. And, Mom, he admitted it!

I thought I'd been struck by lightning. I got so scared, and at the same time it hurt, hurt so badly—really already from the moment I'd said it out loud. It burned like hell on my tongue, and deep inside my chest, I felt this awful pressure. And those eyes of his, if only you'd seen them. They were sad, so terribly sad. And the worst part about it was that it was my fault. Because I'd stopped paying attention to him as a man, if you know what I mean. When Blanka went off to live in the school dorm and would come back to visit on weekends, I was supposed to be getting ready to go away. But I preferred staying at home with her to staying with my guy, who then had no choice but to take care of himself. He said I'd pushed him away for a grown-up kid, and, Mom, one just doesn't do that. So you see, it was all my fault. That's not to say that Rozára's a saint—she's a bitch, and definitely more calculating than my Jára. I can't tell you what a flood of tears I cried over it, before I was finally sure that it was over and that Jára wasn't seeing her anymore. He said he broke it off as soon as I found out, but—you know—it takes a while before you can shake off that uneasiness that keeps you checking pockets for notes or sales receipts or someone else's handkerchief.

But, come to think of it, she wouldn't know. Because for as long as I can remember, Mom didn't have a man, so how could she possibly know what it's like to be losing someone you love so terribly much. And when I was the one losing him, all she could talk about was that apology and the reparations. At the end of one of those rare, unavoidable visits, I was so furious, I thought I was going to scratch her eyes out; that's how much I hated her. How did she spend the last few months of her life? What did she turn those last few weeks into for me—when we'd finally started talking to each other again? The apology. *Apology*—to this day, when I say that word, I feel myself making a face. It oozes out of my mouth like poison, that apology. Even Blanka has picked up on it, so now she tries not to talk about it in front of me anymore. That apology, it was the only thing my mother still cared about—here was a grandma with a daughter and a granddaughter, and all she ever wanted to talk about was that apology. Like a broken record.

She'd spent her whole life trying to deny she was German, and suddenly, out of the clear blue sky, she managed to dig up some old wrongs that had been buried deep inside her and fought like a prize-fighter to see them made right. A fool of a prizefighter, because what was the point of an apology? Especially from people who, when it came to the expulsion, that frigging great stigma on her life, didn't even remember it? Brno. Supposedly, Brno owed her an apology. To her and to Johanna, and on top of it, also to me and to Anni and to Rudi, not to mention all the countless others. Except that I hadn't been affected by it—I had nothing to do with it. That German choke collar, which I only caught a glimpse of now and then, I got rid of it—I didn't fuss with it and straighten it neatly around my neck the way my mother did and at the same time didn't. So now, I could finally tell her exactly what I thought of it, that obsession of hers with Germanness and that apology. In the end, it was all pearls before swine, anyway. If only she knew how slyly they'd managed to get around it—it would've made her die a second time. There was no apology made to the expelled Brno Germans, no reparations. Even coming from the young people in that new group that was standing up for the rights of people like my mom, they hadn't taken the bait. All they did was express regret over the disorderly expulsion of their fellow citizens. Period. They came out with that statement in some back room, very hush-hush, so that it wouldn't cause a lot of speculation, and that was it. And it was obvious why, seeing as all those people sitting in town hall hadn't had anything to do with it. But I think most of the people to whom it was supposed to have been directed were left with their jaws dropping. Regret. What did that even mean? I really believe that for my mom, had she been presented with this version of *the wolf ate, but the goat remained whole*, it would have killed her. And I would have wished it on her. Because of these past few years, when I'd been forced to listen, over and over again, to everything about her, and about how terrible her life had been. Meanwhile, she had absolutely no interest in my problems or Blanka's problems. That time, when I was leaving the ICU where she was lying, I almost told that puny little nurse in charge of her to just go ahead and do it. Take her off. I was so furious at her. And then the next day, I didn't go—that much I remember—I simply couldn't digest that last conversation we'd had. But then the day after that, I did go back, this time with Jára. And I don't know why, but I brought along some flowers that I'd picked in our garden to brighten her room. She had that same expression on her face again, so peaceful—but otherwise she was just lying there with her arms at her sides, completely still. After a while, Jára went out—after all, what else was he going to do there, except stare at an old woman in white bedsheets about whom he'd always had his own opinion. So I stayed there again with her by myself, and somehow I had the feeling that we made up. It's hard to describe. Making up with your mom who's in a coma and who already for days now has been unconscious. But that's what happened. I felt it. Maybe it was also the twitch of her eye right then, just as I was leaving and promising her that I'd come back again. And I really did go back again, and we talked about things that I was interested in. We talked about Blanka, about Jára, about crossword puzzles, and even about how I was feeling—and that I actually wasn't an old woman yet, just a little over fifty-five. And I wasn't even unattractive. And then, at the end of that visit, I read her the letter that had arrived—I couldn't even say exactly when, because lately I really hadn't been paying much attention. But a letter for her had arrived, and it was from the Red Cross. At first, I thought it was probably some kind of a donor drive, maybe for giving blood or something like that. It was only when I noticed that there seemed to be something else stuck inside the envelope that I opened it, read it, and then brought it with me to Mom in the hospital. Inside was a second envelope that had been stamped with an old date, still before the wall had come down, and it was postmarked from Frankfurt. The letter was written in German, which I managed to decipher with the help of a dictionary, and from which I gathered that I had some relatives. I then read it to her in German, because it was clear to me that she'd understand, even though I'd never heard her speak that language.

Adressat: Gertrude Schnirch (1925), Sterngasse 142 in Brünn noch im Jahre 1944

Dear Frau Gerta Schnirch,
I am writing to you on behalf of my husband, Friedrich Schnirch Junior, your brother. Allow me to let you know of his quiet and peaceful passing on the morning of Saturday, October 31, 1980. He departed, having made peace with himself, but not having made peace with you. His final thoughts were of his closest family, among whom throughout his life he always counted you, although he was unable to overcome the barrier that the war had put between you. Furthermore, during the final days of the war, he suffered a loss of memory, which he regained only just before the Lord summoned him to himself. You should know, however, that he wanted to look for you in order to find out whether you had survived the war, and always had in his mind the hope of trying to reunite the family once more, according to God's word. Believe me, the only reason he didn't do so was due to his conscience, by which he was tormented, and because of the fear that he would no longer be able to look you in the eye.

Dear Gerta, should you, thanks to the help of the Red Cross, receive this letter, please grant this request on behalf of my husband, your brother, and forgive him whatever you can. Please know that in doing so, you will have not only his gratitude, may he rest in peace, but also

*mine, Adelheide Schnirch, and our children's, that of your
nephew, Friedrich, and your niece, Barbora. We would
be glad of any word from you, and send you our regards
and best wishes for a good life.*
    The Schnirch Family, Frankfurt am Main

Well, I'm not sure how interesting she found it. In our house,
no one ever talked about an uncle Friedrich, although I knew that
I'd had an uncle who had fallen in the war. She didn't bat an eyelash,
just went on staring at the ceiling from behind her closed eyelids and
saying nothing. Maybe she really wasn't interested anymore, because
if she and that uncle had ever done anything to hurt each other, which
the Czechs and the Germans had a tendency to do, then it was very
possible that she never wanted to hear about him again. The only
thing that occurred to me to do right then was to write back and say
that Mom had died too. But then I felt ashamed of myself, because
Mom was lying there stretched out in front of me and was actually
still alive—because, although she was in a coma, she was still breathing, and I wasn't about to order her death. I tossed that letter into my
backpack and completely forgot about it over the following stretch of
many long days during which I would go to see her in the hospital and
talk to her, up until the moment that she actually died. By that I mean,
when I finally let them take her off life support. The doctors had been
saying that it was a useless battle, that we were just waiting to see how
much her heart could take, and that it was just a matter of time. Jára
said the same. Jára, who was spending long afternoons sitting at home
alone while my mom and I were having conversations like we'd never
had before. I felt terrible when I gave the nod, and then later when
we were all standing around her, together with Blanka and Jára—at
first, we felt she was still there, and then suddenly, she wasn't. It felt as
though she were disappearing little by little, very gradually, her breath
becoming quieter. And then she was gone. I felt it was all my fault that

she suddenly didn't exist anymore, that my mom was gone—ice-queen mom, Gerta Schnirch. But what was I supposed to do? Spend those fleeting moments when my daughter would come home to visit me in the spotless but foul-smelling hospital? Leave Jára alone for days on end, and wait for another Rozára to get wind of it again? I needed to be there for the living, not for the dead. Or the almost dead. And I convinced myself that the doctors knew what they were saying. That she was no longer getting anything out of staying alive. Then a few days later, we went to the cemetery to bring her urn to Grandma Ručková's grave and to light some candles. And that was when it hit me—it hadn't been just those last few weeks, but an entire lifetime out of which she hadn't gotten anything. No man, no warmth—frozen in hatred for this society, and in the end consumed by her yearning for the apology. I can't help it, but I have the feeling that apart from those two or three years with Uncle Karel, my mom lived a completely unfulfilled and futile life.

INDEX OF LOCAL PLACE NAMES

Horst-Wessel-Straße, today Husová Street

Jakobskirche, Church of St. James

Köffillergasse, today Stará Street

Kotgasse, today Körnerova Street; 1918–1939 Blatná Street;
  1940–1946 Schöllerova Street

Mendelplatz, today Mendlovo náměstí (Mendel Square)

Ponawkagasse, today Ponávka Street

Pressburger Straße, today Bratislavská Street

Rathausplatz, today Dominikánské náměstí (Dominican Square);
  1952–1990 náměstí Družby národů (Friendship Among Nations
  Square)

Ratwitplatz, today Žerotínovo náměstí (Žerotín Square)

Richard-Wagner-Platz, today Malinovského náměstí (Malinovsky
  Square) with the National Theater of Brno, formerly called the
  German City Theater

Schöllergasse, today Körnerova Street; see Kotgasse

Silniční (in German Strassengasse), today Hybešova Street

Stadthofplatz, today Šilingrovo náměstí (Šilinger Square)

Sterngasse, today Hvězdová Street

Wiener Straße, today Vídeňská Street

ABOUT THE AUTHOR

Photo © 2012 Vojtěch Vlk

Kateřina Tučková is a Czech playwright, publicist, biographer, art historian, exhibition curator, and bestselling author of *Gerta* and *The Žítková Goddesses*. She has won several literary awards, including the Magnesia Litera Award (for both *Gerta* and *The Žítková Goddesses*), the Brno City Award for literature, the Josef Škvorecký Award, and the Czech Bestseller Award. Kateřina is also the recipient of the Freedom, Democracy, and Human Rights Award by the Institute for the Study of Totalitarian Regimes, and of the Premio Libro d'Europa at the Book Fair in Salerno, Italy. Between 2015 and 2018, she was a founder and first president of the Meeting Brno festival, focusing on international and intercultural dialogue. Kateřina Tučková currently lives in Prague and Brno, Czech Republic. Her books have been translated into seventeen languages. *Gerta* is her first to be translated into English. In December 2020, her novel *Bílá Voda* will be published in Czech. For more information, visit www.katerina-tuckova.cz/en/.

ABOUT THE TRANSLATOR

Photo © 2013 Steve J. Sherman

Born in Switzerland to Czech parents, the late pianist Rudolf Firkusny and his wife, Tatiana, Véronique Firkusny grew up in a trilingual, musical household that sparked a lifelong passion for language, literature, and music. She translates primarily from Czech to English, and her most recently published English translation is Daniela Hodrová's novel *A Kingdom of Souls*, cotranslated with Elena Sokol. Forthcoming publications include, in collaboration with Elena Sokol, Daniela Hodrová's *Puppets*. Firkusny serves as the executive director of the Avery Fisher Artist Program of Lincoln Center and also coaches opera singers in Czech diction. A graduate of Barnard College, where she received a BA in Italian literature, she resides in New York City.